GET WILD

WILD THING

- MAGGIE SHAYNE

  - MARJORIE M. LIU

    - ALYSSA DAY

      - MELJEAN BROOK

B

BERKLEY SENSATION, NEW YORK

THE BERKLEY PUBLISHING GROUP
Published by the Penguin Group
Penguin Group (USA) Inc.
375 Hudson Street, New York, New York 10014, USA

Penguin Group (Canada), 90 Eglinton Avenue East, Suite 700, Toronto, Ontario M4P 2Y3, Canada
(a division of Pearson Penguin Canada Inc.)
Penguin Books Ltd., 80 Strand, London WC2R 0RL, England
Penguin Group Ireland, 25 St. Stephen's Green, Dublin 2, Ireland (a division of Penguin Books Ltd.)
Penguin Group (Australia), 250 Camberwell Road, Camberwell, Victoria 3124, Australia
(a division of Pearson Australia Group Pty. Ltd.)
Penguin Books India Pvt. Ltd., 11 Community Centre, Panchsheel Park, New Delhi—110 017, India
Penguin Group (NZ), 67 Apollo Drive, Rosedale, North Shore 0632, New Zealand
(a division of Pearson New Zealand Ltd.)
Penguin Books (South Africa) (Pty.) Ltd., 24 Sturdee Avenue, Rosebank, Johannesburg 2196,
South Africa

Penguin Books Ltd., Registered Offices: 80 Strand, London WC2R 0RL, England

This is a work of fiction. Names, characters, places, and incidents either are the product of the author's imagination or are used fictitiously, and any resemblance to actual persons, living or dead, business establishments, events, or locales is entirely coincidental. The publisher does not have any control over and does not assume any responsibility for author or third-party websites or their content.

WILD THING

A Berkley Sensation Book / published by arrangement with the authors

PRINTING HISTORY
Berkley Sensation trade paperback edition / May 2007
Berkley Sensation mass-market edition / January 2009

ISBN: 978-0-425-22544-8

BERKLEY® SENSATION
Berkley Sensation Books are published by The Berkley Publishing Group,
a division of Penguin Group (USA) Inc.,
375 Hudson Street, New York, New York 10014.
BERKLEY® SENSATION and the "B" design are trademarks of Penguin Group (USA) Inc.

PRINTED IN THE UNITED STATES OF AMERICA

10   9   8   7   6   5   4   3   2   1

CONTENTS

ANIMAL MAGNETISM

Maggie Shayne

One

Macy McNamara damn near jumped out of her skin when the door burst open and the man stumbled through it, a limp chocolate lab cradled in his arms. There was blood all over both of them.

It only took her a heartbeat to get her bearings, though. She turned to hand the overweight tabby cat to its aging owner. "Keep her on the diet, Alma. Take her on out to Christine, and she'll set up your next appointment." She flicked her eyes to the man's. "You. Put the dog on the table," she said.

He didn't need telling, was already on his way to doing just that, even as Alma Clements, hugging her cat to her chest, scurried away. Macy leaned over the dog, noting the blood coming from the front of its shoulder, grabbed a wad of gauze pads, and applied pressure. "What the hell happened to her?"

"Jesus, lady, you're the vet. Looks to me like a GSW."

She lifted her brows in question.

"Gunshot wound. Sorry. You get used to the lingo."

"So how did you manage to get your dog shot?"

"She's not my dog. She was left at a crime scene, and I got elected to rush her over here."

He referred to the dog as she, not "it." Which told Macy he

was an animal lover, which in turn told her he was probably a decent human being. At least she'd found that to hold true most of her life. There was no time to analyze much more of what he'd said, much less the reaction of her healthy libido to the man's intense green-and-brown-streaked eyes and snug jeans. She had to act if she was going to save the animal's life. It was ebbing at a rapid pace. She nodded toward the door. "Open that."

He opened the door and then jumped when she shouted, "Christine!"

Her curvy blond veterinary-assistant-slash-best-friend came at a dead run. "We need an operating room and an extra pair of hands."

"The room's ready, Macy, and my hands are at your disposal."

"Great." She glanced at the man again. "You. The waiting room is—"

"I know where it is. Can I clean up first?"

She nodded. "Use the sink in here. Better trash that shirt while you're at it. There's a scrub shirt in the drawer there. We'll be a while."

"I'll be here."

She kept pressure on the wound, and Christine wheeled the table, while the guy got the door. As it swung closed, Christine said, "Damn."

"What?"

"What do you mean, what? That's one hot-looking man."

"Is he? I hadn't noticed."

Christine sent her a look as they rushed the dog into surgery. It wasn't skeptical, it was mournful. She thought it a shame her boss preferred the company of animals to people. Especially men. No, she wouldn't have any trouble believing Macy hadn't noticed that the man was gorgeous. She'd probably have more trouble believing that she had.

Two hours later, Macy had washed up and changed out of her surgical scrubs. She was leaning over the lab, stroking the dog gently as she waited for the anesthesia to wear off, when Christine brought the hot stranger in.

He stepped into the recovery room, and Christine backed

out, closing the door behind her. And then he just stood there, silent and waiting.

"She's going to be all right," she said, keeping her voice soft, soothing. "Aren't you, Cassie? Yeah, you're going to be just fine."

"Cassie?"

She glanced over her shoulder. "It's . . . on her tags."

"Oh. I hadn't checked them yet."

I hope to God the name is there when he does, she thought, rolling her eyes at her own slip. "So you're a cop," she said. She'd finally managed to think about what he'd said when he'd first come in—that the dog had been found at a crime scene.

"Yeah."

"Can you tell me what happened?"

He released a slow breath. "Not really. At least, not until it leaks to the press. That way I don't take the blame for releasing it."

She kept stroking, kept petting. "It's not like I would tell."

"Doctor-patient confidentiality?"

She shot him a look. "I never repeat a word my patients say without their permission. It's a rule."

That earned her a smile, but it died when she didn't return it. And then he frowned, studying her face and said, "What's that supposed to mean?"

"She's coming around," she said, and turned her full attention back to the dog. She didn't blame him for not trusting her. She didn't trust people as far as she could throw them.

Her hands moved gently over the dog's uninjured places. "It's all right, Cassie. Everything's just fine. You're safe. No one can hurt you here." The dog was waking, but slowly. She was confused and nervous, but not in pain, and Macy's voice and touch were soothing her. "The bullet missed her heart," she said, still keeping that gentle tone. "I was able to extract it without much further blood loss. Her vitals are still slightly weak, but getting better."

"Glad to hear it." His tone matched hers, easy and low.

"She's wondering what happened to D—to her owner. Probably."

"She's in the hospital, but she's going to be okay."

"There, you hear that, baby? She's going to be just fine. Promise."

As Macy leaned close, still stroking, and Cassie's mind cleared, the animal became agitated. Macy kept petting, kept speaking, trying to calm the dog as the images replayed in the lab's mind. Her leg twitched, and she whined plaintively.

"It's all right, girl. You did great. And she's fine, I promise. She's fine."

The dog sighed, closed her brown eyes, eyes only slightly darker than her coat. Even her nose was reddish brown. "God, you're a beauty, you know that?"

"Thanks. You're not bad yourself."

She turned to the man, forgetting for a moment that her face was still soft, her smile still in place. "I was speaking to the dog."

"I know. I was just feeling left out of the conversation."

She nodded. "She's been traumatized. This crime, it was— something she witnessed?" She made it a question, though she already knew the answer.

"Witnessed. Yeah, I guess you could put it that way."

"And she was shot by the criminal? Maybe as she was trying to protect her owner?"

He frowned. "That's . . . what it looks like. But I really shouldn't be discussing—"

"How badly is she hurt? The owner, I mean."

"She'll be in the hospital for a few days. But they don't expect any permanent damage. It's just a damn shame she didn't get a look at the guy."

Macy bit her lip. "Yeah, that is a shame. Listen, Cassie needs to stay overnight. If you can come back tomorrow, around ten, she should be good to go."

"Perfect." He moved closer to the bed, reached out, and stroked the dog's head. "She's a great dog, isn't she?"

"She really is. See you tomorrow."

He glanced at her, and Macy realized she was sounding a bit eager to get rid of him. Probably because she was.

He didn't leave, though. Instead, he extended a hand. "Thanks. You're good at your job."

"Thanks. I hope you're as good at yours, so you can get that son of a bitch off the streets, Officer . . ."

"Detective, not officer."

"Okay."

She didn't ask his name. That was what he was waiting for, she thought, but she really cared more about the dog's name than his. And *she* wasn't rude enough to make her ask. Humans sucked.

"Detective Harris. You can call me Jay."

Okay, so maybe he wasn't rude enough to make her ask, either. She nodded, did the polite thing. "I'm Dr. McNamara. Macy."

"Yeah, I saw it on the sign out front." He didn't move any closer to the door.

Wait a minute, was he stalling and trying not to leave? Was he . . . flirting with her? Oh, hell, this she did *not* need. And why was she suddenly nervous and a little sick to her stomach?

"Look, Detective Harris—"

"Jay."

"Whatever. I have other patients stacked in the waiting room like cordwood. So—"

"Yeah, I have a load of work waiting, too. I'll get out of your hair."

"Perfect."

"So I'll see you tomorrow, then."

She nodded and returned her attention to the dog.

Cassie adored the man. He'd been great to her on the way over here, kept pressure on her wound, and though it hurt, she knew he'd been trying to help her. Macy figured he'd probably saved the animal's life with his quick thinking and fast action. And no one had saddled him with the job of getting her here. He'd done that all on his own. The way Cassie visualized the handsome detective, he was a hero—a two-legged Rin Tin Tin.

As he left the room, Cassie shot a longing brown gaze after him and sighed almost dreamily. Macy leaned over the dog. "You're not much help, you know."

The dog let her eyes fall closed.

* * *

"Dr. Macy McNamara, huh?"

Jay looked at his partner and nodded. "That's the one."

"You do realize she has earned a reputation as the most unfriendly vet in the county."

"I'd heard that. Which is why I take Fred to a clinic fifteen miles farther away."

"Don't get me wrong. People say she's great with animals, just lousy with people."

Jay smiled. "I witnessed that firsthand, Matt."

"What? Are you saying she was even nasty to you?"

Nodding sheepishly, Jay said, "She addressed me as 'you' and accused me of getting my dog shot." He shrugged. "Just about what I expected."

"Except?"

Jay glanced at his partner, who knew him altogether too well. They sat at their desks over the mound of paperwork the latest in a string of sexual assaults had created for them, wasting time gossiping about the local vet, because it was much more fun than writing police reports. "Except that she's a freaking knockout."

"Uh-oh."

"No, I'm not kidding. Body to die for. Long hair, sleek and dark. And this skin that has a coppery sheen to it. I think comes naturally, not from the sun. But it was her eyes that really kicked my ass. Kind of almond shaped. Exotic."

"Color?"

"Brown. Like milk chocolate."

"So aside from having the personality of a pit bull—"

"Aside from that she's a walking fantasy."

Matt shook his head slowly, emitting a long, low whistle. "So you gonna go for it?"

Jay shot him a scowl.

"Oh, come on, pal, you know I live vicariously through you. If there'd been as many women willing to have casual, meaningless affairs in my day, I'd have been in my glory."

"Sure. They'd have been falling at your feet, for sure."

"Maybe they would. I wasn't always pudgy and balding, you know."

Jay grinned at his older partner. "It's a new day, Matthew Cooper. Full of liberated, independent females who are just as into having a good time as men have always been. No expectations. No demands. They don't need us anymore, except in the sack. Damn, it's good to be a guy in the new millennium."

"So you *are* gonna go for it."

Jay's grin died slowly. "I don't know. There's something . . . odd about her."

"Odd, how?"

"I haven't decided yet."

"Well, you're a detective. Detect."

"I plan to."

Hell, what could it hurt? He was going to have to see her again anyway. He might as well make the most of it. He wondered if he could get her to stroke him and speak to him in that soft tone she had used on the dog.

And then he had trouble focusing on the paperwork for the rest of the afternoon.

Two

Macy spent the night in the clinic, and not for the first time. In fact, it happened so often, she had a cot stashed in the supply closet, complete with bedding and a fresh change of clothes. The clinic's restroom included a shower stall, and she kept it stocked with the same bathroom supplies she kept at home.

That night, she set the cot up in the room where Cassie was staying. She hadn't had the heart to put the poor lab in one of the kennels. She was far too traumatized for that.

And she knew the dog had things on her mind. Things she needed to share. She'd put a dog bed on the freshly mopped floor, and once the dog settled there, without having touched a bite of her dinner, Macy crawled onto the cot. She'd eaten every crumb of her frozen entrée and was wishing for dessert.

The dog stared at her, brown eyes wanting.

Macy sighed, flung back her covers, and got up. She slung her blanket and pillow on the floor and curled up beside the dog bed.

Cassie shifted closer, whined a little because the movement caused pain, but then sighed and laid her head down on Macy's pillow.

"You're shameless, you know that?" Macy stroked the lab's head. "It's okay, you know. I know it was bad today, but you did good. And she's all right." She didn't just say the words, she visualized them as scenes playing out in her mind's eye.

The dog sighed, shivered a little.

"You can tell me about it, if you want," Macy whispered. She shifted on the pillow, lifting her head so she could look Cassie right in the eye. "Go ahead. I really want to know."

Cassie blinked twice, lifted her own head a little, and stared intently into Macy's eyes. And Macy saw it. She saw it all.

Darla. Dark hair, long and curly; a curvy, vivacious figure; a bright, wide smile. The man had followed Darla and Cassie home from the park, and while Cassie had sensed danger, tried to warn Darla, even growled at the man to send him away, Darla had only scolded her for misbehaving and ignored her warnings. It was only moments after they got home—up the stairs to the third floor of the little brownstone, down the hall to the fourth door on the left—through the door into the place Cassie felt safest, with the carpet that smelled of her own comforting scent and of pizza and of Darla, with the sofa she only slept on while Darla was at work, with the windows she liked to stand up in, so she could watch the people and animals passing on the sidewalk below. Only moments. Then the man smashed through the door, grabbed Darla, threw her on the bed, where even Cassie didn't sleep—and began hurting her.

It was confusing to Cassie. The scent of mating was heavy, but those of fear and danger and pain were stronger. And the scent of blood—Darla's blood—sent her into a rage. She lunged at the man and bit his leg, and he turned on her with a black weapon that made a deafening explosion and smelled like smoke and bad eggs and hurt her terribly.

He had left then, limping on his bitten leg. Darla collapsed on the floor beside Cassie, hugging her and fumbling with the telephone. And then Jay was there, and other men, too. Some of them tried to help Darla, and Jay gathered Cassie up in his arms and brought her to Macy.

Macy saw it all. She saw Darla's battered face and torn

clothing. She saw Jay pressing his nose into Cassie's fur and telling her she would be all right. But more important, she saw the rapist.

The one who had been terrorizing her hometown for seven months now, and who still eluded the police. The one the victim hadn't seen clearly enough to identify. He'd worn a ski mask during the attack, but Cassie had seen him earlier, and she had recognized his scent. She knew *exactly* what he looked like.

Macy put a hand to her forehead, because it ached. "Cassie, do you have any idea what you're doing to me here?"

Cassie stared at her, her great big lab heart in her eyes.

"Look, no one knows about this. No people, I mean. Well, except for Sally at the shelter, and I'm not even sure she *really* knows. And I imagine Christine has some notion, by now. But—"

Cassie whined softly.

"If I tell him, he's going to think I'm nuts."

Cassie kept staring. Macy heaved a sigh. "Hell, since when do I care what people think of me, anyway. I'll sleep on it, okay?"

It must have been, because Cassie closed her eyes, and within a minute was snoring softly. Macy kept one hand on the dog's side, so she wouldn't be afraid during the night, and vowed to find a way to show her that her precious Darla was really okay before tomorrow was over. Dogs didn't understand words and sentences. Tone of voice and touch, yes, but mostly, they had to smell things to know them. Cassie needed to see Darla, smell her, to really know her friend was okay. Which meant Macy was going to have to bully her way into the hospital with the dog at her side, a task that would take every pushy, bitchy cell in her body. Fortunately, she had plenty of them.

And while she was at it, she needed to find a way to tell that hot-looking cop that she could talk to animals so she could tell him what he needed to know to get a rapist off the streets. Yeah. She would make a bunch of enemies and convince the best-looking man who'd ever shown an interest in her that she was certifiably insane.

Not that she cared.

Tomorrow was going to be a *hell* of a day.

"What in the *hell* do you think you're doing?"

Jay stood there in the hospital lobby, face-to-face with Macy McNamara and a bandaged and limping chocolate lab on a leash.

"We've tried to tell her she can't bring a dog into a hospital, Detective, but she just won't—"

"He was asking me, not you, sister, so back off and butt out." Macy interrupted the nurse, reminding Jay that she had her reputation for a reason. "Cassie needs to see Darla, and I'm not leaving here until she does."

He tipped his head a little, would have smiled, except that the woman was dead serious. "Cassie needs to see Darla," he repeated.

"She needs to rest in order to heal, Detective Harris—"

"Jay."

"And she can't rest until she sees that Darla is all right."

He stared at her. "That's your professional opinion. As a vet."

"Yes, and it's also a fact."

"Okay."

She blinked as if he'd stunned her. He liked that. Keep her off balance until he decided what to do with her, or whether to do her at all.

"Okay?" she repeated.

"Yeah." He turned to the nurse, notched his smile up to its most charming, and looked her in the eye. "I understand why we can't take the dog to the patient"—he shifted his gaze to her name tag and quickly back again—"Kelly. But could we maybe bring the patient to the dog? Just for a minute or two?"

The nurse smiled, responding to him the way most women did. Young or old, married or single. He was good, and he knew it.

"I'll see what I can do."

She left, and he turned to face the mad vet again, holding his hands out, palms up, as if to say, "You're welcome."

"That was pathetic."

"Excuse me?"

"The way she went to mush just because you smiled at her. God, sometimes my gender makes me want to puke."

"I got you what you wanted, didn't I?"

"I would have gotten it myself, eventually."

"Maybe, maybe not. Either way, you owe me a favor."

She lifted her brows. "Oh, really?"

"Yeah. I was going to say you could repay me by having dinner with me, but I think there's something I want a whole lot more."

"And what, pray tell, would that be, Detective?"

"Jay."

"Whatever. What is it you want more than food? Sex?"

"Usually. But what I want at the moment is for you to tell me how you knew the victim's name."

And *that* shut her up. Instantly and, he thought, thoroughly. She averted her eyes, and he saw her swallow. But then, to his surprise, she faced him head-on, lifted her chin, and said, "I'll tell you later. At dinner."

He'd be damned if he'd let her have the last word, and he managed a comeback he thought would seal the deal. "So that would be, before the sex?"

"*Way* before," she said, and she turned her back to him and started for the exit. "I'll wait for Darla right outside, so these germophobes don't have heart failure."

And that was the last word. Almost. The final one, really, was a sharp little bark from Cassie. If he didn't know better, he would have thought she'd said, "So there."

He sat outside on a bench, watching the happy reunion and trying to figure the woman out. Darla, the rape victim, had been brought out in a wheelchair—not because she couldn't walk, just hospital regulations—and Cassie ran to her, jerking the leash right out of Macy's hands. She didn't jump on her, though. She was gentle, nuzzling Darla's hands and face, giving doggie kisses, and wagging her tail at the speed of sound.

Darla, he thought, benefited as much from the whole encounter as the dog did, if the look on her swollen and bruised face was anything to go by. She really loved that dog. And it was clearly mutual.

He shifted his gaze back to Macy, or, as he was coming to think of her, The Vet from Hell. But the ice queen of a few minutes ago was nowhere to be seen. Instead there was a softly smiling, tender-eyed beauty standing there. Hell, he thought she was getting misty as she watched the two of them. Then she caught him looking and plastered that cold look on her face again, turning away long enough to blink those phenomenally sexy eyes dry.

Yeah. She was a hard, cold bitch all right. And he was celibate. She was soft and tender, deep down. At least, where animals were concerned.

Eventually, the nurse said it was time to go back inside, and Darla turned grateful eyes on Macy. "Thank you," she said. "You don't know what this meant to me. And . . . thank you for taking care of her."

"Thank Detective Harris over there," Macy said. "He saved her life."

Darla smiled at him, teary eyed. "Thanks, Detective."

He nodded. "We'll be in touch. And don't worry about Cassie. She's in good hands."

Darla nodded, and the nurse wheeled her away. He got up, walked to where Macy stood. "So, about that dinner."

"Get some takeout and bring it to my place. I'm not a calorie counter, so make it good. American, greasy garbage. And don't forget dessert. Six o'clock."

He lifted his brows, about to tell her what she could do with her bossy bullshit, but then he looked at her, and knew it would be worth it. "Seven o'clock," he said. "Make sure you have cola on hand. Coke, not Pepsi. And I don't like any of those new flavors, just the classic stuff."

She looked a little surprised.

"You gonna tell me your address, or should I get it from the background check I'm probably going to run on you when I get back to the station?"

She shrugged. "Get it from the background check. I have patients waiting." She turned and started to walk away, but then she stopped, turned back again. "Thanks for helping out in there, Detective. That was . . . actually kind of nice of you."

"It's Jay," he said.

She shrugged again and started walking away.

"Say it," he called after her. She stopped again, but didn't turn. "Say, 'Thanks, Jay.'"

There was a very long pause, during which he saw her back stiffen, but then she seemed to relax, and she said, "Thanks, Jay."

"You're welcome, Macy. See you at seven."

Three

At seven o'clock, he showed up at her door, impressed in spite of himself. Not so much with the house, though it was a great house—a big old Victorian in need of repairs. What impressed him was the amount of work-in-progress on the place. There were ladders and drop cloths, paint cans and rollers everywhere. The intricately carved trimwork was about half painted, and he could see she wasn't going in for the current trend of painting Victorians to look like decorated birthday cakes. She was going with fresh white paint and trim that was a deep forest green. Dignified. Unlike the pink, purple, and violet monstrosity he'd passed on his way to her house.

He rang the bell and heard a dog barking. And then another, and another. She opened the door, and he looked past her at the mob of hounds around her. Okay, maybe it wasn't a mob. Four dogs did not a mob make. And one was a loaner.

"You dog-sitting for more than one patient, doc?"

"Hello, Macy," she said in a mocking tone. "Great to see you again. You look fantastic, by the way."

He glanced at her, then got stuck. She *did* look fantastic. Hair down, and kind of curly all the way to her shoulders.

How did she do that? It had been perfectly straight before. Her eyes looked different, more intense somehow. Makeup, he thought, but he couldn't be more specific than that. She wore jeans and a tank top that revealed more of her than he'd seen before. The tank showed off her arms, slender and sexy and strong, and it hugged her curves. So did the jeans. Damn, she looked good.

"Good to see you too, Jay," she said, still mocking him. "Come on in."

"Sorry. You look so good, I lost my power of speech."

She smiled. "That comment almost makes up for it. Get in here."

She stepped aside to let him in. The dogs were well behaved, didn't jump, just waited, tails wagging, watching him.

"Jay, you already know Cassie. Meet Winkin, Blinkin, and Nod," she said, waving a hand toward an English bulldog, a border collie, and an unidentifiable shaggy brown mix. "And no, they're not patients. They're all mine, as are the fat lazy cat, Sam, lying over there in the bay window, the parakeets, the turtle, the geckos, and all the fish in both tanks."

"Maybe you should live on a farm."

She shrugged. "I like animals, what can I say? You bring food?"

He held up the paper bag he'd been carrying, from a popular home-cooking take-out place he'd always liked. She read the logo on the sack, smiled as if in approval, and took it from him, then hurried through the house. He looked around as he followed, noting a partially spackled wall and a hardwood floor that had been partly stripped. A giant sander and a pile of sawdust sat close by. A ladder stood in the center of the living room, beneath a chandelier with a few of its globes missing. Aside from that were pockets of beauty. Crown molding and elaborately tooled woodwork.

"Nice place," he said. And it was. It was just so . . . unfinished.

"Oh, hell, it's an ongoing project."

"How many contractors have you got working for you? I count at least a half-dozen projects here."

"None," she said. "I like to do it myself."

Surprised yet again, he followed her into the kitchen, where she was unloading the sack onto an already set table. The dogs had beaten him to her, and sat attentively, tails thumping on the floor.

She glanced at them, snapped her fingers, and pointed to the back door. "Out."

The four canines bounded through the doggie door set into the people door, across a nice deck, and into the backyard. Then Macy flipped the dog door's wooden shutter and latched it. Jay glanced through the window and saw that the backyard was fully fenced in and contained lush-looking doghouses, plenty of toys, and numerous food and water dishes, none of which were empty.

"Nice setup."

"Thanks. It works for us."

She opened the fridge, took out a bottle of Classic Coke, and poured it over ice in two tall glasses. She handed him one and sat down. The table was already set, and his offering of roasted chicken with baby potatoes, baby carrots, thick gravy, and still-warm rolls were out and waiting.

She began filling her plate as he sat down. He knew she didn't have an appetite before she even passed him the potatoes, though. She took very little, and ate even less. She was nervous. He would have liked to flatter himself by thinking it was about their date, but he doubted it. She didn't seem the type to get nervous about eating in front of a man. Thank God.

After she toyed with her food and made meaningless small talk for a few minutes, he set his silverware down, got to his feet, and walked around behind her chair. "You're tense tonight, aren't you?" He asked, using one of his standard lines, which he intended to follow up with one of his standard, break-the-ice-and-get-on-with-things moves.

"Yes," she admitted.

"Let's see what we can do about that, hmm?"

She shrugged, then went stiff when he closed his hands on her shoulders and began to massage them. "You don't have to—uh—"

"Try to relax. You want some wine or something?"

She shot to her feet, effectively shaking off his hands in the process. "There's none in the house."

"Hmm. Next time I'll make it a point to bring some."

"What makes you think there'll be a next time?" She turned to face him, and the look on her face wasn't one he was used to seeing on a woman. "Look, Detective—"

"Jay."

"I don't know what you were expecting here—yes, I do. And that's not what I invited you here for."

He lowered his head, deflated. "Don't tell me. This is about the dog."

She nodded.

Well, hell, he guessed his typical tactics would be a bust with this woman. Then again, she was not a typical woman. And instead of feeling repelled, he felt challenged.

He returned to his seat to regroup and start over. "You said you'd tell me how you knew the victim's name. Why don't we start there?"

"I know a lot more than the victim's name. I know what happened to her, and I know it's part of an ongoing series of attacks that appear to be related."

He hoped his expression didn't betray his surprise. "I can't confirm or deny—"

"You don't have to. I know."

"How?" he asked.

She licked her lips, paced a few steps away from him. "I just know. Look, it's not a leap of logic. My clinic is in the neighborhood where the rapes have been happening. Do you have any suspects?"

He mulled her words over, then said, "Why?"

"Because I think Cassie can help us. She saw the guy. Dogs have an excellent memory for individuals. If she saw him again, smelled him again, she would know him."

"I see."

She lowered her gaze from his, just the way someone with something to hide would do. And that piqued his interest. Not as a man, this time, but as a cop. "Do you think that sounds crazy?" she asked.

"Not necessarily."

She sighed, and it was huge and real. Relief. He saw it in her face. "Good," she said. And then she picked up a fork and dug into her food.

Okay, so she was nervous—nervous as hell, for some reason. And she was hiding something. And she'd never really answered the initial question. He watched her eat for a few minutes, before he posed it again.

"So are you going to tell me how you knew the victim's name?"

She stopped with her fork halfway to her mouth, flicked her gaze to his, then off to the side. "I recognized the dog. It took a while for it to click in my memory, but I'd met them at one of the free rabies vaccination clinics I offer a few times a year."

He blinked, because this time, he was certain she was lying. And suddenly, getting close to this woman was a lot more important than just getting into her pants. She knew something about his case. And he had to find out what.

Macy was deflated when Jay told her there were no suspects in the case, because that meant there was no way she could get him to parade them in front of Cassie and let her pick out the rapist. The alternative, though, was impossible. She couldn't just show him the sketches she'd drawn. She couldn't just tell him that she'd seen the man through the dog's eyes and drawn him based on that. She couldn't.

Could she?

Hell, no. He wouldn't believe her anyway.

They finished their dinner, and he helped her wash the dishes, even though she told him they could wait until later. She was uncomfortable with him, because she was attracted to him. Really, powerfully attracted to him. It wasn't a feeling she was used to. When they put the last glass in the cupboard, he said, "So do I get to meet the rest of the family?"

He just didn't want to leave, did he? "Sure," she said. "Follow me." She led him through her home, into a large room that might have been a den or family room once. She'd turned it into pet central. "I love this room," she told him, as he turned, taking in the three giant aquariums, the floor-to-ceiling windows that filled the room with sunlight, the humidifiers shooting mist into the air, the thriving plants that made the place feel like a garden.

"This one is for my freshwater fish," she said, pausing by the hundred-gallon tank that held goldfish, Oscars, guppies.

"That's a huge tank. Seems like you could put a lot more fish in it."

She nodded. "Could. But they like to have room to swim, and I like them to have it. Besides, they grow bigger that way."

"I thought maybe you just overfed them."

"Vets don't overfeed," she said, but she said it too fast, before she realized he'd been teasing her. Sighing at her lack of dating skills, she turned to the equally huge tank in the opposite wall. "This one's for my tropicals," she told him. "Salt water, higher temps. Aren't they gorgeous?"

Every color imaginable filled that tank, and she could see he was impressed. "And the one back there," she said, pointing to an even bigger tank, "is for the geckos."

He moved closer, peered through the glass. "It's like a habitat, isn't it? You've got sand, live plants, a little pool, a miniature tree for them to climb—damn, you really do make good homes for your creatures, don't you?"

"Nah. They make a good home for me."

He glanced at her quickly. "I'd heard a rumor about you," he said. "They say you like animals better than people."

She shrugged. "I suppose that's one of the better rumors going around about me. And probably the most accurate one."

He tipped his head a little to one side. "Care to elaborate? On why you don't like people, I mean?"

She shrugged and averted her eyes. "What's to like about people? They lie, they cheat, they hurt each other. They let you down. Animals don't do any of those things. They love you no matter what. You don't have to shave your legs or have a great hair day. They don't care if your breath stinks or if you're in a crummy mood. They just love you. People suck."

He grinned a little. "I noticed you have a bumper sticker that says that."

"Well, it originally read 'mean people suck,' but I cut off the 'mean' part."

He pursed his lips but didn't say anything.

"What?" she asked.

"Well, I don't know, I guess I was hoping you'd add a disclaimer there at the end. You know. 'Present company excluded' or something to that effect."

"I probably should have." She took a step closer to him. "Cassie likes you. So do my three knotheads, so you can't be all bad."

"You always judge people according to the advice of your dogs?"

"Dogs are the best judges of character in the world."

"So now that I've passed the dog test, do I get to see you again?"

She lowered her eyes. "What for?"

Then she felt his hand on her chin, gently lifting her head until she met his gaze again. "I kind of thought we had . . . a spark. A little . . . chemistry happening between us. Didn't you?"

The way his eyes plumbed hers, she couldn't have denied it if she'd wanted to. "I . . . okay, maybe I did. Do. But I'm not looking for . . . that."

"For what?"

"A relationship. A person in my life. Complications and sticky romantic crap. You know?"

He nodded slowly. There was something about that slow, knowing nod that seemed to tie her belly up in knots. "So who said I was looking for those things?"

She didn't say anything. He slid his hand from her chin, over her jaw, and around to cup her nape, and she shivered.

"Aha. I felt that," he said. "So, no relationships. No people in your life or complications or sticky romantic crap."

"Right." Her throat was dry, and the word came out raspy. "Got it."

"Good."

He leaned closer and kissed her. And she, God help her, kissed him right back.

Four

She kissed like she was born to it. More than that, like she was hungry for it. Starving maybe. He had the feeling a woman like her didn't get a lot of one-on-one interaction of the carnal kind.

The minute his mouth took hers, she curled her arms around his neck, as he tightened his around her waist, and her lips parted, and she let him in. And it was good. Damn good. Maybe a little too good, because when he came up for air, he was breathing as hard as she was.

"Okay," she said with a smile that looked more frightened than eager. "So there's a spark."

"Yeah, and chemistry. Big-time chemistry," he said.

She nodded. "Big-time."

He licked his lips, summoned all his willpower and said, "I should go now."

She looked surprised as hell.

"I just met you, after all," he said. "I barely know you."

"Well, yeah, but if this is just about chemistry, what more do you need to know?"

Whether or not she was somehow involved with a serial rapist, he thought, for starters. But he couldn't very well say so out loud. "I have to know what my dog thinks of you," he said. "I hear dogs are the best judges of character there are."

She took a deep breath. "You have a dog?"

"Yeah—Fred. Well, he claims to be a dog, but does a damn good impression of a throw rug, for the most part. You want to meet him?"

She held his eyes and nodded once. "When?"

"Tomorrow night. Come to my place after you close up shop. I'll introduce you."

She hesitated for a moment. "I'll . . . I'll tell you what. I'll take a cool shower, get my brain working again, and let you know in the morning."

It sounded like an admission to him. That kiss had hit her as hard as it had hit him. And it had hit him like a speeding freight train, so that was saying something. He yanked a pen from his shirt pocket, found an old receipt in his jeans, and scribbled his address and cell phone number on the back of it. Then he pressed it into her hand. "Talk to you in the morning, then," he said.

"Yeah. Okay."

He left her there, found his own way out, and stood in the night air wondering just what the hell he was doing. Getting close to her to find out what she knew? Sure, but since when did a person of interest in a case turn him on like a 300-watt bulb?

He was going to have to be careful here. Very, very careful. Because like it or not, he wanted her. And it was mutual.

This could get damn dicey.

The phone rang, jarring Macy out of a deliciously erotic dream, in which Jay Harris played a major role. She rolled over in the bed, frowning. "Damn. This better be important." Prying her eyes open as the phone bleated again, she glanced at the clock's glowing red numerals: 1:45. Her irritation became worry as she reached for the phone.

"Macy?"

The woman's voice was tear-choked, but not so much that Macy didn't recognize it. "Christine?" Macy sat up in the bed, snapped on the lamp, and clutched the phone tighter. "What's wrong? What's happened?"

"I . . . it was . . . I need you."

"I'll be there in ten minutes. Are you okay?" As she spoke, she jumped out of the bed, yanking a pair of jeans from her drawer and tugging them on with the phone cradled between her ear and her shoulder.

"I don't think so."

"Do you need me to call nine-one-one?"

"I already did. Hurry, Macy."

"I'm on my way." Macy clicked the cutoff button, tossed the phone on the bed, peeled off the dorm shirt she'd been sleeping in, pulled a top from her drawer, and slid into it without even looking at it or bothering with a bra. She crammed her feet into a pair of flip-flops, and yanked a hair tie from her nightstand, bundling her mop into a ponytail on her way down the stairs. She figured it took her about a minute and a half total, before she was backing out her driveway into a blessedly empty road and speeding toward Christine's place. It was a ten-minute drive, but Macy made it there far faster.

Normally, her best friend, Christine, was upbeat, positive, bubbly even. She was smart, and she was strong, the best assistant any vet could want. But she hadn't sounded like any of those things on the phone. She'd sounded . . . beaten. Afraid. Wounded.

A thousand scenarios ran through Macy's mind as she parked the car in a no-parking spot in front of a fire hydrant and ran up the stairs to Christine's second-floor apartment. Had she fallen, had some kind of accident? Had she suffered a heart attack or wrecked her car? There was no sign of a fire in her building, so it wasn't that.

Macy reached the top of the stairs that ran up the outside of the two-family house. Christine rented the entire second floor for an amazingly good—

Oh, God, the door! Its glass was broken. She knocked twice, then not waiting for an answer, gripped the knob and twisted. It wasn't locked. She walked in, avoiding the broken glass, the tipped-over kitchen chair, the teakettle on the floor. Chills ran up her spine. "Christine?"

"Macy?"

She followed Christine's voice into the bedroom and

found her sitting on the floor in a corner. The bed was a wreck, the curtains torn half off the window, and clothes were scattered on the floor. Christine didn't look up at her, just sat there, hugging her knees to her chest, her face hidden. She wore a short blue bathrobe and, apparently, nothing else. "God, Christine, what happened?"

Christine's head lifted slowly. Macy gasped. One of Christine's eyes was swollen almost shut, and blood had run from her nose to her upper lip. Hurrying closer, Macy dropped to her knees, touched her friend's shoulders. "Did he rape you?" she asked.

Christine's answer was a jerky nod, before she dropped her head to her knees again, sobbing.

"Miss Winters?"

Christine let out a sharp cry at the sound of the man's voice coming from the next room.

"It's okay," Macy said. "It's the police. All right?"

Christine sniffled, nodded, and Macy called, "In here, Detective Harris."

Jay recognized the voice, and the first thing that hit him was panic at the thought that Macy McNamara was the victim this time. He burst into the bedroom with her name on his lips. She looked up, met his eyes, and told him without a word that she was okay. He couldn't quite believe it until he forced his gaze away from her, to the woman who rocked on the floor beside her.

"Christine?" Macy said, her tone soft, gentle. "This is Detective Harris. You remember, he brought in that chocolate lab yesterday?"

"Hey, Christine." He moved closer, but not too close. He didn't touch her, knew better. "We have paramedics on the way. I need to ask you a few questions before they take you to the hospital, if you think you're up to that."

She lifted her head, but didn't meet his eyes. He tried not to wince visibly at the evidence of the beating she had taken. From the looks of the place, she'd put up a hell of a fight.

"I was in the shower," she said. "When I heard something

breaking, I grabbed my bathrobe and came out to see. He was in the kitchen."

"What did he look like?"

Christine blinked. "He wore a ski mask. Leather jacket. Jeans. White Reeboks. Black gloves." She frowned. "He had blue eyes, and he smelled like he'd been drinking."

"Good. That's real good, Christine."

"He grabbed me. I fought. He hit me." She lifted a hand to her face, but winced and drew it away as soon as she touched her cheek. "He dragged me into the bedroom, and he raped me and he hit me, and then he left." She glanced only briefly at Jay's eyes. "He was white. About six feet tall. No taller. Maybe a little shorter. Slender, narrow, you know? Built like a young guy, not an older one."

"Good job, Christine." Sirens announced the arrival of the paramedics. His partner, Matt, was in the kitchen, waiting for the forensics team, and there were a pair of uniforms already canvassing the neighbors.

"Do I have to go to the hospital?" Christine asked. "I think I'm all right."

Macy stroked a hand through her friend's hair. "You really should, hon. We need to make sure, and you know . . . there might be evidence."

Christine's eyes opened wide. "He didn't use a condom. What if—?"

"I don't think you need to worry about that, Christine," Jay said, knowing exactly what kind of fear was making its presence known to her. "He never ejaculates, so pregnancy shouldn't be an issue. None of the other victims have tested positive for any STDs. And I'm pretty sure this is the same guy."

Christine sighed, clearly relieved by his words. But then she frowned. "Why haven't you caught him by now?"

"We will," Jay promised. "We will."

The paramedics were trundling into the bedroom, so Jay backed off to give them room. "Be as careful as you can in here," he told them. "Forensics team is on the way."

One of the medics was female, he was relieved to see, and she took the lead, while the others hung back, not touching Christine any more than was necessary. When they finally finished checking her vitals, disinfecting her cuts, and checking her pupils, one of them asked for a gurney. Christine held up a hand. "I can walk."

They helped her to her feet.

"I'll be at the hospital, Christine," Macy said. "I'm gonna follow right behind you in my car."

Christine nodded, and the medics helped her out of her apartment. Macy started to follow, but Jay touched her arm. "Hold up a sec."

She turned, met his eyes. "You were great with her, Jay. Said just what she needed to hear. Thank you for that."

He nodded, thinking it was a shame he'd learned how to deal with traumatized women the way he had. There had been enough of these rapes that he was getting too damn good at it. And he knew they needed to hear the facts, the truth, without delicate euphemisms. They wanted to know if they were going to get sick from something the guy might be carrying, and they needed that information given clearly and succinctly, unvarnished. So there would be no doubt, later, what he'd meant when he'd spoken to them.

Now he had to be just as straight up with Macy. "How is it you got here before I did?" She frowned, and he quickly added, "I have to ask."

"Right. Of course you do, it's your job. She called me, right after she dialed nine-one-one. I'm only a few minutes away, and I didn't exactly take much time getting ready." She looked down at herself as she said it.

Jay looked, too, and became painfully—and inappropriately, given the circumstances—aware that her jeans were zipped but unbuttoned, and that there was no bra underneath the ribbed white tank-style undershirt she wore—the kind popularly known as a *wife beater*, a term that he hated.

"How long do you think they'll keep her at the hospital?" she asked.

"Overnight, I imagine. Unless she has more serious injuries that don't show."

"Meet me after she's settled in. I'll buy you a coffee," she said.

He looked at her, a question in his eyes.

"I think I can help you find this guy," she said.

"All right. I'll come to the hospital when we finish up here."

She gave him a nod and left. He thought she wasn't looking very forward to telling him what she knew, but he believed she was going to do it. And he found himself hoping it wasn't going to be something that would make her an accessory.

Five

"Jay."

He looked up from the notes he'd been reading for the tenth time, to see that Macy had finally made an appearance in the hospital waiting room. She looked tired, haggard. Her hair was coming loose from the ponytail in places, dangling against her neck, hanging over her forehead. She smiled a little when he met her eyes. It was a sad, tired smile that drew him to his feet and straight to her.

"How is she?" he asked.

"Sleeping, finally. They say she'll be okay."

He released a pent-up breath. "I'm glad to hear that."

"So am I." She hiked a bag up higher on her shoulder, one he didn't remember her having before. And then he noticed she was wearing a bra under the tank top now, and a light jacket over it.

"You stopped at home on the way here?"

"Yeah. Had to get something. C'mon, there's a doughnut place around the corner."

"I know it well," he said. "And it's after four a.m. That makes this qualify as breakfast."

"Ahh, the breakfast of champions. Doughnuts and coffee."

"At this hour, we'll make it high test."

He smiled as they walked out of the hospital, around the corner, and into the doughnut shop. But he noticed how tense she was. Her spine was stiff, her hands fisting on and off at her sides, her jaw tight. Of course her friend had just been raped and beaten. But he had the feeling that didn't account for her nerves right now.

They ordered at the counter. He paid, and they carried their loot to a table. He let her lead, noting she chose the one farthest from the counter. Aside from the two of them and the employees, the place was deserted.

Jay took the lid off his coffee to let it cool, then dug into a doughnut. He was starved; it had been a long time since dinner. He noticed though, that she wasn't eating. Or drinking. She was just sitting there, staring at him.

He swallowed, wiped the sugar away from his lips, and met her steady gaze. "You're really working up to something here, aren't you?"

"I like you," she said. "That's a rare thing for me, you know that? I don't like most people. But I like you."

He smiled—couldn't quite help it. "I like you, too."

"I don't want you to think I'm crazy."

"I don't."

"You will."

"Macy, there's no way I'd—"

She held up one hand, while the other dipped into her handbag. Then she pulled out a sheet of white stationery paper with a drawing on one side. Placing it on the table, she slid it across to him.

He glanced down at the drawing—a sketch of a youngish man, probably in his early twenties, with a scruffy, unshaven face, longish hair parted on one side, a scar on his chin, a tiny one.

Then he looked up at her again. "What is this?"

"It's a sketch of the rapist."

His brows shot up, his gaze dropped down to study the drawing again. He stared at it until his eyes watered, until he'd committed that face to memory. Finally, he looked up at Macy again. "Who drew it?"

"I did."

"It's good."

"Yeah, I wanted to be an artist, but I didn't like the starving part. Veterinary medicine was more fun, though. I love animals so much it was a natural fit, and before I knew it, it just sort of took over."

He nodded slowly and knew she was waiting for him to ask the question he really didn't want to ask. But he had to ask. It was his job. "How do you know what he looks like, Macy?"

She drew in a deep breath, lifted her chin, and watched his face, his eyes. "I have . . . a really powerful connection with animals."

"Yeah?"

"Cassie saw this guy. She kind of . . ." She let her voice trail off, lowered her head.

"Cassie. The dog."

She nodded, not looking up.

"You're saying the dog told you what this guy looks like?"

"Showed me, really. I could see the whole thing unfold, through her eyes. Her memory. She'll never forget the guy who hurt Darla. He wore a ski mask during the rape, but he'd been following them earlier in the day, so she saw him without it. He smelled like leather and stale beer and cigarette smoke. He radiated anger and rage. He didn't have to hurt her; he did it because he wanted to. He enjoyed it."

Jay was listening, trying to get every detail here, but damn, his mind was reeling. "You're telling me you can talk to animals."

"Look, I know it sounds crazy, but it's true. And it's not talking, it's . . . communicating. Mental, not verbal. Or maybe *sensory* is the more accurate term. I can see what they saw, smell what they smelled, hear what they heard, feel what they felt—"

"Macy, that's impossible."

She licked her lips and took a deep breath. "That's the guy. I'm telling you. That's him."

He looked at the sketch again. "What am I supposed to do with this? I mean, where do I tell my superiors I got it? What do we tell the press that it's based on?"

"It's based on the description of an eyewitness."

She was freaking serious. Dead serious. Damn, it was a crying shame, too. He'd liked her, once he'd seen beyond her prickly exterior, and he wanted her like he hadn't wanted anything since—since the summer he spent begging his father for his first BB gun.

Damn. He'd had a narrow escape with this one.

"You can't tell anyone about this, Jay. I've kept this secret a long time."

"Don't worry. I'm not going to tell anyone."

The tone in his voice got to her, finally. She stared at him. "You do think I'm crazy."

He sighed. "Look, I can't use this. I'm sorry." He pushed the paper toward her.

"No, keep it." She shoved it back, got up. She still hadn't touched her doughnut, but she took the coffee. "I'm going to find a way to make you believe me, Jay. Not because I care what you think of me. I don't, I've never cared what other people thought of me. I kept the secret to keep my career alive. But you have to believe it, Jay, because it's the truth, and this guy is going to keep on attacking innocent women until you stop him. I can't live with that, and I don't think you can either."

"I'll catch him," he said. "Just . . . not with this."

She held his gaze a moment longer, then lowered hers and left the shop. He wondered if he'd ever see her again and then wondered why he cared. She was a lunatic. A beautiful, sexy, and, he thought, wounded lunatic.

Damn.

That night, after a busy day at the clinic, and a long time spent in her bathroom acting like a girl, Macy stood outside the door to Jay Harris's apartment, drumming up every bit of courage she had inside her and telling herself to ring the bell. Her finger hovered over it. Damn, why was this so hard?

"Because despite what I said earlier, I do give a damn what he thinks of me," she whispered. "Stupid, stupid, stupid."

But she had to make him believe her. It was vital. Women were suffering, and she could help him stop that, prevent more rapes, more beatings. More pain. She knew Jay was attracted to her, more than attracted, the man was hot for her. That was information she could use. She could get to him that way. And he had a dog. Maybe Fred would be helpful as well.

Seducing a man was not something she had much experience doing. She was no blushing virgin. She liked sex. But she usually had it all by herself, while delicious fantasies ran through her mind. Tonight, she was going to have to act on a few of those fantasies. And she was going to have to make it good. Unforgettably good. So good he would be willing to believe she could read the minds of animals.

"So quit shaking and do it, already."

Nodding firmly, she pressed the button, heard the chimes from the other side, then Jay's footsteps coming closer. The door opened, and he looked at her, his eyes registering surprise.

"Don't tell me you forgot our date tonight," she said. And her voice didn't even tremble. Excellent.

"I . . . I guess I thought after this morning, you—"

"You promised to introduce me to your dog."

He looked uncertain. And he hadn't yet looked anywhere except her face. She'd chosen her clothes with sex in mind, and she needed him to notice that before he decided whether or not to shut the door in her face.

"Did I get the seams straight?"

"Seams . . . ? Oh."

Even as he spoke, she was turning her back to him, running a hand over the back seam of the thigh-high black stockings. She couldn't see him looking, but she knew she had his attention. The dress was black, too, low-cut, curve-hugging, and had a slit up one side. She made damn sure the lacy top of one stocking showed through that slit as she pretended to check her back seam.

"I never seem to get them straight."

"They're great. Perfect." His voice was a little hoarse. Good.

"That's a relief." She turned to face him again and found his gaze roaming from her toes, encased in a pair of the most deadly stiletto heels she'd been able to find, to the cleavage that was a result of the highly effective push-up part of the sexy black corset she wore beneath the dress.

"So, you going to let me in, or what?"

"Sure. Come on in."

Score. She walked in slowly, while he stood holding the door, and she made sure to brush close as she passed. He closed the door behind her and stood there, as if he wasn't sure what to do next.

"So? Where's the infamous Fred?"

"Uh . . . in the bedroom. That's pretty much his favorite place. He likes sleeping on the carpet in there."

She glanced down at the hardwood on which she stood, noted the marble in the kitchen, and imagined the bathroom was tiled. It was a small place, neat, but unadorned. There were a couple of framed wildlife prints on the walls—a herd of deer on a snowy night, a flock of geese in flight, a lone wolf howling at a full moon. She couldn't fault his taste. But aside from those prints and the furniture, the place was bare. Venetian blinds, no curtains. Brown velour sofa and chair bearing the standard accent pillows that probably came with them. Plain looking coffee table, a couple of ordinary lamps.

"Nice place. So the bedroom would be . . . ?"

"It's over there." He pointed toward an open door on the far end of the room. "You want something to drink?"

"That would help." She bit her lip, smiled as if she'd just made a joke. "Yes, I'd love one, thanks."

"Wine?"

"Is that all you have?"

He was studying her face, really trying to read her, she thought. "I've got vodka."

"Better. And orange juice?"

"Yeah."

"Perfect."

He nodded toward the sofa and moved through an open archway into the kitchen. She didn't sit. Instead, she followed and stood watching him as he took glasses from a cupboard, ice from the freezer, OJ from the fridge. He mixed two drinks. She watched him move and got a little tingle that reminded her this wasn't such a chore. She wanted him. Was getting warm already.

He turned, caught her staring at his backside, smiled a little self-satisfied smile that told her he liked that she liked looking at him. Good.

She took the glass he offered her and pretended to examine the ordinary kitchen, oak-stained cupboards with little round white knobs, white fridge, range, and dishwasher.

Taking a long drink she hoped looked like a casual sip, she shifted her eyes to him again and found his eyes focused on her chest.

"How's the drink?"

"Perfect." She took another pull to prove it. "So can I meet Fred now?"

"Okay." He took an inordinately large drink from his own glass, downing about half of its contents at once, then walked toward the bedroom with her following.

But he didn't go in, just nodded through the open doorway. "Wake up, Fred. Meet Macy. Macy, Fred."

She had to force her eyes off the bed, a great big, soft-looking thing piled with pillows and blankets that seemed to be inviting her to crawl inside. The dog was lying on the floor at the foot of the bed. A big, slightly overweight, saggy, baggy basset hound, with ears half the length of his body. He lifted his head from his paws, and his ears still touched the floor.

"I need a refill," Jay said, and she noticed he'd finished his drink. "Go ahead and get acquainted."

"Wait a sec." She drained her glass and held it out. "I'll take seconds, too."

"Okay."

He took her glass and returned to the kitchen. Macy watched him go, then walked into the bedroom, sank down onto the floor beside Fred, and hoped he would trust her with anything and everything he'd observed while hanging around in Jay Harris's bedroom.

Six

When Jay returned to the bedroom, it was to find Fred coming out. He frowned down at his pet. "What's up, pal?"

Fred glanced up at him, but sighed and kept walking on his short little legs. He went all the way to the bathroom and sank down onto the plush throw rug in front of the tub.

"I asked him to give us some privacy."

Jay turned from staring at his dog, to staring at the woman who was lying right now in his bed. She'd taken off the dress. The tiny black number she'd been hiding underneath it was like something out of a fantasy, down to the little straps that hung from the bottom and hooked onto the stockings. She hadn't taken off the shoes.

"Just what are you up to, Macy?" he asked.

"Hey, you're the one who said we had a spark. Chemistry. I'm just looking to find out how much."

God she was hot. He wanted her. Bad.

But she's nuts, a little voice whispered.

Who cares? a bigger voice wondered.

She lifted a hand, crooked a finger at him, beckoning him closer. "Come on, Jay. Don't tell me I wasted several days' pay at Victoria's Secret for nothing."

He swallowed the dryness in his throat, told himself he could handle this, he could sleep with her and not let it impact his objectivity, and not get involved or drawn in to her delusions. He could.

And it was a good thing, because his body wasn't giving him much of a choice in the matter.

He moved to the edge of the bed. She got up, linked her arms around his neck, parted her lips, stared into his eyes, moved close, but no closer. Like gravity, her mouth pulled his to it. There was no thought about it, no intention. He just closed the distance and kissed her like there was no tomorrow, while her body rubbed against his. Damn this was going to be good.

Her hands got busy, shoving his T-shirt up, as her palms skimmed his abs, his waist, his chest. He yanked it off and tossed it, and then she was touching his shoulders, his upper arms.

"You're one sexy man," she told him.

"You're one sexy woman."

"Glad you think so."

She clasped his shoulders and turned him around so his back was to the bed, then she pushed until he lay down, and crawled right on top of him. Straddling him, she kissed him again, his mouth, and then his neck and his chest. God, he was on fire. She went on tasting his skin, even as her hands slid up his arms, moving them until they were up over his head, pressing them down to the mattress there, which turned him on so much he moaned.

Then there was cold metal, a familiar snapping sound. His eyes went wider and he gave an experimental tug and found himself bound to the bed with his own handcuffs, which had been on the dresser, where he'd casually tossed them after his shift.

He swore softly and tugged again, but she was already moving down his body, using her mouth to tease him, using her hands to undo his jeans and tug them off. Then, with infinite slowness, his shorts.

"Oh, my," she said, looking at his cock, which was standing at full attention and aching for her touch. "What's got you so worked up?"

"You," he managed.

"Oh, I'm just getting started." Her fingers trailed over him, then closed around him, and she worked him that way for a while, and then she bent and pressed her lips to him. Tiny little kisses, up one side, up the other, all around the tip, but never touching it. And then finally, when he thought he would explode with need, she parted those lips and took him into her mouth.

He wanted to press his hands to her head, but he had to settle for arching his hips and trying to thrust into her more deeply. Dammit, it was too good to bear, and also, one of his most secret sexual fantasies. How could she know? Or maybe she didn't, maybe it was her fantasy, too . . .

He didn't know. He didn't care.

Just when he thought he was going to explode in her mouth, she released him and stretched out in the bed beside him. She trailed her hand up and down over his chest, giving him time to come back down a little. "I'm going to fuck you now," she told him. "I'm going to ride you like a bull. And you'd better make it good, Jay, because you're not getting out of this bed until you do."

He closed his eyes in an agony of heat.

She got up, and standing there, where he could watch every move, she took off her tiny black thong panties. She turned her back to him when she bent over to slide them over the heels she still wore. And he throbbed so hard at the view, he groaned again.

And then she was back, moving over him, straddling him. He thought he hadn't had a chance for any foreplay. He wanted her wet and ready, and she wouldn't be—

But she was. Wet and hot and oh so tight. She slid her body over his, taking him deep, and then still deeper. He shook all over. And she kept her promise, bracing her hands on his shoulders and riding him hard. He couldn't do a damn thing but lie there and arch into her, over and over, while she worked herself on his cock. When she came, she came loudly, crying out, shaking and spasming around him, milking him until he came, too.

And then she collapsed against his chest, trembling all over.

"Unlock me."

She lifted her head. Her eyes were cloudy and unfocused and moist. "What?"

"You need me to hold you while you come back down. Unlock me."

She blinked and turned to fish the keys from the nightstand where she'd apparently placed them. It took her three times to get the key into the lock and twist it so one wrist came free. He took the key from her to remove the other cuff himself, and then he folded her into his arms and held her close.

"That was incredible," he admitted.

"Just like in that video, huh?"

He blinked, but couldn't search her face, because it was resting on his chest.

"You know, the one you keep tucked away in the closet over there? The one you thought no one would ever know about, where the sexy suspect uses the cop's own handcuffs on him and then takes him, the way I just took you?"

"How the hell do you know about that?"

"Fred told me."

Jay rolled his eyes and tried to figure out if she'd had time to search his room, find the video, see what was on it, and put it back when he'd gone out to make them fresh drinks. He didn't see how, but that had to be it.

"Fred didn't think you'd ever done it that way with a woman, not that he's seen anyway. The last one you brought in here barely moved while you were inside her. She was skinny, light hair, blond I'll bet. Fred didn't like her. She had candy in her purse and didn't even offer him any."

He blinked, cupped her head in his hands and lifted it from his chest so he could read her face. But there was no reading it.

"Do you believe me now?" she asked.

Reality crashed in a little harder than he would have liked. "Is that what this was about? You took me to bed just to prove you could read my mind?"

"Your dog's mind. Not yours. And I didn't hear you complaining."

"I wasn't complaining. I'm still not, but I would have liked to have thought it was about me."

She averted her eyes. "It was about you, too." Macy rolled

away from him, an act that left him feeling lonely before she even got all the way out of the bed. "Look, we both wanted this, or did, until one of us decided the other was insane. I had a point to make."

"And you made it."

She was pulling on her dress, and he was regretting every inch of luscious skin she covered from his hungry eyes. But she turned to stare at him, still lying there in the bed with the blanket at his hips.

"I made it?"

He nodded.

"Then you believe me?"

If it would get her back into his arms, into his bed, hell yes. "Yeah. I mean, I don't understand it, but yeah. I believe you." Because saying no at this point would ensure he never got inside her again. Not an option he would even consider, not now.

He had to admit his skepticism was thoroughly shaken. But he was a cop. He didn't believe anything without proof. Ridiculous as it was, he hoped to hell he could find some. The sooner the better.

"Then you're going to use my sketch."

"Unofficially, for now," he said, making things up as he went along. "I'll show it to the other guys in the department, have them keep an eye out for him. We can go deeper from there."

She nodded slowly, but was examining his eyes as if she suspected he might be lying to her.

"Macy? Are you going to climb back into this bed with me?"

She blinked, staring down at him. "No. Not right now."

He studied her, wondering what she was thinking. Was she more comfortable with him bound, guaranteeing she was in complete control? Was she afraid to release that control? He thought that might be the case, and it intrigued him as much as everything else about her did.

"Why not?" he asked her, not expecting her to answer.

She shrugged. "Why rush?"

"Because that was the most amazing sex I've ever had in my life," he told her. And he wasn't lying.

"That's only because I knew your secret fantasy. Anyone

could be the best you'd ever had if they knew exactly what you wanted."

"So if I knew your secret fantasies, I could return the favor?"

She tipped her head sideways and sent him a "keep dreaming" sort of look.

"Will you tell me?"

"No. This isn't about me and my fantasies, or you and yours, for that matter. It's about stopping a serial rapist."

"I know that." He sat up slowly, reached out and took her hands. Deep down he hoped to God she wasn't entirely crazy. And he was already having second thoughts about dumping her if she was. Because, *damn.* "I'm going to keep after you. You'll give in. Give me one, just one fantasy. A little one to start with. Nothing drastic, nothing dangerous. I'll keep after you until you give me something."

She stared down at their clasped hands. "Why?"

"Because I loved this. I want to blow your mind the way you just blew mine. I want to be the best *you've* ever had. Tell me your fantasy, Macy."

She tossed him a glance as she turned and walked away from the bed. "I have too many to even begin."

Heat blasted through him at those words. Then he realized she was walking out of the bedroom, across the apartment, toward the door. She was leaving!

He jumped out of the bed and rushed, naked, into the living room, only to see the apartment door closing and a fresh copy of the sketch she'd drawn lying on the coffee table.

Hell. Okay, okay. He needed to get to the bottom of this, because he needed to find a way to keep this woman around for a while. So if she was nuts, he'd help her find treatment, medication, whatever it took. And if she wasn't—well, hell, there was very little chance she really was some kind of modern-day female Dr. Doolittle.

He'd start in the morning. By following her. It would be interesting to know how Macy McNamara spent every waking moment of her weekend.

Seven

She spent her Saturday morning at the local animal shelter, where she saw a steady stream of patients. Jay sat outside in his car, with a clear view, thanks to his binoculars and a window in the room she used while she was there. He couldn't hear a hell of a lot, but the apparent woman-in-charge at the shelter seemed to love her.

After Macy left, he stuck around, waited to be sure she wasn't coming right back, and then went inside. The reception area was neat, but plain, lined with plastic chairs, some of which held people. Its walls were covered in photos of happy kids with their assumedly adopted pets. A blond woman seated behind a desk rose when he entered. "Hi, I'm Sally. Can I help you find a pet today?"

"Uh, no." He flashed his badge. "Actually I'm here to ask a few questions about a friend of yours—Macy McNamara?"

Her eyebrows rose in undisguised surprise. "She . . . just left."

"I know."

"Well, what could you possibly want to know about Macy?"

"Look, she's not in any trouble. I just . . . she claims to have a certain . . . ability."

The woman's blue eyes widened, telling him she knew exactly what he meant.

"So, this so-called gift of hers—do you believe it's for real?"

She hustled around the desk, gripped his arm, and tugged him with her, through a doorway and into a corridor that was lined on both sides with kennels, most of them holding dogs or cats.

"Okay. First things first. No one knows about Macy's gift," she said, her voice authoritative and utterly earnest. "I think she'd like to keep it that way."

He nodded. "You know about it, though."

She thinned her lips, nodded, just once. "Not that she's told me. Not in so many words, at least. But I've seen it. It's for real, this . . . thing she has."

"Would you elaborate on that?"

She met his eyes. "Not if it's on the record."

"Then it's not."

"Okay." She drew a breath, seemed to gather her thoughts, then nodded. "Okay, we had this stray brought in. Macy came in to give him a checkup. She comes in every weekend, free of charge. We chip in what we can to cover her expenses, but mostly fall short. She doesn't care. She's a good person, officer."

"Detective," he said. "Harris."

"Sorry. Anyway, we had this one little beagle pup, found alongside the highway, no tags. She gave him his checkup, and then said she'd be back on Sunday to help me find his home. She asked me not to tell anyone else. So I didn't."

"And?"

"Sunday she showed up with a drawing. A little house, a river running behind it, a big oak tree on the lawn, a swing set. She said she thought that was where the dog lived. Gave me some lame excuse about thinking she'd seen him before. But the thing was, while she *remembered* every detail of what the place looked like, and even the two little boys who lived there, she didn't know where it was. It just didn't make any sense. So we drove around all day Sunday, looking for this house, and she kept calling the pup Jack. I didn't think much of it, until we found the place."

He suppressed a shiver. "You found the place?"

Sally nodded. "Identical to the one in the picture, right down to the stripes on the legs of the swing set. We got out of the car. Macy was carrying that pup, and before we got halfway to the front door, two kids—boys—came busting out, hollering, 'You found him! You found Jack!'"

Okay. It was odd. But it didn't mean she could talk to animals. "Couldn't it have been true, what she told you?" he asked. "That she'd seen the animal somewhere before? She is a vet, after all."

"Sure, it could have been true. But it's happened too many times, Detective. A dozen times in the past year. And then there was my cat."

"Your cat?"

"I bring him to work sometimes. She came in one Saturday, and he jumped up into her lap when she sat down for a coffee break. She stroked him about three times, and then she got this look on her face and told me to bring him in for a checkup. I told her he was fine, and she insisted he wasn't. There was something wrong with his head."

He knew what was coming next. He wasn't disappointed.

"He had a tiny tumor. Tiny, Detective. She removed it. It could have killed him."

Jay frowned hard. "Again, she's a vet. Maybe she saw symptoms."

"Maybe. Maybe not. I don't think so. I think she sensed it, the way she senses everything any animal is feeling. I've had dogs refusing to eat, only to have her tell me they prefer a different type of food. I've had cats pulling out their fur, only to have her tell me the smell of the disinfectant is upsetting their stomachs and to try a different brand. I've had cases where the family wanted to come and claim their pet, only to have Macy tell me they were abusive to it, and it would be better off elsewhere. She's never been wrong. Not once. It's too much to be coincidence, Detective."

He nodded slowly. "Okay."

"Okay?"

"Yeah. I guess . . . shit, I can't believe I'm saying this. But I guess I'm convinced."

"Is it that important for you to be? I mean, I've never known Macy to care much what anyone thinks of her."

"Yeah. It's pretty important. And if you don't mind, I'd like to keep this conversation between us."

"I can keep it to myself, if you promise me that you will. I don't want this town thinking Macy is some kind of a head case, Detective. It could ruin her practice. And she doesn't deserve that."

"No," he said. "She doesn't." And that was exactly what she was risking by trusting him with her secret. She had to know that. But she'd risked it anyway. "It won't go any further," he promised.

"Good. Now," she flashed a bright smile. "Can I interest you in a pet?" As she spoke, she turned to look through a cage door, to where an ancient-looking bloodhound lay in an utterly relaxed pose, ears draped over his front paws, eyes open, but tired looking. He seemed to be staring right into Jay's eyes.

He stared right back and said, "Absolutely not."

Macy was between patients, struggling to keep up without Christine—hell, it was just the two of them running the place after all, and the temp was ambitious, but just didn't know things the way Christine did—when she stopped to take a phone call.

"Hey," he said.

And that was all it took. Her belly clenched into knots, and her heart started hammering. If she didn't know better, she would have sworn her cheeks went pink. "Hi, Jay. What's up?"

"You ready to tell me one of your fantasies yet?"

"No."

"Please?"

She closed her eyes. "Fine. In an elevator."

He was quiet for a moment. "I need more details."

She opened her eyes and glanced at Rose behind the desk. "I'm at work. Use your imagination."

"Oh, I am. Believe me."

She smiled, in spite of herself. It felt good to be able to turn a man on as much as she seemed to turn him on.

"I wanted to let you know, I've been showing that sketch around to some cops I trust."

"Anything come of it?"

"Not yet. But I could use some more of your input."

"What do you need?"

He hesitated before answering, and she wondered what he'd avoided saying, if anything. "It's involved. Can you come by my place tonight?"

"Depends. Are you going to feed me?"

"I'll be working through dinner. How does dessert sound?"

"Sounds great. Cheesecake. Raspberry topping. Whipped cream. And coffee, good coffee. With half-and-half."

"I like a woman who knows exactly what she wants."

"Yeah, well, only when it comes to food," she said.

"You're not so sure about other aspects of your life, then?"

"I used to be." She bit her lip, wondering how she'd managed to let *that* slip out. "Nine o'clock?"

"See you then."

She hung up the phone and wondered if she was going to regret this. Probably. But living for the moment had its benefits. And she intended to enjoy them tonight.

In an elevator, Jay thought. No details. Damn, she was putting him on the spot to come through for her. It would have to be fast and furious, that was for sure. What was it about an elevator that turned her on, he wondered. The possibility of getting caught? The idea that it was simply not done? The motion? All of the above? Maybe it was the fast and furious part. It would have to be sudden, out of the blue, no foreplay, no leading up to it, no time for undressing. Just one big explosion. Okay. He could handle that.

"Jay?"

He looked up from his desk and smiled at Matt as he came in. "Hey, pal. Just the guy I wanted to see. Where you been?"

"Ahh, family shit. Had to come in late. You getting anywhere with the lady vet?"

"I think so, yeah." He rummaged in his desk drawer, pulled out the sketch, and handed it to his partner.

Matt stared at it and frowned. "What is this?"

"A sketch of the rapist."

His partner's balding head came up fast, his eyes narrow. "According to who?"

"An anonymous source," he said. "Sorry, pal, that's all I can tell you right now. But I think it's legit. He look familiar?"

"No." Matt blinked. "But uh—can I keep this?"

"Hold on, I have a copy for you. That's the original, I want that one." He returned to his desk drawer, while Matt turned the drawing over, as if there would be further information on the back. Jay pulled out a copy of the drawing and handed it to Matt, taking the original from him. "I've been showing it around, but only to a select few. Guys we've been working with on this, mostly. It has to stay discreet, at least until we have more to go on."

"I think that's the smartest way to go, for now. Anonymous sources aren't exactly dependable," Matt said. He folded the sheet, tucked it into his pants pocket. "She an eyewitness, this source?"

"No. She drew the sketch from the description of an eyewitness, but they can't come forward."

"Why not?"

He shrugged and looked away, aware he'd just confirmed for his friend that the source was a woman. "It's not important. Just keep an eye out, okay?"

"Will do." Matt started for the office door, then paused and glanced back. "Anyone think he looks familiar so far?"

"Nope. I'm hitting a big fat zero, here. Just like every other lead in this mess."

"We'll get there, pal."

"Yeah, we always do, sooner or later. This guy's gonna fuck up, and when he does, we're gonna be there to collar his ass. You and me, partner."

"You and me, Jay."

Eight

She stepped into the elevator at Jay's building, turned around and pushed the button, then waited as the doors slid closed. But just before they met, an arm thrust in between them to keep them open.

A male arm.

And as the doors parted again, she saw the male to which it was attached. Jay. He wore what she used to refer to as a "muscle shirt" back in her high school days—tight, black T with cap sleeves. Faded jeans. She'd never seen him dressed so casually before. It was hot. *He* was hot. And he was just standing there, staring at her.

"Hi," she said, because somebody had to say something.

He only smiled, a sexy smile full of suggestions she didn't even want to think about. Hell, she'd told him about her elevator fantasy. Did he intend—?

The doors slid closed, and the car started its bumpy ascent. Jay made a fist and thumped it on the emergency stop button without taking his eyes off her. Then he moved toward her, snapped his arms around her, and kissed her as if his pants were on fire. He didn't say a word, just held her against him, ravaging her mouth while his hands slid down over her ass to the short skirt she wore. When they slid up again, they took the skirt with them. He arched into her, gripped and kneaded her butt cheeks, and held her to him.

"Jay, this isn't—I mean, we *can't*."

He was shoving her panties down, though. Down her thighs, until they went the rest of the way on their own, and when he bent his head to start sucking on her neck, she stepped out of them and kicked them aside. God damn, she liked that.

He caught her thighs in his hands and lifted them, anchoring her legs around his waist, as he backed her up against the wall. Then he let go with one hand and shoved it in between them to undo those sexy jeans.

"Jay, there must be an alarm going off somewhere."

"Yeah. Right here." He shoved himself inside her, driving the breath right out of her lungs. She sucked in a sharp breath, as he drew back and drove again.

"Someone could come."

"I'll make sure of that."

Enough said. She held on for dear life, as he pounded into her, her back and a few times even her head, thumping on the wall behind her. She linked her ankles and curled her toes, arms twined around his neck, bouncing up and down on him like she was riding a wild stallion.

He bent his head, hiking her up higher as he did, and started mouthing her breasts through the blouse she wore. She helped him out, releasing the stranglehold she had on his neck long enough to undo a few buttons, so she could tug the blouse down far enough to expose a breast. And he made good use of it.

She moaned when he sucked her there, and the sensations magnified until she thought she'd lose her mind. "Oh, God. Oh, God. Oh, God."

He bucked harder, drove deeper, held her tighter so she took the full impact of every thrust, and bit her nipple just a little. Just enough.

She screamed when the orgasm ripped through her. She couldn't help it, barely recognized the sound as her own voice. And he kept going, the bastard, driving her to a state of quivering sensations almost too intense to bear, before he groaned and climaxed in one all-consuming thrust that was so deep she swore he was reaching her belly button.

Then he held her there while the sensations went on and on, and finally began to ebb.

She unlocked her ankles from behind his back, and he held her as she lowered her legs to the floor. But her legs didn't want to cooperate, and she was glad the wall was behind her, because it was the only thing holding her up. God, she was shaking all over.

Jay fixed his jeans. Then he picked up her panties and knelt in front of her, sliding them over one foot, then the other, finally pulling them up and smoothing down her skirt. She struggled to right her blouse, but he wound up pushing her hands away and doing that for her as well, when she couldn't fasten a single button.

Then he just turned around as if nothing had happened and hit the emergency button again. The elevator lurched into motion, and about three seconds later, it came to a stop and its doors opened.

Two people stood in the hall, waiting to get on the elevator. Jay smiled and greeted them, as if everything were perfectly normal, as he slid an arm around Macy to help her stay upright as she exited. She tried to look normal. Might even have succeeded, though her blood was still churning, her body still pulsing, her hands still shaking.

The couple got in, and the doors closed behind them, as Jay walked her to the door of his apartment. He'd left it unlocked, she noticed. He swung the door open and glanced down at her face, and then he smiled just a little. "I take it that was good for you, too?"

"Gee, how could you tell?" Hell, even her voice was shaking.

His smile got bigger, and he scooped her off her feet and carried her into his apartment, kicking the door closed behind him. He took her straight to the sofa, sank down onto it, and held her in his arms, nice and tight, as if he knew how much she needed that right then.

She snuggled closer, relaxed her head on his shoulder. "Just until I stop shaking," she whispered.

"I know. I've got you. Take your time."

"That was incredible, Jay. What was that, five minutes? I can't get *myself* off in five minutes."

"Maybe I've just got the touch."

"You've got something."

He stroked her hair a little, and she opened her eyes and saw the way he was looking at her. His eyes were soft, heavy lidded, and kind of dreamy. A little alarm went off in her head. That look scared her. It was almost . . . loving.

She was *not* ready for that.

"I think I'm okay now." And she needed a little space. She needed to think.

Of course, as soon as he eased her off his lap and got up, what she needed was his arms around her again. Immediately. But she didn't say so. She changed the subject instead. "You said you needed my input on something."

"Yeah. It's over there." He pointed.

She looked and then sat up and looked again. A buff-colored, tired-looking bloodhound lay smack in the center of the living room floor. Fred sat in front of him, staring down at him, even though the hound was snoring.

"Who is that?" she asked.

"That's what I'd like your input on. I've tried a dozen names, and he doesn't seem to respond to any of them. I don't know anything about his past. It's tough to build a relationship that way, you know?"

She sent him a look, wondering if there was a message in there for her.

"Have a chat with him, will you? I'll get the dessert and make fresh coffee while you do."

And then he left the room. Staring after him, Macy tipped her head to one side. He was asking her to talk to the dog as if it were nothing unusual. As if he believed her.

God, he believed her.

When Jay returned to the living room with two slices of the requested cheesecake, complete with raspberry topping and whipped cream and two freshly brewed cups of coffee—Dunkin' Donuts brand, nice and strong—he found Macy sitting on the floor between the two dogs. Fred sat right up against her right side, and her arm was around him. The bloodhound was still lying down, but his head was in Macy's lap, and he was awake.

"You get anywhere with him?" he asked, lowering the tray to the coffee table and unloading it there.

"Yep. Damn, that looks good. Excuse me, guys." She eased the hound's head off her lap and got up, came to the couch and sat down, immediately claiming a dessert plate and fork. She took her first bite, closed her eyes, and said "Mmmmm." Then she licked her lips.

Jay fought down the heat that watching her created in him and tried to focus on his own dessert. But it wasn't what he really wanted. And what had it been, ten, fifteen minutes since he'd taken her hard and fast in the elevator? Since when was he ready for another round this fast? Not since he was a teenager, if memory served.

She took another bite, then set the plate down and tried the coffee. Again, she closed her eyes. "Perfect," she said.

"Yeah."

She sent him an odd smile, reclaimed her cheesecake, and said, "His name is Henry."

"Henry?"

As soon as he said it, more loudly than she had, the dog lifted his head and released a deep "woof."

"Well, I'll be—"

"He lived with an old man for a long, long time. He doesn't think of him by any name, and I suspect that's because they were mostly loners, just the two of them. There was never anyone around calling the old man by name, so Henry never associated a name with him. They were walking in the park one day when the old man just keeled over. Henry tried licking his face, then resorted to baying for help. So many people came around that he got scared and backed off to watch. The sirens came next, and those really shook him, so he hid. When everything was quiet again, he came out to investigate, but the old man was gone."

"Wait a minute . . . that happened just four days ago. An old man collapsed in the park—I remember the call."

She nodded. "Did he make it?"

"No. He was DOA. Heart just gave out."

She looked sad for a moment. "He followed the old man's scent to the hospital—you know a bloodhound has a nose like nothing else alive. He could smell him, even though the old fellow was in the back of an ambulance. Anyway, he waited outside the hospital through one long night, and that's where he was found. He's been at Sally's—uh, at the animal shelter, that is—since then."

He nodded. "No wonder he looks so sad."

"He likes you. Likes this place. He misses his friend, but he's already feeling loads better. And he adores Fred."

"They're like two peas in a pod."

She nodded, but he noticed she was looking at him closely now.

"What?"

She shrugged. "Just wondering what you were doing at the shelter. That is where you got him, isn't it?"

"I needed another dog around, to keep Fred company."

"Sally will tell me, you know."

"I know."

"You were checking up on me, weren't you?"

He sighed, hoping the truth wouldn't piss her off too much. "I'm a cop, Macy. It's what I do."

She nodded. "So you went there to see if I was a complete lunatic, and you came home with a new dog. That Sally, she'll get you every time."

"No shit. She's good. And, just so you know, she had nothing but praise for you. And she knows about your . . . abilities, and believes in them. Hell, by the time she finished telling me enough anecdotes to fill a book, I was believing in them, too."

"Really?"

He looked her right in the eye, because he knew this was important to her. "Yeah. Really."

"That means a lot to me."

He could tell it did. He saw the way her throat swelled a little as she tried to swallow, and the way her eyes got damp.

"And you know what else?" she asked.

"What?"

"I like that you couldn't say no to Sally, or to Henry. That tells me an awful lot about you."

"I'd like to tell you more."

"I'd like to hear more."

"You would?"

She nodded.

"And will you return the favor and tell me about you?"

She studied his face for a long moment. "Yeah. I think maybe I will."

Matthew Cooper sat in his study with the drawing his partner had given him on the desk in front of him. A drawing of his son, Adam.

He'd known for three months now that his son was behind the crimes. Hell, he'd found the lighter at the scene of the second attack—the one he'd bought for Adam himself, engraved with Adam's initials. Fortunately, he and Jay had been the first on the scene, and he'd managed to pocket the thing before Jay had seen it.

He'd had to do likewise several times since, with bits of evidence his idiot kid left lying around. Yeah, there was a reason they were hitting a brick wall with this case. It was because he was sanitizing every crime scene as best he could without getting caught, all before the forensics team could arrive.

Hell, he'd tried everything. Beat the kid bloody, threatened to expose him and let him go down. And for a while, the string of rapes had stopped. But now they were happening again.

And now there was a sketch of the rapist. An accurate sketch, right down to the scar on Adam's chin. Sooner or later, someone at the department was going to recognize that drawing. So he had to take care of this, and do it soon.

It was that damn lady vet. Matt knew it, because the original had been done on the back side of a sheet of office stationery, with her name, office address, and phone number printed on it. She'd drawn on the opposite side, and maybe Jay hadn't noticed the identifying information, or maybe he had forgotten. Or maybe he just trusted Matt so much he hadn't been worried.

He looked toward the corner of the room, where Adam

was still huddled on the floor, pinching his nose to stop the bleeding. "This ends, now," Matt told his son.

"Dad, I tried. I swear I did. I just . . . there's something wrong with me."

"Yeah. I know there is. I'm gonna get you some help, son. You're going into a facility, and if you argue with me on this, I'll expose you. You understand?"

"I'm already exposed. That picture—"

"Is going to be meaningless once the real rapist is caught."

"The real—?"

"Yeah. See, there's gonna be one more rape. Just one. And you aren't doing it, so get that out of your sick head right now. I'll set it up. I know a guy, registered sex offender, paroled six months ago. He's in town, basically a useless boil on the ass of society. I'll plant enough evidence at the scene to put this squarely on him and ensure a conviction. But I'll only do it if you agree to inpatient treatment. I can't keep covering up for you, forever."

Adam nodded his head, though his movements were jerky. "Thanks, Dad. But . . . what about the lady vet? She knows what I look like."

Matt lowered his eyes. There were some things he couldn't say out loud. Not even to his lowlife son. No one needed to know just yet that he'd already picked out the final rape victim. And that this time, the rapist was going to go too far, and kill her.

"You just let me worry about that," he said. Then he sighed. "I'm sorry I hit you."

Adam lowered his head. "Yeah. So am I."

Nine

Matt followed the woman. It made sense to case things out, first, before he moved on with his plan. Nothing could go wrong.

His son was all he had, everything. And deep down, he felt partly responsible for the way Adam had turned out. He'd beaten the hell out of the boy's mother for years, and though he liked to think Adam had been too young to remember, he supposed there was some chance he might. Maybe it was buried down deep in his head someplace.

In the end, she'd offed herself—used his service revolver to do it. Useless and stupid of her. He'd promised he wouldn't hit her again, and he'd meant it, that time. Adam was seven, getting too big to let it slide, had begun turning on his father, looking at him with hate in his eyes. He knew he had to change, for his son. And he would have, too, if the bitch had stuck around and given him the chance.

There was nothing he wouldn't do for Adam.

Including what he was going to do next. But damn, it wasn't going to be easy. Hell, beating her up wouldn't bother him. But rape wasn't in him, and murder—he just had to keep reminding himself he had to do it. It was her or Adam. Period.

The lady vet spent most of the night at Jay's apartment, while Matt parked outside waiting to follow her home, check out her place, see what kind of security she had on it. But she didn't come out for a long time. And damn, it was going to make this harder, knowing Jay was sleeping with the woman. But not impossible. Jay had never been serious about a female in all the time Matt had known him. This one was nothing special to him. He'd get over it.

"So you basically had a Beaver Cleaver childhood," Macy said. She was curled up on the sofa, a glass of wine in one hand, Jay's oversize white terry robe wrapped snugly around her.

Jay sat beside her, an arm around her shoulders, her head in the crook of his neck. "Basically, yeah. No major trauma, no deep, dark secrets."

He'd told her all about himself, his history, his family, high school, college, his career in law enforcement—and even that had been remarkably drama free. A few big cases, sure. A lot of stress, she imagined, but nothing dramatic enough to send him into therapy or to the nearest bar.

"You've had a remarkably ordinary life," she said.

"Hope you don't find that boring."

She shook her head. "Refreshing, really. I like it. You're stable. Normal, even."

"Used to be. I've been bouncing off the walls since I met you."

She lifted her head to look up into his eyes. "What about women?"

"What about them?"

"Come on, you said you'd tell me all about yourself. So tell me about your . . . romantic history."

He sighed, clearly not comfortable with the topic. "I haven't really had one."

"Oh, come on. What about the skinny blonde Fred told me about?"

"Okay, okay. I've been with women. A lot of women, I guess. What I meant was, I wouldn't classify any of those relationships as 'romantic.' Hell, I wouldn't even classify them as relationships."

"So you're a player."

He shot her a nervous look. "Don't think that. I'm not like that. I just tend to gravitate toward women who want the same thing I do."

"Which is?"

"Which *was* a good time. A few laughs. A lot of sex. Careful, safe sex, Macy. I've never been stupid about that."

She didn't doubt it. "I'm not judging you. I'm just curious." And worried. Because of the way he'd emphasized that those things were what he used to want, which seemed to suggest they were not what he wanted anymore. "And I don't see anything wrong with dating just for fun, so long as both parties understand that from the beginning."

"Neither did I. I don't know, now it all seems pretty shallow and pointless. I think maybe what I want is changing."

She felt herself stiffen, knew he had to feel it, too.

"I'm not pushing, Macy, I just think you should know—"

"I guess it's my turn, then."

He tipped his head slightly to one side, searching her face.

"To tell you about me, I mean. It's not nearly as pretty as your life story, I'm afraid. But I did promise."

He nodded. Oh, she knew he could see through her by now. He had to know she'd cut him off for a reason, and she'd been up front enough with him about not wanting a relationship, that he probably knew what that reason was. He'd been perilously close to turning this into one of those sticky romantic things she'd deliberately avoided all her life. And that would just ruin it.

"Okay," he said. "Tell me. I'll bet it's not nearly as boring as my story was."

She sighed. "My mother died giving birth to me, so I never knew her. My dad was kind of—I don't know, distant. Cold. Looking back, I think maybe he blamed me on some level. Or maybe not, maybe I just served as a constant reminder of what he had lost. Either way, we were never close. He remarried when I was five, to a woman I hated, and who hated me right back. Beverly." She made a face, expected Jay to smile at it, but he didn't. He was searching her face, instead.

"Was she abusive?"

"I thought so, though most people wouldn't call it that.

She made me get rid of my pets. Said she was allergic. My big, fat, long-haired, half-Persian cat, Buffy. My mixed-up mongrel dog, Buttons. My guinea pig, Marty."

"Marty?"

She smiled. "It fit him."

"Were you . . . you know, communicating with the animals, even then?"

She shrugged. "If I was, I wasn't aware of it. But those three were my only friends. I didn't connect with kids in school. I didn't make friends easily, wasn't popular. All I thought about all day was getting home to my pets. And then she came, and I had to let them go. I never forgave my father for siding with her on that."

"He let you down."

She nodded.

"So when did you realize you had this gift of yours?"

She bit her lip, lowered her head. "I don't . . . talk about that."

His hand came to her chin, tipping her head up. "You don't have to, if you don't want to. But I'd really like to know. And you can trust me, Macy. I promise."

She frowned at him, not because she didn't understand what he was saying, but because she didn't understand what she was feeling. She did trust him. She realized it right then, and that was so shocking to her that she could barely process it. Why? Why *him*?

She took a sip of her wine, set the glass down, and words started spilling out of her mouth, before she even realized that she'd decided to tell him.

"I was seven. Two years with Beverly, and I hated it. Dad took us on a camping trip—a weekend at Yellowstone. It was, maybe, his way of trying to make things up to me. He knew I'd love it. Beverly threw a fit. She hated nature, hated the outdoors, but in the end, she gave in. For once, Dad held his ground, took my side. I was so happy, so excited. But then . . . well, everything went wrong."

She lowered her feet to the floor and got up from the sofa, pacing slowly away from him, her vision turned inward, her wineglass in her hand. "We'd gone hiking. Beverly forgot her precious bug repellent and bitched until Dad went back to

camp to get it. While he was gone, we wandered off the trail
to check out some wildflowers and then farther, to a stream,
and then a tree, and then some tracks in the ground. I don't
know, it was one thing after another, and I was like a kid in a
candy store. So excited, and kind of amazed that I was actually having a good time with my stepmother. And then all of
the sudden, she was just . . . gone."

She turned to glance at Jay. He was still sitting on the sofa,
staring at her, his eyes dark and probing. "Gone?"

"I couldn't find her. I called, and I searched, but I couldn't
find her. And I couldn't find the trail, either. I thought I knew
the way back, but only wound up wandering farther into the
forest. It got dark. I was hungry and cold and scared out of my
mind. Spent that entire night alone in the forest, and I was
pretty sure I'd never find my way back to my dad."

"You must have been terrified."

She nodded. "I finally stopped wandering, probably just
because I was too tired to go on. I spent the night under a pine
tree, listening to the animals all around me. Birds and squir-
rels and chipmunks and field mice. And after a while, I got
this feeling that I could understand them. That they were
telling me to wait right there until morning, that I was safe
there." She shook her head slowly at the memory. "I believed
it. I believed it was real, even though deep down there was
this little part of my mind telling me it was just my imagination. I needed to believe it right then, and I let myself. I felt
safe, and protected. And in the morning, when the songbirds
started chirping and little deer were tripping through the
woods, I was sure they were telling me where the trail was. I
was just sure of it. Not with words, just feelings. So I followed those feelings, and I found the trail. I started back
toward camp, and was only a mile or so away when the park
rangers found me."

She glanced down at the floor, where the two dogs lay, not
sleeping, but watching her as if they, too, were listening to her
story. "I've never said this out loud before, Jay, but I've
always believed Beverly lost me on purpose. I think she was
trying to get rid of me. I was sure of it, even then. So sure that
after that trip, I told my father I'd prefer to live with my
grandparents."

"But you didn't tell him why?"

"No. But he'd have to be an idiot not to have at least suspected the same thing I did." She shrugged. "He didn't do anything about it, though. Just let me go. So I guess, even though I found my way back, Beverly got what she wanted in the end."

"She should have done time," Jay muttered. He sounded angry, then got to his feet, came to her, and wrapped her up in his strong, soothing arms. "I'm sorry you went through that, Macy."

"I'm not," she said, relaxing and holding him and wondering why it felt so damn good. "I've been talking to animals ever since. It's what made me decide to become a vet, so I could spend more time with them. It was only as I got older that I came to understand that I wasn't really talking to them, but picking up things the same way they did. Through their senses—through smells, feelings, instincts—sight and sound and taste. That camping trip really was the defining moment of my life."

"Yeah. Unfortunately, it had a down side, too. It taught you not to trust people, because they would only betray you, not to get close to them because they would only hurt you, not to depend on them, because they would only let you down."

She nodded. "All that's true. But those lessons have served me well, Jay. They've kept me from being betrayed, hurt, and let down ever again."

"But they haven't kept you from being lonely."

She looked up at him, into his eyes. "I have the life I want. The life I chose, Jay."

"You could have a lot more."

She lowered her head quickly, swallowed the lump in her throat, and wondered why her heart was pounding and her blood thrumming as if she'd just run a marathon. She felt the way she would feel if she were utterly terrified of something. And maybe she was.

"I should go," she said. "It's getting late."

"I'm sorry. I was pushing again, I'm sorry, Macy."

She sighed deeply. "It's okay. I just—"

"I know. Kiss me good night?"

The fear went away when she nodded, and his mouth

descended to cover and capture hers. He kissed her slowly, gently, deeply, not pushing but teasing until she forgot everything except his taste and the way he made her feel. By the time they stopped kissing, her heart was racing for all the right reasons, and she wasn't afraid anymore.

"I need another fantasy, Macy. You said you had plenty. Give me one more."

She shook her head. "I'll sleep on it."

"I'll hold you to that. And I want to see you tomorrow."

She wasn't sure it was such a great idea to see him again so soon. He was already starting to feel more than she wanted him to. But instead of saying that, she found herself nodding, and feeling as eager to see him again as he seemed to be to see her. And then she wrapped her arms around his neck and kissed him one last time, before turning to throw on her clothes and leave the apartment, fast, before she could change her mind.

Ten

Finally, the woman—Macy McNamara—left Jay's apartment, got into her car, and drove away. Matt had been half asleep when she'd emerged, but had come fully awake by the time her car's headlights snapped on. His heart pounded, and his blood rushed. Every cell in his body came to life in anticipation of what he had to do. There was fear, yes, but there was something else. Some forbidden feeling of excited anticipation. Even though it wouldn't be tonight. Tonight was for laying the groundwork.

He followed her.

She lived in a big Victorian house in a suburb that was littered with them. He was careful to note the landmarks particular to hers, so he wouldn't get the wrong place by mistake tomorrow night. It was white, with dark trim. Not black, quite. Maybe green. Tough to tell with only the headlights illuminating it.

He watched as she shut the car off and went inside, unlocking the door. She was greeted by several barking dogs, and Matt thanked his lucky stars he'd checked the place out first. Those dogs would need to be dealt with, or he'd never get to her.

He waited outside for a while, until all the lights went out and she'd had ample time to settle into bed. Then he got out of his SUV and walked around the house, making as little noise as possible, and keeping to the hedges and shrubs that separated her property from her neighbors. Most of the flora were tall enough to conceal a grown man creeping around in the darkness. Good.

In the back he saw a fenced-in yard, four-foot-high chain link. Easy to scale. Inside were doghouses and dishes and toys. A deck lined the back of the house. And in the back door—yes. A doggie-door. Perfect.

As he stared at it, he heard barking, and three canines came charging through it—which told him it was left open at night while she slept, so the dogs could go in and out. Sure it was. She wouldn't expect anyone to gain access that way. They'd have to climb into the fenced-in yard and get past all those mutts to do so. She probably felt perfectly secure.

The dogs barked up a storm, and he backed away, hurrying along the shrubbery wall to the sidewalk, as an upstairs light popped on. Then, casually, he walked a block down to where he'd left his car and drove it home.

Adam was in bed. Good. Matt had set up an appointment for him with a very expensive, very discreet psychiatrist who would get him the help he needed. Since Matt knew about the man's addiction problem and had enough evidence to put him away for quite a while, he had no doubt the shrink would do what he was told.

Tomorrow, he would pick up his scapegoat to question him about some unrelated case and collect his fingerprints, a couple of hairs, whatever else he could get. Then he'd plant the evidence at the scene. The two-time loser would be caught and convicted, the case closed, and since the rapes would end once he was put away—because Adam would be in a mental hospital by then—no one would ever question his guilt.

It was perfect.

Matt was ready. And he wasn't even dreading the task ahead all that much.

The next day was completely insane. Macy had three emergency patients in addition to a full schedule of regulars and wound up working straight through lunch and still falling behind. Thank God Christine was back on the job. She had bruises and seemed skittish, not her usual confident, bubbly self, but just as efficient as ever. Macy didn't know what she would do without her.

It was after five, and her stomach was as empty as a desert. She was hurrying through the reception area, from one treatment room to the next, when Christine held out the telephone and covered up the mouthpiece. "Jay Harris. The cop," she said. "I thought he was calling for me, at first, the way he asked how I was doing, and filled me in on the case before even asking for you." She shrugged. "I think he's kinda sweet. You two have something going on?"

Macy shrugged, proud that she'd finally managed to stop wincing every time she looked at Christine's bruised face. "Something. I'm just not sure what." She took the phone. "Hi, Jay."

"Hey. You're still at the office. I take it that's bad news for me, huh?"

"Why, what did you have in mind?"

"Depends. How long are you gonna be?"

She looked around the waiting room—three cats and two dogs. All routine. A couple of vaccines, a hairball, a rash. "Another hour and a half, by my best guess. I worked straight through lunch, and I'm still behind."

"You must be starved. How about I make you dinner, have it waiting when you get here?"

She frowned in thought. "You know, I hate to ask, but—"

"Ask."

"Would you mind if we did it at my place? That way you could feed the gang for me, the dogs, anyway. If they don't get dinner on time, they tend to start chewing the furniture."

He laughed, and the deep, sexy sound of it stroked every nerve ending in her body. "I'd be glad to. Think they'll let me in?"

"They love you. There's a key in the fuschia plant that's hanging on the front porch."

"Okay. Any preference for dinner?"

"Nothing foreign. Simple and filling."

"Got it. Steak, salad, baked potatoes with sour cream and chives, and maybe chocolate cake for dessert. Sound good?"

"God, I want you," she said with a laugh, as her stomach rumbled.

"You just want me for my meat. I'll see you soon."

He hung up before she could reply, and when she turned to return the phone to Christine, she realized she hadn't exactly been discreet. Christine was grinning at her, and Macy would have resented it, if it hadn't been the first time she'd seen her friend smile since the rape. "Shut up," she said, and hurried back to work.

Jay found the key right where Macy had told him it would be and let himself in, to the delight of the dogs. The chocolate lab was gone, as he'd expected. He knew her owner had been released from the hospital the day before, and he imagined reclaiming her dog had been the first thing on her to-do list. But Winkin, Blinkin, and Nod greeted him at the door, barking happily as he made his way past them, juggling grocery bags and closing the door with his foot.

There had been little progress on Macy's various remodeling projects. A bit here, a bit there. Were he tackling the place himself, he'd have been more deliberate about it, more disciplined. He'd have planned out each bit of work, then completed it before moving on to the next. Not Macy, though. She worked according to what inspired her at any given moment.

A man would never know quite what to expect from a woman like her. Some men might find that irritating. He found himself challenged by it, and even excited. Then again there wasn't much about Macy McNamara that he didn't find challenging and exciting.

He carried the groceries into the kitchen, then went to work feeding the dogs as she had requested, and as the pack of them seemed to expect. Macy had assured him that her dogs sensed he was a decent person and liked him, and he hoped that was why they were so willing to let him traipse around her place when she wasn't home. He'd hate to think just anyone could walk in here without being challenged.

With the dogs fed and in their yard, Jay busied himself

scrubbing the potatoes. It was when he was looking through various drawers for the skewers, and coming up empty that he found a well-worn paperback novel with dog-eared corners that suggested it had been read over and over. The title, *A Woman's Passion*, intrigued him, as did the cover art, a nude woman with one arm crossing her chest, the other stretched downward, so her palm covered her center, her back arched, head tipped up, eyes closed. She was superimposed by translucent flames.

"Hmm."

He flipped through the pages, stopping in a place where the upper corner was folded down to mark the spot. And then he sat down and began to read the scene Macy apparently liked enough to read over and over.

When he finished, he smiled and went back to cooking dinner.

Eleven

Macy arrived home to the succulent smells of food wafting from her kitchen and walked in to find the table set, candles gleaming, and Jay waiting with a dangerously smug expression on his handsome face.

He kept smiling—almost as if he knew something she didn't—as he came across the kitchen to greet her with an all-too-brief kiss.

"Dinner's ready."

"Everything looks great," she told him. "Thank you, Jay. This was above and beyond."

"Oh, you just wait."

She frowned, searching his face. "For what?"

"Later. You ready to eat, or do you need to relax first? Maybe have a drink?"

"I'm starved, but I'd love a drink with dinner."

He nodded, and within the space of a few more heartbeats, had poured her wine and served her dinner. "You don't need to wait on me hand and foot, you know."

"I had an easy day. You had a hard one. I figure when the tables are turned, you'll do the same for me."

"Such a sense of fair play."

"That's what you get when you date a cop."

She smiled as they both dug into the food, which was amazing. When she finished chewing her first bite and washed the food down with a sip of wine, she said, "I think there are a few other things I'm getting from dating a cop," she said. "Like paranoid."

He lifted his brows. "How so?"

"Take last night, for example. I could have sworn someone followed me home from your place."

Jay stopped with a forkful of steak halfway to his mouth, and his expression turned serious. "Someone followed you?"

"Like I said, paranoia."

"What kind of vehicle?"

"An SUV. Dark blue or black. It was too dark to be sure. Still, it was all in my head. Whoever it was kept right on going when I pulled in here."

"You pulled in here? Jesus, Macy, when you think you're being followed, you should never go home. Go somewhere public, somewhere crowded. Hell, you should have turned right around and come back to my place. Or at least called."

"Easy, big guy." She reached across the table to pat his hand. "Nothing happened. Though I have to admit, when the dogs started going nuts an hour later, they had me wondering."

He set his fork down. Hard.

"It was nothing. I got up, looked around. No one in sight. I think someone must have been out for a late night stroll or something."

"For God's sake, Macy—"

"It's fine. I'm fine."

"Right. Just not too smart when it comes to your own safety."

"I locked all my doors."

"There's a serial rapist on the loose, Macy. Or did you forget that?"

"Bring him on. My dogs would tear him apart. I promise you, no one intending me harm would ever make it beyond the front door."

His jaw remained tight, his brow furrowed.

"Don't be mad at me, Jay. Tonight started out so nice, let's not ruin it."

Drawing in a deep breath, he sighed, and it seemed he let go of his anger with the breath. "Promise me you'll be more careful from now on."

"I promise."

"And if you ever get so much as an inkling like that again, you'll call me."

"I will."

"Immediately."

"I promise."

"You know if more people paid attention to their instincts, there would be far fewer victims in this world."

"You're right. I mean, it turned out to be nothing, but I should have been more cautious."

He sighed again and seemed satisfied. She changed the subject, talking about her day, her patients, listening to him talk about his, and his progress—or lack thereof, to be more accurate—on the rape cases.

When they'd finished eating, he excused himself and went upstairs. It was only after they'd cleaned up the kitchen that she found out why.

"Come on upstairs. I want to show you something," he said.

Shrugging, she let him take her hand and pull her from the kitchen. Then he led the way up the stairs, which told her he'd become pretty familiar with her home while he'd been there on his own. He led her through her bedroom, opened the bathroom door for her. She stepped inside and stood there, blinking.

The place was dark, except for candles lining every possible surface. The tub was full, and lavender-scented steam rose from it in twisting spirals. He let her precede him in, and as she looked around, soft music came on, and she turned to see he'd set a CD player on the counter.

Blinking at him, she said, "What is all this?"

"One of your fantasies."

"But . . . how did you—what did you—"

"Shhh." He pressed a finger to her lips, and then he began undressing her. She wanted to argue, to question, but when he ran his fingertips from her lips, over her chin, and down the front of her neck to the opening in her blouse, she didn't want to do anything but feel. That touch sent shivers right down her spine. God, she loved when he touched her. Even so slightly. When his fingers went to work unbuttoning her blouse, she lifted a hand to help, but he covered it with one of his own.

She understood, lowered her hand, and tried not to melt into a puddle at his feet while he continued. His fingers brushed her skin with every button he freed. And when he pushed the blouse's sleeves down over her arms, his hands skimmed her flesh, and she drew an unsteady breath as her stomach clenched up.

He pressed his hands to her sides, slid them slowly around to her back to unfasten her bra, and tugged it off her, caressing her every step of the way. His hands never left her skin as he undressed her, and in a moment, his lips followed suit, beginning at the crook of her neck and following her curves. Shoulders, chest, breasts, waist, belly. *Damn*.

He undid her pants and pushed them down her legs, rubbing her thighs on the way, then did the same with her panties. Touching, kissing—every inch of skin he exposed was treated to his special brand of pleasure. Almost as if he were worshipping her.

When she finally stood naked in front of him, he rose, kissing his way up her body until he was standing again, and then he scooped her off her feet and lowered her gently into the tub.

"Lay back, baby. Let me take care of you tonight."

She felt her eyes widen, because the words were so familiar, and then she sat upright in the tub. "You found my favorite book!"

He smiled. "Lie back. Close your eyes. Let me do this, I'm getting such a charge out of it."

She stared at him. But those sexy eyes of his, combined with the hot, scented water convinced her to just go with this. And in a moment, she relaxed, leaned back, and closed her eyes. A second later, she felt him lifting her head to tuck a small, soft pillow behind it.

"Better?"

"Mmmm."

"Open your mouth."

She obeyed, didn't question him. Though she didn't remember this part from the story she'd read so often she'd worn the ink off some of the pages.

He held something to her lips, and she tasted it, smelled it. A strawberry. Plump, ripe, sweet. She bit down, savored it, and licked its juice from her lips.

"That wasn't in the book," she whispered.

"Well, you know, you have to make it your own."

She sighed. God, he was good.

He washed her, gently, making the entire bath into the most elaborate and erotic kind of foreplay she could imagine. He poured water over her head, careful not to get any in her eyes, totally disregarding the pillow, which would dry anyway, and washed her hair.

She closed her eyes tighter, as involuntary whimpers of pleasure whispered from her lips. His fingers massaged her scalp, her head, working the shampoo through her hair. Running through it again as he rinsed, and conditioned, and rinsed again.

It was incredible. Tender and loving and absolutely incredible.

Eventually, she opened her eyes again, to see that he'd taken off his shirt, probably to keep it from being soaked. And that made the sensation of him scooping her, dripping wet from the tub, even better, when he held her against his naked chest. He carried her into the darkened bedroom and laid her on the bed, which he'd lined with thick, soft towels. And then he joined her there, stretching out beside her, wrapping his arms around her, kissing her so deeply she almost climaxed right there.

But then he was backing away, and when he came back, he had another strawberry in his hand. She could barely make it out in the darkness. "Now it's your turn to feed me one," he said.

Smiling, she lifted a hand, reached for the fruit.

"Not like that."

He moved his hand and the strawberry, and before she knew what he intended, he was sliding it between her legs.

"Jay . . ."

"Uh-uh. Just go with it. I promise, you won't regret it." He pushed the strawberry into her, just a little, and then he was kissing his way down her body as she slowly went up in flames.

When he bent between her thighs and began nibbling at the berry, she thought she would explode. He worked on the fruit, then on other places, licking and tasting her, teasing and sucking her. She started to shake. He felt it, and it seemed to drive him to take more. Burying his face in her, he devoured the strawberry, and then he proceeded to devour her, until she came in a blinding orgasm so powerful she shook all over.

And kept shaking, for a long time afterward, while he crawled up her body, wrapped her up tight in his arms, drove his rock hard erection into her, and made her scream all over again.

He was holding her, waiting for her to come back to Earth, caressing her gently as she did, when he said the words she did not want to hear.

"I think I love you, Macy."

She lay there, saying nothing, blinking in shock as a sense of icy panic and fear slowly replaced the delicious heat with which he'd filled her.

After a moment, he said, "You don't have to say anything. I mean, I know it's too soon, but—"

"Yeah, I do have to say something." She took a breath, closed her eyes. "I don't want this. I'm not ready, Jay. I'm just . . . I'm not ready."

"You don't love me." He looked at her, but she just couldn't bring herself to meet his eyes, or even look at his face.

"I . . . I—*can't.*"

He got out of the bed, was pulling on his clothes before she could manage to find words to explain her feelings to him. And then she realized she couldn't explain what she felt to him, not when she didn't even know it herself.

"Dammit, Jay, don't be angry," she whispered.

"I'm not." But he was. "I just . . . need . . . look, I'm going. We'll talk. If you still want to. Call me, okay? I won't push you any further. You don't call—hell, I'll survive, I guess."

She sat up in the bed as he left the room. "Jay, wait."

But he didn't wait. She got out of bed, wrapping one of the

towels around her and ran to the doorway, but he was already down the stairs and heading out her front door. And even as angry as he was, she saw him pause and turn the lock, before he pulled the door closed behind him.

Macy lowered her head, closed her eyes, and let the tears come. Most women would be over the moon to have a man like Jay say he loved them.

Unfortunately, Macy McNamara wasn't most women.

Twelve

Finally! Matt had been beginning to think Jay would never leave.

He didn't wait long. It was getting late, and he wanted this over with. Besides, it didn't particularly matter if she were sleeping or not. She'd be awake before long anyway. And a short time after that, she'd be asleep again.

Permanently.

He tossed the steaks over the fence to the dogs, watched while they fought good-naturedly for them, watched while they ate the meat, and then watched while the tranquilizers took effect. The dogs' movements slowed. Their eyes glazed over, rolled, closed, and one by one, they sank down into the grass.

Matt pulled his ski mask on, climbed over the fence, and tiptoed past the unconscious canines, up the back steps, and across the deck. He crawled through the doggie door and started for the stairs.

Jay was halfway home when his cell phone went off, interrupting a damn good pity party. He could not believe Macy didn't feel anything for him. But if she did, she would have said so, wouldn't she? She would have softened the blow a little by telling him she may not love him—yet—but that she did feel something. She cared for him, was fond of him, liked him a whole lot, wanted him, missed him when they were apart, burned for him, thought he was hot. Hell, *anything*. She'd given him nothing.

Well, except for the most amazing sexual surrender he'd ever been given.

Damn, the woman was incredible.

The phone rang again, and he snapped it up, glad for the distraction. He was pretty sure she would never call him again. She'd been very clear about what she wanted up front, and he'd ignored it and blurted his feelings anyway. Idiot.

Again, the phone rang.

He flipped it open. "What?"

"Uh—is this Jay Harris?"

"Yeah. Why?"

"This is Bobby Ketchum. We've worked a couple cases together."

He frowned, his attention caught. "Officer Ketchum," he said, remembering the raw rookie with a smile. The kid had enthusiasm and a keen instinct. He'd made an impression. "We were both on the scene of that pickup-versus-motorcycle wreck last month, right?"

"Yeah, that's me. I'm calling about your serial rapist. I saw that drawing you sent out and—"

"Whoa, whoa. How? I only showed that to a handful of people."

"Yeah, well, it's a big case. People know other people, and you know cops talk to each other. Anyway, it's a good thing they did, because I know the guy."

"You what?"

"Yeah. And I think you've made a serious mistake. Figured you should know about it before this goes any further. It's Adam Cooper."

"What?"

"Yeah, I figured you must not realize it. It's your partner's son, Detective. He didn't say anything?"

His partner. Matt.

Jay hit the brakes and jerked the wheel, bringing the car to a stop on the shoulder. He flashed back to the way Matt had looked at the drawing, the way he'd turned it over and looked at the back. Scrambling for the drawing, Jay opened the glove compartment and yanked it out, turned it over and saw, by the dashboard lights, Macy's name and office address printed on the back.

"You still there?" Ketchum demanded.

"Black SUV," he said.

"Huh?"

"Matt drives a black SUV. Shit."

"Detective Harris?"

"Call for backup, kid. Tell them to get out to 817 Oak Street. Tell them he's probably there."

"Who?"

"The rapist. Make it fast. Better send medics, too. I'm on my way."

"Got it."

"And kid?"

"Yeah?"

"Good work."

Jay snapped the phone closed and dropped it onto the passenger seat, while whipping the car around. Matt's kid must have been using his old man's car last night, when Macy thought she was followed home. He'd been casing the place, which meant he was planning to go back. Did that mean he knew it was Macy who knew his face? Had Matt told him? Would his friend betray him that way?

Jay pressed the accelerator to the floor, speeding back toward Macy's place and praying he would make it in time.

Macy lay in her bed, trying to quell the flow of tears and finally succeeding. She was very afraid that she had blown it with Jay, and that hurt. She wasn't ready to lose him, not yet. But maybe it was for the best. It wouldn't be fair to him, to be with a woman who was incapable of loving him.

And she'd survive. She always had. Though she didn't

think she'd felt pain this intense since the night her stepmother had tried to lose her for good.

And that begged a question, didn't it? Why did the thought of losing him hurt so much?

She rolled onto her back, blinking up at the ceiling and letting that question roll around in her head for a minute. Finding no answers, she told herself to forget about it, but it refused to stop repeating itself in her mind. Why did it hurt so much?

"Enough, already. Pity party is over." She swung out of the bed, yanked a short silky robe from the back of a nearby chair, and pulled it on. Then she decided to head downstairs to call the dogs in, lock up the house, and maybe fix a cup of warm milk or something. Otherwise, she doubted she'd sleep all night.

She twisted her bedroom doorknob and pulled it open. A fist plowed into her face. Pain exploded, blood spattered from her nose, and her back hit the floor so hard her breath was forced from her lungs and she couldn't draw another. Blinking, gasping, she stared up at the figure who had stepped into the bedroom, as he reached down to clasp the front of her robe and pull her to her feet again. He wore a ski mask and gloves. She finally caught her breath and used it to scream, while kicking at his shins and twisting away from his grip.

It didn't matter, he only hit her again, knocking her onto the bed this time. Then he gripped her shoulders, rolled her onto her stomach, and pushed the robe up to bare her to him, as he knelt on the bed behind her.

She tried to scramble free. He gripped her by the hair with one hand and punched her in the temple with the other. Everything went dim. Not dark, not quite, but her body was no longer responding to her mind's commands. She needed a minute.

Unfortunately, she didn't have one. He was unzipping his fly and climbing onto her. She felt his flaccid member brush her flesh, as he tried to put on a condom, one-handed. The other hand clutched her nape in a brutal grip and kept her head forced into the pillows. She could barely breathe.

And then she realized that's what he intended. He was trying to suffocate her. Grinding against her backside in an effort to stimulate an erection that wasn't cooperating and mashing her face into the pillows with both hands now. He was trying to kill her.

He was going to rape her and kill her, and he didn't seem to care in which order.

She tried to twist her head to one side, sucked in a desperate, if minuscule, breath and glimpsed the nightstand, her eyes desperate for a weapon—all in the instant before he forced her face back into the pillow again.

She'd seen no weapon. Only a Sharpie marker, a plastic water bottle, and an alarm clock far too small to be effective. The phone was there, but too far to reach from her current position. Jay. God, if only she could call Jay.

It occurred to her as she became dizzy from lack of oxygen that tonight was the last time she would ever see him. His final memory would be of her telling him she couldn't love him, when the truth was, she already did.

She loved him.

And he would never know.

The man behind her cussed, still trying, still too soft to make it work. Hoping his dilemma provided enough of a distraction to keep him from noticing, she inched her right arm toward the nightstand, sucking what precious air she could through the pillow, not getting enough, losing the battle. She closed her hand on the Sharpie and brought it back to her, moving her hands over her head, which meant letting go of her resistance, letting the bastard jam her face even more deeply into the pillow. Above her she found another pillow, slid her hands beneath it, and used the Sharpie to write on her left hand, hoping the words would be legible when they found her body.

The man behind her had managed to get it up. She felt him, poking her, off target, but close. Dammit, she wished she would have passed out before she had to endure this.

He leaned all his weight on the back of her head, groaning as he searched for his target. She couldn't breathe at all, and a second later, she was out cold.

* * *

Jay saw the SUV parked a block past Macy's place, and his blood went cold. He dove out of his car, ran up to the door, and kicked it open, barely breaking his stride. Then he was racing through the house, up the stairs, into her bedroom. He grabbed the bastard by the shoulders and flung him off her with a burst of pure animal rage that had nothing to do with training or procedure. The rapist crashed into a chair, breaking it to bits. He started to push himself up again.

Jay was on him before he could even begin, pounding him mercilessly until the man no longer lifted his gloved hands to try to block the blows, and his head hung limp, blood dripping from the edges of the ski mask.

Sirens sounded. The cops were here, the bastard wasn't going anywhere. Jay turned and went to the bed, where Macy lay still, her face pressed into the pillows. She wasn't moving. He gripped her shoulders, carefully rolling her onto her back, using one hand to smooth the robe down into place as he did. "Macy? Can you hear me?" He shook her a little, fury and fear mingling in his belly when he saw her face. She'd been pummeled. And she didn't respond. In between the blood and bruises, he noticed that her face was slightly blue, and panic took hold of his heart as he leaned closer.

She wasn't breathing. He could feel a pulse, but not a breath whispered from her lips.

"Dammit!" Jay tipped her chin up, pinched her nostrils closed, and put his mouth over hers, blowing into her lungs until he felt her chest rise, and then again, and then again, and then—

She sucked in a desperate, noisy gasp, and her eyes flew open.

"It's okay, Macy. It's okay, babe, it's me. I'm here. You're safe."

She was disoriented, unfocused. She blinked at him a few times, and then her eyes started to fall closed again, probably due to the beating she'd taken. And she muttered something that didn't make any sense.

"I'm here. Don't try to talk, baby, you're safe now."

"Read my hand," she murmured again.

Then she passed out, even as cops were flooding the house. One came into the bedroom—one he recognized. Bobby Ketchum, the rookie who'd busted this thing wide open. "Paramedics are outside until we clear the place. Is that him?"

"Yeah. He was alone. Let the medics in, Ketchum. She needs 'em."

"On it." He backed out of the room. Jay glanced at the man on the floor, noting for the first time his build, his size. What the hell?

Rising from the bed, he moved to the man and tugged the ski cap off. Then his heart tripped over itself. It was Matt. Not his son. Matt, himself.

Matt lifted his head, swollen eyes struggling to focus on Jay.

"What the hell is this, Matt?" Jay demanded. "What are you thinking, man?"

"Had to . . . protect Adam."

Jay closed his eyes as it all fell into place. "You were gonna get caught and take the fall for him?"

He shook his head. "Was gonna . . . kill her, plant evidence pointing elsewhere, get Adam . . . get Adam the help he needs."

"You were going to kill her? Even knowing that she and I—"

"Blood and water, Jay. He's my kid." He paused, glancing at the woman in the bed. "I'm sorry."

"Fuck you."

By then other cops had arrived in the bedroom. They'd heard, got the gist of things and were hauling Matt up and cuffing him, as Jay turned back to Macy. He saw something black on one of her hands just as the cops hauled Matt out of the room and the medics came hurrying in.

They were about to swarm around Macy, blocking him from access, so he held up a hand. "Just one sec." And then he moved closer, clasped her hand, and gently turned it until he could see what was scrawled there in black marker.

"I love you, too, Jay."

He closed his eyes, had to, because they got real wet, real fast. Then he had to back off and let the medics do their jobs.

"Take care of her, guys. You wouldn't even believe how special she is."

One of the medics glimpsed her hand, then glanced at Jay with a knowing expression. "You got it, Detective Harris."

"Yeah," he said. "I do. And I don't intend to lose it."

Epilogue

When Macy opened her eyes, she was in a clean, comfortable hospital bed, and Jay was sitting in a chair beside it.

She blinked and tried to remember—then did and wished she hadn't.

Jay watched her face, seemed to be reading every emotion that crossed it—the horror, the pain, the fear—all of it. And then she focused on his eyes. "I passed out before . . . did he . . . ?"

"He never penetrated you, Macy. The doctors are sure, and the condom showed no trace."

She closed her eyes, relieved. "You got him?"

"We got him. And his son, and I'll fill you in on the details whenever you're ready."

She nodded, thinking, and then her eyes widened. "The dogs! What did he do to the dogs, they never would have let him in—"

"Drugged them. But they're fine, Macy. They're all fine."

Sighing in relief, she whispered. "Thank God. All of this could have been so much worse. He wanted to kill me, Jay! He tried to suffocate me."

"I know. But he didn't. He didn't rape you, and he didn't kill you. And he'll never hurt anyone again. Still, I know that doesn't make what happened any less traumatic. I'll understand if you need time and space—without me hanging around, I mean—to work through this."

Frowning, she studied him, and then she remembered what she'd done and brought her hand down to see if her message to Jay was still there. Someone had done their best to scrub it away, but the letters, though faint, remained.

Then she glanced at him, found him looking at her hand, too, and there was a softness in his eyes that told her he had found the message, had read it and understood.

"Given how I feel about you," she said, "Space and time without you hanging around are the last things I want." She shrugged. "In fact, I think having you around—a lot—would do me more good than anything else I can think of."

"Yeah?" He smiled and clasped her hand in both of his.

"Yeah. I've finally found a guy I like as much as my dogs."

"Like?" He turned her hand in his, tracing the letters L-O-V-E with a fingertip.

She met his eyes. "It's true, you know. I love you, Jay. I didn't think I could, but I do. And I'm sorry I hurt you. And I hope you'll give me another chance."

He leaned closer and whispered, "Promise me one thing?"

She nodded, expecting a serious and deep request.

"That you'll make a habit of writing love letters to me on various parts of your body."

Her lips pulled into a relieved smile, just before his covered them.

PARADISE

Meljean Brook

To Mom and Dad,
with all my love

One

Will you tell the court the events leading up to the night of August twelfth?

He couldn't remember. Lucas Marsden glanced from the hammer in his right hand to the nail through the back of his left, and had no idea how he'd managed to pin himself to the backstage scaffolding—or why, despite his three years of law school and countless hours studying proper witness examination techniques, it was Perry Mason's made-for-TV query that echoed in his head.

Or why he answered it.

I was dismantling the set from our latest production at the Paradise Theater— The wound had stopped bleeding; pale skin healed over the head of the nail, embedding it into his flesh like a round hungry tick. *—The Glass Menagerie, which was doing well until last month, when our lead actress, Olivia Jordan, was murdered.*

And could you describe the nature of this murder?

She was staked out in the forest, decapitated, and left to burn to ashes in the sun.

She wasn't just an actress, was she, Mr. Marsden? And her

death is the reason why you've nailed yourself to a four-by-four—

And the reason why he was interrogating himself with leading questions. Jesus Christ. He wasn't as strong as he'd thought; the cow blood had already turned him into an idiot. With a shake of his head, Lucas focused.

Drops of perspiration gathered at the dark hair near his temples, over his brow. The scent of his blood lay heavy in the theater's stifling air. He'd not yet fed that evening; typically, the fragrance would have aroused the bloodlust . . . but a month without a living food source had slowed its response.

And, apparently, damaged his hearing and psychic senses—he did not notice the woman until she appeared in his peripheral view. Endless tanned legs, sun-streaked blond hair, and probably not even of legal age to drink.

Or to drink from.

Thank God his eyesight still functioned; Lucas wasn't as certain about his brain. He was suddenly grateful he was stuck to a post—the ache in his fangs told him the bloodlust had decided to rise, after all.

Fortunately, his flesh didn't react in the same way. She was edible, but obviously human. The last thing he needed was for the vampire community to learn he'd lost control and taken one.

His hearing worked, too: The even thrum of her heart reverberated in his ears.

Lucas frowned, struck by the peculiarity of that steady beat, the smoothness of her expression. She was alone in a pitch-black theater with a strange—and by no means small and harmless—man, and she didn't evince the slightest fear. Nor could he detect any in her psychic scent.

He couldn't sense *anything* from her. The animal blood must have muddled his ability to read her. Or she possessed a disturbing level of vapidity, and there was nothing to read.

"I'm sorry, miss," he said, forcing away his unease. How many gorgeous young women had arrived at the Paradise since Olivia had been killed? The drama department at Southern Oregon University was bursting with them, and he'd received several inquiries from actresses up in Portland and Seattle—all eager for a chance to tread the boards at one of Ashland's private stages. Granted, most of them did not come in at midnight, but he usually wasn't impaled on a nail. "The theater is closed until next season. We'll be holding auditions in October."

Her gaze held his before dropping to his hand, and his apprehension returned, knotting in his gut. His estimation of her age increased drastically. Those quiet blue eyes didn't belong to an insipid young woman . . . and no human could have made out his shape so clearly in the darkness.

"I'm not here for an audition," she said in a voice made of clarified honey: thick and sweet, the tones golden and clear. A smile deepened the indentation in her top lip, emphasized the lush curve of the bottom. A cupid's bow. He'd thought such lips were as mythical as their namesake, but now he realized that any vampire who'd encountered them had likely hidden the woman away and fed from her mouth for eternity.

She approached him slowly, as she might have a trapped animal. She wore those strappy sandal-things Olivia had sighed over in magazines, ordered, and then left in their boxes at the bottom of her closet. Wine-red ribbons wound from ankle to knee like a ballerina's slippers gone wild, the ends dancing the length of her sleek calves.

Her heels clicked against the floorboards. How had he *not* heard her come in?

"I'm here to help. Though I didn't expect it to take this form, or for you to need it so quickly."

Lucas looked up from her feet, swallowing hard. "Psychiatric help, I hope. I apparently suffer from a severe self-persecution complex."

"No." Her smile widened; her teeth formed a straight white line. No fangs.

Careful to keep his own from showing, Lucas pressed his lips together, bent his head, and concentrated as he returned the hammer to the loop in his carpenter's pants. It shook against his thigh before he steadied it and slid the handle through.

She wasn't a vampire; perhaps she'd grown up too quickly, and it had left that long-lived patience in her eyes.

He searched for another reason for her visit, and his addled mind came up with, "The air-conditioning system, then." It had failed earlier in the week, but Lucas hadn't found a repairman with an open schedule in the midst of the August heat wave.

"No." She stood next to him now. She was tall, her chin on level with his throat. Her gauzy white sleeve brushed his forearm as she lifted his hand from the hammer and studied the tremor in his fingers.

His palm was cool, and in the stagnant theater a light film of perspiration had settled over his skin. A human would call his touch cold, clammy; this woman didn't give any indication that she found it disgusting.

"How long have you had the shakes?"

Dark beads circled her neck, dripped between her breasts to her waist. Her burgundy shorts tied closed below her navel with a large bow; a wide satin band around the hem of each leg held them tight against her upper thighs, the material between billowing slightly like a pair of old-fashioned bloomers.

But there was nothing old-fashioned or prudish about the long stretch of bare leg beneath.

"They started two days ago." He closed his eyes. Her skin was warm; lifeblood pulsed just beneath the surface of her upturned wrist. "You have to leave, miss. Now."

"You can't hurt me." A gentle prick at the flesh covering the nail in his opposite hand accompanied the statement. Tepid crimson blood trickled from the reopened wound. Surprised, he looked up again.

A dagger glinted in her hand before disappearing. Lucas blinked, certain he'd been mistaken.

"What would you say your mental faculties are at? Sixty percent? Seventy?" She pinched the head of the nail between her forefinger and thumb. The wood screeched as she pulled. Quick, merciful—he barely felt the rip of the flesh that had healed around it. She slanted a glance up at him and dropped the nail to the floor. "Are you typically so unresponsive? You haven't completely descended into 'big dumb ox,' but hammering yourself to scaffolding doesn't venture into genius territory, either. What has it been, two weeks or so that you've been drinking the animal blood?"

He must be hallucinating. First Perry Mason, and now a ridiculously strong, impossibly perfect *human* who knew far too much about vampires. "A month."

Her head tilted as she regarded him; her lashes were thick and black. He couldn't smell any mascara. She didn't have any odor, except the light scent of sunshine and heat and blood.

"A month? That's an extraordinarily long time for a vampire to—" A crease formed between her dark golden brows. "Are you nosferatu-born?"

Nosferatu. A white naked hairless figure. Enormous and skittering out of nowhere in the depths of the cave: pointed ears, gleaming fangs. The tearing of flesh—Olivia's screams. A teenager in a monk's robe, wielding a sword.

The images flashed in front of him; this time Lucas was certain they didn't exist. It was a memory, a nightmare. One he'd had far too often in the twenty years since his transformation.

"Lucas? Are you well?" Her frown disrupted the bow of her lips. "Where's your partner?"

Dead. Grief and remembrance centered him. He wasn't a dizzy, drooling boy faced with a sexual fantasy come-to-life; he'd stop acting like one.

The pale skin on the back of his hand closed again. He wiped the blood onto his navy T-shirt and said flatly, "You know who I am. *What* I am."

She nodded slowly. She slid her thumbs into the front of her waistband; her fingers fanned across her lower abdomen. Her weight rested on her right leg, her hip cocked. Her relaxed posture didn't indicate wariness, but he could almost feel the speed and readiness coiled within that lithe frame.

"Yes. Lucas Marsden, formerly an officer with the Salem Police Department. A graduate of Willamette University's law school, and a prosecuting attorney for Marion County, but after two years, you gave up your position in the DA's office. Now, you are the owner of the Paradise Theater and head of the vampire community in Ashland, Oregon."

Probably not either for much longer. "But you aren't here looking for a role. Are you searching for immortality?"

If so, she'd arrived at exactly the right time; he was almost desperate enough to be reckless in selecting his new consort.

And if desperation weren't enough, the temptation in the slow curve of her lips might be. "No. I found that several centuries ago." She untucked her right thumb, held out her hand. "I'm Selah. I'm a Guardian."

"A Guardian." Lucas clasped her hand briefly. "And what is it you guard, Selah?"

"Humans, usually. But a lot of things have changed of late."

He arched a brow. "You protect vampires now?"

"Typically, I slay those who end up crossing my path." Before he could respond, she shook her head and continued, "*Typically*, those who cross my path are not part of a community, but are endangering humans."

His tension eased. He'd had to do the same to several rogues; and in the last three months, more than in the past twenty years combined.

"If you aren't here to kill us, then—" He stopped himself. Was he truly having this conversation? With a warm sun-kissed woman possessing a vampire's strength?

But her touch had been real; so was the unwavering blue stare she leveled at him. "I believe you have a demon in Ashland, Mr. Marsden, and I have every intention of slaying it." Her gaze swept his length. "But you won't be much help to me like this. Where's your partner, or someone you can feed from?"

A demon? How many holes did she think the animal blood had riddled in his brain? Lucas clenched his jaw, embarrassment and frustration rising hot within him. And anger, though—like the bloodlust—it was slow to respond. "I'll show you."

He didn't believe her.

Selah followed Lucas Marsden through the sleeping city. She'd scented his odor coming from a Jeep parked in front of the theater, but they traveled on foot.

Was he testing her? If so, she was probably learning more of him than he was of her. He *must* be nosferatu-born; though tall and broad-shouldered, with a lean swimmer's build, those physical traits were only indicative of his human life. Normal vampires—those transformed by an exchange of blood with another vampire—couldn't have moved as swiftly as he did, no matter what their shape.

And it was a fine shape indeed. Selah watched it as she jogged along behind him, not bothering to conceal her appreciation. She hated walking, loathed running, and if she had to follow him at this between-hate-and-loathing pace, she might as well get as much pleasure as she could out of it.

If she teleported them there, it might have persuaded him that she spoke the truth. But Lucas was at the stage where he was aware he wasn't thinking clearly and so doubted his perception; such shock-and-awe tactics could push him over the edge and convince him she was nothing but a figment of his imagination.

Taking more time wouldn't hurt, and considering the direction they were heading, she suspected she wouldn't like what he had to show her.

She shook her head as they left the smooth pavement behind, entering a wooded area north of the city. The sharp fragrance of pine sap, the sweetness of ripening blackberries, and the rich scent of volcanic soil rose around her.

Her heels would catch on any protruding root; she vanished her shoes with regret and created boots that matched his. They clomped, though she tried to keep her steps light. God, she *despised* jogging.

Lucas turned to glance over his shoulder, his dark brows lifting in surprise. He no longer radiated anger and shame, but curiosity. Good. He wouldn't be difficult to work with, once he'd fed. A month of animal blood, but his shakes weren't in the advanced stages, his verbalization was coherent—it should only take one or two feedings for him to return to normal.

But no matter how handsome his face and figure, Selah hoped it wouldn't have to be from her. The last time she'd been a beautiful vampire's meal it had ended . . . badly.

Lucas came to a sudden halt, scenting the air. Tension gripped his form. Drawing up beside him, Selah caught it on the faint breeze, metallic and dark: vampire blood.

She focused, performed a psychic sweep of the forest around them. Only the Gate, resonating its soothing hum within her—and tinged by sulphur and rot. Nothing unexpected.

But a demon could hide its psychic presence from her. From both of them.

"Stay here," Lucas said softly. Without much apparent effort, he suppressed the trembling. His palm rested steadily on the hammer at his thigh.

He must be accustomed to his orders being followed; assuming her compliance, he took a step forward.

"Lucas." Selah stopped him with her hand on his forearm. The muscles were cool and hard beneath her fingers. She brought in a sword from her invisible cache of weapons; his breath caught when it appeared in her grip. "Have you any fencing experience?"

He stared at the sword for a long moment. His throat worked, and he swallowed before saying hoarsely, "I had to take on the part of Laertes for an evening."

"Stage fighting?" She smiled. How was it that almost everyone she knew—vampire, Guardian, or halfling demon—had such a dramatic streak? "We don't want to *pretend* to hurt him." A semiautomatic pistol replaced the sword. "Can you shoot?"

He recovered quickly. "It's been a while, but"—he took the gun from her, efficiently chambered a bullet—"yes."

"Aim for the head, especially the eyes. Shooting him won't kill him, but it will slow him down. Don't hesitate to use it. It might keep you alive until I can get to you. Go ahead; I'll be at your back." She could still watch for an attack from the front and protect them both if it came from behind.

Armed now, his attention never strayed from his search of the forest ahead of them. She'd always liked that in nosferatu-born vampires: their predatory instincts.

The crunch of pine needles was loud beneath their feet. There was no possibility of hiding their location with silence when they had to walk—he must have realized it, too.

"What are you? What's a Guardian?" he asked quietly, just as they came upon a break in the trees, allowing a glimpse of a small clearing.

A body lay in the center. The odor of blood was overpowering.

A vampire who hadn't yet fed might be distracted by such a strong scent; no vampire could control the bloodlust. And already, she could feel the hunger and need heightening within him.

With barely a thought, Selah formed her wings. The white feathers shone beneath the silvery moonlight, increasing her mass and providing a bright target. Hopefully, it would divert attention away from Lucas.

"We're like angels"—she slanted Lucas a quick glance, found him staring at her; his emotions slid from disbelief to wonder and fascination, underscored by wariness and the nascent heat of his bloodlust—"only much better."

Two

Pine needles and soil clung to the vampire's long hair as Lucas rolled the head over. Half-open brown eyes, round freckled face, fangs. "I don't recognize her."

Selah crouched beside the naked body, her wings in an arching sweep behind her. The tips trailed on the ground, and the sight of those pristine white feathers dragging through the dirt was almost offensive.

Almost. The death here *was* offensive; it eclipsed the reverence he might have otherwise felt, faced with such a being.

"These symbols . . ." she murmured to herself before looking up at him. "I've seen something like this before. Will you photograph her position before we move her? I want to look around, see if he's written anything anywhere else."

"Yes, but—" He broke off as a digital camera appeared in her hand. Taking it, he lowered to his heels next to her. "Where have you seen them?"

Symbols had been carved into the vampire's flesh; some geometric in shape, others curving in a macabre script. He hadn't found Olivia's remains until after she'd disintegrated into ash. Had this been her fate as well?

Selah's gaze rested on his face. Lucas glanced away, but

was certain he could not hide his anger-laden frustration from her.

"It was in San Francisco," she said quietly. "In May, a series of ritualized murders. The media coverage was extensive—you must have seen it."

"Yes. You're speaking of the cult of humans who'd tried to become vampires." Two university students and one professor had been dismembered and mutilated; four more students had been rescued from sacrifice at the last moment.

And in the same month, dozens of vampires had flooded into Ashland from San Francisco, stretching resources and tempers. Many had reports of enormous blood-drinking creatures—who weren't vampires—slaughtering the city's elders. Most had left Oregon shortly after the media had reported an end to the ritual slayings.

Lucas had been forced to kill several who hadn't had a bloodsharing partner and refused to take animal blood until they'd found one. Maddened and starving, they'd attacked other vampires in the community for blood; it wouldn't have been long before they'd turned to humans for feeding.

The camera's flash left bright spots behind his eyes. Gathering evidence, but there was no need to establish a chain of possession, no need to follow official collection methods. There would never be a police investigation, no trial, no sentence—except that which Lucas conferred.

"There was no cult. A horde of nosferatu tried to make a bargain with a demon—with Lucifer. The story in the media was just a cover."

He understood the last bit; the truth had to be hidden from humans. But to believe that *Lucifer* . . . ?

As if anticipating his doubt, she caught his gaze. Unfolding her wings, she waved them a little and lifted her brows.

Lucas bit back his smile when the feathers' movement stirred the scent of blood and death.

Tamping down the bloodlust did not prove so easy.

"Anyway, Lucifer failed," she continued, rising to her feet and walking a slow circuit around Lucas and the body. "And he lost a wager; the Gates to Hell are closed for five hundred years. But a couple of hundred demons fled Hell before they could be trapped in that realm."

"And you think it was one of those demons who killed her?" White light illuminated the vampire's gaping neck. No ragged skin. The edges of the wound were too clean to have been made by a knife or saw. Perhaps an ax . . . or a sword. Lucas looked up. Selah was kneeling near the decapitated head; she touched the ground, brought her fingers to her nose and sniffed.

"I'm not sure," she said, frowning. "Lucifer didn't share knowledge of his magic. I'm surprised that another demon would know to use the symbols. On the other hand, that it's a vampire lying here—in copious amounts of her own blood— makes me think that it must be a demon who murdered her."

"Why is that?"

"The Rules forbid demons and Guardians from killing humans, but we can kill vampires." She stood, surveyed the clearing with her hands on her hips. "And she wasn't raped. Demons can simulate sex, but they have no sexual drive. Nosferatu and vampires do, particularly when blood is involved. A nosferatu would have torn her apart rather than have sex with her. And nosferatu and vampires aren't bound by the Rules, so if it had been either, I would've expected to find humans here and the blood missing. But instead of that, I find decapitation and the remains of five vampires: this one, and the ashes of four others."

His brows drew together. "Four?"

"Yes." She watched him quietly before asking, "One was your partner?"

"Yes."

"You have no one else to feed from?"

Resignation tinged her question; Lucas bristled at the realization. "I did not ask you—"

"You don't have to." She sighed, took a last look around. "Do you need to examine the body further?"

"No." His teeth clenched, and he rose abruptly to his feet. Spots danced wildly around his vision.

The vampire and her head vanished from the ground, and the odor of her blood disappeared. Selah shuddered. Disgust emanated from her psychic scent, and she wiped her hands down the sides of her shorts. "I'm taking her to San Francisco. I can't read the symbols, but I have two colleagues who can. Would you like to accompany me?"

Three hundred and fifty miles? Lucas eyed her wings doubtfully. "You'd have to be very fast." Dawn was only five hours away. As soon as the sun rose, whether he was protected from its burning rays or vulnerable, he'd succumb to the daysleep; he couldn't awaken until it set again.

Unless a trip had been carefully planned or the reason for traveling dire, few vampires went far from home.

"I can fly the distance in half an hour—but we won't go that way." Amusement creased the corners of her mouth, though she didn't give voice to it. "I promise I'll have you back home before curfew."

He blinked. Was she flirting with him? Or ridiculing him for his hesitation?

And what had he descended into, that he couldn't trust his interpretation of a woman's tone?

He must have projected his confusion; Selah tilted her head, brushing her hair back over her shoulder and exposing the long sweep of her neck. "You need to feed first, though. You're hungry, and your mental faculties will be sharper after you've eaten."

She was right. He *knew* it, but he replied stiffly, "I'm fine."

Her features softened; he didn't know if it was with understanding or pity. "Trust me," she said. Her dark lashes swept down, but not before he saw the sudden sparkle of humor in her eyes. "You don't want to meet with my colleagues with your head at seventy or sixty percent. They can be . . . difficult."

So could the bloodlust. So could desire and grief and a sense of duty. He'd experienced "difficult"—nothing this quiet woman had to throw at him could be worse. "No."

He sensed a brief flare of irritation from her before she shrugged; her wings swayed with the movement. "Very well. I won't force you. Are you ready?"

"Y—" Lucas didn't see her move, only felt the warmth of her hand on his arm. The world rolled dizzily around him.

When it stopped, there was concrete under his feet. "Yes," he finished, and decided that he might just vomit on it.

If she *had* been flirting with him, she wasn't likely to continue in about a second.

* * *

Teleporting always thrilled Selah—not so her passengers. It hit Lucas worse than most: the animal blood intensified the disorientation. He shook off her hand and staggered toward the wall, bracing his forearm against it, his shoulders heaving.

He was probably glad he hadn't yet fed that night.

After bringing in her cell phone from her cache, she dialed Hugh's number and listened to Lucas's deep, steadying breaths as it rang. He turned to face her again, his gaze narrowing on the phone as Hugh answered. Nosferatu-born, Lucas was able to hear both ends of the conversation.

"Selah."

"I found a dead vampire near the Gate. I'm at the warehouse with Marsden," she said and hung up, then vanished the phone. Hugh had been her mentor for a hundred years; they'd worked together two and a half centuries. There was no need for more explanation than that. "They'll be here in about twenty minutes."

Lucas looked away from her, ran his hand over the nail-pocked surface of the unfinished wall. Eventually, this room would be an office; now, it was a collection of sawdust, drywall, and exposed wiring.

"We're in San Francisco?" He angled his head, and his eyes unfocused, as if he listened to the noise from outside the warehouse.

"Yes. In the Department of Homeland Security's soon-to-be-finished Special Investigations headquarters. Hugh Castleford—who you just heard me speak with—and his partner, Lilith, will be directing operations here."

Tucking her thumbs into the front of her shorts, she watched him circle the room. He moved quietly, like a man accustomed to observing in a manner that didn't draw attention to himself. Predators moved that way.

Most of them.

He glanced back at her. His black hair was overlong and slightly curling, as if he hadn't bothered to cut it in the past few years, and it fell in a thick uneven wave across his forehead with the movement. "What type of operations?"

"Acting as liaison between Caelum and Earth. Tracking

down any rogue demons that have escaped Hell and hopefully slay them. Keeping knowledge of our kind from humans—beyond the few in Washington, D.C., who know of us, that is."

He turned, slowly approached her. His hands were broad, strong. His fingers were trembling again. *"Caelum?"* He formed the word carefully, as if he wasn't certain he'd heard it correctly. His fangs gleamed sharp behind the firmness of his lips.

Her mouth dried. "It's the Guardians' home. In a different realm than Earth. Like Hell, or Chaos—"

She broke off, closing her eyes. *Chaos.* Some days, she could still hear the screams.

But they were not so terrible compared with what had befallen the vampire whom she'd teleported there—the vampire whom she hadn't had the strength to teleport back out.

And she didn't want to think about Chaos now, when in a couple of hours she'd very likely be feeding another vampire.

Silence hung between them. When she looked up at him, he was studying her face. His eyes were a moss green; how strange that such a soft color could be so direct.

"You can"—he hesitated for an instant—"'jump' anywhere? On Earth and between these realms?"

"Teleport. Yes."

"Show me this Caelum," he said softly.

Shaking her head, she said, "It's very sunny."

His lips tilted, but he didn't return her smile. Instead, he stepped close enough that she had to tip her head back. "Why did we come here? Obviously this facility isn't ready for a postmortem examination. Why not take me directly to your colleague's location? Why waste twenty minutes?"

Because she didn't like to hop unannounced into people's homes. Because Lilith and her hellhound might not have appreciated a strange vampire suddenly appearing in their living room. But primarily— "Because I don't know you."

His brows rose. "You're going to use this time to learn about me?"

She doubted twenty minutes would suffice for that. "You didn't feed. I don't know you well enough to determine whether you'd have control when I take the body and the blood out of my cache."

A muscle in his jaw worked; the roughly hewn planes of his cheeks flushed with color. Despite his anger, he didn't argue. Stubborn, but he recognized it within himself and accepted the consequences of the choices he made.

"And if I lose control here?"

"I'll teleport you to safety," she said.

He blinked in surprise.

"I would've at their house, too," she explained, "but if I have to stop Lilith from killing you, I'd rather do it here. It's neutral ground. She might consider it an insult if I save you from her at her own house." A mischievous grin pulled at her lips. She fought to subdue it and only partially succeeded. "Which is *almost* reason enough to take you there and hope you go insane with hunger, but not quite."

His gaze dropped to her mouth. His bloodlust swelled, a heated caress over her nerves before he strengthened his psychic shields. It wasn't burning—not yet—but he couldn't completely conceal it, either.

Why was he so adamantly opposed to taking her blood? His grief was deep, but not tinged with the excruciating pain and loneliness she'd sensed from countless widowers and separated lovers over the centuries.

He dragged in a lungful of air; during his long silence, he hadn't been breathing. A rarity among vampires and Guardians—most did it automatically, a habit left over from life.

"I think I might already be insane," he said. His focus shifted from her face to her wings. His hand rose over her shoulder, but he paused before touching them. "May I?"

She nodded, her lips parting in a quiet assent. His shirt stretched across his chest as he reached; he smelled of lumber and pine.

The frame of her wings jutted up from her shoulder blades, rounded and thick with muscle at the base, tapering into the arch. His cool fingers trailed along the sensitive, downy surface. She couldn't quite stifle the shiver that raced over her skin.

His eyes met hers, his lashes crinkling together in amusement. His psychic scent held a hint of masculine interest. Animal blood suppressed libido; once he'd fed, how potent would it be? "Ticklish?"

A short laugh escaped her. Her reaction hadn't confused him *that* much. "Something like that."

"You said that you found immortality. You used to be human?" His arm at full extension, he smoothed his hand through the feathers meshed together at her left wing's apex, two feet above her head.

She resisted the urge to fold them closed, trap his hand between them. "Once."

"I assume this isn't the result of being bitten by a bird. Or biting one."

His lashes lowered as his gaze dropped to her neck. He quickly stepped back, crossing his arms over his chest.

The effect of his touch lingered; her skin felt tight, cold. Her body warmed in response, a slow rising heat. "No. They aren't animal in nature."

"Angelic?" The tips of his fangs appeared briefly.

"Yes." Selah shifted her weight to her right leg; the boots were heavy, clunky. Rocking up onto her toes, she changed them back to her ribboned heels. When she lowered to the ground, she was only an inch or two shorter than Lucas again. "Guardians aren't angels, though the powers we receive during transformation originated in Heaven. The Guardian corps was formed to take the angels' place, protecting humans from demons and nosferatu."

He blinked. After a quick glance at her feet, he examined her face. "How long ago?"

"At least two thousand years." She didn't know for certain. In Caelum's library was an archive of Scrolls detailing the Guardians' history—but they didn't tell all of it. Only Michael, the first Guardian, knew what had occurred after the angels had relinquished Caelum to him and before the Scrolls had been recorded.

"Two thou—" Lucas shook his head. "How could we not have met with your kind before?"

"Most vampires haven't, but *you* must have," she said. "You're nosferatu-born, but a nosferatu would never have left a human alive. A Guardian must have interfered, and saved you—made you drink the blood."

"You?" Even as he asked, he knew it hadn't been Selah.

The cave. A youth in a monk's robe—but no wings. A flashing sword.

"No. I've arrived early enough to slay a nosferatu before he could kill a human, and I've been too late. But never at the critical moment, when the nosferatu's blood is the difference between life and death." And she'd never have forgotten turning Lucas, even if she'd transformed hundreds. "How old are you?" Hugh hadn't been specific about dates when he'd given her Lucas's background information.

"In human years, fifty-five. I've been a vampire twenty."

She absently ran her fingers the length of her beads, thinking. After World War II, Hugh had operated primarily in the western United States. He might know who had transformed Lucas. She could discover more about him from that Guardian—assuming, of course, he hadn't been a part of the mass Ascension that had reduced their number.

Twenty years. Not long, but he'd taken over leadership of the Ashland community. His strength couldn't completely account for that; if he hadn't been successful, the vampires would have removed him. A community could be vicious when it perceived its leadership as weak.

Confidence, then. Intelligence. Both dulled by the use of animal blood, yet he hadn't taken a new consort and secured his position. And he resisted feeding from her, even though it would halt the degenerative effects.

Selah met his eyes; he returned her stare with an expectant lift of his brow. Realizing that he was waiting for her response, she belatedly offered, "I was born in sixteen hundred and eighty four. In what's now Maine."

And lived the whole of her life in one settlement, never venturing five miles beyond the bed she'd been birthed in.

A Guardian's Gift reflected their human life; Selah couldn't have been more grateful for the one she'd received. She could escape from and go anywhere, just on a thought.

Except to and from Chaos.

Only the slight clench of Lucas's hands betrayed his shock. "You're older than any vampire I've met."

"That doesn't surprise me. There aren't many who've lived more than a century or two." Nosferatu and demons slaughtered vampires like livestock; only in the last hundred and fifty years had the vampire population expanded. Ashland's community of thirty vampires was small—but a century ago, Selah would have been hard-pressed to find such a large group in Paris, London, or New York.

Apparently, her statement didn't contradict anything he'd heard. He nodded, and his gaze slid her length. The bloodlust flared before he repressed it. It came more frequently now—and each was successively stronger than the last. "You must have been young. Twenty-two? Twenty-three?"

She shook her head. With demons and Guardians, appearances were almost always deceiving. "No. I was transformed in the mid-eighteenth century."

His brows drew together, frustration hardening his jaw; obviously, he didn't trust the calculation he'd made. She saw the moment he accepted the number: His mouth dropped open.

Smiling, she took a step forward, tapped his chin up with her forefinger. His teeth snapped together.

"I promise not to pinch your cheek, if you promise not to call me Grandmama," she said. "I had enough of that when I was human."

Three

It took the remainder of the twenty minutes for Selah to recount the origin of the Guardian corps to him. Lucas listened in silence, trying to take it all in—and certain the mental overload he was experiencing had little to do with the animal blood.

The first part held little surprises; he'd heard the story countless times. Lucifer, an angel, led a failed rebellion against Heaven. As punishment, he and his companions had been transformed into demons and thrown down to Hell.

More difficult to believe was that the nosferatu had also been angels, but had abstained from taking sides during the battle. They had been tossed from Heaven along with the Morningstar and his cohorts; but instead of taking up residence Below, He had cursed the nosferatu with bloodlust and vulnerability to daylight and cast them to Earth.

Lucas rubbed his forehead. "But wouldn't nosferatu endanger the humans who lived here? Why would He send them to Earth?"

A smile quirked Selah's mouth, and she disappeared, instantaneously arriving a few feet from where she'd been standing. "Avoiding the lightning," she said when he raised a brow.

He glanced uneasily upward.

Her laughter was soft, and her feathers rustled slightly when she shrugged. "Honestly, I don't know. Angels protected Earth then. Perhaps there wasn't any danger; perhaps angels were always on time. And both demons and angels slaughtered nosferatu whenever they found them. Those that are left usually hide in caves or underground. Angels—now Guardians—and demons have hunted them almost to extinction. Both sides are rather unforgiving. Though," she added, "it's with good reason. Without exception, nosferatu love the kill. So do demons, but they can't hurt or kill humans. Demons are as evil, just less the immediate threat."

"But not to vampires."

Her gaze was direct. "No. Not to vampires. But that's why we're here."

Guardians. Lucas shoved his hands into his pockets and crossed the room. Opaque plastic covered an unfinished window. He pulled it to the side. The buildings around them were in poor repair . . . not what he'd have expected for beings who said they were connected with Heaven.

"Caelum *isn't* Heaven?"

"No. Not in the sense that you're probably thinking of it."

He smiled slightly, glancing down at the buckling asphalt in the fenced parking lot. "No streets paved with gold? A chorus of angels singing in the background?"

Amusement lightened her voice. "Hardly. Though angels once lived there, I don't know that they sang."

"Why leave?"

"According to the Scrolls, the angels who protected Earth could take human shapes, but mankind never mistook them for something human. More like gods."

Recalling the astonishment and awe that had torn through him at the first glimpse of her wings, Lucas could easily believe it. "Have you seen one?"

"No. They left Earth after the Second Battle. I don't even know that Michael—the first Guardian—has actually seen an angel."

"The Second Battle?"

"Lucifer took exception to his former brethren being perceived as gods—so he led his demons against the angels in a second war, with Earth the battlefield," Selah said from behind him. Closer now. "And brought creatures he'd summoned from the Chaos realm with him. A dragon, and hellhounds that he bred from wyrmwolves. They slaughtered the angels."

Her voice was strained, just as it had been the first time she'd mentioned Chaos. Lucas would have asked more about that realm, but was distracted when a large dog trotted into the lot, his nails clicking against the asphalt. It was huge, but its size didn't account for the sudden uneasiness that slid through him.

He shook himself when, like any other dog would, it headed to the garbage Dumpster and began to sniff around the bottom. Perhaps it was mention of these creatures, combined with the animal blood. He was beginning to see demons and monsters everywhere.

"The angels were losing? What happened to change that?"

"Men joined on the side of the angels and helped defeat the demons. One—Michael, who killed the dragon—was given angelic powers and access to Caelum. And he created the Guardian corps, because we can protect, but also pass as human. We still are human, in many ways." Her tone changed; wry humor darkened the honeyed notes.

He turned, found Selah watching him. Her gaze lifted to his; her blue eyes sparkled.

Not watching him—she'd been *ogling* him.

It had been a while since that had happened. And despite her age, ogling her in return made him feel like a dirty old man. He pulled his hand through his hair. Thick, still black— he only had to look into a mirror to confirm that at least he didn't look like a dirty old man.

A glance at his dusty boots, his stained pants and shirt made him amend it to "old man."

But she obviously found him attractive. The knowledge had more effect on him than the bloodlust—and now it was rising, too. He swallowed to ease the sudden thirst. His body did not harden, but the tips of his fangs ached. He caressed them, soothed them with the flat of his tongue.

The laughter slowly left her gaze, replaced by heat. Then frustration, as she cocked her head.

"They're almost here." Her expression smoothed. Her shirt and shorts vanished; she exchanged them for a white gown. The material gathered over her shoulders and at her waist like a toga. Her ribboned shoes peeked beneath the hem at her ankles.

He listened, but it took a few more moments before he heard it: the sharp whine of a motorcycle engine, the deep purr of an expensive, powerful car motor.

"Colin must be with them." She shook her head. "They're racing."

Lucas looked out the window, surprised. "They can't teleport here?"

"No. Teleportation is my Gift; I'm one of two Guardians who can."

He glanced back at her wings. "Why not fly?"

"They aren't Guardians."

There was a screech of tires, and a Bentley careened into the lot. A motorcycle followed, narrowly missing the car's bumper as it sped past. Then another motorcycle, at a slightly more sedate speed.

His psychic probe revealed nothing from any of them. "What are they?"

She joined him at the window and pointed to the dark-haired man on the second motorcycle. "That's Hugh Castleford. He used to be a Guardian, but he Fell and became a human again. Colin Ames-Beaumont—the blond in the car—is a vampire. Kind of. The woman is Lilith, and there's her hellhound."

The woman had long, black hair, wore leather pants and a tight corset. The giant dog ran up to her. Lucas blinked . . . then blinked again, but he hadn't been mistaken. It had three heads now.

"What is she?"

Selah sighed. "Lucifer's daughter."

"Selah, my dear," Colin said as he leaned over and pressed a warm kiss to her cheek. "The shoes are positively smashing, but the gown is on par with the bloody horrid sack Castleford used to wear."

His voice lowered below a whisper; only Selah could have heard him. And Lucas, but he was still staring dumbstruck at Colin's face. She couldn't blame him—it had taken several days before Colin's impossible beauty had stopped having the same effect on Selah. Fortunately, she'd had her eyes closed much of the time, pretending to be unconscious whenever he'd fed from her.

"Confess. You only wear it to irritate Lilith."

She looked past him. Lilith and Hugh were poring over the vampire's corpse; the former demon's features were set, the line of her body taut as she read the symbols. Lilith's shields prevented Selah from sensing her emotions, but it was easy enough to see that Lilith was as troubled as Selah was by the vampire's fate—and that Lilith was determined it wouldn't happen again.

"Sometimes," Selah admitted. "Not today."

Colin turned, examined Lucas with a quick glance. "He thinks me beautiful. Therefore, I've decided that I shall like him very much."

With a visible shake, Lucas gathered himself. "I'm not certain," he said slowly, "whether I should fall at your feet and beg for your blood or ask Selah to teleport me away as quickly as possible. I think the second."

Fighting laughter, Selah averted her face and tried to keep her expression impassive. Despite the awe the blond vampire's appearance elicited, he'd read Colin perfectly.

"You're obviously not an idiot yet," Lilith said as she stood. "But it won't be long." She looked at Selah. "Are you going to feed him? Given what I've just read, we can't waste a nosferatu-born vampire's strength."

Flat denial radiated from Lucas's psyche, stiffened his long frame.

Selah bit off her angry response. Nothing was going to make Lilith tactful, and the insulting manner of her delivery didn't mean she wasn't right. "Yes. What did it say?"

"I won't be certain until I can confirm it with Michael, but I think the ritual is designed to change the resonance of the Gate, linking it to Hell instead of Caelum. Half of the symbols reference the Gates, and the rest are about transformation."

Lucas's jaw clenched. He stared at Selah a moment before

he said, "I was told Lucifer had been required by a wager to keep the Gates to Hell closed for five hundred years."

"Yes," Selah said quietly. "But he might be trying to twist the terms of the wager. He closed the Gates, fulfilling his part in it—but if he were to create a new Gate, it wouldn't be included in the wager."

"A Gate to Hell in your backyard," Lilith said. "And it would be the *only* Gate. Every demon going in and out would travel through Ashland."

Hugh met Selah's gaze. "Has the effect on the Gate increased since this last ritual?"

She nodded. "I can still sense Caelum, but it feels . . . off. Rotted around the edges. Worse than it was last week, when Jake first noticed it."

The young Guardian had used the Gate to travel from Caelum to Earth. Except for Michael and Selah, every Guardian had to move between the two realms using one of the portals. The Gate in Ashland was the nearest one to San Francisco—once this facility was completed, they'd be using the portal regularly.

But an increase in flight distance was hardly as alarming as the thought that Lucifer might have access to Earth again.

Hugh slid his hands into his pockets and glanced at Lilith. Neither had psychic abilities, but they might as well have communicated. A single look, and they agreed upon a course.

"Selah, you'll stay in Ashland," Hugh said. "Find the demon, kill it. Make certain it doesn't take any more vampires."

"Yes." Nothing different than what she'd intended. Lucas watched her, his eyes dark beneath his brows. "I'll benefit from your assistance," she said. "You know the community."

His expression was like iron, but he gave a short nod.

Lilith gestured to the dead vampire. "Did you know this one?"

"No."

Colin strode across the room and lifted the head by its tangle of hair. "I've seen her. It's been four or five years, perhaps."

"Here, in San Francisco?"

"Yes. She had a partner. A youngish bloke, if I recall correctly. Auburn hair, tattered denim jacket. They ran into me near Polidori's nightclub, protested my feeding from a human." He dropped the head back to the floor; his teeth flashed in a sharp grin, startling white against his tanned skin. "Protested until they got a look at me, that is. Then they wanted their turn."

Lucas went rigid. "You feed from humans?"

"They enjoy it," Colin said easily. "Quite a bit. Ask Selah; even chained to a bed, she thought it a wonderful experience."

Her lips pursed. "It might have been good. I barely remember." *Only what came after*.

Colin arched a brow at Lucas; his gray eyes glinted with laughter when Lucas quickly repressed his anger—and his bloodlust. "She saved me from the animal blood, too. She's quite adept at sacrificing herself for the cause, no matter the trouble it lands her in." His features darkened at the last.

"All Guardians are," Lilith said. "Martyrdom is a requirement for the job."

Selah closed her eyes and prayed for patience.

"Selah." Hugh's voice immediately calmed her. Though she hardly understood some of the choices he'd made, he still understood her. Maybe too well. "We'll speak tomorrow?"

"Yes. I'll find you at noon." She drew in a long breath then looked at Lucas. "Are you ready to go?"

For a second, she was certain he was going to walk out and find his own way back to Ashland. His gaze ran over her, then to Colin . . . and the corpse. "Yes," he said tightly.

Had she ever been so glad to leave a place—even Chaos? But at least this time, she was able to take the vampire back with her.

Four

Lucas thought he was better prepared for teleportation, but the forest clearing still quaked at the edges of his perception when they arrived.

Selah released him. The mild expression that had over-taken her features in San Francisco sharpened into concern when he swayed on his feet, but he waved her hand off.

It dropped to her side, fisted.

He swallowed and forced himself to steady. "Why are we here?"

The scent of the vampire's blood exploded around him, appearing from nowhere and quickly soaking into the ground. Selah shuddered. "I wanted it out of my cache. This is the best place to dump it. And I thought I'd show you the Gate's location."

The rich fragrance coated his lungs, his mouth, his tongue. His gaze narrowed as she turned. Instinct demanded that he pursue her. He fought it, but couldn't tear his eyes from her hips, their supple roll.

Her wings were outstretched. She'd shed her gown and replaced it with the clothing she'd worn earlier.

Ribbons dangled and fluttered behind her knees, her calves.

"Here," she said, stopping at the northern edge of the clearing. She lifted her arm out in front of her.

Her hand and wrist disappeared.

The blood wasn't so overpowering when he moved away from it. He stood beside her and remained silent so that he wouldn't have to breathe.

"It won't do anything to you," she said.

And it didn't; his hand remained intact. He looked at her wrist, saw the cross-section of bones and veins and muscle as if it had been sheared through with a blade. Though she held herself still, the tissues quivered: motion at a cellular level, and the flow of blood. Life at its most basic, but it was . . . disturbing.

Her brow arched when he responded with a grimace. "That's why I like to 'port," she said dryly and pulled her arm back. "A novice in Caelum was probably wondering why a disembodied hand was waving at her."

His laughter caught him by surprise. Her, too. She blinked before smiling; her eyes were clear and blue, bright with humor. So different from her attitude when she was with her colleagues, when emotion had fallen awkwardly over her features and was swept away like litter.

Too soon, her amusement faded, and she sighed. "A portal to Hell is most often created by human sacrifice—less frequently, at a site of violent human death and negative energy. There is . . . *was* a Gate to Hell in San Francisco like that."

"But this isn't human sacrifice."

"No. A demon can't kill a human; perhaps that's why he's using vampires to transform an existing Gate instead of making a new one."

Lucas turned, examined the distance to the center of the clearing. "Why isn't he performing the murders over here?"

Her brow furrowed. "Demons can only sense Hell's Gates, and Guardians only Caelum's. He must have followed a Guardian at some point—most likely a novice. He wouldn't have wanted to let slip his presence by getting close enough to see exactly where the Gate was. And apparently, it doesn't have to be right on top of the Gate, because the rituals are working."

"And this one? Was it created the same way?"

She shook her head. "I don't know. And though Guardians are linked to them by sacrifice, it's their own sacrifice, and it's a willing one."

Lucas frowned. *Martyrdom is a requirement for the job*, Lucifer's daughter had said. He'd assumed from Selah's exasperation—one of the few emotional responses she'd allowed to slip through her psychic shields when they'd been in San Francisco—that the comment had simply been an overused jab, or a joke Selah had heard too many times. "What kind of sacrifice?"

Her gaze was steady on his face as her hand rose to her neck, and her fingers ran along the beads. She'd done that before, just prior to telling him her age. Did she always hesitate and debate the consequences before revealing anything of herself?

She pulled the length of the necklace away from her chest, let it drop. "A Guardian has to willingly sacrifice herself saving another human's life—or soul—from a demon or nosferatu." Her lips pursed. "Or vampire. Mine was a demon."

In the mid-eighteenth century. "What happened?"

"We—I lived with my daughter and granddaughter—quartered an injured soldier while their husbands were off fighting the French in the Seven Years' War." Her brows arched, and the tilt of her eyes suggested that she was laughing at herself.

"But he wasn't a soldier," Lucas guessed. "Do you think you should have recognized him for what he was?"

"No. It is just . . ." She trailed off and blinked up at him. "It's odd to remember those days. I was a widow, more than seventy years of age, and my life was incredibly different. It's as if I'm speaking of someone else." She studied him for a moment, her blue eyes piercing, intense. "You didn't."

He held her gaze, took a step forward. "Didn't I . . . separate my human life from this one?"

Her chin lifted slightly at his approach, her lips parting gently to form that soft, perfect bow. "Yes."

No, he hadn't. But there were differences that ran deeper than a liquid diet and an aversion to daylight, and too much of himself that he'd pushed even more deeply. "Not completely."

Hardly an answer, but she nodded and blew out a breath,

her focus turning inward. "My granddaughter, Mary, had a little boy, not yet six months old. She'd been suffering from melancholy—postpartum depression, I imagine—and was the perfect target for a demon."

It took him a moment to realize what she meant. "To manipulate the depression into something else? Murder?"

"Or suicide. The demon was good—he nearly got both. Luckily, his arrogance got the better of him. He was bragging of his victory before she'd followed through on it. But we were still almost too late."

"Almost?" he asked in a low voice.

Her lashes fell, hiding her eyes, and she looked down at her hands. "She went to the river. My daughter took the baby, but Mary just . . . jumped in."

"And you went after her?"

"Yes." She smiled faintly, brushing a lock of hair back from her forehead. "I didn't stop and think about it overmuch. And by the time I reached Mary, she'd changed her mind." She pressed her lips together, but the corners curved upward despite her attempt to repress a smile. "She was a good girl, but slow sometimes. The river's current was *not* slow, however—and it was cold. We'd brought a rope, and my daughter was trying to pull us out, but she couldn't pull two. And I was tired." Her chest rose and fell on a long sigh. "Very tired."

His gut twisted into a tight, heavy knot. "So you let go."

"So I let go," she echoed. "And Michael picked me up about a mile downriver."

"Jesus." He had no idea what else to say to that. "But they were saved?"

"Yes. And it wasn't too bad. I had a nice nap." She invited his smile with her own. "I imagine it's better than being attacked by a nosferatu."

The tips of his fangs pressed against his lips when he returned the smile. "Perhaps. I've heard fish had big teeth back then."

She laughed softly. "Enormous. Shall we go?" Her fingers brushed his forearm. "Dawn is but a couple of hours away, and you need to eat."

His amusement died a quick and violent death. "We'll go, but not for that. We'll look for your demon and be rid of him."

She tilted her head to the right, studying him; the beads clinked softly against the inside swell of her breasts. Beneath the dark circle they made around her neck, he could see— feel—the pulsing through her veins. "We probably won't find him tonight. It'll strengthen you for when we do."

Look anywhere but at her, he told himself. He stared over her shoulder, past the wings. The depths of the forest were dark. With his preternatural sight, he should have been able to see clearly into them.

"I don't want this sacrifice from you," he said tautly.

"It's not a sacrifice. It's freely given." Her voice hardened. "What happened to that girl is a sacrifice."

To Olivia, too. For twenty years. "Do you want to do everything that goes along with it? Is that given freely, too?" He crowded close and showed his fangs. "If you desire me, the bloodlust will take over. I'll fuck you. Once I've begun feeding, I won't be able to stop myself."

"I can stop you," she said quietly. Her gaze held his before it lowered, skimming his length, pausing at his groin.

Still no reaction from his flesh; thank God for the animal blood.

Her jaw firmed, and she glanced back up. "And if I had a choice, no, I wouldn't do it. Not right away. I'd wait until I knew you better. But I don't have one. Neither do you. You're shaky; from this point on, the degeneration is quick if you don't take living blood. Can you protect your community like that?"

No. "I don't want it," he repeated from between clenched teeth.

Her face became shuttered. Her wings vanished. "We're too vulnerable here. Would you feel more comfortable feeding at your house?"

In his home? *In his bed*—with a woman who was there because she had to. Because of duty. He stared at her, his rage and humiliation warring with his bloodlust. Anger won. He turned and stalked across the clearing.

From behind him, he heard her sigh. His next step sent him crashing against her. Her hands cupped his jaw.

Jesus Christ, she was unbelievably strong. To his astonishment, he couldn't pull away.

She shoved her thumb into his mouth, slicing it on his fangs. Her blood flowed over his tongue, a brilliant shock of light and rich, heady life after a month without flavor.

And so warm.

Not enough of it. The wounds were closing, the liquid trickling to nothing. He slashed through the vein in the heel of her hand and drank in rough swallows.

The ground dropped from under his feet. She withdrew her hand; he grasped at it, growls tearing from his chest, his throat. His knees folded beneath him, sank into his mattress.

His bedroom?

Selah stood in front of him, her heels digging craters into the sheets. Her lips were parted. Her breasts moved in time with her quick breaths, her nipples peaked against the gauzy shirt.

The hunger roared within him; impossible to resist it now that he'd had a taste. *Damn her* for taking away this choice.

The hemline of her satin shorts was at his chin. Her inner thigh was leanly muscled, and an artery carried sweet living blood through its sleek length.

He leaned forward and bit deep.

Selah fell back against the pillows, stifling her blissful moan when Lucas slipped into her blood. He didn't have to make it good for her. He could have let it be a rip at her flesh and pain.

Considering that she'd forced him, it was what she'd expected. Probably what she'd deserved.

What was she becoming? A demon might do something like this.

But a demon could never feel this arousal. Her fingers clenched into fists, her back arched. She'd already acted against his will; she wouldn't add selfishness and take her pleasure through touch. But her knees rose of their own accord, sliding up Lucas's arms, hooking over his broad shoulders.

He lifted his head, and the stream of exquisite sensation through her blood halted, but not the need. Her nipples puckered with it, and she wanted his lips on them, or anywhere . . .

His powerful hands circled her thigh, gripped her opposite

hip, as if he could hold her in place. His mouth dipped low, and he reopened the punctures with his fangs and continued drinking.

His lips were cool, his tongue a shivery press against her skin. His fingers, curling beneath her waistband, a perfect contrast to her heat.

Denial shrieked from his psyche. Her eyes flew open; Lucas ripped the seam at the inside of her thigh.

She vanished the shorts, instantly replaced them. "Lucas!"

But he was lost to the bloodlust. The suction against her thigh increased; erotic pleasure speared through her. The predator was lulling the prey into complacency.

His palm cupped her sex, began a slow rhythmic caress through satin.

She lifted her hips to meet his touch. Gentle, gentle. Don't move too quickly. Let him think she wouldn't resist. Use her psychic blocks to conceal her intention. Don't hurt him— don't let him hurt himself.

The punctures on her thigh healed shut.

She teleported. Straddled his back an instant later. Her dagger flashed; the blade opened the inside of her wrist, and she pressed it to his lips.

"Just drink," she said quietly into his ear.

His mouth fastened on the wound, and he sent the pleasure rushing through her again. His helplessness and horror crawled into her veins. He pivoted, rolled. Her arm twisted in front of her; his hips shoved between her thighs.

She cupped the back of his head with her free hand. "You aren't hard," she said breathlessly against his temple. "Your thirst is so overwhelming because you were taking the animal blood for too long, but it has also suppressed your libido. Even if you wanted to, you couldn't have sex with me. And you can't hurt me."

He yanked her arm over her head, sank his fangs into her throat. Her legs wrapped around his waist. Tight. He couldn't reach between them, couldn't remove his pants.

He tried. His hungry growls filled the room. Her necklace snapped. Beads rattled across the floor. His shirt ripped, then hers. Cold bare skin. Her nipples tightened. His desperation spiked.

"Lucas. Just drink." The bloodlust wouldn't respond to his will; it only responded to her desire. And she couldn't will that away, but she could ease his fear. "I'll stop the rest."

He shuddered against her. The bloodlust didn't allow him to halt his attempts to get inside her, but relief replaced his despair when she parried every thrust of his hands and body, resisted every psychic barrage through her veins.

Lucas drank. And drank. He took far more blood than a human could have survived. Perhaps more than a normal vampire could have.

Though almost lost in her own need and arousal, Selah felt the moment the bloodlust broke.

He stiffened. Pulled back, his face a mask of fury. He took a deep breath and said simply, harshly, "Go."

Easy enough to do.

She teleported out from under him.

Selah didn't go far.

Though he couldn't hear her, Lucas felt her psychic presence as he showered, soaping death and dirt from his skin. As he stripped the bloodstained pillowslip and blankets from the bed. As he climbed the stairs from his room in the basement, his muscles still tight with anger.

Tight, but no longer shaking.

He found her in front of the large picture window in the living room, looking out over the porch. The house was old, built on the outskirts of the city when Ashland had been little more than a logging town. Giant firs edged the property and, in the darkness, rose like shadowed sentinels around the yard.

Selah, in her wings and white column of a dress, stood almost as broad and unyielding.

Her face was smooth when she turned, without expression. Her arms were folded defensively below her breasts, her shoulders and back rigid. "I forced the feeding on you," she said quietly. "And I apologize. That was not who I am."

It apparently was. Had it surprised her? After three hundred years, she should have known what lurked inside her.

"If it comforts you to believe that, go ahead. Tell yourself that it was for my good, and that I was too stupid to make the decision for myself. I don't care."

Frustration and shame deepened her voice. "That was not what a Guardian is."

His gaze held hers. "*I don't care*. Let's go find your demon so that you can fulfill your duty, kill it, and get the hell out of my town."

Selah stared at him for a long moment before nodding. Her blue eyes were carefully blank. Rather than offer protection, the shields she formed over her face and around her mind exposed a deep vulnerability, provided evidence that something inside her *needed* to be guarded.

He turned away from her, his jaw clenching. Goddammit, he shouldn't care. He shouldn't be wondering why she was smiling and soft one moment, then a woman of marble and ice the next. Why she looked at her colleagues with a combination of affection and the expectation that they'd rip her guts open if she showed the slightest emotion.

His weapons were in the coat closet by the entryway. He retrieved the wooden stakes and the hand ax and tossed them in a canvas pack.

She didn't move from her post by the window, but she must have been watching him. "You use stakes?"

"Of course. What do you use?"

"My sword, usually. It doesn't have to be wood. All that matters is that you bisect the heart, cut off the head, or completely drain them of blood. Demons, too."

A wry smile crossed his lips. That knowledge could have saved him a lot of trouble; even with his strength, it was difficult to kill a vampire with a piece of sharpened oak.

Of course, his power was nothing compared to hers. Remembering the ease with which she'd held him on the bed, he glanced over his shoulder. "And Guardians?"

"The same. But you won't need to kill any."

"We'll be seeing more of you when you begin using the Gate. If they threaten my community—"

"You won't see more of us, nor are we likely to threaten you if your community lives as quietly as it does now. Most vampires won't be able to sense the difference between a

Guardian and human." She sighed. "Unfortunately, the same is true of demons."

"*Most* vampires? But not me." Even on the animal blood, he'd been able to tell she wasn't human. He simply hadn't trusted his instincts.

"You're nosferatu-born. You have greater psychic strength than normal vampires, and I can teach you to differentiate between us."

"And to use a sword?"

He thought he felt approval from her, but it was impossible to determine from that blank expression. Did she think he'd completely shunned his responsibilities because he'd refused her blood?

He'd simply drawn a line between desire and duty; she'd pushed him over it. It didn't matter if she hadn't been herself when she'd done it. The desperate creature in that bed hadn't been him, either.

Would she be prepared if he pushed back?

"Yes. Though Hugh is more qualified to teach you. And it's best learned for defense; demons are as fast and as strong as I am. It's better to call for help from the Guardians than try to fight one."

Lucas nodded and glanced down at the pack in his hands. Stakes and an ax required that he get close before he could strike effectively. Useless against a demon, then. The weapons clattered together when he threw the pack into the closet.

"What's the plan for this evening?" He turned as he asked and had to suppress his astonished curse. Selah's skin had lost its golden glow; she was as pale as he was. Her incisors lengthened into fangs.

"A sweep of the city." She frowned slightly, swiped her tongue over her bottom lip. Scarlet dotted the soft pink flesh. Humor brightened her gaze. "Hugh would have my ass for not practicing with these more often."

Lucas would, too. He inhaled, felt the rising ache as her blood scented the air. Not bloodlust—that had been sated.

He approached her slowly. This close, he could detect his masculine odor lingering on her skin. The fragrance of arousal was hers.

There was no doubt she'd wanted him; she hadn't simply

thought him attractive. It had been accompanied by willingness to follow it through to consummation. His need to have her wouldn't have been so overwhelming if she hadn't been willing, but the bloodlust wasn't responsible for the craving he felt now.

Yes, if she tried to feed him again without his consent he had every intention of pushing back—hard.

Selah didn't move as he lifted his hand to her cheek. Warm. The appearance of vampirism, but only a thin mask.

"Why the disguise?" He kept his voice as light as his touch. Her skin was heated silk beneath his fingertips. He let them remain a moment longer than necessary, skimmed them over her pulse when he dropped his hand away.

Her breath shuddered past her lips before she swallowed and said evenly, "If we're seen by a vampire—which is probable, given that it's three o'clock in the morning—you won't have the community wondering if you've slipped and hunted a human."

Or give them knowledge the Guardians existed. They wouldn't think she was anything but a vampire with extraordinary psychic shields, as long as they didn't touch her skin— or smell her.

"You don't have a vampire's scent," he said.

"Unfortunately, I can't fake one. Perfume might cover it, but I don't have any in my cache." Her gaze swept the room, narrowed on something behind him. "That will work, though."

She vanished. Lucas spun around; Selah stood next to the sofa table, a women's magazine in her hands. Glossy paper caught the light as she flipped through the pages.

She paused at an advertisement. Her lips parted; her eyes widened in feminine delight. "Oh. That's gorgeous." Her wings disappeared; a slim indigo top and flouncy knee-length skirt replaced the gown.

His mouth dried. The shirt hugged the ripe curve of her breasts. Her stomach was flat, taut beneath the clinging material. Beyond gorgeous. Beyond alluring.

And impossible. "You made that—looking at a picture?"

"Yes. I just imagine it, and wear it." Paper ripped; she rubbed the magazine down her front, up the length of her neck. A perfume sample. Light and breezy, as if the ocean had been captured in the scent. "I spent half my human life sewing. I consider the ability my eternal reward."

Amusement and arousal hit him with equal force. Best to go with one rather than suppress both. Lucas pinched the bridge of his nose, a deep laugh breaking from his chest.

Her teeth flashed when she grinned. She slapped the magazine closed, took a second to look at the cover. "I like this one, too. I'll have to remember it." Her smile faded, and her thumb smoothed over the mailing label glued to the bottom corner. "Olivia Jordan? She was your partner?"

"Yes. My consort." A partnership suggested equality; there'd been little between them. Friendship, yes. But he'd never been equal to her memories of something more.

Selah glanced around the living room. He knew what she'd see—the dark colors, the heavy rustic furniture. It had been the same in his bedroom. There were no feminine touches; that magazine was the only indication a woman had lived with him for twenty years. There'd never been any evidence of her in this house, except in her room.

A room that Lucas had never visited. It and the theater had served as her sanctuaries when friendship hadn't been enough—when the bloodlust had been too much. He hadn't intruded on them.

She carefully tucked the opened perfume strip back between the pages. "I think I'll enjoy giving the demon *his* eternal reward."

So would Lucas.

Five

Once again, they went on foot. Walking.

Or maybe it was a stroll. A slow amble. Whatever it was, after an hour of it in Lucas's company, Selah knew it was far more pleasurable than *walking* could possibly be.

He'd been relentless in his interrogation about demons—particularly their weaknesses. To her surprise, he hadn't fixated on their physical vulnerabilities, but on their mental ones. And as she'd never met a demon she hadn't wanted to kill, Selah had no compunction against describing the personality flaws and the demise of those she'd slain.

In explicit detail.

But she shouldn't have been surprised, she mused when a brief silence fell between them. Once he'd realized his weapons would be useless against a demon, he'd left them behind. Though accustomed to being the most powerful of his kind, he wasn't completely dependent on his strength to protect them. Now he looked for other means of defeating the demon and anything else that threatened his community—including Guardians.

It was ridiculously appealing.

He drew to a halt at an intersection. "Cross?"

"No." The street was a clear demarcation between the theater district and a modest residential neighborhood. "It would be a slam to his ego to operate from there. Not rich enough."

They'd concentrated their search downtown, focusing on the more expensive hotels. A demon probably wouldn't have bothered with permanent accommodations, and most preferred luxurious and moneyed surroundings.

She'd sensed several vampires, but the demon's psychic presence eluded her. Either he was shielding, or he wasn't within her search radius.

Lucas's sigh of frustration echoed hers. "Do we know that he'll be in Ashland?"

"No." A single streetlight illuminated the corner, tingeing his pale skin with yellow. He should have looked sallow in such a light, but his features were too strong, his gaze too sharp for the light to weaken his appearance. "He could have picked that girl up in San Francisco. Or anywhere in between, if she'd fled San Francisco in May and hadn't yet returned."

"Four others, but only one—Olivia—from this community. I'd have known if any others had gone missing." His jaw tightened, and he passed his hand through his hair. "I returned to the site several times in the two weeks after she was killed, but I couldn't find any evidence, and no odor but hers."

"You tracked her by scent?" *Impressive.*

"Yes. The next evening, when I realized she wasn't home. Her scent went directly from the theater to the forest. She walked. There were prints from her shoes, and from a male's." He tucked his hands into his pockets, and they began retracing their path back to the heart of the city. Maintaining the illusion of a couple out for an early morning stroll. "She wasn't careless. And I'd warned her to be careful—we'd had too many unfamiliar vampires in town."

Some of them looking to challenge him, Selah guessed. His consort would've been a target if any other vampire sought his position. "He could've resembled someone she knew. Or imitated you."

He stilled. "How well?"

It was easier to demonstrate, and no one was on the street to see it. Selah shifted her form, created a mirror image of

Lucas. His black hair, the green eyes. Copied his dark cotton shirt, the flat-front trousers, and his shoes.

"Jesus Christ." He circled her, taking in her appearance from each angle. He faced her as she regained her shape, and drew in a long breath between his teeth. "I don't think he impersonated me. The day before, she said she thought she'd seen David." He exhaled, shook his head. "Do you have to see the person to duplicate them?"

"It helps, but I can also use a picture. It's not as good that way, though, because I have to fill in a lot of the details. What the back of the person's head looks like, for example."

He stopped in front of a café, staring at his reflection in the darkened window. His eyes closed; his chin dropped. "Goddammit. Poor Olivia. She never had a chance."

Grief again, but this was older. And though it was less painful, it was also more deeply entrenched.

And beneath it, a sense of failure. Of betrayal.

He might not want comfort from her, or her touch, but she offered it. Her hand slid over his shoulder, and she stared at his set profile. "David. He was someone she'd known?" Someone dead. A brother, perhaps. Or a lover. A demon's deception was more effective—and more painful for the victim—when he took the form of a loved one.

"Olivia's husband."

That wasn't reason enough for the emotions she felt pouring from him. "Your friend."

He lifted his head. His voice was like stone. "Yes."

"I *will* kill him, Lucas." It seemed a poor reassurance.

"No." He backed up a step, and her hand dropped to her side. "You'll help me find him, and I'll do it."

She knew it wouldn't be that simple, but she nodded.

Lucas studied her for a long moment. "Dawn isn't far off. An hour. Do you need a place to stay? I have an extra room."

He only suggested it out of politeness; she could feel the reluctance that accompanied the offer.

But she had only herself to blame for it, and for the tightness in her throat. "I don't sleep." She forced a smile. "Do you want me to 'port you home?"

"No. I have a set to tear down." His hands flexed at his

sides. Strong, powerful. And though he kept his emotions well contained, she hadn't any doubt he would forego the use of his tools this time. "Will you remain in the city during the day?"

Where else would she go? She had to meet with Hugh, but other than that . . . what was there to do but this?

And why did telling herself there was nothing, which had always pleased her before, seem so inadequate now? It was a Guardian's role to protect, to slay, to watch. It had always been enough. It had always been *everything*.

Many things had changed of late, but that shouldn't have.

"Yes." She pointed to the sky. "I'll make another sweep before the sun comes up. If I'm called away and won't be back before sunset, I'll try to leave a message for you."

"Can you find me if I'm not home?"

"Yes."

"But you can't find the demon?"

"No. I don't have an anchor to him. I can teleport anywhere, but to go directly to a person I need a physical link to them and their psychic shields must be down—or at least lowered slightly." She sighed when his hard stare asked the question he didn't voice. "I took your blood off the nail. It's in my cache. But I won't intrude on your privacy. I won't pop in unannounced."

Most vampires woke at sundown, but there were rituals to follow: showering, dressing. And though she'd have enjoyed teleporting into a hot, steaming room with a naked Lucas, she doubted he'd have appreciated the surprise.

Apparently, a similar scenario occurred to him. His eyes glittered with sudden heat, and his gaze swept her length. "At least you'd be certain that you got everything right."

Her mouth dropped open, and she laughed. "I would show you what I imagined, but I'd risk crushing your ego."

His lips firmed, and he cast an accusing glance at her pelvis.

Grinning, she added, "Not because it was small. It's because reality might not live up to it."

She teleported before he could respond. Hovering a hundred feet in the air, she heard his startled, reluctant laughter. She watched silently over him as he returned to his theater, then an hour later, as he emerged covered in sweat and saw-dust, and drove home beneath a lightening sky.

Home. The breeze slid through her wings, a cold and wel-come caress. How strange, though she could go anywhere in the world, that in two hundred and fifty years it was the first time she wished she had a place to go *to*.

At noon, Selah teleported into a park. It had sun-warmed green grass, a lake, dogs fighting against their leashes—and humans who exercised. Hugh ran past her, then jogged in place, waiting.

"You *knew* I was coming." She instantly changed from the white gown into a pair of sweats that were as ragged as his. Then made them fluorescent pink, hoping the color would blind him.

A smile tugged at his mouth, but his blue eyes were hard and flat. "Yes," he said before he continued down the trail. With a sigh, she fell into step beside him. It was several miles before he spoke again. "Did he take the blood?"

"Yes."

He slanted a glance over his shoulder, read her in an instant. "But not willingly."

"No." Her chest ached. Not from running; she didn't need to breathe and didn't physically tire.

Silence fell between them again, only broken by the quick rhythm of their feet. They were running much faster than humans could have, but though several watched them pass, none remarked on it.

She hated this. Hated it, and he knew it.

"Why did you?"

Her teeth ground together. He'd had to Fall after denying a human's free will—to save a little girl—and he wondered why she would deny a vampire's will? "Because he can't pro-tect his community if he's not strong."

She felt his cold disappointment before he said, "That's a lie, Selah."

Blades of grass smashed beneath her skidding shoes, releasing their verdant odor. He stopped as suddenly, though without the same awkwardness.

Or the shock. Hugh could determine the truth of any statement; it had been his Gift as a Guardian, and he'd retained the ability after his Fall. She couldn't doubt his assessment—but neither could she understand it. "How is it a lie? He can't protect them if he's on animal blood."

"*That's* truth." His breathing was ragged; sweat dampened his T-shirt. "But it wasn't your reason."

"Then what was?"

Grooves formed beside his mouth as if he was suppressing laughter. "I don't read minds."

"But you read people. You *see*." Better than anyone Selah had known. And he was more honest in his evaluation than anyone; he didn't mince words. There was never any fudging of truth to save hurt feelings.

"You want to know? Truly?"

It could be brutal, but she wanted—needed—to know. "Yes."

His face hardened. "I saw that you came here wearing angelic clothes that you've set up as armor. I'll admit I was angry. And—"

He broke off, but he didn't need to tell her. He opened his shields, let her sense it.

Hurt. Frustration. *She'd* created that in him? Her hands clenched at her sides. "Why?"

"You always embraced being a Guardian. Left everything you'd been as a human behind. And you took to it better than anyone else, internalized everything it stood for."

"And you rejected it," she said flatly.

He stilled for a long second, his jaw tight. Then he gripped the hem of his shirt in his fist and dragged it up to his collarbone. His voice was hoarse. "You can say that to me?"

She made herself look at the scars on his chest, the symbols written there. Three months before, she'd watched him stand and willingly accept the pain as they were carved into his flesh, to save a human's soul, to save Caelum.

"No," she whispered. "I'm sorry." Twice, in less than a day's time, she was apologizing with shame thick in her throat.

Hugh deserved better. Lucas had deserved better.

He sighed and let go of the shirt. "Yet you obviously feel

the need to have that armor between us. Not just *us*—you've put it between yourself and every other Guardian."

"So you forced me out of it?" So that she'd be vulnerable?

His dark brows drew together. "How can I force you to do anything?"

She waved her arm in a wide arc, indicating the park, the humans. "Circumstances forced it—circumstances that *you* chose. And because I can't run around with wings and a gown without risking someone seeing me."

"That reason is truth. Though they'd never assume it was anything but a costume, unless you flew."

"Better than running. You could have made me change clothes by meeting me in a restaurant. Why would you do it this way if you know I hate it?" Someone like Lilith might do it for that reason, but Hugh wasn't vicious or petty. Or he hadn't been.

His blue eyes warmed. "Why didn't you ask me to stop?"

She stared at him, her lips parting in surprise. Why hadn't she? If she'd requested they quit, he would've immediately assented.

A short laugh escaped her, and she tilted her head back. The sky was pale, the sun high. Summer in western San Francisco—it would probably be obscured by afternoon fog before much longer.

She glanced at Hugh, noted that his strong, quiet stance was exactly the same as it had been when he'd covered his body with a staid brown robe. It was the same as every time he'd forced her to discover a truth by working through it.

He'd give her tools, but he wouldn't dig her out. That she had to do on her own.

"Do you ever stop mentoring?"

"No." His mouth quirked into a brief smile. "Though there are many I don't have an opportunity to teach."

She blinked as she caught his meaning, but she wasn't truly surprised. "Lucas?"

Hugh might not have remembered the name, but he likely wouldn't have forgotten the face—especially once he realized Lucas was nosferatu-born. There weren't many.

The vampire hadn't recognized Hugh, but the former

Guardian had aged since he'd Fallen. In human years, she guessed he was thirty-two or -three. No longer the teenaged boy.

Hugh nodded. "I made him, and helped him transform a woman. One—a male—I couldn't save. I'll tell you at the house."

"I'm not walking back."

His deep laughter echoed across the grounds. "Good," he said as he held out his hand. "Because you wore me out."

"You're just old." She slid her palm against his; she didn't need to prepare him. They'd done this hundreds of times.

"That's true, too."

Six

Selah waited until twilight stained the sky violet before knocking at Lucas's front door. His absent reply came from deep within the house.

Mentally anchoring to his blood gave her a better sense of his location than his voice did. He didn't startle when she teleported in. His black hair was damp, curling slightly. The scent of disuse hung stale in the air, enlivened only by the smell of his soap.

She leaned closer to him and inhaled the woodsy fragrance, then masked her appreciation with a melodramatic sigh. "I missed the shower."

He glanced up from the framed photo in his hands. A wedding picture; the cut of the groom's tuxedo and the bride's stiffly sprayed bangs and makeup suggested it was at least twenty years old. "I would've lingered for another hour, waiting, but if you'd mimicked me in cold water it would've done very little for my ego."

She smiled, but her amusement faded as she looked about the room. Theater posters and memorabilia patterned the walls. The furniture was upholstered in soft cream and blue; the coverlet on the bed was delicate lace. A woman's bedroom. Heavy drapes covered the windows. A vampire's bedroom.

They were upstairs; the ceiling peaked in the center. For someone with a vampire's speed, it wasn't an inconvenient distance from the basement—but its existence implied a separation much wider than the physical.

Perhaps it was disrespectful to think ill of the dead, but Selah had never witnessed anyone struck down by the heavens for doing so.

Olivia Jordan had been an idiot.

A beautiful idiot. The bride was the same woman fronting many of the cast photos sitting atop the dresser. A haunted, ethereal melancholy had replaced the exuberant joy in the wedding picture.

Lucas wasn't in any of them.

"How is it that you went from police officer, to lawyer, to theater owner?" Two of the occupations required an assertive personality, yet as a vampire he'd remained in the background.

He replaced the frame on the nightstand. "How is it that you have knowledge of what I was then, but not what happened to Olivia a month ago? Or even that she was my consort?"

"You didn't file a joint return with the IRS. I'm serious," she protested when his lips tightened. "Guardians don't keep tabs on the vampire communities." Not any longer. After the Ascension, Michael hadn't assigned any of the remaining Guardians to observe the vampires. When thousands populated Caelum, Guardians had monitored the vampires' internal power struggles and provided the communities silent protection from demons and nosferatu. Now, with less than fifty in the Guardian corps, they simply didn't have the ability.

"But you did know how to find me."

"It wasn't difficult. Once we discovered the problem with the Gate, I came to Ashland, shifted into a vampire form, and asked the first vampire I saw who the community's head was. Once I had your name, I took it to Hugh. He got the background info."

"How?"

Selah smiled slightly. "A computer, I imagine."

Lucas nodded, seeming to accept that explanation. He hadn't asked these particulars the previous evening, but perhaps the animal blood—or the surprise of discovering that Guardians existed—had overcome his caution.

His attention shifted. Stepping away from the bed, he tapped a poster on the wall. "*Tartuffe*. It was our first."

In the summer of 1987, the same year Hugh had transformed him. "But you don't perform."

"Not if I can help it." As if he was amused by the notion, a soft chuckle escaped him. "The few appearances I made in the courtroom made it very clear that I'd never be a good actor."

"You didn't win?"

"Win, yes, but only because my arguments and cases were solid. If a guilty verdict had depended upon my skill as an orator and playing my audience, I wouldn't have earned a single conviction."

"You bored the jury?" Selah had a difficult time believing that. Just watching him pace a path from the wall to her side was mesmerizing. All fluid muscle and silent pursuit.

"No. I was too single-minded." His gaze met hers, and wariness had her flexing her hands, as if in preparation to call in her sword. She saw what he didn't add: Relentless. Merciless. "If a jury had been any less certain of a defendant's guilt, they'd have set him free."

As compassionate humans would any helpless, trapped animal. Selah swallowed, forced moisture onto her tongue. "Obviously you couldn't have remained an attorney." Courts didn't operate on a vampire's schedule.

"No. When I came to Ashland—"

"When you were brought here."

He paused. "You know that as well?"

"Hugh was the one who transformed you—and Olivia. He told me about the cave and about bringing you to the elders here." Whose position Lucas had quickly taken. Had he been forced to kill them in self-defense after they recognized his strength? Most vampires wouldn't appreciate knowing they'd invited their successor in through the front door.

"Then he has a better memory of it than I do."

"It must have been terrifying," she said softly.

His firm lips tilted in a smile. "Yes. I haven't spelunked many caves in the past twenty years."

Three months ago, she had. Run through them, scrambling and scratching through caves so deep that the screams of the damned hadn't penetrated the stone walls. Through corridors so small she'd had to vanish her wings and crawl. Through caverns so black, even with her angelic sight, the darkness had been as unyielding as death.

But in Chaos, the dark was less frightening than what had been living.

"Selah?" It was only her name, and spoken quietly, but it pulled her back. His gaze was intent on her face.

She glanced away, tracing her fingers over the bedpost's scrolled woodwork. Cool and smooth. She'd have preferred to sit on the mattress rather than stand, but Lucas's focus on her hadn't shifted away, and he had enough advantage with his size. He did not touch the bed, but he stared down at her from less than an arm's length away. His shoulders seemed very broad, and her height and heels and Guardian strength did not negate the overpowering *presence* of him.

She swallowed. "Did the theater pass to you when you defeated the elders?"

It wasn't unusual for a community's economy to center around a theater or a nightclub. It provided employment and a place to congregate. Typically, those venues were in the elders' possession, and younger vampires were discouraged from buying their own—with the explanation that it might splinter the community. But Selah knew no one truly believed that. It simply kept the power in the elders' hands.

His brow furrowed, and for a moment she thought he might pursue her reaction instead of her response. But he only said, "I bought the theater from one of the elders. Pierre—the former community head. And once he realized my physical capabilities, he relinquished his position and I acceded to it."

Selah shook her head in disbelief. "You didn't have to kill him?"

"No. Ashland isn't your typical vampire community. There are no squabbles for power. Most concentrate on the theater. Some produce art and sell it in the tourist shops. Pierre wants only to direct; he was content to pass the business side of the theater to me—along with the duties required of the head."

Such as protection and punishment for those who disregarded community rules. Given his background, Lucas would have been well suited for both. "But even the most easygoing vampires won't allow you to continue like this indefinitely—without a consort."

"No."

She smoothed her expression. "I could inquire within the San Francisco community. After the nosferatu slaughtered the elders, many vampires were left unattached."

Lucas gripped the carved bedpost, his hand six inches above hers; his thumb rubbed firmly over the surface, as if to polish away a spot. His mouth tightened with a combination of humor and frustration. "No. Thank you."

Selah halted her fingers' restless movements and dropped her fist to her side. He looked down at her hand, and his body stilled. Selah's breath drew in raggedly between her teeth.

She'd retreated. Not in fear, or from discomfort caused by his proximity, but because her fidgeting betrayed her uncertainty of how to handle him—and of her response.

But stopping had called attention to it just as well.

"And who would you have asked to procure a consort for me? Your vampire?"

His voice had deepened, a silken prowl the length of her spine. She suppressed the shiver that ran through her. "Colin?" At his nod, she shook her head, her laugh sticking in her throat. "He has no connections. The vampires in San Francisco like his feeding from humans no better than you did."

"Why do you allow him?"

"We don't *allow* him anything. He does what he needs to survive, and we don't stop him." She tilted her head; his gaze fell to her neck before meeting her eyes again. His bloodlust hadn't yet risen, but she couldn't mistake the hunger in his psychic scent. "And he's a friend," she added.

It was best Lucas didn't misinterpret her relationship with Colin. He was charming, entertaining, and she'd welcome him at her side in a battle—but with a selfish streak that reminded her, at times, of a spoiled child.

She preferred men.

Judging by the narrowing of his eyes, the satisfaction in

that steady gaze, he didn't misunderstand. "As the others are friends?"

"I'm undecided about Lilith." Her lips quirked. "But, yes, Hugh is."

"It was difficult to tell."

She lifted her brows, glanced pointedly at Olivia's bed. "Friendships can be complicated."

A wry smile touched his mouth. "Yes. Why is yours?"

He added the question smoothly, familiarly, as if it would be the most natural thing in the world for her to bare herself to him. And perhaps it was. By forcing him to feed, she'd already exposed something she'd never shown anyone else . . . hadn't been aware it was in her.

Was it new, or had the recent upheavals in the Guardian corps brought it to the surface? Had Lucas?

She stared up at him. His features were strong, handsome—but as seconds passed and she didn't answer, it was the slight wrinkling at the corners of his eyes that appealed most. Humor, when he realized she hadn't fallen for his slippery tactic.

His fangs glistened as his smile widened, and he leaned his shoulder against the bedpost, crossing his arms. It was a relaxed, masculine pose—and with it, he invaded oh-so-casually into the cushion of space she'd maintained between them.

Yes, he could easily be a life-changing force. An upheaval.

And maybe she needed one. A *good* one. "I mentioned last night that Hugh gave up his immortality and Fell."

If Lucas was surprised she'd answered him after all, he didn't show it. He simply nodded.

"Hugh was the best of us. No question of it; if Michael assigned us rank, Hugh would have been his lieutenant general. And he was a mentor to many of us. So when he lost faith in his role as a Guardian and transformed back into human . . . it was devastating."

"But he's working with you again."

"Yes. And living with a demon."

"You consider it a betrayal? Lucifer's daughter—and his Fall?"

She glanced down at the lace coverlet, straightened a fold

at the corner. "No," she said truthfully. "He did what he had to do. There are others whose actions I'd consider—"

"'He did what he *had to do*'?" The cool press of his fingertips beneath her chin startled her. More in surprise than at his insistence, she looked up. His fangs gleamed in a hard smile. "You said almost the same of the vampire, and his feeding from humans. If doing what one 'has to do' is your criterion for excusing behavior you don't sanction, little wonder you forced me last evening. Whose reluctance infuriated you more—mine or yours?"

"That question assumes I did it because I was angry." Had she been?

"And now evasion."

"Uncertainty."

"And this?" He tugged the pendant dangling from her wide velvet choker. "*I* am uncertain if this is supposed to act as enticement for me or protection for you."

"It is neither. It's just a pretty piece of jewelry I saw in *Vogue*." She caught his wrist. "You want to know if I'll force you again."

"Yes." He didn't try to escape her grasp.

"I prefer not to."

"But you would."

Yes, but this time for the right reason. "Why do I need to?" But she knew the answer to that. This bedroom screamed it. "A demon is sacrificing vampires in your city. *Will* I need to?"

His jaw clenched. "No."

"Good." She didn't realize how tension had knotted inside her until his answer eased it, and she released it in a short laugh. "I haven't provided supper according to a schedule since I died, but I'll make an exception for you. And the best part is that I won't be on my feet for hours preparing it."

Brief amusement sweetened his psychic scent, but his voice was flat. "Because you have to."

"Yes, though it would be just as easy for me to find a vampire to do it." Her grip tightened. "It's also because I *want* to. Why does it have to be one or the other?"

Lucas didn't have the strength to break her hold, but even

without hundreds of years of training, he knew how to turn it to his advantage. He pulled her toward him.

And she knew a dozen ways to reclaim it, but she let herself fall against him. Her silk top was thin; her nipples drew taut against the chilled cotton of his shirt, the hardness of his chest.

His hand cupped her jaw, the splay of his fingers a delicious pressure on the skin of her cheek, below her ear. "I've been twisted up for twenty years. I want something uncomplicated."

His touch was cold, but heat built in his psychic scent and curled like a slow smoking flame deep within her. Hot and moist.

"So do I." She lowered her shields slightly, let him feel her response. "And *this* is."

This was enticement. Not a necklace or even blood, but the warm press of her body. Her smile, a cupid's bow fully drawn. Lucas had always thought his fangs lethal, but her mouth was far more dangerous.

And it was best to approach it with caution. Her bottom lip softened beneath his. Willingly. Without a recoil of guilt and shame, without a reminder that a kiss wasn't necessary—or wanted.

Selah had been correct: This was simple. Necessity *and* want. Not one or the other, but both.

Her long exhalation spoke of her pleasure. Of her desire for more. It had been twenty years, but he recognized that silent confession. The plea.

Her lips closed over his tongue, and need arrowed sharply through him. He took her mouth with deep strokes. His fangs scraped wet silken skin. Blood, just a taste, but he wielded the bolt of electric flavor like an erotic sword, struck her with it.

She moaned low in her throat; her fingers tightened painfully on his shoulders. She'd already healed, but the effect lingered. Her back arched. Her knee rose alongside his thigh, a warm smooth glide over rough denim, and hooked over his hip. He rocked back slightly when she rose onto her toes, as if she were trying to get closer—trying to crawl *onto* him.

And the best part is that I won't be on my feet . . .

He slid his hands to the firm swell of her ass, lifted her. Selah apparently liked that—better than she had the bliss he'd sent singing through her veins. Fierce arousal darkened her psychic scent. Her fingers buried in his hair. Her wrists were a heated brand against his neck.

He tumbled her onto the bed. Her legs encircled him, drew him down with her. Fragile lace crumpled beneath his fisting hands, and he set up an easy rhythm of his body over hers.

He froze above her. Clenched his teeth.

His unresponsive body.

Goddammit.

Selah moved; the next instant, he was on his back. She straddled his hips, braced her hands on his shoulders. The tips of her hair brushed his chin. Her face was devoid of expression, but he could smell—feel—the heat and wet of her, see the flush on her skin. "We might have to slay this particular demon another time."

He blinked; had she thought he'd stopped because this was Olivia's bed? But he had no time to ask.

The skirt of her white gown suddenly pooled around her knees, over his stomach and thighs. The mattress creaked as she formed her wings, doubling her weight.

"How many?" she said over her shoulder.

Lucas tried to sit up; she held him fast.

"Seven." The deep masculine voice made a melody of two syllables. Lucas's psychic probe revealed nothing, and he couldn't see past the arch of thick white feathers.

The muscles in her thighs tensed beneath his hands. She met his eyes; fear flickered in their blue depths before she swept it away with the fall of her lashes. "Will you leave two for me?"

"If you hurry."

"I'll find you in twenty seconds."

Lucas knew the moment their visitor left by the shifting of her features, the reclamation of emotion.

"Michael. A rout of demons. I'll be back as soon as I can."

He nodded. There was nothing else to do; he'd been a cop. He knew that "*if* I can" was attached to that statement.

She sat up fully, releasing him. He rose onto his elbows.

Two swords appeared in her hands. "And I'll tell him to knock next time."

He grinned. And *now* his shaft responded with a subtle ache when anticipation flared through her psychic scent, when she vanished one of her swords to brush her thumb against his left fang and slide it into his mouth. A drop of blood fell on his tongue. He forced himself not to catch her wrist, to prevent her from withdrawing her hand.

He swallowed; his voice was thick. "Or to bring a dose of Viagra. I'm at that age, you realize—"

Her smiling mouth caught his in a kiss. And then she was gone.

Seven

Jesus Christ. A limp dick and a lame joke. As he parked the Jeep near Pierre's apartment, Lucas tried to decide which had been worse. He wasn't even certain if he could blame it on the animal blood.

Erectile dysfunction, yes. But inanity?

It must have been her mouth. Or the brief vulnerability she'd shown him. Seven demons against two Guardians, but she'd gone because she'd had to. Because of duty.

And he'd found his attraction instantly deepening into something beyond physical, into admiration and an unexpected kinship. Self-disgust followed it, that she'd had to force him into accepting the same. Concern, that whatever fear she'd had would be realized and she wouldn't return.

So he was twisted up, once again. But without shame, without guilt. He didn't think he wanted to be straightened out just yet.

Marguerite waited for him on the sidewalk, her portfolio case in one hand, a mound of flowers tucked beneath her chin. Lucas automatically took both from her, though their weight was negligible to any vampire.

"Ah, chivalry isn't dead. Not five minutes ago, I despaired

every man but Pierre had driven a stake through its gallant heart."

Roses. Not his favorite—too sweet and cloying. He drew in a breath through his mouth and followed her up the stairs. Pierre and Marguerite leased the second floor of the Parisian-inspired building. A wrought-iron balcony overlooked the street; a human couple window-shopped in front of the art gallery on the first level.

"What occurred five minutes ago?"

She paused in front of the door. A knot of gray hair pulled at the corners of her eyes; clothed in unrelenting black, she looked as severe and thin as a nightstick. "Victor closed the gallery, interrupting Julianne and me, just as she began relating the most fascinating bit of gossip I've heard in ages. I was distraught, until I looked out the window and saw the subject of our little tête-à-tête."

Lucas wasn't surprised. There were a lot of eyes in Ashland; many of them had excellent night vision. "The evening has cooled nicely, hasn't it? I saw that it was a record high today."

"Cheeky vampire. Don't smile like that. You'll frighten the children."

Once inside, frigid air surrounded him, the hum of air-conditioning units. Aside from that modern convenience, it was like stepping into a luxurious Old World salon. They'd spared no expense on their collection of furniture and art—and they'd had more than a century to collect them.

"Lucas. Pardon me, Scott." His dark hair shining beneath the lamp, Pierre rose from the ivory-inlaid game table in the corner of the room. The young male vampire nodded, his gaze fixing on Marguerite for a long moment before he returned his attention to the chess set in front of him.

Lucas suppressed his amusement. Scott was one of Marguerite's "children," but the latent sexual hunger coming from the vampire wasn't remotely familial. He'd buried it, hidden it well; Lucas doubted that either Marguerite or Pierre were aware of the kid's interest.

Or Scott's partner, Andrea. Though Lucas thought even if Andrea had known, she probably wouldn't have cared.

She sat at the window, her chin resting on her crossed arms

as she stared through the pane, her hair a pale wispy crown, her eyes blank. Not much emanated from her psychic scent.

They were refugees from San Francisco, where both had lost their partners to the nosferatu. They'd arrived in Ashland a month after most of the other vampires had left and had been unwilling to return to California. Their bloodsharing arrangement had arisen from necessity, but it was easy to see that little affection had developed between them in spite of the forced intimacy. Even Andrea's clothing acted as a barrier; she'd covered every inch of her skin.

Marguerite had made it her mission to support them until they found suitable employment, and probably thought the mock turtleneck and slim pants were a flattering emulation of her style—but Lucas had experienced exactly the same from Olivia in their first years together.

"Since sundown, I have been bombarded with telephone calls from the elders," Pierre said as he took Lucas's hand in greeting. His unlined skin retained some of his natural olive color; his Gallic nose and eyes were sharp. "Cora is demanding to know whether you've taken Vampire Barbie as your consort."

Despite the humor in Pierre's tone, Lucas didn't mistake the gravity behind it. The community's anxiety over the situation was increasing. Unfortunately, he couldn't yet reassure them. "No."

Marguerite made a sound of dismay, but she directed it at Pierre. "You'd heard this *on dit* and didn't journey downstairs to share it with me?" She pursed her thin lips, shaking her head. "Chivalry *is* dead, and the elders can rest easy for at least another day. Lucas has obviously fed."

Pierre nodded, studying him. "Who is she?"

Conscious of the children, Lucas said cryptically, "A friend of the man who left me on your doorstep twenty years ago."

Pierre and Marguerite exchanged swift, startled glances.

"You knew what he was," Lucas realized.

"We suspected, but didn't truly imagine—" Marguerite's mouth softened; disbelief filled her scent.

"We'd only heard rumors of their existence," Pierre said. "We knew of the nosferatu, but the others? No one was certain."

Lucas looked behind him. Though Scott stared at the board, his attention was clearly not on calculating his next move. Andrea's apathy was palpable. He'd have preferred privacy for this discussion, but there was nowhere within the apartment the two vampires couldn't overhear them.

"Apparently, the 'others' include those not as willing to save us. I found another in the woods last evening," he said quietly. "A female from San Francisco."

"Who?"

Lucas turned. Andrea's eyes were wide with alarm. "She didn't have any identification. Long brown hair, freckles. Her partner was a male. Redhead, wore a ratty denim jacket."

"You found him?" Her voice was low, a soft fearful whisper. She darted an uneasy glance at her partner.

"No. But there were the remains of several others. A total of five," Lucas said and frowned at Scott. The vampire had begun to actively shield his thoughts. He wouldn't meet Lucas's gaze; his fingers clenched tightly around a pawn.

What was the kid hiding? Had Andrea sensed something odd while feeding from him, and only now pieced it together? If Lucas could only read Andrea better and determine the source of her anxiety—detecting Scott's unusual sexual proclivity had been easier than penetrating her blank psyche. But Scott's behavior created a reasonable suspicion, enough to—

Realization slammed into him, and Lucas snapped his psychic shields into place.

And lowered them . . . slightly.

Lucas immediately pushed thoughts of the demon to the back of his mind, but Marguerite and Pierre knew him too well. They formed their mental blocks in response to his—but Lucas couldn't answer the questions that lurked in their eyes.

What would a demon do if they showed alarm or fled? Perhaps its only enjoyment stemmed from their fear. And it wouldn't know that Selah was returning; it might decide to prolong their dread.

Marguerite touched his shoulder. Though her expression was neutral, the fine lines radiating around her eyes and mouth had deepened. "This is terrible, disturbing news," she said. "We should discuss this with the elders. Shall we walk to Victor's?"

Out of the apartment . . . where they wouldn't be over-heard. Leaving Scott alone with Andrea. His gut tightened. Andrea turned to stare out the window again, her body trembling. Her hands disappeared into her sleeves as she hugged her arms to her chest.

"No," Lucas said. "We'll wait."

He hoped it wouldn't be long.

The rising sun was in her eyes, the traffic below her loud. Early morning Rome. Dangerous to fly so low and openly, but at this speed few humans would notice. The maze of buildings blurred around her. A few miles to the south, Michael probably still battled the three demons left in the church's catacombs. Selah had taken off in pursuit of the one who'd fled.

But she couldn't find the damned thing. Worse, she couldn't hide from him. Her mind was guarded, but the blood spilling from her side advertised her location better than—

Il Vittoriano passed below in a flash of boxy white marble. She blinked.

A new figure straddled one of the equestrian statues on the roof, his wings spread as wide as Victoria's. His crimson scales gleamed in the sunlight; his horns curled like polished jet. A demon, hoping she wouldn't look too closely. He'd have had better luck posing as a tourist in the crowded piazza.

She teleported behind him.

Stupid of her. Arrogant. She'd lost the advantage of surprise in the catacombs when she'd beheaded his demon brother. He'd seen her use her Gift; he was ready for it.

His ax cut through her bicep. She teleported before the blade could slide past her ribs into her heart.

She appeared on his left side. She couldn't use her strongest arm; it lay useless on the roof. He was still in motion, following through on the strike that should have killed her. He couldn't defend himself in time.

His horns struck sparks from the stone. His blood spurted across her face and feet, and the pain finally hit her, ripping up through her shoulder. She ground her teeth together to stop the scream, squeezed her eyes shut.

Push it away. Need to get back to—

No. No need. A familiar psychic presence filled her senses, but only because he allowed it. Letting her know he was there.

"It was well done," Michael said. She didn't look up. The clatter of her sword told her what he was doing: picking up her arm. A psychic touch eased over her stomach, strong enough that it actually *felt* like touch. The dull ache in her side disappeared.

She staggered as a burst of healing power slammed through her. Her fingers tingled and burned. All of them.

Selah sucked in a long, relieved breath and glanced up. Michael had already changed his clothes, trading his blood-stained toga and giant black wings for a white linen tunic and loose pants.

Italy. And she was still alive. It called for strappy heels and a sundress.

She looked down at her toes and vanished the demon's corpse, shuddering; nothing felt more disgusting than a body and blood in her cache. "I guess it's better than carrying my arm back to you to be Healed, though. Or waiting for it to regenerate."

His mouth pulled into a brief smile, but his humor quickly faded. His dark gaze swept over the city.

"Rome," she murmured, absently massaging her bicep to erase the bite of the ax. A phantom pain, probably more mental than physical. "I haven't had to come here before." She'd visited on her own, briefly.

"No. It's usually well protected."

"We've been stretched thin since the Ascension, and the nearest Gate is—" She had to think about it. She didn't use them. "—outside of Paris? It's hardly a surprise that demons would congregate here."

He shook his head; his closely cropped black hair seemed to absorb the sunlight. "No. Protected by one who calls it her own."

"A Guardian?" Selah hadn't known, but she wasn't surprised. There had been so many Guardians before the Ascension. Only Michael kept track of them all.

"Yes."

"Where is she?"

"I don't know." His back was rigid, his broad form motionless. Like Lucas, he didn't breathe unless he was speaking. "I have spoken with Lilith about the sacrifices in Oregon. Her interpretation of the symbols was correct."

"Will it work?"

His mouth firmed, and he gave a short nod. "Like every being who was once human, vampires have a natural connection to Hell. As they do Caelum. If enough are sacrificed, and it is not self-sacrifice . . . it will work."

"Would Lucifer have relinquished knowledge of the symbols so easily?"

"No. The Morningstar likely made a bargain to ensure secrecy—and to ascertain the demon would complete his task." Michael's obsidian gaze met hers. "And he probably limited the time in which to complete it. Opening the Gate four centuries from now would not serve him."

Then she needed to get back. But she hesitated. Seven demons; two Guardians. She'd barely survived, and she was one of the strongest remaining.

"Are we going to make it through the next five hundred years?"

He tilted his face back, closed his eyes. The pale sun burnished his skin a deep bronze. "Yes. But we have to change."

Dammit. "I'm not very good at that."

His brows lifted, and he shot her an amused glance. "Neither am I."

Cool morning air in Rome, to cool evening air in Ashland. Nothing else was similar. Selah hovered above the small, quiet city, letting the breeze slip through her skirt, over her thighs and arms.

Lucas was directly below her. She'd anchored to him, and then teleported several hundred feet into the sky. And a good thing that she had: he wasn't home. Her dropping in to a stranger's apartment would have been difficult to explain away.

She frowned, listening. A male with a faint Parisian accent inquired about a doll's accessories; Lucas replied with light, offhand laughter.

To all appearances, a casual and friendly conversation, yet, except for Lucas's, each mind in the apartment was tightly shielded.

Her psychic focus narrowed, pierced through the first. A female vampire, who kept her fear well contained with her maturity. On to her consort. Selah sensed his concern for the first vampire and moved on. The young vampire, filled with dread. And the other—

Barely a touch to that mind, and it slithered over her skin. Demon. Aware of her now.

It didn't speak, and she was too distant to hear its heartbeat. She couldn't determine its location. Dammit. Protection, then, at least in the first moment.

She teleported in front of Lucas, snapped her wings wide. There, by the window—

Lucas said with obvious relief, "And she comes with swords."

So did the demon. A tiny pale girl . . . no longer. She shifted as she leaped. Not toward Selah, but across a table. Her taloned hand closed around the young vampire's neck. The point of her blade drew blood from his pale skin.

"Guardian."

Only a demon could make a hiss of the word, sliding it from her forked tongue. Black membranous wings flared from her back. Her glowing scarlet gaze never wavered from Selah's face.

And why would it? The vampires weren't armed. But Selah could change that. "Lucas, hold out your hand."

Selah glanced swiftly at the others; the male's arms had wrapped around his consort, and he was pulling her toward the door.

"Gather up the others, Pierre. Get them to the Paradise and lock it down." Lucas stood next to her, the gun she'd given him aimed at the demon's face. His stance was relaxed and confident, his concentration cold.

Selah teleported.

Save the boy. She appeared to the right of the demon, provoking her instinctive defense and drawing the sword away from the vampire's throat. It was impossible for Selah to strike an effective blow without hurting the kid; his body shielded the demon's. Selah touched him and teleported again.

She dumped him by the others, just outside the apartment door. The female gasped "Scott!" and gripped his arm as they began to run. Selah didn't wait to see where they ran to—a puff of air signaled Lucas's shot.

A silencer. Loud to Selah's ears. Back in, but not to block the sword she'd expected; the demon, reeling back from the impact of a bullet in her forehead, had replaced her weapon with a crossbow. She'd already fired it.

Protection first. Selah teleported in front of Lucas, and the bolt embedded in her throat, knocked her into his arms. The second bolt slammed into her chest, her blood filling her mouth and burning her lungs like Hell.

Weakening, dizzy—she couldn't fight like this. Couldn't protect him. They had to go.

Caelum.

Eight

Get it out get it out *getitout*—

Selah fell to her knees, grabbed the feathered shaft.

Not enough Healers. She didn't dare teleport to Michael or one of the few others who had the Gift. She didn't know where they were; if they weren't in Caelum and didn't have privacy from humans, appearing before them risked exposure.

It hurt, but it wouldn't kill her.

"No! Selah . . . wait." The rigid cast of Lucas's face tightened as his hands covered hers. Blood dripped between his fingers, between hers, dotted the white marble floor with irregular circles. Ever-widening circles. "Let me break off the point first. Jesus fucking Christ. You're insane."

His arm circled her shoulders; he leaned forward and lifted the hair from the back of her neck. His grip was gentle, the snap decisive and quick. She yanked, and the pressure inside her throat eased, pouring out as easily as the blood.

She slapped her hand over the small hole, staunching the flow. Tried to smile. "Hungry?" It came out as a bubbling wheeze.

In the instant his incredulous gaze met hers, she tore the second shaft from her chest. She couldn't halt her scream or the tears that made his moss green eyes blur and soften in front of her.

"Jesus! Hold on." His fingers threaded into the hair by her temple; his palm cupped her cheek. "Goddammit, Selah. *Let me help.*"

The scent of his blood hit her, darker and richer than her own; he'd opened his left wrist with his fangs, was pressing it between her breasts.

Her sigh of gratitude was lost in her ruptured throat. She already healed quickly, but a vampire's blood would speed the process.

She saw him bite his tongue before he dipped his head. He nudged her chin up with a push of his jaw, pulled her hand from her neck. His mouth covered the entrance wound; his tongue pressed wet against her skin.

It wasn't erotic. Selah tipped her face to the ceiling to allow him better access. There were no windows, but Caelum's never-setting sun warmed the white stone above her and beneath her, its heat soaking through the marble. She had always found it soothing, but now Lucas's cool lips, his strong embrace comforted her more.

She could stay here forever.

She shut her eyes. No. No, she couldn't.

His fingers tightened in her hair. The bloodlust swelled, rasped over raw nerves. His shields were down. She felt him struggle against the urge to feed before he tore his mouth from her throat.

His voice was harsh. "I'm sorry. I won't be able to stop if—"

"I know," she said, and this time they sounded like words instead of the slap of a sheep's stomach against a butcher's block.

His gaze fell; he quickly met her eyes again. "It's closed." He lifted his hand from her chest. "This, too."

She nodded and watched as he gathered himself and looked around the room.

"Where are we?"

"Caelum. My apartment." She couldn't read his expression or his scent and didn't know how he'd interpret what he saw.

It was bare. Everything she needed or wanted she kept in her cache. No bed was in the room, because she didn't sleep. There was only one long, ruby red sofa that Colin, horrified by the lack of decoration, had asked her to pick from a magazine and then purchased for her. She rarely sat on it; she was rarely here.

And white. A *lot* of white.

She'd have hated it when she was human; white invariably became ivory, then yellow, then dingy. But nothing in Caelum was dirty or needed cleaning.

Except for them. She vanished the blood and created a new dress, then sank back on her heels. "Do you want to change?" She couldn't take his possessions without permission.

He drew in a breath. "I need to get back."

She probed his psyche, felt his resistance before he allowed her in. He also needed to feed. The bloodlust would be a distraction; his hunger was a weakness the demon might use against him.

"Your vampires have locked themselves in the theater? How secure is it?"

"It's a large studio we've reinforced with steel. It could keep me out," Lucas said. "I don't think it would Andrea."

But it would take effort for the demon to reach the vampires . . . and anything that took effort would be noticed. "I'll send two Guardians through the Gate; they can watch over the building until we return."

His mouth hardened, and he rose fluidly to his feet. "How long?"

She didn't stand. "When my chest stops feeling like a demon shot me with a crossbow. When my body replaces some of the blood I lost. Maybe when I don't feel so damn *tired.*"

Her muscles tensed, locked into place. The last had fallen from her tongue without thought, but it was true. And her lungs were tight, but it had nothing to do with a demon.

Nothing to do with Lucas, either. Except that, for a short time, he'd held on to her, and it had been *good.* It had been what she'd used to get from Caelum, from simply being a Guardian.

She glanced up. His large body was motionless, in his

quiet predatory stance. His eyes were alert, searching her expression, seeking . . . what?

She wasn't certain what she was looking for anymore, either. Just something different than what she had. Something for herself.

"Send them through the Gate," he said softly.

Don't open the door.

She'd said the sun was up; why wasn't he in the daysleep? Lucas prowled the length of the room. And what kind of apartment was this? Spacious, open, clean—empty. Marble columns divided the large room into living areas, but obviously nothing *lived* here.

The silence was absolute. He thought he'd known quiet. Leave the city behind, and there was only the whisper of the wind and the rustle of life.

Caelum was beyond quiet. Eerily so.

Selah arrived soundlessly, but the rhythm of her heartbeat made him aware of her presence before he turned to face her, before she said, "I managed to find four available. Two are novices, but they can keep watch over the theater while the other two sweep the city."

Though she'd met with other Guardians, she hadn't changed from her dress into the white gown. The skirt swirled around her knees when she shifted her weight to her right leg.

A thin jeweled strap circled her ankle; another crossed the top of her foot. Her toenails were unpainted.

"Why," he said as he stalked toward her, "do you say that as if it's a miracle in itself? Why is no one available and no one here?"

Her fingers hooked into the wave of blond hair above her forehead. She brushed it back, uncertainty firming her lips, hesitation clouding her psychic scent. "We're trying to keep knowledge of it from the demons."

He could easily guess what lay unspoken in that statement: To keep this secret from the demons, the Guardians told no one. Yet whatever the secret, she was revealing it to him. He'd seen her caution with her friends; she didn't offer her trust lightly.

And he didn't know what had made her decide that he deserved it, but he couldn't deny his fierce rising pleasure. She'd let him in. "'It'?"

"An Ascension. Most demons assume we are still a force of thousands. If they knew the truth—and without Lucifer to check them—they might become too bold. Particularly in their aggression against vampires, because killing them doesn't break the Rules."

Her chin tilted up at his approach, and his gut clenched. A pink, quarter-sized blotch marred the golden skin at the base of her throat.

It should have been his mark. Her breath whispered out on a sigh when he smoothed his thumb across the spot.

Still healing. He'd fed well the previous night. He could ignore his hunger until she'd regained her strength, and as long as he didn't have her blood, he could resist the bloodlust. Giving in wasn't inevitable until that first sip.

But her throat was a near-irresistible temptation; it was best to keep his mouth filled with questions. "An Ascension?"

"When a Guardian no longer wants to serve—oh!" Her hands clasped over his shoulders when he lifted her against him, and she laughed breathily before she continued, "He can become human again and Fall, or choose to Ascend and go on to Heaven. Or Hell, if he's damned. Either way, they go on to Judgment."

Her legs slid over his hips as he strode to the sofa. His arousal confronted his softened flesh, and the resulting ache told him desire was slowly winning. Ah, thank God. He wouldn't take her now, but damn if it wasn't good to know it still worked.

He lowered her to the cushion, arranged her lengthwise before sitting and draping her legs over his thighs. "So, essentially, they choose to die."

"Yes." Her toes curled as he lifted her ankle, unbuckled the strap. "There's nothing left. They just disappear. Essentially," she said on a soft moan as he ran his thumbs over the ball of her foot, "Michael has to kill them. Sometimes, they don't do it individually. Last time, it was several thousand who'd decided we didn't have a place in modern society or a role protecting humans from demons any longer. I think I'm falling in love with you."

His heart stopped for an instant, until he realized it was the motion of his hands over her sole that had drawn the declaration from her. Not, he mused, unlike a man in bed at the moment of climax. In moments of extreme pleasure, it probably really was love.

And it just gave him more reason to continue pleasuring her. "Did they not realize demons had escaped Hell?"

Her eyes were closed, her head supported by the armrest. "They did it before Lucifer lost his wager."

He pressed his thumbs against her heel. Her back arched, her hips canting down and her knees bending as if she'd just accepted a lover into her body, taken that first deep thrust.

Yes, everything was working perfectly. He struggled to recall why, why, *why* he was touching only her feet.

There was no reason. He ran his palms up the length of her calves.

"And I despise them for that," she said softly. With a touch of wonder, as if she'd just realized it.

His voice was equally low. "Because they didn't do their duty?"

"Yes." Her unapologetic gaze met his. "It was their choice, their right. But considering how few of us remain and how many demons there were—still *are*—it was also unforgivably selfish."

He didn't reply, massaging the indentations below her knees, skimming his fingers behind and relishing her shiver. He pressed them farther apart, until her left thigh was flush against the back of the sofa. The skirt of her dress slid up, bunched at her hips.

Smooth, absolutely bare. Glistening with moisture.

His mind went blank.

His mouth was supposed to be doing *something*. Not what he suddenly wanted to do, but talking. Asking. His tongue was heavy, but he managed to say, "So I was correct." No. That wasn't a question.

Her breath was coming in sharp pulls. Her nipples beaded, rising against the thin cotton bodice with each quick inhalation. "Yes. I was angry with myself for being reluctant to feed you. I wasn't doing my duty."

"And upset with me." Her thighs trembled beneath his hands. His mouth cheated and spoke against her inner knee. Still not a question. "It doesn't have to be one or the other. It was both."

"Yes." It was almost a laugh. "Yes."

"Yes?" Lucas wasn't certain what he was asking now. Answering.

She was staring at his mouth, the slide of his tongue over her skin. "Feed from me. This time, because you want to."

Unbearable need ripped through him. Hunger. His erection strained within the confines of his jeans. His gaze lifted to her neck. Beneath the pink circle in the hollow of her throat, her pulse beat a rapid pace.

That was why he had intended to wait. Why he still would. "I will. Later. Why so reluctant? You knew you could stop me if you didn't want to have sex."

A light flush of arousal stained her shoulders, her chest, her cheeks. The tension within her was high, but he didn't mistake her sudden stillness for simple desire. "I couldn't save him."

What did that have to do with feeding . . . ? Ah, yes. "The vampire—Colin?"

"Yes. In Chaos."

"He looked alive and well to me." He shouldn't have begun this line of questioning. He didn't want her thinking of another vampire now. Not a warm and tanned vampire. Not an unbelievably beautiful one, who'd made Lucas reconsider his own sexuality for about half a minute.

He blinked in realization. Jesus Christ, he was *jealous*. Of someone she'd already told him was a friend.

But his jealousy and the surprise it produced faded when a sad and frightened smile touched her mouth. "Appearances are deceiving."

She'd said that of her appearance, too. Of her perfect, angelic form. "So, because you didn't save him, you thought you'd fail with me?"

"That it would end badly." Her shoulders lifted; embarrassment fluttered through her psychic scent. "Irrational, maybe."

As was his jealousy. "So you aren't perfect."

"No." Her eyes sparkled with amusement. "I suppose I am not. Are you disappointed?"

"That you aren't Vampire Barbie? No."

Her soft laughter held no surprise, no offense.

"You've heard that before," Lucas realized.

"Yes."

"Many times?" Idiots. She had an exquisite face, a flawless body—but they weren't artificial or plastic.

"Enough. In different variations, depending on the human culture." She regarded him through lowered lashes. "When I learned to shape-shift, I chose to be this. It fit what I imagined a Guardian to be. Two hundred and fifty years ago, it might have been fake. Just an image. Now, it's me."

He'd assumed that, like him, Guardians simply stopped aging—or in Selah's case, regressed to an earlier form. "This isn't you when you were young?"

She shook her head. "I don't even remember what that was. I know what I looked like when I was old and when I died. But it's more natural to hold this form—and the wings—than to shift to my human one."

"Considering that you were the same age as my mother is now, and I wouldn't want to associate her with you"—he grazed his fingertips down the inside of her thigh—"like *this* in any way, it's best that you don't."

Her laughter filled the room with its golden tones. Empty, surrounded by hard white walls, but the sound didn't echo. And as she rose up, curling her legs beneath her, the sofa erased the whisper of her movement.

"No Grandmama jokes," she murmured against his jaw. "I'm no longer dizzy. And I don't know how you've done it, but I don't feel tired now. We ought to get back to Ashland."

"Yes," he said, but not yet. He cupped the curve of her ass, brought her up, over him. Not to his mouth, he hadn't that much strength; his will wasn't so powerful that he could resist a bite. But his hands . . .

He slipped them in between their bodies, down. So unbelievably silky and warm and slick. His groan was rough, harsh. He closed his mouth and drew in a long breath, filled his lungs with her sweet feminine scent, and wondered why he didn't breathe more often.

Selah panted his name and rolled her hips toward him. His fingers slid through wet and heat. *Into* wet and heat. Unadulterated pleasure speared through him, just from this touch.

His hands were falling in love with her.

And his mouth. He nibbled at the upper bow of her lips, teased the lush bottom before sweeping in, devouring. Thank God for older, experienced women who could take the hunger in his kiss and still accept more, *insist* on more. Strong women, who could prevent him from doing the same when the bloodlust flared and burned. *Not now, not yet.*

As if she'd heard him, Selah ripped her mouth from his and buried her face in his neck. She didn't allow him the same angle, though the bloodlust demanded he bend his head and drink.

Her lips moved, and she licked beneath his jaw, her every exhalation a short burst of heated air over his skin. His fingers stroked and parted. His thumb found the slippery taut bud that made her tense, made her hips jerk in a frantic slide against him.

"Lucas—I want . . . I want . . ."

He didn't know when her soft moans had become words, only that they were explosive fuel to his inflamed senses. He tried to hold on. The effort of his response made his voice a growl. "To come?"

He couldn't, not without blood. And if he took hers, he wouldn't be able to help himself. He would lose control to the bloodlust.

"You."

Her reply, her body—they were like honey, warm and sticky, dripping and tugging. Enticing him to feed. God, but he'd love to help himself.

She met his lips, spoke against them. Waiting. Her voice was thick. "Do you want it?"

A groan rumbled up from his chest. She must know he did. Why had he made her ask?

"Yes." This was either going to be very torturous, or very good. Or both. He drew back slightly when she would have deepened the kiss. "Don't let me feed, Selah."

A smile tilted the corners of her mouth. "For how long?"

Older, knowledgeable women . . . who understood vampires. "Until you can't stop me."

She bit her lip, rocking forward against his hand. Her clothes vanished. His mouth dried. Gorgeous edible nipples, buds of coral swaying amidst an ocean of pale gold. "It won't be long," she said.

"No." For her, for him.

"Next time."

"Yes."

He should make her promise there would be a next time. He would have, but the shock and pleasure of her naked skin against his stole his breath. The thrust of her tongue into his mouth prevented his taking another.

Her hands circled his shaft and stroked him from base to tip. The sound of her appreciative murmur was lost beneath the blood pounding in his head.

And he should have known. He should have realized how she'd do it. All at once, as she'd taken the nail from his hand, the bolt from her chest.

She rose and fell and her body swallowed him with a tight push of her hips and thighs.

She muffled her cry against his lips. His hands clenched on her waist, and for an instant he was frozen, impaled within her, his stomach trembling and his head spinning as if she'd taken him somewhere new and extraordinary.

"Lucas," she said, and though she didn't move, she sank further onto him, lodging him deep, surrounding him with slick flesh. Heavier. Soft feathers swept his legs. Amazement and euphoria coiled through her psychic scent; she was breathless, quaking. "It's *so* good."

He lifted her, chasing the movement with an upward plunge. So wet. Her back arched, and they were enfolded in white. Unbelievable.

Her hair tumbled away from her throat. His arousal spiked, tearing at his fangs and gut. His arms shook with the need to pull her to his lips, to feed.

Talk. Fill his mouth with words. "Selah. Hold me down."

It should have been a battle. It might have looked like one as she pushed him flat on the length of the sofa and leaned forward, drawing his hands over his head, pinning them.

Captured, by appearance. Trapped. But it was release. Lucas surged against her, into her, without resistance.

He didn't fight the bloodlust, but let it rage. He reveled in the ecstasy, the ache. Desperate with need, he delivered silken promises and threats.

And when she shuddered and tightened around him, collapsed against him with a hoarse moan and the whisper of her wings, he finally used his mouth to make good on them.

Nine

Selah was crouching in Pierre's opulent parlor when she realized that she'd worn the ribboned shoes again not because she liked them, but because she'd known how much Lucas did.

She'd never done that before.

Bemused, she stared at the rug beneath her feet. No stains marred its thick weave; Andrea must have vanished any blood that had spilled from the bullet wound.

"No traces of blood in their rooms," Lucas said. A shiver tingled over her skin—not just from the surprise of his announcement after his silent approach, but also because of the rough velvet lingering in his voice, abrading her nerves like the stroke of his tongue.

Warmth curled through her womb, licked at her sex. She clenched her thighs, but instead of easing the sweet ache, the pressure served to remind her of how his tongue *had* stroked—and how very good he was at it.

She shook herself, focused. "Nor here."

"Are you?" he said softly.

Selah glanced up. There was something different in him,

too. His features had not changed; the planes and angles were as sharp, his gaze as quietly intense. "Am I . . . ?"

"Here." Amusement glittered in his eyes. The same color, but harder now. An effect of the feeding erasing the vestiges of animal blood? "A moment ago, I don't think you were."

Her lips curved. She hadn't been. She'd been on a red sofa, her wings folded tight beneath her, lifting her hips to his mouth. "I wasn't," she admitted. "I shouldn't disappear like that."

He held out his hand. She accepted the courtesy and rose with her palm against his. "Not without taking me with you," he said in a low voice.

Pleasure slid through her, heated and full, lightening her legs, her feet. She wanted to inch her way onto him, weightless. "And not while hunting demons."

"Yes." His fangs gleamed, and the anticipation she saw in his smile was not wholly for her.

Excitement twisted through her belly, shortened her breath. *That* was the difference. The predator was still there, but he'd unleashed it.

That was good, too. They'd need it. "How did you know?"

"The demon?" At her nod, he said, "I initially thought it was Scott—"

"The kid?"

"Yes. Until I realized I couldn't penetrate Andrea's psychic shields—and until I remembered that demons don't experience sexual need. Scott has an interest I don't encounter often."

"Oh?"

His lips quirked. "Do you want to know because it'll help us find Andrea?"

She shook her head, grinning.

"I can't tell you. You've forbidden grandma jokes."

Her eyes widened in surprise. "An obsession with someone who looks older? That *is* different. Particularly in a vampire community." If anything, vampires were often transformed too young, by older vampires trying to reclaim their youth by taking an immature partner. They never physically aged, but after fifty or sixty years, they felt it in other ways.

He shrugged, then lifted his hand to brush a strand of hair

back from her throat. "It's Ashland. And I apparently have the same fetish," he said.

He smiled when she burst into laughter. He trailed his fingers from her shoulder to her wrist, his gaze following the movement. Pleasure emanated from his scent, but it wasn't simply erotic.

He liked to touch, Selah realized. He enjoyed the physical connection.

So did she. Still laughing softly, she leaned into him, pressed a kiss to his mouth. "We'll keep knowledge of that quiet. Andrea might use it to her advantage." She sobered as she recognized the truth in that. "Not that she'd get far. Even if you didn't sense it psychically, you'd know. Their skin is hot—warmer than a human's."

"She covered hers. Long sleeves, high-necked shirts, pants."

Selah nodded. "And once you took her blood, she couldn't have hidden it. Scott was recently transformed?"

"Yes."

"She played on that, then. He was too young, knew nothing of demons and probably not much about his psychic abilities. It allowed her to live right in the heart of the community without being found out." Selah glanced around the room. It was luxurious, elegant. Yes, exactly the type of place a demon would like. "Pretending to be a vampire would have amused her, I think. The knowledge that she was deceiving you all in plain sight. Posing as a human or hiding wouldn't have been as gratifying to her ego."

"Demons drink blood?"

Selah grimaced. "They *can*. Just as they can fake being vampire or human. Or fake sex. What is it?" His brows had drawn together, a frown creasing his forehead. "I'm not disgusted by the idea of drinking blood in general. Just demons doing it."

He shook his head. "I was thinking of the sex."

"While hunting demons?"

His smile didn't reach his eyes, and the slick probe he sent through her mind startled her with its strength . . . and the resolve beneath it, wrapped around an overwhelming instinct to protect. "While feeding. Your response in Caelum was not just duty."

She stepped back, studying his face. She couldn't read it: she could only sense the tension coiling within him. Preparation to defend her . . . but from what? "No."

"What consequences are there?" His jaw tightened. "For lust? Fornication?"

Her lips parted in surprise, then slipped into an impish grin. "Thirty lashes. It's excruciating."

His stance relaxed, but slightly. "It's allowed?"

"I cannot count the number of orgies I stumbled across before the Ascension." Her smile faded. "But it's not *allowed*. That suggests permission, as if Guardians live and act by another's will—by Michael's will. Free will is honored in humans always, and Guardians and vampires whenever it's possible. There's not always a choice. But we don't judge or determine what is moral."

"I find that difficult to believe. You slay. You must judge."

"Demons and nosferatu were judged, but not by Guardians."

"And vampires?" he asked quietly. Very quietly.

"*Being* a vampire isn't immoral. But if one breaks the Rules and denies a human free will or kills one—yes, I'd judge him. I'd slay him. Humans can't."

"And a vampire who kills another vampire? Or denies another's free will?"

"That depends on the circumstances. If Andrea was a vampire and you couldn't slay her, I would. But I wouldn't slay a vampire for killing another in a bid for leadership. Nor for protecting and policing within his community, unless the methods he used were cruel and no other vampire had the strength to stop him." She knew Lucas had killed others; did he think she would slay him for that? "It's all intent. It's not the action; it's the reason behind it. Not just killing—anything. Even sex. The only immorality in sex is hurting someone with it. And even that isn't simple, especially if more than one person is involved. People can be careless. Or just concerned with protecting themselves more than someone else."

"Yes." His gaze held hers, unyielding. "So you will leave us to police ourselves?"

Her chest was tight. "What are you asking?" Was he speaking in general terms, meaning all Guardians and all vampires? Or Selah, specifically?

And why did the thought of leaving pull at her throat and lungs, burning like the bolts from the crossbow? A phantom pain.

He exhaled a short breath through his nose, a self-deprecating laugh quickly stifled. "Nothing. And we're ignoring our duty. I've got a roomful of vampires who need to know a demon is impersonating and sacrificing us."

"Yes. We ought to go." But she didn't want to. Not yet. Not until she discovered exactly what he'd meant.

Lucas turned away, glancing around the room. His back was rigid. "Is there anything I can give them? Any protection they can use if she takes them and a Guardian isn't available?"

"No."

His hands fisted. "There must be something. Some hope."

"A scream, and perhaps I or someone else might hear it and get help. It won't do any good to run, or to fight—but they might get lucky. I'll leave weapons. It could give them time. They *should* fight for as long as they can, but then . . ."

He swung around, his features taut. "What?" he rasped.

"If it's the end, they've got to give in. Die willingly." It sounded horrible, even to her ears. And she knew how easy it was, to make the decision. Letting go had been, too. But when it happened, when the cold and dark had taken her down, she'd fought it. "It would disrupt the Gate's transformation. Guardians are linked to Caelum's Gates through their self-sacrifice. Opening one to Hell depends on resistance—and that the victim isn't dying of their free will."

The edges of his lips were white. "I can't ask that of them."

"It might save others. If the Gate opens—" Selah broke off, closing her eyes. It didn't bear thinking about. The vampires would be slaughtered. So would many Guardians. "I'll be here, looking for her. I'll check the clearing frequently."

"Unless you're needed elsewhere."

Her teeth clenched, but there was no response to that. "Andrea can't take them out to the site during the day. She can't behead a pile of ashes. I'll do my best to be here, particularly after sunset. If I can't, I'll have someone else come."

Frustration poured from his psyche. "Will she feed me as well? I'd better change my goddamn sheets." He passed his hand through his hair, a muscle in his jaw flexing. He glanced up at her face and stilled. "Jesus. That was uncalled for. I'm sorry."

It was a struggle to force emotion into her expression; she finally managed indifference. "It's fair. You have no reason to think otherwise." She ran over whatever response he'd have made, slipping into her vampire form. "We'd best go. Is there a way in aside from teleportation?"

"No. Selah—"

"I won't be able to hide what I am, then. Will that be problematic for you? Undermine your authority?"

"Undermine . . . ? No. Hold on, just one damn second." He moved swiftly, silently, stepping forward and capturing her face with both hands, preventing her from looking away.

No, he couldn't do that. This was where she wanted to be, even with her chest and throat aching.

"All right. All right. We have to go. But first . . . listen," he said, and while she was still waiting for him to continue, Lucas covered her mouth with his.

She hadn't expected a kiss. And not one that was a gentle taste, an apology. But she'd been the one to put that anger in him, born of her own, so she lifted onto her toes, offered her apology in return.

All too soon, he drew back. His voice was harsh. "I'm twisted up. Not only you—it's the circumstances."

Not an excuse. Just a reason. "I am, too."

He nodded slowly, and she felt the tension easing from his solid form. His thumbs smoothed over her lips, pressed against her fangs. "Get rid of these. Go as you are."

She searched his face, found nothing but determination. "Are you certain?"

A smile touched his eyes, his mouth. "They'll appreciate it," he said dryly.

Lucas knew his vampires well.

Wearing her wings, Selah teleported into the small, crowded room. Per his request, they were unfolded. The apex of her left wing framed Lucas's head like a halo, her feathers a snowy backdrop.

She'd anticipated the stunned silence, but not the applause or the cries of "Bravo!"

Startled, she looked over at Lucas. He raised his brows, wry amusement filtering through his shields. They'd certainly appreciated it, she realized—but more the theatricality of their entrance than the display of strength behind him.

Until Lucas began outlining the danger the demon posed. Then their gazes became speculative, moving between Lucas and Selah, often pausing at her neck. Selah watched equally quietly, observing their reactions.

Perhaps Lucas was not a good actor, but he commanded their attention and silence—something that, Selah intuited, was not easy with this group. He spoke with authority, with confidence . . . and underscored it with concern, which they responded to more readily than his power.

A strange community. A leader who protected because he cared for them, rather than the control it gave him. And the vampires . . . Selah quickly touched each of their minds, came away astonished.

Though their physical appearances ranged from the teens to thirty-somethings, with a few—such as Marguerite—approaching up to sixty years of age, all but a few had been vampires for more than half a century.

They were almost all elders, but there was no tension among them. No viperous glances, no subtle backstabbing.

And though a wave of dismay and fear swept through the room when Lucas asked them to meet the end willingly, there was also determination and protection beneath it. If it saved their friends, they would do what was necessary.

A close-knit vampire community. It was . . . extraordinary. Different.

So, too, could their defense be. "Lucas," she said softly. "There might be another precaution you can take. Even if Andrea imitates one of you, her psychic blocks will be up. But if your community leaves their shields down, their minds open . . ."

"We'll know of the danger because hers won't be," he said, his gaze narrowing thoughtfully.

"Yes." She couldn't think of any other vampires who would

willingly do so; there was too much infighting, too much hidden. "And if any other vampires are near and open, they might sense the fear and have time to alert us before Andrea can get them out to the clearing."

Lucas nodded, then looked back at the others. She saw the brief shudder of laughter that shook through him.

"This might be worse than death," he said.

By the time Selah teleported the twenty-ninth and thirtieth vampires from the secured room into their homes and left them a selection of weapons, her head was aching—and she knew far more about the members of Ashland's vampire community than she'd ever wanted to know.

She'd been wrong: They *were* in competition with one another, with a need to prove they could be the most outrageous, possess the most angst, the darkest soul, the greatest drama—and to see who could mentally project each accomplishment the hardest.

It was entertaining, she decided—but exhausting. When she returned to the theater and found Lucas alone, she couldn't contain her sigh of relief. His face was set, drawn. Tired. Dawn wasn't far off, and it had been a difficult evening. A difficult month.

The studio was empty. She and Lucas reflected in the mirror at the opposite end, and her voice echoed against the hardwood floors. "They walked home?"

Pierre, Marguerite, and Scott had been in the room when Selah had left, but there was little danger in their leaving on foot: Their apartment was directly down the street.

"Yes." Humor slid from his scent. "I think Scott's going to be happy with the new arrangement he'll have with Pierre and Marguerite."

"A threesome?" Not unusual among vampires, but she wouldn't have guessed they would participate in one.

"I don't think they're strangers to a ménage. Marguerite would not allow Pierre to transform her until her children were grown and had no further need of her. But they lived together for decades before that."

"Oh." Pierre must have had a vampire partner in those years.

A human couldn't feed a vampire every day. "Your community surprises me," she admitted. "I think they must have surprised Andrea, too."

"Why is that?" Lucas glanced at her face before his gaze moved to her wings. He reached, and his fingers trailed over the downy frame, the feathers below.

"She would've expected that killing Olivia would throw everyone into disarray—and that in the ensuing chaos and battle over leadership, she'd be able to carry out the other sacrifices. *And* set it up so that the deaths could be blamed on that, instead of something outside the community. Instead, she had to look elsewhere for her victims, or risk you becoming suspicious."

"Why Olivia then? Why not me? I'm more of a threat."

"Yes, you are the strongest, the community's protector . . . but you couldn't save Olivia. Demons love guilt." She hesitated. "Did everyone know about the complications in your relationship?"

His hand stilled on the outside sweep of her wing. "It's not something you can conceal for twenty years. And she never hid her love for David, though she was openly grateful to me for saving her life—and willingly performed her duty as my consort. It was . . . beautifully tragic." His mouth twisted. "And I fucked my best friend's wife every night."

Her heart contracted, tight and heavy. "Andrea must have been hoping to exacerbate your guilt, then."

His features hardened, stark anguish in the rigid set of his face. "It worked."

"Lucas," she said softly. "Whatever Olivia told you afterward, or during, so that she could preserve that fantasy . . . she wanted you, too."

"I know." It was harsh, ripped from him. "Otherwise I would have been able to stop it."

As Selah had been strong enough to stop him. She wound her arms around his neck, hugged him close. His hands fisted behind her back, between her wings, his embrace strong enough to make her lungs burn. She pressed her mouth to the skin below his ear, inhaled the masculine scent of him.

He drew back, his eyes like green flame as he stared down at her. "Selah," he said, and kissed her as thoroughly as she'd ever been kissed. Each silken plunge shivered through her, a dip into a cool refreshing well.

Cleansed. Awakened. Renewed.

Her pulse was racing when he finished, her legs trembling. His hands cradled her jaw, and she looked at him, shaken to her core.

She was falling for him.

Her fingers clenched on his shoulders. Did that mean another kind of Fall was in her future? How could she choose—*was* there a choice? He could give her immortality again, but she wouldn't be a Guardian. And could she live with herself if she left them *now*?

"Selah?"

She swallowed past the ache in her throat. It wasn't a decision she could make immediately, anyway. "We should go . . . through the city. Look for Andrea. Until dawn."

Lucas touched her brow. "What is it?"

"Nothing." She turned her cheek against his hand, glanced up at him from under her lashes. "Shall we walk?"

Ten

It was good with him. As they made a slow circuit of downtown, Selah pushed away everything but the search for the demon.

And Lucas.

"Does your mother live in Ashland?" She paused in front of an ice cream shop, testing the lingering scent of waffle cones.

Lucas halted a few feet farther. His hair fell over his forehead as he glanced back at her. "No. In Seattle, near my sister and her children. I visit them twice a year, but it's safer they don't come here." His nostrils flared slightly. "Can you taste?"

Selah nodded. Vampires couldn't—only blood. "I don't need to eat, and usually don't. Now and then, however, something smells so incredible it's irresistible. Popcorn. The satay in the open-air markets in Bangkok. Have you been to any?"

"Not Thailand. In Nepal and India." A shadow passed over his face. "With David, the summer after our second year of law school."

She watched him stroll back to her side, his hands tucked into his pockets. "The Himalayas?"

"Yes." A smile deepened the firm curve of his mouth. "Mountains and caves. We spent most of our free time climbing up them, skiing down them, or going through them." A crease appeared between his brows, and his gaze searched her face. "What is it? Whenever I speak of caves—or *you* mention the Chaos realm—you get this expression that reminds me of a defendant just prior to the reading of a verdict."

She smiled a little. "You weren't a lawyer *that* long," she said, and began walking again.

He adopted a tone as light as hers was, but she could feel his disappointment. "No. But late-night TV is much better than it used to be, even if the commercials are as bad."

She caught his hand and met his eyes. "I don't want it overheard," she said quietly. "I trust you, I'll tell you . . . but not here."

Lucas's palm was cool; his fingers tightened around hers. "Thank you." He didn't relinquish her hand as they continued walking. "Will Andrea abandon her plan? She's been found out, the vampires are watching for her, and you are protecting the city."

"No." They passed an all-night café. Bitter coffee and the light, sweet scent of marijuana. Snippets of a conversation debating the merits of hemp. Amused, Selah shook her head and explained, "Many demons are cowards, but Michael said she is likely bound by a bargain. If that's true, she'll be desperate to complete it."

"Why?"

"In Hell, there's a territory for people—and demons—who don't fulfill their bargains. It's a field of the damned, and they are frozen into the ground with only their faces exposed. Frozen for eternity, but aware and able to feel."

He stopped, stared at her. "You're serious."

"Yes."

"Have you seen it?"

Her lungs felt pierced by a skewer. "Yes. There's a Pit, too, and the tortures there are bad enough. Just as you probably think of it, too—fiery, rotting, and stinking. But the field and those faces are . . ." She couldn't think of a description terrible enough to convey the horror of it. "But a few months ago, I learned that the Punishment for failure is even worse than that."

"How did you learn it?" Lucas asked, his voice deep and

rough—and then he frowned, turning to the east. "Goddammit. The sun's coming up."

"Good." When he glanced at her in surprise, she said, "Prepare yourself."

She teleported into thick, warm air. The heavy fragrance of tropical vegetation. The tumbling rush of a waterfall.

Lucas blinked quickly. "Shit." A laugh rumbled through the word, and he dragged his free hand through his hair. "I should get used to that. Where are we?"

Selah tried not to think about how much she wanted him to become accustomed to it. "An island in the Pacific. Two time zones west."

"And alone?" His focus shifted, closed in on her. A predator, with the target in sight. And this time not to kill or devour—but to defend.

"Yes." She drew in a long breath. "The Chaos realm. Lucifer brought his dragon from there, but he hasn't been able to access it for centuries. But Colin's blood is tainted—and it anchors him to the realm."

"And that's why you don't want the demon to overhear," he said.

She nodded. "If they knew, they'd try to gain access, and the power of it . . . I can imagine what they'd do to him." She closed her eyes. "Anyway, I fed him. Or rather, Colin fed from me."

Lucas stiffened. "What do you mean?"

She couldn't halt her blush. "Lilith knocked me unconscious and gave me to him." Her brows lifted when his face darkened. "*That* didn't happen. He likes them awake so they can appreciate his beauty. And even after I regained consciousness, I didn't want him, so it wasn't an issue. But later, we were attacked by a demon and a few nosferatu—and I tried to teleport us to safety. His anchor was too strong. We ended up in Chaos; I couldn't teleport us back out."

"Were you weakened by the feeding?" His voice was rough.

"No. And it's a matter of will rather than physical strength." Even Michael could not journey to Chaos without an anchor. "But we weren't certain of that then, so he refused to feed from me. And I refused to leave him there alone. We were both terrified. It's—" She broke off, had to swallow. "The sky isn't of air. It's a frozen mass of dangling bodies. Their faces are frozen into the ceiling, but they're constantly screaming. And the dragons eat them. And their bodies regrow, and they're eaten again."

She was shaking; Lucas circled his arms around her, dropped his forehead against hers. "And you think this is what happens to the people who didn't fulfill their bargains—who are frozen in that field in Hell? They span the two realms?"

"Yes. And there are other creatures. Wyrmwolves. We had to flee from them—to a mountain and the caves. But they still came after us."

"How long?"

"Almost a week," she whispered. "Colin was starving by the end of it. And he finally told me to leave on my own. To see if I could teleport back to Earth without him. I could. I found Michael, and he brought Colin back. Michael told me he had to heal him, first. A lot of healing. I don't know what happened, but I keep thinking if I had just forced Colin to feed, then he wouldn't have been so weak . . . maybe would have been able to fight."

He drew back. "Does he blame you?"

"No. But that doesn't make it easier. I'm a Guardian. I have this Gift. I should have been able to save him; instead I left him alone."

He smiled slightly. "It sounds to me that you did what you had to do."

A short laugh broke from her, but it ended on a long sigh. "Maybe."

"Yes," he said, and held her against him until her trembling eased. "Better?"

She pressed her lips together and nodded, unable to say anything. It would have probably been a declaration of something she didn't yet know she could have.

Letting go of her hand, Lucas stepped out onto the edge of the cliff, looking out over the night-darkened beach. She joined him. Two hundred feet below, waves broke against a narrow line of black sand. To their left, a stream of water slipped over the edge and frothed into a pool before spilling across a stone shelf into the ocean.

He grinned, and his fangs gleamed in the pale moonlight. "If I fall, will you catch me? My personal hang glider?"

She formed her wings. "Yes. Always."

His grin failed. He looked from her wings to the rocks below, and the jesting tone in his voice was replaced with a note of wonder. "I haven't done this in far too long," he murmured.

Lucas didn't fall. He jumped.

Her heart stopped before pounding into sudden, exhilarating life again. She dove, her feathers tight against her body, arrowing after him.

Streamlined. But Lucas had his arms and legs outspread, his body positioned to catch the most air, to create the greatest resistance and slow his descent. He'd obviously done this before. Parachuting?

She caught up to him halfway down the side of the cliff, slamming into his back and wrapping her arms around his chest. She tripled the size of her wings, but didn't unfold them. Her shout was nearly lost beneath the rush of air through the mass of feathers. "Tell me when!"

His laughter vibrated against her breasts, her belly; the sound was whipped away by the wind.

A breathless second passed. Two. And at the moment Selah knew she would have to open her wings or risk injuring him, she heard his "Now!" and snapped them wide, felt the strain across her back, painless but incredibly strong, and still going so fast though not just down, down.

She angled her wingtip, and they banked to the left, gliding now. The beach was dotted with rocks and gravel. There was no smooth landing there. "The ocean or the pool?"

"The pool," he said, his voice a low growl, and she skimmed above it before letting him go and vanishing her wings. She dropped like a tossed stone and splashed into cool, churning water.

Lucas dragged her against him before she surfaced.

The water roared in her ears. Her hair floated in front of her face, obscuring her vision before he anchored it back to capture her lips.

So incredibly good. The suction of his mouth pulled at the line of nerves from her tongue to her sex, streaking a path of heat and need. She wrapped her legs around his hips, felt the powerful flex of his muscles, the thick ridge of his erection as he pushed away from the bottom of the pool.

She was still kissing him as they broke the surface, and didn't draw breath. Her palms slicked his hair from his forehead; wet, his pale skin shone pearlescent beneath the moon.

Like Caelum's marble might have, had that realm ever been touched by moonlight.

A moan of protest rose in her throat when he stiffened and lifted his head. Her skirt billowed and drifted up between them, teasing her gently kicking legs as she treaded water.

"Selah." He said it on a rough inhalation. "No bad moments? Under water?"

Her lips parted. He'd thought of *that* when even she didn't? When arousal raged through his psychic scent? "No." Smiling, she added, "And I notice that the cold water had no ill effects on your ego, either."

His brows tilted at a wicked angle, as he pulled her close to murmur against her lips, "There was a reason Olivia wanted me."

She gasped and buried her face in his neck, her body shaking. Guilt tinged his scent, but if he could laugh at himself, make a joke of it, then even that might wane.

And as pleasing as his size was, Selah thought it had been his quiet predatory nature—and how easily he used it for defense as well as the hunt. Olivia must have felt secure with him. Probably couldn't help but admire the strength of him, inside and out.

If she hadn't, then she truly had been an idiot.

Selah's laughter slowly faded. When he tried to find her mouth again, she slipped away, submerging herself. She clenched her thighs around his calf to hold steady and fumbled at the buttons of his jeans. Easier to vanish them, but though her hands were awkward on the soaked denim, baring him to her sight one button at a time seemed the most erotic, miraculous discovery.

She surrounded him with the heat of her mouth, took him deep. His hoarse groan carried through the density of the water. Her fingers dug into the tight muscle of his ass, felt the tremors ripping through him as she suckled and licked.

But not to completion. He couldn't come without blood, and she could offer him none from there. It would be torture to stay too long, though the sounds he made and the pleasure radiating from him tempted her to continue.

She kissed her way back up his torso, broke the surface, and found herself hauled to the end of the pool, where the water slid over the shelf before tumbling onto the beach. Her nipples pebbled beneath his lips, his teeth. The smooth stone was cool against her back, his mouth a perfect match. His tongue was a glorious shock to her heated flesh, the slick folds of her sex.

His hand clasped her hip, lifted her to him as he rose above her, positioned himself. His skin was taut, his jaw clenching. His eyes closed as he pressed inside. "God. Selah." His chin dropped to his chest. "So hot."

And tight. Her back arched against the thick intrusion. Easier to do it fast, but lacking this exquisite anticipation, the slow stretch of her body around his length. She moaned when he finished the long stroke, and she didn't know if it was in pleasure, or disappointment that it was done.

But Lucas wasn't done. She wouldn't have tortured him, but he must have himself, and he wrung cries from her until she twisted beneath him, shuddering her ecstasy. And still he took more, another thrust and another, each one better than the first.

She barely felt the prick of his fangs, but the rush of euphoria tore another orgasm from her. And this time, he went with her.

Eleven

Lucas woke with Selah pressed naked and warm against his side. He blinked rapidly in surprise; his last memory was of walking through the surf with her and sensing the tingling on the back of his neck that told him dawn was approaching.

"You're up," she said, turning and propping herself up on her elbow. Her breasts were firm and round and perfect.

"Not yet." He had to force moisture onto his tongue. "But I'm certain I will be soon."

"That's bad." Her nose wrinkled when she grinned. "I'm not nude."

He looked. The edge of the sheet rose to her sleek waist. "It's difficult to tell."

She slid it over her hip. Bare. "I'm wearing my shoes," she explained, lifting her leg and pointing her toes. Winding black satin, tied behind her knee and trailing all the way down her thigh to . . .

Oh, Jesus Christ. He swallowed. Tried to think. Those ribbons were more destructive than animal blood. "Were you in bed with me all day?"

"No." Her lashes fell. "I wanted to be here when you woke

up. The daysleep took you immediately after we teleported back."

"Ah," he said. It was all he could manage when her fist wrapped around him.

"But I can't stay long. The sun's set. I should make another sweep of the city, keep watch at the clearing."

He closed his eyes, his hands clenching in the mattress at his sides. "All right."

"Lucas."

"Just a moment. I'm being touched by an angel."

"I've heard that one before, too," she said dryly. Her palm circled the crown of his shaft, and she tugged lightly. "Will you be here alone?"

Concern lay beneath the question and arrested his attention. He searched her gaze, found humor and arousal in the quiet blue . . . and something darker. Something that made his stomach tighten with need, that provoked an instinct to hunt and trap and keep.

He pounced, pinned her under him. And knew she stayed because she wanted to. "I'm not hungry," he said softly.

Her skin was flushed, her reply breathless. "I'm not here to feed you. But we have to hurry. And I need to know where you'll be tonight."

He could do both at once. "Marguerite is inviting everyone over. Easier to protect them if they're in one place." Pushing inside her was like heaven.

Her head tilted back against the pillows, her body a strung bow beneath him. "Is that wise?" she gasped. "With all of them open?"

Open. His hand found her ribboned calf, and he drew it up, hooked her knee over his arm. Shoved deep. "No. But entertaining." His voice was a rough growl. "Let me in."

Her eyes were glazed. She answered, but he wasn't certain what it meant. Or if it was even language.

"Your blocks."

"Oh," she whispered. And then he was enfolded in her, his mind encompassed by a psychic scent so powerful he could almost smell it. Almost taste it. Sunshine and heat.

The bloodlust ripped through him. He sank into her with his body and fangs and dropped his own shields.

She trembled, shook. Her heel scraped over his back. "Lucas!" It was a ragged cry, and it echoed through her veins. *Lucas.*

He almost drew back in shock, but delved deeper, drinking. Listening. Not a voice, but it was Selah, a brush of warmth and light.

—so good so good so good—

Unbearably arousing, to hear her pleasure. To feel it. He braced his arm and rocked hard into her, against her. Her blood was lightning over his tongue, winding electric tendrils down his spine, charging his nerves, drawing tight and sparking over his skin, in his gut.

Her trembling abruptly stopped, and she arched beneath him. Her slick heat clasped rhythmically around him; ecstasy shot into his mouth, and he couldn't hold on. His climax rushed through his blood, released a storm of sensation. And beneath it he heard—

—falling in love with you I think I could love you—

But it could have been his voice. It could have been his.

He was taking too long.

Lucas glanced at his watch, shook his head. At his feet, the box of theater paraphernalia was half-full.

Olivia's walls were half-bare.

He knew what had possessed him to start this task, but he didn't have to finish it that evening. It was enough that he'd begun.

He turned and found his reason watching him, a smile curving her cupid's-bow mouth. "You're late," she said. "Everyone's expecting you. And I believe every one of them sensed what we were doing in bed earlier."

Perhaps that was why her shields were up. Not completely, but tight and strong. He gestured to the box. "Marguerite and Pierre might want a few of the posters or photos; I'll mitigate the damage with this."

She glanced around the room. She stood evenly on both feet, her thumbs tucked into the waistband of her skirt. "If you give me permission, I can vanish it all into my cache. Dump it at a charity."

"Maybe another time," he said easily, though apprehension coiled in his stomach. *Dump it*. Such a careless phrase. He'd sensed that Selah didn't think much of Olivia, but she'd kept it well hidden. For his sake. He knelt and lifted the box. "Perhaps my next consort will enjoy feeding and fucking me in her predecessor's bed."

The hurt that crossed her features and projected from her psychic scent was well done. Olivia, in her best role, had never come as close to convincing him.

But Selah would have shown nothing at all. "That wasn't kind of me. I'm sorry," Lucas said. "I'm just wound up."

Her face brightened. "I can think of a way to unwind you." She formed her wings. "Flying . . . and we can swing by and check the Gate on the way to Pierre's."

"I think a walk might be what I need, actually." *A slow walk. Take as much time as possible.* "To clear my head." His shields would be down; he had to fill his mind with thoughts of Selah.

The real one.

The demon's smile widened. "That sounds lovely."

His gun was downstairs. He had nothing to fight with. And he'd seen her speed, her strength.

Go willingly, he thought.

It was the hardest damn thing he'd ever done.

On her second pass over the city, Selah flew low over Pierre and Marguerite's apartment. Voices and minds and music were all at high volume; she teleported to the balcony, then raised her shields as high as she could without alarming the vampires.

"That made me want to puke," said one from the shadows. "The beaming from one place to another."

Selah turned, recognized the teenager. Scott. An unlit cigarette was in his hand. "It does many people."

"And vampires. But not Guardians?"

"Some."

"Demons?"

She smiled and glanced through the balcony doors into the apartment. She didn't see Lucas in the crowd, and it was too loud—in every possible way—to pinpoint him by sound or psyche. "I don't teleport many."

"Why not just send them back to Hell?"

"They'd be able to return through the Gates . . ." She broke off, shaking her head. "Not anymore. But before, it was better just to try to kill them than risk them coming back."

"Can't you drop them into a volcano?"

"If they couldn't fly, and if lava would kill them, I would," she said, trying not to laugh. "And I have to touch them; getting that close makes me too vulnerable."

"You can't just beam their head off?"

"That would be nice." She sighed, imagining it. A simple, quick death. "But no. I can't take bits. Nor can I teleport them *into* something . . . like halfway through a wall, cutting them in two."

His disappointment was palpable. "That sucks."

"Yes." She searched the faces inside again.

"Mr. Marsden isn't here yet. After that psychic blast we got from you guys, Marguerite says that he's probably frozen in a sexual stupor. Her words, not mine," he hastily added.

Her sword glinted in the spill of light from the apartment. "Get inside," she said and teleported.

And hovered above a forest of conical fir trees, their branches thick with needles. She couldn't see through them to the ground.

But she could hear Lucas. Could hear his heavy steps.

Heard her voice answering him.

Her heart pounded; a cold sweat broke over her skin. Lucas wouldn't have been tricked by imitation. Very possibly, the demon had her sword at his back. At his neck.

And Selah couldn't see him to protect him. She flew up, silently—and waited for them to reach the clearing.

Lucas glanced up once, and saw a shadow moving across the top of the trees.

"What is it?" the demon asked, her chin tilting back. Her palm was warm—hot—against his. Her hair was a long blond cascade down her back.

"An owl, perhaps. Maybe a vulture." He prayed it was a

gorgeous winged woman with the sexiest lips and shoes he'd ever seen. Tugging her forward again, he said, "Did you find any evidence that Andrea is still in Ashland?"

"No. Perhaps she'll give up."

"Yes," he said in a contemplative tone. "Once she realizes all of us will submit, negating the effect of the ritual, she'll look elsewhere." Her fingers tightened on his. He was a terrible actor, but he pretended to shake himself and added, "No. She'd already taken four victims in other cities. Any others she finds won't know to give in."

He felt the speculative gaze she ran over his features, but kept his focus on the path ahead of them.

"Yes," she finally said.

"I wonder what sort of bargain it was," he said. "What kind of terms could be set? What sort of negotiations does a demon have with *Lucifer*?"

Her voice was sweet, light. It set his teeth on edge. "He probably caught her as she tried to flee through the Gates before they were closed. I imagine he said something very much like: Return to Hell within six months, or I'll torture you for eternity within the Pit."

His brows rose. "That's a *bargain*?"

"She wouldn't have much choice. And he allowed her to live, allowed her through the Gate to Earth; returning is equivalent to going, and an eternity of torture is still life. In Lucifer's mind, it's an equal bargain." She angled her head, looked at him from below her lashes. "Is it true? That a willing sacrifice can upset the ritual?"

A chill swept over his skin. "Yes."

Her eyes began to shine, the whites changing to red, glowing crimson ringing the blue. "I shall have to make it very, very difficult for you not to resist me, then."

She squeezed; a bone in his hand snapped. Another. He ground his teeth together, white-hot pain streaking up his arm.

"Make it painful enough, and I'll *beg* you to kill me," he gritted out.

"That won't do," she said. "But it'll be fascinating to discover where your threshold between resistance and pleading lies. I'll admit I didn't take the time to find Olivia's. It was just 'off with her head!'"

"I'm relieved to hear that." And he was.

She dragged him forward; he couldn't shake her grip, so he walked. His wrist was next. Dots danced in front of his eyes.

"I'm saving the blood for the Gate. And I'll do it right on top of the portal this time; your Guardian was so kind to show you where it was while I was watching." She sounded like a girl expecting praise for a task well done. "Why aren't you afraid? I know you're in pain."

"I'm an adrenaline junkie."

"Vampires are affected by adrenaline?"

"I don't know." His breathing was harsh; he couldn't control it. "Maybe I'm just anticipating the moment Selah pops in front of you and stabs you through your heart. How much blood do you need for the Gate?"

Her teeth gleamed. "A whole lot of it."

"That's unfortunate," he said, and used his fangs to rip open his opposite wrist. A willing sacrifice.

"You stupid fuck!" she hissed, then yanked him forward by his broken wrist. Fast—dragging him over the ground toward the clearing.

They breached the treeline. He looked up, and his heart jumped into his throat.

Selah stared down at them, her wings outstretched, holding her aloft with a slow steady beat. Her crossbow was aimed at the demon's throat.

Cold steel landed on his palm. A gun. The blood made the grip slippery, it was in his left hand, but the demon was in close range. No need for precise targeting.

She whipped around, her sword raised over his head, and he unloaded the clip into her chest.

It wasn't going to be enough.

Two bolts from Selah's crossbow tore through the demon's bicep and forearm, forcing her to drop her sword—but there would be another in the demon's cache.

And she was still dragging Lucas toward the Gate. Within a second, she was *at* the Gate. Steel glinted against his throat, and she embraced Lucas against her chest like a lover, showing Selah her back . . . and Selah realized the brilliance of it.

She couldn't reach Lucas. The Gate prevented her from teleporting in front of the demon and taking him away. And if she teleported behind the demon, tried to kill her, she'd cut off Lucas's head.

The demon screamed in pain; Lucas had torn up the top of her arm and part of her shoulder with his fangs.

The demon would kill him for that. Would anyway.

Selah teleported, wrapped her arms around them both, preventing the demon from using her blade—and teleported again.

Shrieks. Fire and sulphur. Hell.

The Pit.

The demon staggered dizzily, and Selah used her second of disorientation to haul Lucas from the demon's grasp. Selah teleported into the air, out of reach.

"Jesus Christ," Lucas whispered in horror.

The demon stared up at them, her face a mask of terror. Selah leveled the crossbow on her heart.

Another demon, covered in scarlet gleaming scales and wearing huge membranous wings, abandoned his torture of a pale, naked figure. A human, once. Not much remained, except the organs needed to scream. Lucas's body heaved in her grip as he fought not to vomit.

The new demon didn't look at them, but beyond them. He spoke in a sibilant tongue: the Old Language. Selah didn't know it, but she recognized one word. *Morningstar*.

"He's coming," the demon with Selah's face said. "Have mercy, Guardian."

"Her bargain is fulfilled. She's come back to Hell," Lucas said, his voice raw. "It won't be the field."

She glanced down at his hand. Thought of Olivia and the vampire with the freckles. Others she hadn't known. "Mercy," she said. "But not for you."

She adjusted her aim, firing the bolt through the heart of the once-human. Then she teleported her vampire away.

She floated with him in a warm sea. The Caribbean, just north of the Yucatan. He needed blood; he needed to heal. He drank from her amidst the soft swell of waves.

"You should have let me take you to Michael," Selah said quietly.

Lucas held up his arm. The bones had fused back together. "It just aches a little." A wave rolled beneath them, a slow lift and drop. "I should return to Ashland soon. Tell them it's over."

Over. She couldn't speak for a long moment. "Yes," she finally said. "And I need to return to Caelum. Soon."

"Yes."

Making love in the ocean wasn't as easy as in a pool; she used her wings to steady them, to act as a raft. Afterward, they drifted in the path of the moonlight.

After a while, she said again, "Soon. There are sharks in the water."

He turned lazily and stared at her with a bemused expression. "Is that a lawyer joke?"

"Maybe a vampire one, because they're probably drawn by the blood. From when you bit me."

"I can't fault them for wanting a nibble of you, too," he said as they landed on his bed in a wet tangle. "I need to call Pierre and Marguerite."

She lowered her shields, felt the surge of power when he dropped his. "I think they'll know."

Selah left Lucas sleeping at dawn and teleported directly to Michael's side. She arrived in the center of Caelum, in a courtyard that only she and the Doyen could access. A fountain was before him, and he stood at the low wall, holding a sword.

Not, Selah noted with a sudden lump in her throat, one of his swords. "Was that Jeremiah's?"

The Doyen's eyes were fully obsidian. His enormous black wings arched over his head. "Yes." He let go the weapon. It slipped soundlessly into the fountain's pool and sank. His bronze hands fisted; his knuckles were white.

She looked away. Around them, Caelum rose in a corus-cating vision of white. Temples and domes, spires and columns. The sun hung in a brilliant blue sky.

"If you have come to tell me you want to Fall or Ascend," he said softly, "I might kill you."

She blinked, then caught the slight curving of his hard mouth. Her laughter didn't echo in the marble courtyard; his did.

"I know you are too much the Guardian to do either," he said when it faded. "But you *are* here for something." He vanished his wings and toga, replaced them with his linen tunic and trousers. His arms crossed over his broad chest.

"To change," she said. "The others, those who Ascended— they didn't have anything but this." She waved her arm in a wide arc.

"You do not think it is enough?"

She couldn't read his expression. "No. Not after a while. They needed something of their own, but there was only this."

"Yes. That's what they thought, but they never asked. I cannot decide if their determination to have no other life but a Guardian's was an indication that I chose well when I transformed them, or if their assumption that I would deny their wills if they wanted more than a Guardian's life was my failure. Perhaps it is both." He studied her for a long moment. "What is it you want, Selah?"

"Both," she said. "I want both."

She wasn't beside him when he awoke. Lucas sat on the edge of the bed, waiting for the hollow pain of her absence to fade.

It didn't.

He called Pierre first. Calculated distance and time. Made a reservation at a hotel. Packed a bag.

Thirty minutes after sunset, he was on the road. He had two names: Hugh Castleford and Colin Ames-Beaumont.

The second would be easier to find; any member of the San Francisco community would probably know where to find a beautiful, warm, tanned, human-drinking, nosferatu-born vampire.

And that vampire would know how to find Selah.

"Where are we going?" she said from the passenger seat, her heels propped against the dashboard, and he almost drove off the highway.

"Holy mother of God! Fuck me!" He screeched to a halt on the side of the road.

"Is that an angel joke?" She closed her eyes. "That was bad. I'm going to Hell."

He stared at her. "You've been. And back."

"That I have. You, too. It probably won't be the last time, either." Her blue eyes were sparkling with amusement. "So where are you going?"

He ran his hands through his hair, then slapped them back down on the steering wheel. "Nowhere. Now. What are you doing here?"

She pursed her lips. "Feeding you? You've got no one else."

"No."

"Doing my duty? Protecting Ashland from further demon attacks?"

Her impish grin nearly undid him. "No," he said.

"Splitting my time between you and Caelum? Half of eternity is still eternity. So I've got evenings off now. Though," she added softly, "you might say that I'm on call. If I'm needed. But there are a lot of time zones if we need to make up for hours lost; half of them are always dark. You didn't get my message?"

He shook his head. "What message?"

She palmed her cell phone, then made it disappear. "On your answering machine. I called to say I'd be late. Nosferatu in Denmark."

"I didn't check." Something in his chest swelled, a bright electric ache. And it felt incredible. "You're staying?"

"I've got a Gift," she said quietly, and brushed her fingers over his lips. "Not just to escape whenever I want, and not just to go—but to return."

"And you will?"

"Every night." Her gaze searched his. "I don't know what this is yet. I do know that being with you is good . . . better than anything else. I think I know what it'll become."

What was it? Extraordinary pleasure, just from her presence. Every moment.

He thought he knew what it was, too. And his brain was working perfectly well. His body.

His heart.

She kissed him. Those lips *had* been dangerous. But they

were his now, and he'd risk Hell again for another taste of them.

"Let's go home, then," he said when she pulled away.

"That's exactly where I want to be," she said. And this time, he was the one to take her there.

HUNTER KISS

Marjorie M. Liu

To my mom and dad,
with love

One

My mother used to say that the tale of the world is drawn in blood, blood in flesh, veins forking into destiny like the branches of the tree from which the apple hung and the serpent danced, trading whispers for the corruption of innocents. Good and evil, knowledge and choice. And there, at the root of history, the world tumbled down.

History is legend. Legend is blood. And I am totally fucked.

My mother was murdered on the day I turned twenty-one. It was at night. She served me cake. When I blew out the candles, she died. Shotgun blast to the head, aimed right through the kitchen window. I walked away without a scratch. I suppose I killed her, just as much as the zombie who pulled the trigger did. I try not to think about it.

Since then, though, I've kept to the road. No home, no roots. Just me and the boys. I suppose they deserve some of the blame, too. All of it, really. But hating them is the same as hating myself, and my mother would not want that.

So, like I said, I try not to think about it.

It is a rainy evening in Seattle. Beyond the drizzle, sunset is coming. Best time of day, or the worst—depending on where I am. Right now, it is pretty bad. I know the sun is setting because my tattoos are ready to peel. Puts me in a bind because I've got no place to go and nowhere to hide. I am standing beneath the arcade on the crowded upper level of Pike Place Market, only a step away from the wet cobblestones and idling traffic of First Street. There is an echo beneath my feet; the lower levels of the Market, sinking into the hill, resonating with the footsteps of tourists and locals; voices chattering around the antique dealers, the comic book sellers, the head shops and farmers and crafts and kitsch. A combination meant to evoke nostalgia, perhaps. An emotion lost on me, at this particular moment.

I blame the zombies. I am surrounded by them. They are breathing down my neck. And they are not happy to see me.

The zombies are mixed plain as day within the tourist jungle, and they are as diverse as they are deceptive. I see an old woman, torso swallowed up in a loud embroidered jacket; men with beer bellies and fanny packs, a college-type with glasses sliding down her greasy nose. Others, ordinary and respectable—and some worse: a young boy, a skinny blond thing with a hollow gaze. He must be a terror. The circles under his mother's eyes seem to indicate as much. I hope she keeps all her sharp objects secured away.

In all, I count ten zombies. Could be more. Most of them study me sideways, quick glances beneath their eyelashes. A few have the balls to look me in the eyes. They do not hold my stare for long.

I call them zombies because I like the name, not because that is what they are. A game, from long ago, when my mother told me to name the myriad species of spirits and demons who invade this world from across the prison veil.

Name something, give it power. Name something, take it away.

Zombie rolls off the tongue. I was ten. It was Halloween. I had a book of scary stories and went down the list. And the zombies in front of me, as in the movies, are easy to see. Crowns of shadow pulse and flicker above their heads. Dark auras: the only way to tell if a human has been possessed. Zombies, after all, look normal. Regular. Alive and human. No point to anything else. *My* zombies—no matter how much I love the art of George Romero—are not dead. They do not rise from graves, rotting and stinking and leaking guts. They do not groan and shamble, mindless as coma victims on remote control. Zombies hold jobs. They laugh, they cry. They look like the people you love. They *are* the people you love. That is why they are so dangerous. Zombies get under your skin, and you never know it. Not until they hurt you. Not until they kill you. Not until they use words to tear you apart, breaking you down, destroying your heart.

The dark spirits I call zombies are demons, parasites, and they are very patient. They lurk on the fringes of human minds, sniffing out who is weak and broken—choosing just the right fit, the perfect life and body—until finally, quietly, they steal inside to squeeze, slowly command, control, and seize. Altering, irrevocably, the personality of the person who has been taken.

Possession never ends well. The demons who create zombies feed off strong emotions. Not flesh or brains—just heart. Anger is good. Pain is better. The pain and terror of others best of all.

I lean against a pillar in the arcade and watch the zombies. They watch me. I can feel the sun dipping low to the horizon. I need to run, fast, and hide. I do not move, though. I have never seen so many zombies gathered in one place. Not right, not right. Zombies do not cooperate. They do not swap tales of possession. They have territory, and that is sacrosanct. Zombies do not poach pain.

And they do not show themselves to me. Not without running. Or fighting.

So, I have a problem. More than one if I am still here when the sun goes down. Bad luck. I did not come here looking for trouble. All I wanted was an afternoon stroll in the rain, sipping Starbucks and window-shopping; a grim Pollyanna in cowboy boots, a little Miss Sunshine in jeans and old leather. Good times, minding my own business, playing the tourist game—taking in my last hour before the boys wake up. We are leaving town tonight. I am all paid up at the Hyatt. My bags are in the car.

I should have stayed in my room. Clint Eastwood was on. I could have ordered steak.

I push off the pillar and wind through the crowd, taking the long way to the street. I force myself to go slow, memorizing faces, tracking the zombies, as they do the same to me. A cool wet breeze from the street stirs my hair. I wish it could do more. My turtleneck and leather jacket feel too warm; sweat rolls down my back; my palms are sweaty beneath my black kid gloves.

The boys, after a moment, absorb the moisture. Little heartbeats skip a beat as they begin to wake. Early, even for them, but I blame the zombies. Zee and the others always know when wicked is near, even when asleep. Part of their natures: like calling to like. I do not want to think about what that makes me.

I bump hard into the mother of the young zombie boy, steadying her with an apology. I meet the gaze of the grim pale child at her side. I cannot imagine how—or why—he convinced his mother to bring him here, but he has a demon inside him now, and they are master manipulators.

The zombie child looks at me with death in his eyes, and I give him a smile. Compliment his mother on having a good boy. A good boy with an aura so dark I want to pin him down and crawl a spell inside his head.

Maybe later. I walk away. With his mother's wallet in my pocket.

I make it to the street. I have, if I am lucky, five minutes before the sun dips below the horizon. Not enough time to reach the hotel, even at a run, but this is the city—there must be a bathroom nearby. A parking garage. A hole in the ground or some slip of space behind a Dumpster. Someplace I can hide when the boys wake up.

The man across the street changes everything.

The only reason I notice him is because I turn to check one last time on the zombies and find them no longer watching me. All of them, even the child—who is being tugged away by his clueless mother—are staring at a point over my shoulder, their gazes so intense, so hungry, I take several steps into the road before turning my back to study the evening crowd behind me.

I see the man through the rain, which is coming down harder; the world dim, gray, full of shining headlights and slick concrete; splashes of color dancing from clothes and nearby restaurant windows. The man is human. No dark aura.

But he stands out. I cannot explain how, just that looking at him feels like seeing a wolf in a pack of Chihuahuas. Wet brown hair tumbles past the collar of his navy windbreaker, hanging unzipped over a large flannel shirt and thermal. His jeans are old, his work boots older. His face is too angular to be called pretty, but he is tall and his body full of hard planes and lines. Youngish, in his thirties. He leans on a carved wooden cane, a backpack hanging loose over his shoulder.

Near him sits an old homeless man huddled on a flat sheet of cardboard, a blue plastic tarp spread over his grizzled silver head and bound belongings. His face is lost in shadow, but my eyes are sharp: I see a mouth, set in a grim line—a mouth that relaxes when the man with the cane crouches beside him. Lips move, heads bob, arms gesture at the worsening weather. Familiar, easy. Those two know each other's names.

The cane is set aside, and the man digs into his backpack. A bottle of water and a white box emerge, quickly passed over. The old homeless fellow tucks them both into his lap. Smiles.

The young man picks up his cane and stands, swaying slightly. He looks across the street, his gaze roving over the Market crowd walking dry beneath the golden-lit arcade behind me. His scrutiny seems to falter when he sees the zombies. But when he looks at me, he stops entirely.

He stares. He stares as though startled, as though he knows me, as though there is a line of history between us—a life-line—and I cannot look away. I cannot blink. I am falling, falling, but the ground is firm beneath my feet and my knees are strong and I know it is all in my head—*only there*—but I cannot help myself, because all that matters are his eyes. His eyes are so warm.

It does not last. I sense movement, all around; the zombies stirring in the thinning crowd, gathering together. Dark auras, rubbing. The boys roll more urgently against my skin, peeling with the sun that is grazing the horizon beyond the clouds.

I have to go now. I have to run like hell.

The zombies are still staring at the man. The little boy is gone. An elderly woman teeters close. She is dressed in black silk, with a gaze like fingernails on a chalkboard and lips so red she looks as though she has been sucking blood from the sea on the other side of the prison veil. I wonder how much of the real woman is left, whether her mind, any part not subjugated by her possessor, is screaming.

She opens her purse and tilts it toward me. I see a gun inside. I am not impressed. I am inclined to take that gun and ram it down her wrinkled throat. Every zombie—every *demon*—knows how my mother died. It is the same way *her* mother died, and her mother before that. The same way I will die, unless someone becomes creative. And I doubt that. Seriously.

"What do you want?" I ask the zombies, though I look only at the old woman. She, like the others, stare at me as though they can taste the future bullet marked for my brain. Not that anyone else notices. The tourist crowd, thinning as it is, flows around us. Some of the zombies receive odd looks, but that is all; not a single passerby seems to see beyond the surface, to question, to wonder if there is a problem.

But the gun that old woman finally hauls from her purse certainly spins some heads. Her hand shakes. Violent tremors. I see some fear in her eyes, confusion. Fighting the compulsion, struggling against the demon inside her. Maybe. I like to give people credit.

"Hey," rasps the zombie. She has a low hard voice—a chain-smoker. "Hey, Hunter. Hunter Kiss. Bang, bang."

She points the weapon, but not at me. I spin and there—just behind, limping his way across the cobblestone street, is the man with the cane. He still stands out—a wolf among dogs—and is taller than I realized, even broader, stronger.

All it takes is two steps. I throw myself at the man, and somehow he is ready for me, arms coming up to hold me as I take him down, my hands cushioning the back of his skull.

The gun fires. I feel the bullet bounce off my body as we crash into the road. I hear a rough grunt beneath me, a harsh intake of breath—and then around us, screams, cars honking, the patter of rain against stone. I try to roll free, but the man is strong; he holds me so tight I cannot breathe.

And then he does let go, a shout gurgling up from his throat, and I feel something hard press against the back of my skull. Same gun, same old zombie. This time she does not shift her aim to the man. She pulls the trigger on me.

The world erupts. I stop breathing. I go deaf, blind—all I see for a moment is a sheet of shining light—and I cannot move. I cannot think. Not until I feel my body shift—the man, rolling—pressing on top of me, shouting, his hands cradling my head. His eyes are wild and dark, his body hot and long and hard. I take a breath, another after that—gasping—and I force myself to push against the man. This is not safe. He is not safe.

But oh—*oh*—that old zombie woman falls down beside us, gasping and shrieking, writhing like a pale wrinkled eel. Blood pours from the side of her neck, blood that is nothing compared to the fountain gushing from the remains of her mangled hand. The gun is gone. Blown to shrapnel when the bullet backblasted into the barrel. So stupid. Stupid to shoot me. Stupid to place the gun so close against my body.

Bullets ricochet. Bullets boomerang. Bullets and other projectiles do not like my tattoos. The boys are good body-guards. The demon inside the old woman should have known that. I have a reputation.

Her blood soaks my coat, spatters my face. I can see the demon in her dying gaze, but loose now, distant. The creature is going to make a run for it. Find another host. Leave this old woman to die alone, wondering what she just did, her name blackened forever, destined to live on as an Evening News Special Report: *Random violence in America on the rise.* The elderly, snapping.

And me—if I am caught here—I will be in that report, as well.

The man rolls off me, and I roll with him, grabbing his hand and pulling him with me as I force myself to stand. I smell like blood. I touch the back of my head, pushing through thick hair to find unbroken skin, hot to the touch. I remember my mother, and I want to vomit. My legs shake. The man reaches around me and places his big warm hand on the back of my neck. He stares into my eyes.

I have to look away. The zombies are gone, scattered, lost in the trampling mob of frightened people racing from the violence. I see faces behind windshields staring, gape-mouthed.

The man still touches me. "You okay?"

"Are you?" I sound as shaken as I feel. *Shot in the head, shot in the head.* I shrug off his hand, and he takes a step, following. His knee buckles. He brings up his cane in time, but I also grab his arm, tugging him close, holding him. His body feels hard, strong. He smells good, too. Like cinnamon and sunlight. Home scents, warm.

"Sorry," he murmurs, but I say nothing. I have no time, and I cannot leave him. I pull on his hand, but he pulls back, looking at the old woman—that zombie—dying on the ground.

"We have to go," I tell him. *We.* Not a word I have used in a long time. Not about anyone other than the boys.

"She's hurt," he says.

"She tried to kill you."

"Doesn't matter." He looks at me, and his face hardens. "Go on, then. Leave."

But I do not. I get in his face and grab his collar, pressing so close I can almost taste his lips. His face is wet with rain, the shadow of his jaw sharp and dark. I should leave. I should run and abandon him. I should dump this city and every other like it, give up the mystery of demons and zombies—prisons and veils and guns and murder—and go hide on a mountain at the top of the world. Hide and pretend that I was not born to kill.

"Please," I whisper.

His jaw tightens. His fingers skim my back, and then he reaches up and covers my hand with his own. I let go of his collar. He does not let go of me.

I pull him beneath the arcade. He limps, but I simply drag him with me—fast, without hesitation—and I do not look back. I leave the old woman to bleed out. I leave the demon free to find a new host. I hate that. My mother would hate that. In a perfect world I would do neither, nothing but the right thing. But this is not a perfect world. This is a prison, and the inmates do not even know it.

I have no time. I do not know where I am going, but I see stairs and take them. The man lets go of my hand, but I grab his sleeve. I cannot let him get away from me.

He says something—a protest, maybe—but I do not hear. Somewhere above us the sun is clipping below the horizon, and I can count the seconds, feel them ticking in my heart as a burn flashes over my entire body, from scalp to fingertips to toes: a quicksilver fire, the ritual trial.

The boys wake up. All at once, with a shudder that is worse than the impact of the bullets. I see a sign for a restroom and dive inside, dragging the man after me. The place reeks of piss and mildew. The floor is covered in soiled black and white tile, and the doors on the stalls only come up to my waist. Inside one of them is a gray wiry fellow all sinew and bone with a needle in his arm, shaking and moaning. He is the only other person in the bathroom. Nothing I can do about him. No lock on the main door, either. I brace my shoulder against it and tear off my gloves.

The man with the cane makes a low guttural sound, but I do not look at him. All I see are my hands. Smoke writhes against my skin, pulsing with flickers of red lightning that only seconds ago were nothing more than the lines of an intricate tattoo.

The front of my sweater bulges. I yank it up. Silver smoke winds around my torso, peeling away from my ribs and back, stealing the dark mist covering my hands—and lower, the smoke that I know covers my thighs and legs and feet. Tattoos, dissolving into demon flesh, coalescing into three small dark bodies: Zee, Aaz, and Raw, all of whom slide down my legs to the floor. They peer into my eyes, long claws rattling. Beneath my hair, two more tiny demons wriggle free. Dek and Mal, slender black snakes with the heads of baby hyenas. They curl around my neck, purring, whispering nonsense I do not understand and never will; only, that it is soothing, warm, familiar as a lullaby. I slump against the bathroom door, exhausted, heart thundering. I reach out and small hands touch my hands.

My boys. The only friends I have in this world.

Zee's angular face is the color of smeared soot. The spikes of his hair resemble thousands of tiny bobbing silver needles, while his spindly arms are edged in razor scales and claws bright and metallic. He opens his mouth, and his white teeth are jagged, tongue black and long.

"Maxine?" Zee rasps quietly, but the others tug on his sharp hair, and we all look across the bathroom at the man I brought here, the man I could not abandon. I left a zombie to die, but not him. Not him.

I stop breathing. The man stares, and the world contracts around me as I look into his eyes, his straight gaze. He does not look at the boys, but only me. Just me.

Zee and the others make a humming sound, like tiny chain saws revving their engines.

"Hot damn," whispers the little demon. "Trouble."

Two

Trouble. Yes. I am in a lot of it.

It takes me a long time to move. I do not want to. But the man draws in a sharp breath and leans so far upon his cane I am afraid he will fall. So I go to him. I take my own deep breath and cross the bathroom, stopping with some distance between us. I do not know if the man can handle standing close to me. I do not know if I can handle being close to him. If there have ever been witnesses to the daily ritual of the boys' awakening, I have run before being forced to deal with the terrified aftermath.

But all I do now is stand, unable to speak. His eyes are so keen. I feel as though he can see right through me, though his attention is momentarily drawn to Aaz, who sticks his face in a urinal to eat the cake. Farther down I hear a lapping sound from one of the stalls. Raw shambles out, wiping his mouth. The man's lips twitch.

"Maxine," Zee says again. He hops from foot to foot, pointing to the bathroom door. I hear loud footsteps and click my fingers. Aaz and Raw dart across the tile floor and lean their heavy bodies against the old wood door, bracing themselves as someone pushes from the other side. The boys do not budge.

They are heavy, dense, lean, and twisted, ribbed with muscles and sinew and sharp objects; gray and silver spikes run down their spines, organic metal that has no equal on this side of the prison veil. Perhaps no equal anywhere, though only the boys understand what they are. All I know for certain is that they are as immortal as their host—born to be weapons, little deaths.

And I am their Mistress. I am their Huntress, and they are my Hounds. For now.

The door is pushed again, this time with more force. I hear a shout, followed by pounding fists. The commotion is short lived, but Aaz and Raw do not move from the door.

The man touches my arm. I jump. I did not hear him move. Dek and Mal rise up from their resting place on my shoulder, hissing; the narrow furred ruffs of their scaled necks tremble. The man flinches, but does not let go. I cannot imagine what his nerves are made of.

"What is this?" His eyes are brown, his brow strong, furrowed. I feel lightheaded. This is my worst nightmare. I glance away from him and catch a glimpse of myself in the long mirror above the sinks. *Snow White*, my mother used to call me. White skin, red lips, hair as black as a raven's wing. My eyes are hollow, though. Tired. Face spattered with blood. No crystal coffins or kisses for me.

I shake the man's hand loose, keenly aware of the boys; Dek and Mal are still poised to strike. I reach up and stroke their backs, trying to calm them. The man watches me, and I watch back, taking his measure, finding no fear. No fear in his eyes, in the set of his mouth. Just his hand, still trembling. A bead of sweat on his brow, in the hollow of his throat. I see some blood on his cheek.

I walk backward to the sink and turn on the faucet. Rip off a paper towel and soak it. I hold it out to the man and point at the mirror. He stares at it, then me, and then his reflection. I look, too. We are strangers, watching each other, and I cannot read his eyes.

"Someone tried to kill you," I tell him.

"Yes. You saved my life." He hesitates. "Two bullets. You should have died."

I try not to think about that bullet bouncing off my skull. I hate being shot in the head. For obvious reasons. Nor is there a good explanation for my survival, nothing that would make sense. All I can do is look at the man. I have never wanted anyone to be afraid of me—until now—and I cannot explain it except that this man's odd edgy calm, his rigid control, is not right. Not right at all.

His eyes narrow. "You're not human."

"Human enough." I push away thoughts of my mother. "Who are you? Your name."

"You first."

I hesitate. "Maxine. Maxine Kiss."

"Maxine," he says slowly. "My name is Grant. Grant Cooperon."

"Grant." I draw out his name, tasting it. "Grant, this must be very strange to you."

"Yes."

"Yes. So, if you need to . . . to . . ."

"Freak out?" he says, voice strained. "Run screaming? No. No, *ma'am*. I don't think that would be a good idea at all. But try not to look so disappointed."

"Disappointed," I mutter. "You're too calm."

"*Calm.*" He spits out the word. "*This* is not calm."

"Fine." My cheeks are hot. I toss him the wet paper towel and then fix my own. I scrub my face in the mirror, washing away the old zombie woman's blood, watching his reflection as he stares at me and then Zee, who is prowling close to his feet, sniffing the air around his body. Grant stands very still, but except for one brief grimace, shows no fear.

"We have to leave," I tell him, drying my hands on my jeans. "It's not safe here."

"For you or me?" Grant's knuckles are white around the knobby head of his cane. "What is this? What is going on?"

I turn to go to him, but falter at the last moment and lean against the sink, studying his face, mustering all my strength to match his piercing stare. He does not look away. Neither do I.

"You tell me," I say quietly. "Why would someone want to kill you?"

"And why would someone like you save me?" Grant tilts his head. "Peculiar, isn't it?"

"Everything about this is strange." I push myself off the

sink and take a step toward him. "No doubt stranger to you than it is to me."

"No doubt." He glances down at Zee and raises his eyebrow. "Hello."

"Boo," Zee replies, regarding him thoughtfully, sticking the tip of a silver claw into his mouth, sucking lightly. "You got odd eyes, hu-maan. Deep sea seeing eyes. Bet they taste *good*."

"Bet you'll never get a chance to try," Grant replies, surprising the hell out of me. He glances my way. "I think *you* might have a word or two to say about eyeball snatching."

"Depends," I tell him. "You don't know me."

He shrugs. "I take faith in small gestures. Like saving my life."

"Even if that savior is me? Covered in demons?"

"Demons." He tastes the word, something hard and resolute settling in his gaze. "Demons don't frighten me."

I have to catch my breath. "The old woman who tried to kill you was possessed by one. A creature controlling her actions. There were others, too. All of them there for you. Waiting."

I listen for his response—some kind of denial, fury. Anything. But all I receive is that same steady stare, so thoughtful I find myself wondering if *I* am not the one insane.

Something hard slams against the bathroom door. It has been quiet for the past minute, but no longer. There are new voices now. I think of the zombies upstairs; there could be more of them outside this room, also with weapons. Nothing is safe.

"Hey!" yells a man. "This is security! Open the fuck up!"

Zee's nostrils flare. He cracks his knuckles. "Three, Maxine. Just three. All hu-maan."

"Wait," Grant says, but I take his arm and push him into the empty stall next to the heroin addict. The floor is slick, the toilet seat slimy. I almost gag on the smell as I crowd in with the man. Dek and Mal slither deeper into my hair.

Grant yanks his arm free. "Stop. I need answers."

"Why?" I shoot back. "You already seem to have a grasp on things."

"Don't confuse calm with comprehension."

"Why not?" I stare up into his face. He is big, all man. Breathtaking. "You aren't phased by this, are you? Not one bit."

"The bullet was a surprise," he says, eyes narrowing. "And you. Definitely you."

I push away from him, but there is nowhere left to go—and all I can think of are the odds. One man in a city of millions. One market, full of zombies—who never gather, never gang. And me, there, on the cusp of sunset. Of course. Just my luck.

I swallow hard. "You're not human either. Or if you are, you're not like any human I've ever met."

"Human enough." He steals my words, presenting a bitter smile. "Though having humanity and being human are two different things."

"And what are you?"

"A man of both, I hope." Grant sways close. "And you?"

"This is ridiculous," I mutter.

"No," he says. "Tell me. Please."

"I don't know," I whisper, anger stirring—at him, at myself for being so weak with words, so easily cornered when I have never been cornered before. "I don't know what I am. But right now I don't give a damn. I want some answers, too. So you tell me, Mr. Cooperon . . . how did you know? How did you know what those people were?"

Grant sways close. For a moment I forget he is a stranger, a mystery, because the regret and uncertainty in his dark gaze suddenly feels like a mirror, a hard reflection of my own emotions. I do not feel sorry for him.

"I see things," he tells me, with a deep breath that sounds like an anchor dropping into his chest. "Color. Or the lack of it. Up there, darkness. Darkness in most of that crowd. And then you." He leans even closer, his gaze flickering over my face, my mouth, until, soft, *"You."*

He says the word like it means something, like it means everything. It scares me. Everything about this is wrong.

"My presence was an accident," I tell him, barely able to drag my voice above a whisper. "But that darkness you saw . . . that was a sign of possession. Demons, a certain kind of parasite. And they were there for you. They wanted you dead, no questions asked. I cannot understand why. No one draws that kind of attention, Mr. Cooperon. No one."

"Not even you?" Grant says gravely.

The bathroom door slams open. I hear three muffled

screams, followed by silence and hard successive thumps. Grant and I tumble out of the stall. Two men in uniforms are sprawled face-first on the filthy floor, and a third, in street clothes, rests on his back. They are breathing. No dark auras, either, just as Zee promised. Aaz and Raw sniff their faces. Zee pokes a thick round belly with his silver claw.

"Juicy," he says, sly. "Very juicy, Maxine."

"No," I warn him. "I'll get you dinner later."

"A better dinner," Grant says, surprising me again, "if that fellow there tastes like he looks."

Zee grins, rubbing his little shards of hair. "Not picky, humaan. You want to give *your* finger for a pinch and a taste?"

"Give me yours, and we'll call it even," Grant replies, and this time he is rewarded by tiny chimes of laughter. He does not smile, but merely looks at me—challenging—as though daring me to say something.

All I can do is stare. Zee tugs on my sleeve, and I scoop him into my arms. He hugs me, pressing his sharp mouth to my ear.

"You smell like fear," he murmurs. "Like blood battle. We dream, and we remember as dream, but Aaz says something bad cut you down. A big bad zombie cutter."

I move away from Grant, toward the bathroom door. "Can you tell me what this is about?" Zee shakes his head. I breathe, "And the man?"

Again Zee says nothing, but the purr rumbling through his chest stops. I hold my breath. It would not be the first time I have misjudged character, human or otherwise, though the boys are good authorities on trust, ready to pass verdict whether or not it is required. The last time I met a man the boys did not like, I had to pack a body part on ice for paramedics to find.

And now? They are laughing at jokes.

Grant, leaning on his cane, stoops to check the pulses of the unconscious men. "Fierce. Care to explain the best way to stay off their bad sides?"

"Do not fuck with me." I give him a long hard look. "Do not fuck with anyone who doesn't deserve it."

"Fighting on the side of light, huh? Wonder Woman, be still my heart." Grant's smile is grim. "Of course, that doesn't explain how to stay off *your* bad side."

"That might be impossible for you."

"So harsh."

"Compared to demons wanting you dead?"

"That last bullet was for you." Grant's gaze flickers over the boys, all of whom watch him with red eyes, coiled bodies hunched light over their gray and silver haunches. "Care to explain that? Or how you survived?"

Aaz and Raw drag their claws over the tiles, hissing softly. Zee puffs out his little chest. "In your daylight, hu-maan, our skin is her skin. Cutters got no glory over us old boys. Cutters got nothing but pain."

"By cutter . . . you mean demon?" Grant's jaw tightens. "And what are *you*, little man? Aren't you the same?"

"No," I cut in. "They are not the same. The boys are family, the only family I've got. I take care of them, and they take care of me. They *protect* me."

For now. The boys, after all, did not protect my mother on her last night. Or her mother. Or her mother before that, or any of the women in our line. Survival always wins out in the end. Always, for them.

Grant studies my face. This is the longest conversation I have had with anyone in almost five years. It is also, without a doubt, the worst mistake of my life.

He looks at the boys, his gaze lingering on their upturned faces. I try to see them as he must, but I have grown up with them, and there is nothing left about their bodies or personalities that can startle me.

"Are you ready?" I ask him, wanting to run, to scream. "Do you have some place I can take you?"

"Let's get out of here first," Grant says.

I reach for the door. He stops me. His hand is warm.

"Thank you," he says quietly. "I don't know why you saved me, but thank you."

"Don't thank me yet," I tell him, just as softly. "You could still be dead by morning."

"Such an optimist."

"Yes," I reply, without humor. "I wouldn't still be standing here if I wasn't."

Behind us, the stall door rattles. The gray wiry fellow slouches out, a trail of blood running down his coarse arm.

He glances at us and then takes in the men on the floor, the boys.

"Fuck *me*," he whispers, rubbing his eyes.

"Get out of here," Grant says to him. "Right after us, get out. You don't want to be here when someone finds those men."

The man nods. I hope he listens.

I crack open the door. Raw peers out and clicks his claws. We leave fast.

Traveling with demons is not so difficult as one might think. It all depends on the particular demons, but in my case the boys are experts at shadow-jumping. Fortunately, the dim lighting of Pike Place Market's lower level offers many opportunities to use their skills.

Zee, Aaz, and Raw leap into the first dark spot they find— a dirty corner filled with the lazy remains of some janitor's work: soda cans, a syringe, candy wrappers. One minute here, and in the next, gone. Swallowed by shadows. Dek and Mal, hidden as they are in my hair, stay with me. They press against my skin with warm purrs, tangled and nesting like very small, very serpentine, cats.

Grant, leaning on his carved wooden cane, watches the boys disappear. "Interesting."

"You are a master of understatement," I tell him. "Unless your life is more strange than what you've already told me."

"Strange enough. Where did they go?"

"I'm not sure. They jump short distances, from one shadow to another. When we hit the street, as long as it's dark out, they'll be able to travel beside us without anyone seeing them."

"Interesting," he says again, and pins me with a brief heavy stare. "Still doesn't explain you."

"Not much does." I start climbing the stairs. Grant, after a moment, follows. For a man with a limp, he moves surprisingly fast. He looks too strong to need a walking device, but the weakness in his right leg is no act. I point at the cane. "Accident?"

"No," Grant says. "Not in the slightest."

Before I can ask—before I can wonder at myself for wanting to ask—I hear the static of a walkie-talkie. We are still on the stairs, not quite at the upper Market level. The radio is tuned to a police frequency. I hear other voices, muted tones, very serious. Somewhere close, the wail of sirens.

Grant throws me a look. "I might be the victim here, but why is it I feel like a criminal?"

"A guilt complex is an ugly thing, Mr. Cooperon."

"Call me Grant."

I ignore him. "It's your choice. If you want to go to the police and introduce yourself, go right ahead. Tell them you were there."

"Really. Just like that."

"You're not my prisoner."

"No," he agrees slowly. "I don't quite know *what* we are."

I look away. "You should know that I don't usually do this."

"Save lives? Kidnap men?"

"Hang around afterward."

"Ah." Grant studies me for a moment, then peers down at his hands, his feet. "So, cops. You talk about choice, but why do I get the feeling that introducing myself to those uniforms would be a bad idea?"

"The same reason Zee and the others knocked out those security guards. There's nothing they could pin on us, but it would eat time."

"And they would ask uncomfortable questions." I feel him finger my back, and jump as he makes contact with skin. I reach around. There is a sizeable hole in my jacket, right down to my spine.

"Your hair covers it," Grant says quietly. "But I knew where to look."

I swallow hard. "I still say you're handling this remarkably well."

"I'm too much a man for hysterics."

I shoot him a quick glance and catch the dry tilt of his mouth. It takes me so off-guard I almost smile—almost—and Grant's mouth curves a fraction more.

"Got you," he says softly.

"You got nothing." I search his face, trying hard not to be affected. Tables are turning, turning fast. I feel like prey when

I look at this man. Wolf among dogs. And here I thought I was the Hunter.

"I don't know why you haven't tried to run yet," I say, my voice barely above a whisper.

"I thought you wanted me here."

"You don't know what I want."

Grant's smile softens. "If I tried to get away from you, I think you would come after me. I'm no fish to be thrown back to the water. Not after all the trouble you've gone to in order to keep me safe."

No argument there. "I have questions about why you're a target. Unless, of course, you already know. You, who can see demons peel off a woman's body and somehow treat it as sane. You, who can see other kinds of demons when everyone else in this world doesn't have a clue."

"*Sane* is a relative term." Grant sways close. "As for the other, I suppose that could have something to do with why those things, whatever you say they are, want me dead. I've . . . seen them before. The darkness."

"And you knew they were possessed?"

Grant hesitates. Before he can answer, Zee pokes his head from the shadows of an alcove above us—like a demonic otter cutting the surface of dark water—and tests the surface of the ceiling with the tip of his tongue. Hisses instantly, spitting out the taste. Specks of red saliva spatter my face. I wipe it off.

"Maxine," he rasps. "Hot spot. Whole place is burning. Fucking red hot."

"Damn," I mutter.

Grant frowns. "What does that mean?"

I study him, wondering how much I can say—wondering, too, if I have passed the point of no return, where hesitation is nothing more than stupid pride, keeping up with illusion. My secrets, the things I know, have always been mine and mine alone. At least since my mother died. Sharing that with someone else—a stranger, no less—feels wrong. Then again, *wrong* is suddenly becoming my new normal.

I glance up the stairs, but do not hear anyone coming toward us. I pull Grant to the side, next to the railing. "You already know a little, right? You've seen things. I don't want to know how much, not yet, but the bottom line is that there are demons in this world, and they are not supposed to be here. There's a barrier, a prison—several prisons—keeping them locked away, but sometimes they still manage to get through. Push enough, and a crack will form. Push enough, and that crack will become a temporary door."

"A . . . hot spot."

"Yes. Some locales make more than others. Cities are always bad. Too many humans, too much emotion, too juicy of a lure for all those dark spirits. Problem is, the numbers of hot spots are growing. The veil is getting weak."

"And if all those demons come through?"

I just look at him. "Humans do bad things all on their own, Mr. Cooperon. Some are worse than others. Some need help becoming monsters. There are more of those than you might think. Watch the news at night."

"I do watch," he says grimly. "And I see."

"Then you know what would happen, on a worldwide scale, if the barrier I told you about goes down. And those are just the demons who possess humans. There are others kinds, too, but they all feed off strong emotions. Anger, hate, fear."

And some that are worse than that, demons I cannot speak of. My mother's voice echoes inside my head, with her stories of the outer ring beyond the prison veils. The First Ward, home of the worst, the most dangerous. World Reapers.

I chew the inside of my cheek, still studying him. "I want to know why those demons up there wanted you dead. It could be the fact that you can see them. But that doesn't seem like a threat worth risking their hosts over."

"If you say so." Grant rubs his forehead. "This is too much information."

"Too much to believe?"

His hand stills. "No. Just . . . more than I wanted to know. Though I wouldn't complain if you planned on being my body-guard."

He manages to say it without sounding sleazy. A feat. And the only reason I do not steal his cane and push him down the stairs. I take a step up, listening to the crackle of radios. Zee has already disappeared. "Why were you coming here today?"

"I make flutes," he says.

"Flutes." I turn to stare at him.

"Wooden ones," he clarifies. "I don't sell them myself. There's a man who does it for me. I come down here to play on the weekends. I have a corner."

"Huh." I peer around the wall. Most of the arcade has been cleared of shoppers; at the very end, I see yellow tape, cops and news crews everywhere. None near us, though. "Where did you learn to do that?"

"I've played the flute since I was young, but I learned to make them in Nepal. China, after that. The mountain people produce incredible sounds."

"Really." I try to imagine leaving the continent, and get stuck on the mystery of setting suns and horizons. *National Geographic* and the Discovery channel are the closest I will ever come to exploration. "Did you always want to do that? Travel? Be a . . . flute maker?"

"No," Grant replies. "Before I did that, I was a priest."

Expectations are a liability at this point. I lean against the wall, staring. Grant smiles. "I don't fit the profile, huh?"

I take in his long lean lines, his damp hair, the angles of his face, and those dark warm eyes that carry the edge of something sharp. A big strong handsome man—a good man, the longer I look at him—but impossible to reconcile with the idea of contemplation and devotion to a higher power.

"No," I say weakly. "Why did you change?"

His smile turns brittle. "Complicated. I counsel now. Without the collar."

I do not say a word. My ears are ringing. Demons hunting a former priest? A flute maker? A man who walks in the rain and feeds the homeless? It makes no sense. I slowly push out my breath and meet Grant's eyes. The edge has faded from his smile, though not the humor.

"I'm sorry," he says. "I scared you, didn't I?"

"No, not scared. You're just . . . confusing."

"And you're not?" He shakes his head. "Never mind."

All is clear around us. Without thinking, I take his hand and pull him toward the street in front of us. When I try to let go, his fingers tighten—but only for a moment. One squeeze, as though to say, *I am here*. He lets go, but the sensation lingers.

It is still drizzling. We weave around the stopped traffic on

First Street, headlights illuminating the light mist soothing the flushed skin of my face and throat. It feels so good. I want to just stand beneath the rain and close my eyes—breathe slow and deep. I want to forget violence, mystery, responsibility. I am so tired.

"Maxine," Grant says quietly, and oh, it is strange hearing him say my name. Hearing it breathe off his tongue. I do not answer him, but instead curl deeper inside my jacket. I forgot to check if the old zombie woman's blood is visible on the black leather, but the street is dim, growing darker by the minute. I do not think anyone will notice.

I try to stay alert, but I trust the boys to keep an eye on things. They are good at that. They have to be, to keep me safe at night when my body is vulnerable. Their sleep is my armor, their freedom my weakness. Day and night. It is a pattern my mother warned me about, but I never understood until I had to live it myself.

I glance at Grant and find him watching me. He sways close, and I do not move away. "I see the darkness, too," I tell him. "It's how I knew that old woman, and all the others around her, had been possessed. But you say you see other things, too. Colors. Has it always been that way for you?"

"I suppose so. I've seen colors—auras—since I was young. At first it started with music. I would play the piano or flute, and each note would have a hue. There's a neurological condition that causes that. Synesthesia. Stimulation in one sense creates a response in another."

"Except yours goes a step further."

"My ability to see colors in people started later, but because of the other, I thought it was natural. Until I started talking about it. Then . . . it caused problems." He shrugs. "Like I said, there was a darkness around that old woman. A lot of those people."

"You've seen it before."

"Like a crown of night," he says quietly. "A crown on the head of a creature who does not belong."

"No." I think of that old woman dying on the street. "They do not belong at all."

"Neither do you." His gaze travels over my face and shoulders. "No offense."

I could ask him what my aura looks like—he clearly expects me to—but I do not want to know. "And are you going to judge *me*, former Father Cooperon? Are you going to judge me for my demons—or worse, for not *belonging*?"

"If not belonging was a sin, Maxine, we would all be in Hell."

"And what makes you think we aren't?" I remember my mother's stories, her tales of our beginnings, of the world, this sweet prison. "What makes you think that the very thing that makes us human, that *sets us apart*, isn't what also makes us prey? What makes you think that we haven't already been judged?"

Grant stops walking, his eyes turning so grave I almost wonder if I have made a mistake, if I have found the one thing that will make him angry. He leans close, rain dripping off his lashes, glittering like diamonds in the headlights of passing cars. "If we have been judged, Maxine, then there is no hope. There is no hope of anything, regardless of whether or not one believes in God or Heaven. And if we have been judged, then why, *why*, are we capable of change? Why are we capable of becoming more?"

"And if that capability is its own judgment?" I close the distance between us. "If that capability to hope and dream, to be tempted for good or bad, makes us so vulnerable that without protection we would be nothing more than victims? Hunted into self-destruction? That our weak natures are what imprison us? Demand, even, isolation from all kinds of creatures, and for nothing more than survival?"

Grant says nothing for a long time. He stares at me, but I do not think he sees my face; only something else: memory, dream. And then his gaze clears, and he looks at me—looks hard—and says, "And you, Maxine? You speak of yourself as human, but you can't be. Not entirely. Am I supposed to believe that your ability to hope and change is set apart from mine? Or that the demons you live with are any different? That *any* sentient creature, demonic or not, is incapable of becoming something more than what it was born to be?"

I start walking again. "You're not bringing up any questions I haven't already asked myself."

"And?"

"And nothing." Which is a lie, but better than facing the alternative. I glance sideways at Grant, watching him watch me. "You sure you don't want to tell me why you stopped being a priest? Seeing as how you're still so opinionated on matters of religion."

"I don't think we're discussing any religion approved of by the Church," Grant says wryly, "and as for my history, maybe I'll tell you later. After *you* explain why there are demons living on your body."

"Or why I saved your life?"

"I choose to think it's because you're a good person."

"And if you're wrong?"

He smiles. "I have faith."

I bite back another laugh. A police cruiser appears at the crest of the hill, lights flashing, sirens off, and speeds down the street past us. An ambulance follows. I hope it is the second, and not the first to arrive on the scene. I do not want to think of that old woman lying in the road. A zombie, yes; but a human woman first. Bleeding to death, without anyone to help her. Help I could have given if I were willing to expose myself and the boys. Which I was not—until Grant. And that, I still cannot explain to myself.

"You think she died." Grant's voice is heavy. He looks back over his shoulder at the disappearing vehicle.

"I hope she didn't. She deserved better."

"Everyone does. You don't blame her for being possessed?"

I shoot him a dirty look. "Do I blame women who wear short skirts for being raped? Give me a break."

Grant shrugs. "You might be surprised at how unforgiving some people are. Stray just a hair from the path that has been declared, and *pow*. You deserve what you get."

"Let me guess. You strayed."

"I was *told* I strayed. There's a difference."

I sway close—an accident, I tell myself—and brush his elbow. "Still bitter?"

"*Bitter* is such an ugly word, Maxine."

"How about pissed off?"

"Better." He smiles. "But not anymore. I find this life to be less . . . stifling. I enjoy my intellectual freedom."

"Is that all you enjoy?"

Grant laughs. "What's your life like?"

"Fine. Ordinary." The first two words out of my mouth, and they are utterly ridiculous. I shrug, searching for something better, but in the end, all I can say is, "I don't know. No one's ever asked me."

"You're kidding." Grant shakes his head. "Wow."

Wow, indeed. "Can we talk about something else?"

"Do we have to?"

"Grant."

"My, I believe that's the first time you've used my name." I roll my eyes, and he adds, "I think I've got a right to be persistently nosy when it comes to you."

"You should be more worried about yourself."

"And you seem to have a lot of expectations about how people should react to things, Maxine." Grant stops walking and leans close. Heat radiates from his body. I try to imagine him in black, with the collar, and I cannot. Or rather, I can— but I do not think I should.

I expect him to keep pushing—again—but instead he surprises me by reaching out and gently pulling up the collar of my leather jacket. He brushes aside a strand of wet hair from my cheek, and the heat that trails from his fingers reaches down into my gut.

I am not used to being touched. I like it. Which is dangerous, stupid. Men are a death sentence for me. Literally. And I am too young to start that clock ticking on the Grim Reaper's time.

Grant clears his throat. "Without this sounding like a line, do you want to go back to my place?"

I bite the inside of my cheek. "You have a ride?"

His smile is slow, warm. "I am a humble man. My legs have always sufficed."

I jingle my car keys inside my pocket, nestled against the stolen wallet. "I've got wheels. If you don't mind making a pit stop first."

Grant checks his watch. "I need to be home by ten."

"Curfew?"

"Not for me," he says, and I have to ask. I have to.

"Children?" I say to him.

His mouth curves. "Now who's fishing?"

Heat spreads over my face. I spin on my heel and walk fast up the hill. Grant catches up with me after a moment, his hand sliding over my shoulder. I feel the heat of each individual finger through the layers of my clothing.

"I'm sorry," he says. "I didn't mean to embarrass you."

"You didn't," I lie.

"Good." He hesitates, glancing at me. "And no, I don't have children. I'm not married, either. No girlfriend. I've been single since before I joined the Church, more than eight years ago."

This time I let myself smile. "Are you sure you're not still a priest?"

His hand gently squeezes my shoulder. "I wonder about that myself, sometimes."

Three

Fifteen minutes later, Grant and I find ourselves seated in my little red Mustang. It is very strange being with another person inside my car. The windows are tinted, and the boys are in the backseat, having slipped from the shadows of the Mustang's interior to join us in the flesh. They have their things out, along with soft old blankets and pillows. Dek and Mal untangle themselves from my hair to join their brothers.

"Nice wheels," Grant says, sliding his hand along the smooth leather interior. He fiddles with the CD player I installed several years back, and Bon Jovi roars to life. The boys let out a cheer from the backseat.

Grant laughs. "Fans?"

"Groupies. They made me follow his last tour."

"Best seat in the house?"

"Rafters directly above their heads."

"And you?"

"The other rafters." I bite back a smile. "After a while, I just waited for them in the parking lot."

He hums a few strains of "Wanted Dead or Alive," and twists in his seat to look at the boys. Aaz and Raw have rope and scissors; they are mangling their teddy bears, the ones with the cowboy hats sewn on. Zee lays over their laps flipping through a row of magazines. He pats Dek and Mal on their heads as they slither past him.

Grant peers down. *"National Geographic? Vogue? Playboy?"*

My cheeks get hot. "They like the pictures. I don't know why."

"I do," he mutters.

I dig into my pocket for the wallet I lifted. My gloves are still on. I do not touch the cash or credit cards, but instead pull out the license to peer at it under the dome light.

Katherine Campbell. Born August 2, 1967. Still very photogenic. Organ donor. Mother of a demonically possessed child. A zombie.

I peer at the address, memorizing it, and then hand the license to Grant. "I don't suppose you know where that is, do you?"

He frowns. "This isn't yours."

"Yes, I know. I confess my sins. Now, address?"

His frown deepens. "Capitol Hill. It's close. Just head up Pine Street." He stops, hesitating, and I can almost hear the wheels spinning in his head.

"I don't steal for a living, if that's what you're wondering." I put the car in gear and slide out of the parking space. "I inherited money from my mother. That's how I live."

"Ah," Grant says slowly. "How long has it been?"

"Five years." I glance into the rearview mirror. Zee is watching me. "I never knew my father."

"And . . . them?"

"The boys?" I smile. "Like I said, they're family. Everything I've got left."

"No home?"

"You're looking at it."

He blinks. "What about friends?"

"Are you asking me if I have any?"

"Do you?"

"I have friends. I just don't talk to them. Much."

The corner of Grant's mouth curves ever so slightly, but that is no consolation, because his eyes will not stop looking at me, not even to blink.

"What?" I say. My palms are sweaty, and there is a low warm ache in my stomach that has been growing ever since we got into this car together. His stare makes it worse, makes me scared and hungry for something I know I should not have—or contemplate.

"It's nothing," he finally replies, quiet. "Except that I believe I would prefer being your enemy to your friend, if it meant getting to talk with you more."

My cheeks warm. I look away, but when I steal another glance he is still watching me, and it is too much. His eyes are too gentle.

"*Stop.*" My voice breaks on that word. "Please."

He finally does, but I do not feel any better, and except for him giving me minimal directions, we do not talk. I glance at him once, find him staring out the window, mouth covered by his hand, the other holding the cane. He looks thoughtful.

I am afraid to check the backseat. The boys are too quiet. They take men very seriously. Their survival depends on it, just as surely as mine does not.

Twenty minutes later we pull down a residential street filled with fine expensive homes. There are no streetlights, but it is only seven-thirty. I drive past the house listed on the driver's license. It is very bright inside. I see people moving behind the curtains.

I park one street over and roll down the window. I need air. "Zee, check the place out. Aaz and Raw, go with him."

They slide into the shadows of the backseat, while Dek and Mal slither along the floor until they reach my foot. They climb my leg into my lap, curling and twisting as I stroke their backs. Their purrs are loud.

Grant reaches out and very carefully touches them. No one bites. He hesitates again, and then scratches the furred ruffs of their slender necks. Their purrs roughen, turning into low chortles.

"You are the first man to ever do that," I tell him. "I'm surprised you still have your finger."

"You weren't going to warn me?"

"Consider it a trial by fire."

Grant smiles, and stops petting Dek and Mal. "Maybe you can explain why we're here."

I tap the driver's license and slide it back into the wallet. "This woman has a son who was at the Market today. He's a zombie."

"A zombie."

"Sorry. That's my term. I mean he's been possessed. By a demon. The same kind that wants you dead."

His mouth curves down, the furrow between his eyes deepening. "And you think this boy—or the creature inside him—will know why?"

"It's worth a try. Even if the demon won't talk, I need to remove it from the child."

Grant studies his hands. His jaw tightens. "You're an exorcist?"

"When I have to be." I study his hands, too. They look strong, accustomed to hard work. I see history in those long elegant lines, in the turn of his wrist, the sensitivity of his fingers as they begin to tap, tap, tap against the hard wood of his carved cane.

But there is an uneasy energy coming off him; I sense a crack in his calm, and that bothers me almost as much as his unruffled reaction to our first meeting.

I touch the smooth knob of the cane, caressing the outline of a leaf. Grant's fingers freeze in mid tap. "How much do you know about demons?"

"Not a lot," Grant's fingers start moving again, only this time they skim a trail over my wrist. The ache inside my stomach becomes a tremor; worse, as his exploration moves to the skin between my fingers; light, so light. "I've . . . been motivated to study the subject from a variety of cultural viewpoints."

"Before today, you believed they existed."

"I learned to believe. So I studied. It was impossible to know if anything I read was accurate. Now . . . I think not so much."

"If you think about what you learned as a whole, some of it might make sense."

"Searching for connections?"

"Lowest common denominator. The perpetuation of hate. The war against compassion. That's what it all comes down to."

"Not always." His fingers slide up my wrist. "Not you."

His touch feels too good. "You don't know me."

"I don't have to." He looks into my eyes. "Someone else tried to kill me. A hit and run. It happened a month ago. I was headed to the Market that time, too."

I have to take a moment. "And you don't know why?"

He shakes his head, but only after a brief and significant hesitation. It reminds me of the silent treatment Zee gave me when I asked him about Grant. It reminds me of someone who is thinking about telling a lie.

The boys return, flowing from the shadows into the back-seat, breathless, chests heaving with subvocal chatter and clicking claws. I snatch back my hand from Grant as Zee says, "We found him. Bad runner, Maxine. Cutter got a good one when he found that boy. Rotten, rotten."

"What does that mean?" Grant reaches down into the back-pack stashed between his feet and the cane. He removes a slender black case.

"It means that the boy was already damaged when the demon possessed him. More than damaged. A psychopath, maybe." I look at Zee. "Best way to him?"

"Now. Right now. Outside, Maxine. Playing."

"In the dark?" Grant mutters. I can taste his uneasiness. For a moment I think of telling him to stay behind, but he gives me a look so stubborn I know anything I say will carry little weight. He wants to go. He has to go. End of story, even though I could force him. Leave one of the boys behind to watch him, with that bad leg as my excuse. With anyone else I would. But this man . . .

I do not know what it is about him. About us. I do not want to shake him, even for a moment. First time in my life I have ever felt that way. Even with my mother there were times I wanted to run. I tried, too. The boys always brought me home.

We get out of the car and walk. Dek and Mal tuck away inside my hair, still purring, while Zee, Aaz, and Raw hop between shadows. The rain is coming down harder; the side-walk is empty. Windows are bright and golden.

A nice neighborhood. Comfortable and rich. People who live in areas like this feel safe inside their homes. Safe outside their homes, as well. They are confident in their safety. So confident, that if a man and woman are seen strolling down the street before eight in the evening, at ease, one of them crippled, they cannot be a threat. No danger. No need to be afraid.

Unless you are a demon.

The Campbell home has a narrow walkway leading from their driveway to the backyard. For a fraction of an instant, Grant hesitates, but I take his hand and pull him along as though we live there. Confidence is the key, even if it just an act. There is so much that could go wrong right now.

"Don't turn around," I murmur. "Just keep your eyes forward. You live here, you're a guest here—"

"You are far too practiced at this," Grant says. "Have you ever been in jail?"

"Not yet," I mutter. "But if I get there because of you, we are going to have words."

We follow the line of the driveway toward the back of the house. No one stops us. Zee disappears into its shadows first, and after a moment is followed by Aaz. Raw waits, nose tilted to the sky, red eyes whirling. He takes the path. But not before clicking his claws at us.

The path is narrow and wet. On our left, the house—on our right, rosebushes drooping and heavy with rain. The air smells sweet. Ahead of us, I hear the muffled scrape of a body across grass. I walk faster.

Raw appears in front of me and grabs my hand. He pulls, I follow—dragging Grant behind me—and suddenly we are in a backyard filled with bushes and trees, thick roses, and a large playhouse with a full-sized camping tent staked in front of it.

That is where we go. I can hear pots clanging in the house behind us; a woman's voice, calling something to her husband. The back door hangs open; she must feel very safe to let her son play outside at night, in such weather. That, or she is relieved to have him away from her.

Grant and I crawl into the plastic tent. It smells like dirty socks, and the ground is wet beneath us. The boy is stretched out flat on his back, held down by Zee and Raw. His mouth is covered. Dark aura aside, he looks frightened and angry, and so very young.

I hate this. I hate this part so much.

Aaz carefully peels back a layer of cut sod and reaches beneath to dig one-handed in the dirt. There is no light, but my eyes are good. I see him pull something furry from the ground. A squirrel wrapped in duct tape, with only its head and tail still free. The little thing is dead now, but I have a very bad feeling it was still breathing when placed in all that dirt. I also have a feeling there might be more little bodies buried around us. I see tools inside the tent.

There is barely enough space. I lay down on one side of the boy, while Grant crouches on the other, putting down his cane. The zombie child's eyes roll white in his head when he sees me, but when he looks at Grant a shudder races through his slender frame, a violent shiver that makes his heels drum against the ground. He starts to fight. Aaz sits on his ankles.

"The boy knows you," I murmur, watching emotion flicker across Grant's face. "Why is that?"

Grant says nothing. Uneasy, I press my palm against the zombie child's forehead. I can feel the demon inside of him, curled like a fist around his soul, and I coax it up and up to the surface of his mind. I do not know exactly how; only, I feel a hook in my hands, a hook I send through flesh to snag and prick. A trick my mother taught me. I use it to snare the darkness and hold it in place.

But the boy still stares at Grant. I feel like a second fiddle—a real first for me—and I glance at Zee, who is also watching the man. His red eyes are thoughtful, which is dangerous for everyone. Grant merely looks upset. He reaches into the slender black case he looped over his shoulder and pulls out a slender wooden flute.

"What are you doing?" I ask him. Grant hesitates. Zee makes a low sound in his throat, while the zombie boy arches his back in a muffled scream, staring at that flute like it is a red-hot brand.

I do not have time for this. I mutter words my mother taught me—gibberish, strange, more music than speech—and the boy's eyes flutter shut into sleep. Just the boy, though, the host. The demon begins to fight like crazy beneath my hand, but with no body to control, it is helpless. I drag my palm away from the child's forehead, like drawing out a rope of thick snot, and I grimace as I pull and pull, waiting for that *snap*, that break from the child's soul.

When it comes, Zee pounces. He stuffs the demon inside his mouth. I can hear it screaming.

"Come on," I mutter, breathless. "We're done here."

But Grant does not move. He keeps staring at the boy.

"His aura," he murmurs. "It's still dark, Maxine."

The boy, in my eyes, appears clean—but the only auras I can see are those that belong to demons.

"He is not a good child," I say to Grant. "There's nothing you can do about it."

But Grant lifts the flute to his lips, and before I can stop him, he breathes into the instrument. I hear a note. Just one, and it shoots through me like a blade of ice dropped from the top of my head to the soles of my feet. My fingers tingle. He plays another note, soft as a dream, and then more and more, the music whispering through the air as though poured from a fairy tale of moon dust and starlight. Zee and the others push against me, growling. The child, resting on the ground, stirs and mumbles.

Grant stops playing. He is breathing hard, his eyes wild, and I hear him murmur, "Better," just as the back door of the house slams open.

"Peter!" calls the child's mother, her voice tentative, hollow. "Peter, it's time to come in."

I stop breathing. Grant clamps his mouth shut. The boys go still. The woman says the child's name again, her voice dropping almost to a whisper, and I cringe as I hear her move across the grass toward the tent. I wave at Grant and hold up one finger. At the same time, I tap Aaz on the shoulder. When he looks at me, I cover my eyes, then my mouth. The little demon nods and disappears into the shadows of the tent. Raw follows him.

A moment later I hear a muffled scream. I scrabble for the tent entrance, hauling Grant after me. Katherine Campbell is down face-first on the grass, squirming and fighting as Aaz sits on her back with his little hand clamped around her mouth. Raw holds down her legs, the long spikes of his spine raised in agitation.

Grant and I run. We run down the path, down the driveway, down the sidewalk to my car, arms pumping, cane tapping, breath rasping in the cool night air. I hear a distant scream just as I unlock our doors, and then we are in and all the boys are there, slipping from the shadows to crowd into the backseat. I start that engine and go.

No one talks. Not at first. Even the boys are quiet. I glance back and find them all staring at the Grant. And his flute.

"So," he finally says, clearing his throat. "That's an exorcism."

I want to kill him. I see a McDonald's and swerve into the parking lot, choosing a spot as far from all the other cars as possible. I slam on the brake, cut the engine, and turn. Grant stares at me. I point at the flute.

Zee, in the backseat, makes a sound and waves his claws over his mouth.

"Spit him out," I tell the demon, though my eyes never leave Grant's face. I hear a wet smack, the sound of drool being slurped back into a mouth. A very tiny snarl.

I look. Held in Zee's gray fist is a wisp of nothing; dark air, shadows congealing into a writhing smoke that pulses and pounds. The boys gather around like cats to a mouse. I reach beneath my seat, pull the lever, and slide back until I am practically in the back with them. Dek and Mal uncoil from around my neck for a better look, and I put my face right up to Zee's fist, keenly aware of Grant watching, his knuckles white around his cane and flute.

The demon stops struggling, its wispy body settling into still air, a hiss. "Hunter Kiss."

"Yes," I whisper. "If you know who I am, you know what this means."

A high fine snarl fills the car. "Talk or torture. No choice."

"No choice," I agree. "None at all."

The demon screams and screams, but I have been through this before, and I know eventually the screaming will stop. I think of my mother as it wails. I think of holding my mother's body, drenched in her blood, sitting in a wet hot pool with nothing and no one, feeling my own scream building, my own scream cutting, and I remember the boys snarling in the backyard, the boys hunting, the boys killing. I remember them coming into the kitchen covered in a different person's blood. Zombie blood. Human blood. I remember them weeping blood. Huddled against the body of the woman who carried them for almost thirty years.

My past, my future. The demon, the little zombie-maker, stops crying.

"Talk to me," I say. "Tell me how you know this man and why you want him dead." I point at Grant, who does not flinch, but looks at me with his jaw set, gaze heavy.

"Piper," rasps the demon. "Twister. Perverter."

"Really." I look at Grant. "All those things?"

"Maxine—"

I cut him off with a wave of my hand and look at the demon. "Give me more."

"He steals us." The smoky air clenched in Zee's fist wavers. "He corrupts us. Takes us from our mother."

"Your mother."

"The Dark Queen," whispers the demon. "Blood Mama."

Blood Mama. I stop breathing. The boys mutter beneath their breath. Grant looks at them, then me. "Who is that?"

"Trouble," I mutter.

"Big bad cutter trouble," Zee adds.

Grant still looks confused. I do not feel sorry for him. "I've told you there are other dimensions, all of them prisons, all of them separated by barriers, veils. On the other side of us is a place called the Blood Sea, which is where *this*"—I jab my finger at the smoky demon—"crossed over from. And the Blood Sea, supposedly, is ruled by a queen. She is, as you can imagine, a demon." And not just any demon. Blood Mama is the most powerful voice of the dark spirits who cross the prison veil. But until tonight, I have never heard her name spoken out loud, only read of it in the diaries kept by my mother and her mother, and all those women before us.

Legend. Another kind of myth.

I look at Grant. "You know what this thing is talking about. Corruption, being stolen away." When he hesitates, I lean right up into his face, searching his eyes. All I see is uncertainty, regret, and it makes my heart ache. Makes me wish, all over again, that this day had never happened.

"Tell me," I whisper. "No games."

"Tell her," rasps the demon softly. "Tell her what you do to us."

Grant sways away from me and takes a deep breath. Holds my gaze as he lifts up his flute, laid flat upon his palms like an offering.

"I make them good," he says in a low voice. "I make those demons very good."

Four

I need to think, and the boys are hungry. I go into the McDonald's. Grant follows. The lights are too bright, the interior looks like it has not been renovated since the early eighties, but the floors and tables are clean and mostly empty. That is all I need. Some quiet normalcy, even if it is nothing more than an illusion.

"I'm sorry," Grant says. I ignore him and wait for someone to come to the cash register.

"Maxine." He leans on the counter, forcing me to look at him. "It's not like you told me all your secrets."

"I asked if you knew why *demons* might want to kill you. And you said *no*. You lied."

"I evaded. There's a difference."

"Whatever. Man of God, my ass."

"Former," he snaps. "Give me a chance to explain."

Someone clears her throat, and I find a girl standing behind the register, staring at us like we are some kind of circus act. I wonder what Grant and I look like together. The thought irritates me. I start tapping the plastic counter with my fingernail. Grant covers my hand and holds me there when I try to jerk away.

The girl frowns. "Um, are you guys going to order?"

"I'm buying," Grant says.

"Serves you right," I mutter, and ask the girl for twenty double cheeseburgers, twenty apple pies, twenty sets of fries, and four Sprites. I am not a complete bitch. I order off the dollar menu.

I keep expecting Grant to protest. He never does. The cheeseburgers make his mouth twitch, the pies make it curve, and the French fries tug a slow blooming smile from his lips that is just so damn beautiful I cannot look away.

When I order the drinks he laughs, a deep and masculine rumble, and by the time that sound travels down my spine into my stomach, I am not quite so angry anymore. A miracle. This man is no good for me.

"Is any of that for you?" Grant asks. I shake my head, and he sighs, pointing at the menu. "Anything you want?"

"Fudge sundae," I hear myself say.

"Make it two," Grant tells the girl, and glances at me as he takes out his debit card. "This, apparently, is how I'm going to celebrate the second nervous breakdown of my life."

"What was the first?" The order total is quite high. I watch him swipe his card. "I'll pay you back for this, by the way."

"No," he says firmly, then leans close and presses his mouth to my ear. "The first has to do with a certain change of profession I had some years back. I think you might know what I'm talking about."

The heat of his breath against my skin is electric, crazy, though I manage to scrape together enough brain cells to look him in the eye. Grant brushes a strand of hair away from my face. His fingers linger, trailing a path down my cheek.

"I'm sorry," he says again, so softly I can barely hear him. "I was not trying to play you for a fool. I was not trying to deceive you. I wasn't even certain there was a connection, though I began to suspect."

"You could have told me."

"I didn't know you."

"You still don't," I whisper. The girl behind the counter clears her throat and slides the fudge sundaes toward us, giving notice that it will take about ten minutes for our order to be completed.

We pick up our sundaes and walk to a battered table next to the window. I look out at my car. Everything seems normal. Everything in the McDonald's appears normal, too. No dark auras. No zombies. Dek and Mal purr against my scalp.

The fudge sundae tastes good. It has been a long time since I have had one. A long time, too, since I sat with someone over a meal. I wish it could be under better circumstances. I study Grant, watching him concentrate on his food. I want to smooth away the furrow between his eyes. "Tell me what you do. Tell me why those demons are upset enough to risk their hosts and kill you."

"It's complicated. I didn't know I was putting myself into danger." Grant shoves a heavy spoonful of soft serve into his mouth and swallows. "You remember what I said about music and color? Auras? Well, aura reflects personality, the core of who and what a person is, and I learned early on how to look at someone and know their heart based on nothing more than energy. Helps in other ways, too. If someone lies to me, for instance, I can tell."

"And the connection to the demons?"

"That's where it gets complicated. In my mid-twenties I discovered I could use music to . . . change the colors I saw. Change the . . . language . . . of a person's personality."

I set down my spoon. "Mind control?"

Grant hesitates. "I don't know. Based on the people I've affected, all I seem to do is give a shift in perspective. A new way of looking at things. A choice."

"That boy tonight. What choice did you give him?"

His expression darkens. "The child was sick, just like you and Zee said. His aura did not change when you took the demon from him. It simply became more . . . transparent. All I did was infuse that darkness with color, as much of it as I could in the time I had. It might last, if the boy is willing to let it, but auras and personalities are like muscles, Maxine. The more you commit yourself to a certain way of being, the harder it is to turn away from it. You keep wanting to flex."

"And you're sure this works?"

"Better with some than others. And not just humans." Grant gives me a rueful smile that does nothing to smooth the stress lines in his forehead. "Those things want me dead. What just happened in the car confirmed the reason. It's because I can change them, Maxine. Give them a choice to be something different."

I almost laugh, but only to cover the sickness in my throat. "No such thing as a choice like that. Not for demons. Not for *those* demons. Born evil, bred evil. You can't change what they are, no matter how hard you try. And if you do, the reason they change will not be through free will. Not through choice. Not anything close."

"And Zee and the others? Are you going to condemn them, too?"

"They're different."

"But were they always different?" Grant leans forward, narrowing his eyes. "How do you know, Maxine? How can you be so sure?"

"Because there's no alternative." My voice is hard, cold. "Not for what I do."

"Which is?"

I do not answer him. I had a purpose, once, and I suppose I still do—but there is no destiny screaming in my ear. I am just a girl. A girl with a horde of demons living on her body. A killer.

"Maxine," he says.

"Every prison needs a guard," I tell him.

"I thought this wasn't a prison."

"It might as well be. That, or a feeding ground. Humans aren't equipped to protect themselves against demons."

"But you are," he says, thoughtful. "Do you have help?"

I think of my mother. "The boys."

"No. More than them."

I remember cake and candles, white frosting sprayed with blood. "I'm the only one. There are no other Hunters." No others at all, not for centuries. I am the very last of the human hybrids created to act as wardens, guards, and protectors of this soft sweet spot inside the prison rings. And while I do not know much about *how* I exist, I do know this: I am not enough.

"You've seen some of what I do." I force myself to hold his gaze. "I hunt demons. I kill as many of them as I can find."

"Just like that? So easy?"

"Yes."

"Liar." Grant traces the air above my head. "You're no murderer."

Murderer. The word hurts. No good pretending otherwise. It is a word wrapped in guilt and fear, a lingering unease that has followed me no matter how hard I try to shoot it down. My mother never questioned herself—not to me—but *murder* is a word I dream of often. Murder is an old nightmare.

I dig my nails into my thigh. "Demons are parasites. Predators. In simplest terms, they are hardwired to cause humans pain, because that is what keeps them alive. So I kill them. I kill them because *they* kill. I hunt them because *they* hunt. If I find a demon looking for a host, I cut it dead. If I find a demon inside a host, I force it out and do the same. The boys are my weapons, but I am the assassin. And after seeing the damage those demons leave behind—the broken homes, the strings of murders and rape victims, children molested and neglected—I consider it a *public service*."

Grant's gaze remains steady, unwavering. "So you're helping others. But are you helping yourself? What price do *you* pay, Maxine? Only psychopaths take lives without conscience, and you're no psycho. I can tell that much. So it must be costing you something, even if you're just . . . killing demons."

"What's the alternative? Your way?"

"Maybe."

"Maybe," I murmur bitterly. "You wouldn't say that if you had experienced what I have. You wouldn't dream of it."

"Then tell me," he says, searching my face. "Please, Maxine. Help me understand."

"Help you understand what?" I whisper. "How long have you even known these things exist?"

Grant pushes away his sundae. "I wasn't sure they did. Not until today. All I knew for certain was that people who had dark auras—no matter how kind or gentle they acted—had an equal darkness in their hearts. So I tried to fix them. First with words, my counsel, and then with music."

"You were with the Church at the time? How did you find out you could change people?"

"An accident. I was playing my flute, and someone

wandered into my vicinity. A particularly disturbed man, an older fellow who hung around the Church. Not possessed, just crazy. He stopped to listen to me, and I remember thinking, *I wish I could help him.* Not long after, I saw the colors of my music inside his aura. And he changed, Maxine. For a little while." Grant stares at his hands. "I experimented. Maybe it was wrong of me. I prayed, asked for guidance—forgiveness, even—but I couldn't help myself."

"Power will do that."

"Maybe." Grant gives me a bitter smile. "I might have been seduced by my hold over people. I like to think that I wasn't. I did, after all, try to help."

"I'm not casting blame. Just saying." I rub my face, weary. "And the possessed? How did you encounter them?"

"Also by accident. Sometimes, not always, I would find two distinct auras in the same individual, layered on top of the other. And by fixing one, I could fix the other."

"Tell me what you mean by fix."

"For all intents and purposes, every 'possessed' man and woman I played for, the ones who had the double auras, who demonstrated the most destructive tendencies, suddenly . . . stopped. Not overnight, and not without a persistent dose of my music, but I saw acts of compassion where I couldn't have found any before, shifts in lifestyle and interaction that were so radically different, and so . . . beneficial . . . that it was like a whole new personality took over."

"And then?" I lean close. "What made you leave the Church?"

Pain flashes through his face, so sharp I reach out and touch his hand, but before I can say anything to him, two girls wearing McDonald's uniforms arrive with our bags of food. I tell them to leave it all on the table nearby, which they do, watching us warily. Grant does not seem to notice. When the girls are gone, I move around the table and sit beside him. I stay quiet, waiting.

"I thought I had a gift," he finally says. "A true gift from God, something that could allow me to help people in a very real way. So I told a friend. A very trusted friend, a fellow priest."

"He betrayed you."

"In a way. He refused to believe me. At first. But I was so naive, so stupid, and I kept at him until he finally did believe. Only, instead of seeing it as a gift, he became convinced that it was the work of the Devil, that I had become possessed by . . . dark and arcane powers. It was crazy, Maxine. I felt like I was in the middle of the Inquisition, and it made no sense. I hadn't done anything wrong. I had only helped people."

"They didn't hurt you, did they?"

Grant's jaw tightens. "They wanted to exorcise me. They wanted to drive the music out of me. They said I was stealing free will. And maybe I was. Maybe I still am. But they called it the work of the Devil. Even sent someone from the Vatican to cleanse me."

My mouth curves into a faint smile. "Did he?"

Grant leans against me. "Guess not. I ran away before he arrived. Hardest choice of my life, but I had to go."

"Did you have family to turn to?"

Grant shakes his head and takes a bite of his sundae. He gives me his spoon. I go for the fudge. "I don't have much family, Maxine. After I left the Church, I went to Europe and followed a line around the world. Italy, Israel, India, Nepal, China. I even lived with a Navajo Shaman for a time. Everywhere I went, I tried to learn more about life, about all the different ways to believe in a higher power. And when I finally made my home—here, in Seattle—I had enough confidence in myself to believe that whatever I was, it was my choice to be good or evil. My choice to uplift or destroy. And I chose the light."

"And part of that light is converting demons."

"Like I said, I didn't know that's what they were. Despite my former calling, I always questioned the dark side of my religion. I did not want to believe in true evil. I thought it was just . . . an excuse, a way to cast blame away from bad deeds. The Devil made me do it. Blah."

"But you suspected something before tonight. You must have. You were too calm. Even after seeing the boys come off my body, you were too calm."

Grant hesitates. "Before I left the Church, I encountered one of the people I had helped. I could see that something had changed. One of the auras was darker than the other. Like it was reverting. When I tried to fix it, that second shadow . . . ran."

"Ran."

"Left the body and disappeared. And when it did, there was only one aura left."

I lean back in my chair. Grant's sundae is gone, but he keeps scraping the plastic cup with his spoon. I reach across the table for my unfinished ice cream and slide it over to him. He takes it with a raised brow, but I wave him on, and that is that. No more soft serve. Grant stabs his spoon into the cup. I wait for a moment, just watching him.

"You really think you can change those demons?" I ask him quietly.

"I'd like to believe so."

"And you still call it free will? Their choice?"

"I don't know." He looks at me, and his eyes are tired. "But if they are as bad as you make them out to be, does it matter?"

Yes, I say to myself, and not because I fear for the rights of demons. I am only afraid for myself. Because if demons can change, if they can—through choice or force—be altered in a way that takes away their ability to harm humans, then what am I? What am I, except a true murderer?

I close my eyes. Grant says my name. When I do not answer him, he wraps his arm around my shoulders and pulls me into the curve of his side. It feels natural to lay my hand on his chest. It feels good and safe, and when his lips touch the crown of my head, the heat that travels through my body makes me sigh.

"Maxine," Grant says again. "Tell me."

"What do I tell you?" I murmur, suddenly achingly weary. "There's too much, Grant."

His mouth travels to my temple, pressing light and sweet against my skin. "You said my name again. I like it when you do that."

"You're too easy to please."

"No," he says, kissing me again. "Not at all."

Five

When we go back to the car, dragging our bags of food, there is a police officer waiting for us. He has no aura that I can see, but that does not make me feel better. He is a tall lean man with an olive complexion and a buzz cut. Serious mouth. Suspicious eyes. His cruiser is parked on the other side of the lot, and he is standing so that the Mustang is between him and the McDonald's. I did not see him from inside.

"Are you the owner of this vehicle?" he asks Grant.

"The car is mine." I cannot see through the tinted windows. I wonder if the boys are still in there.

The officer looks at the bags in our hands. "Party?"

"Big eaters," Grant says. "Is there a problem?"

"I have some questions about this Mustang," says the man. "One just like it was seen driving away near the scene of an assault tonight. A place not far from here, in fact."

"That's terrible," Grant says, and damn if he does not sound like he means it, from the bottom of his heart. "Where did it happen?"

"Capitol Hill. Fifth and Tunney."

Grant blinks, frowning. "We were in Capitol Hill not long ago."

"Got a reason why?"

"My friend here is from out of town. She's thinking of moving to the area. We were out for a drive, and I thought I would show her the local neighborhoods." Grant's aura must be flashing fireworks; the man is a master liar. Some priest he must have been.

The officer frowns, his gaze flickering between Grant and me. "Can't see much at night."

"Places have a different feel after dark," I tell him. "You know. Sometimes scary, sometimes not."

He gives me a hard look. "Driver's license?"

I set down my bags and pull a slim leather card case from the back pocket of my jeans. My hand bumps against the hard lump in my jacket; Katherine Campbell's wallet. Shit.

The police officer slides a Mag-lite from his belt and shines it on my license. "You're a long way from home, Ms. . . . Kiss."

"Texas isn't all that far," I tell him, trying to sound winsome, pleasant. He gives me another piercing look and asks for Grant's identification. Turns and strolls back to his vehicle. I hear the static of a radio as he opens his door. He sits inside, one leg hanging out. Works on finding out if we are criminals. Which I am. Not that I have ever been caught.

Of course, there is always a first time for everything.

"Maxine," Grant says, under his breath. "This is not going to turn into an episode of *COPS*, is it?"

"I prefer *Prison Break*, personally."

"Maxine."

"You're an excellent liar," I tell him. "Did you learn that in priest school?"

"Try kindergarten," he mutters, and then, softer, "He's coming back."

I steady myself, Dek and Mal shifting beneath my hair. I see a flicker of movement beneath the Mustang; the tip of a claw, wagging at me. I look away and force myself to greet the police officer with a questioning smile. Dumb, sweet, and hopelessly innocent.

No effect. His expression is impossibly grim. He hands back our driver's licenses and gives the cane a fleeting glance before meeting Grant's eyes. "Sorry. You can go now."

Grant and I look at each other. The officer shifts his feet, a distinctly uncomfortable expression passing over his face. "Gilda says hello."

"Gilda." Grant blinks. "Ah. I remember her. Is she . . . doing well?"

"She's good in dispatch. Got a mouth on her, though."

"Feisty. But very . . . pious."

The cop grunts. "She, uh, recognized your name when I called it in. Gave me an earful." He backs away, giving me one last distrustful look before tipping his chin at Grant. "Have a good evening, Father Cooperon. Ma'am."

"Um," Grant says, but thankfully, lets it go. And just like that, we are free. Hallelujah, Amen. The cop gets into his car. I reach for my keys and pretend not to watch him as he drives away. My heart feels like it is going to explode from my chest. This is not the closest I have come to the law since my mother died—but once was more than enough.

"Gilda?" I ask mildly.

"Long story." Grant tilts his head up to the drizzling sky and closes his eyes. "I helped her once."

"Apparently so."

He smiles, but not for long. Just keeps watching the road where that police car disappeared. Shakes himself and takes a deep breath. "Let's go home, Maxine."

He says it so naturally, like I belong with him. Like I have a home. With him. Makes me breathless, though I do not say a word. Just unlock the doors and climb in. The boys melt into the backseat, quiet, and we give them the drinks and food.

The demon, the little zombie maker, is gone. Grant starts to ask, but I shake my head. Better for him not to know. Zee and the boys have sharp teeth. Not even little demon wisps can escape their bites. And, it is enough that there be will be one less possession to cure after tonight. No matter what Grant can do—or how he feels—in the end, that is all that is important.

He gives me directions. I put the car in gear and drive to the sounds of tearing paper, wet slurps. No music, no talk. I remember my mother and I—another night like this—driving and eating through a strange city, surrounded by that odd settled hush that comes from comfortable silence, an easy way.

It has been a long time since I felt that kind of contentment. A very long time.

I look at Grant, the clean lines and shadows of his face. I think of his story, his ability to twist darkness into good. I think of what the demon said.

"Piper," I murmur, and Grant looks at me. "Piper. That's what the demon called you."

The skin around his eyes crinkles. "Piper of the Damned?"

"I was thinking more along the lines of the original Pied Piper. Except with demons instead of rats. Or children."

"Alas, alas, for Hamelin," he says.

We drive. The drizzle turns into a hard rain. Lightning flashes outside the car, a sudden burst of brilliance so close and bright that everyone, even the boys, flinch. Thunder breaks the world, a crack and rumble that rattles the car. I feel it in my chest. Unease crawls up my spine, Zee responding with a low hiss. Nothing happens, though. Nothing springs from the shadows into the road; no strange car follows us. I am on edge, that is all. It has been a bad night.

Grant lives in the warehouse district just outside of Chinatown. An area of old brick, wide panes of glass, the docks and dirty ocean on the other side of I-5. And in the center, a gritty oasis—an upbeat stone building surrounded by old-fashioned pewter lanterns that line a landscaped walkway, which crisscrosses a larger piece of grassy property bordering a gritty burnout of chain link, cracked cement, and broken glass.

Following Grant's instructions, I slow down in front of the main structure, which is cleaner than its neighbors, and rambles into several smaller facilities, one of which looks suspiciously like a church.

I park in the small lot. "What is this place?"

Grant shrugs. "Depends on who you talk to, though it's mainly a homeless shelter. A place for people to get back on their feet."

"And you live here?"

"I own the place." Grant smiles and climbs out of the car, leaning heavily on his cane. I take a moment, staring at his back, and shake my head.

I do not bother grabbing my suitcase from the trunk. I turn up my collar, duck my face against the cold rain, and run after him, jogging down a narrow sidewalk to a plain metal door set within an alcove just off the core building. The boys melt from the shadows beside us, eyes glowing, claws clicking. Keys jingle in Grant's hand.

"I have a private entrance," he says, and then we are inside a dry dark space where the only way forward is up a steep flight of stairs, lit by a dim light somewhere far above us. Grant moves slowly, his cane thunking loudly on each step.

"Were you injured in the hit-and-run you mentioned?" My voice is loud in the hush of the darkness surrounding us. I feel the boys brush past my leg, and I watch the outlines of their sharp spines as they dart ahead to scout and explore.

Grant glances back at me. His eyes are hooded, shrouded in shadow. "All I received from that incident were some scrapes and bruises. The leg happened five years ago. I got on the wrong end of a tire iron."

I suck in my breath. "What happened?"

Grant pauses on the stairs, and I join him, close but not touching. Rainwater drips from the tips of his hair, the air is cold—but his body radiates a heat I feel down to my bones. We stare at each other, soaking in silence.

"There are risks to helping people," he finally says, softly, with an edge of pain. "It's safer to walk away. Turn a blind eye. You know that better than anyone."

"I do." I hesitate, then reach up and touch his wet cheek. Grant closes his eyes. His skin feels bristly, hot. So good. "People are never who they seem. Not even to themselves."

He captures my hand and presses my palm to his lips. "But you accept the risks. No choice, no alternative."

"Commitment. Dedication." I edge close, swallowing hard.

"Saving lives," Grant whispers, lowering his head. Our lips touch. Fire spreads down my throat into my breasts, my stomach. His strong arm curls around my waist, hugging me close. I cling to him. I let myself hold and be held, and though I am risking my life, my heart, I do not care. For the first time in my life, I do not give a damn. I want this. I want *him*. I lean in harder, tighter, and Grant makes a sound; low, guttural. He breaks off the kiss. We are both breathing heavy.

"Upstairs," he rasps, and we stumble up together, hands clasped tight. Grant slides his palm against the wall, and lights come on. The brightness hurts my eyes at first, but I can see well enough to take in the pleasantly large room at the top of the stairs. I see large windows of clouded glass, deep couches, and long massive bookshelves; a grand piano, several guitars, and a very large Triumph motorcycle polished to a loving red sheen. No doubt Grant's pride and joy, once upon a time— though I cannot imagine how anyone could have hauled it up those stairs we just climbed.

The room is nice, warm and cozy. It feels like a home, though a bit more luxurious than anything I imagine a former priest being able to afford. The austere life, no more. Grant gave up more than the collar when he left the Church.

I walk to the piano. I have not been near one since I left home, and an ache soars through my throat with the memory of my mother giving me lessons; dark hair tumbling loose over her face, her long neck, brushing it out of her eyes, away from her red mouth. Daytime, her arms bare, skin covered in tattoos that I would trace and trace with my fingers; naming them, crooning lullabies.

I like to think I resemble her. I like to imagine I am as strong.

The boys are prowling. Grant moves close, and his fingers trail a path up my ribs, making me shiver. "Do you play, Maxine?"

"A long time ago." I capture one of his hands against my side and use the other to press down on a high C. The note drifts sweetly in the air. Grant reaches around my body. I go very still as he wraps his hand around my own. When I press down on another note, his hand is still there with me, resting large and heavy on top of my wrist.

"I'd play a duet with you," he whispers in my ear, "but I think that might be dangerous."

I cannot talk. All I can do is nudge his hip, and he sits down, slowly, on the piano bench. I join him, on his lap. Grant makes a sound, low in his throat, and I bite my bottom lip as I move very gently against him, savoring the hard sensation of his body against my own.

I touch the piano. I play a sonata. Grant reaches around me and lays his hands over my hands. I carry him across the music, his mouth touching my ear, my neck, trailing kisses across my skin. I miss a note, then two and three. Grant's hands slip over my skin to the keys, fingers slow and dancing, and for a moment we play together, a duet, sweet and light, until the melody shifts, and I rest my palms on his strong wrists and let him be the one to carry me, rocking us both into music that is mournful and hot, hot like the hard cradle of his body.

Grant finishes the song and wraps his arms around me. I listen to his heartbeat, his slow breathing; more distant, the boys dragging and unzipping, rattling paper. His chest rumbles. "Are they going to burn this building down?"

"Not yet," I murmur, biting back a smile when he laughs, low. His fingers thread through my hair, holding me close, tight, my face pressed near the crook of his neck. His skin smells so good. I touch him with my lips. Grant's breath catches, and then his mouth slides next to mine, light and warm.

"Maxine," he whispers. "I want to take you to my bed."

I close my eyes. Nod my head.

He cannot carry me—his leg is too weak to support that effort—but he clutches me so tight against his side he might as well be carrying me, and we stagger into his bedroom, a clean place with only a bed and little else. The covers are rumpled, unmade, but I do not care. I fall onto the mattress, breathless.

Grant glances around, taking off his jacket. "Where are the boys?"

I look and do not see them. Probably close, though. I reach into my hair and pull out Dek and Mal. Their eyes are very solemn, and when I place them on the floor they slither from the room without hesitation. Grant closes the door. "They're not voyeurs, are they?"

"Not about this," I tell him, though in all honestly, I do not know for certain. I have become too used to not having any privacy in my life.

I swallow hard, watching him. Grant hesitates, then very deliberately walks to the bed and perches on the edge beside me. He twines his hand around my own.

"We don't have to do this," he says quietly. "Not tonight. Not ever, if you don't want."

"Change your mind?" I try to smile, to pretend, but Grant

is not fooled. He kisses my palm and presses it to his chest. Holds it there, watching me with those dark wild eyes.

"I want you," he says, in a voice so low and rough it makes me shudder, makes Grant shudder, both of us shaking against each other like a hard hot wind is blowing through the room.

I almost tell him. I almost tell him what might happen if we do this, but I am afraid he will stop, and I do not want to. Before tonight I would never have thought I could change my mind, break the old promise to myself—not like this, so willingly—but being with this man has changed something inside me. I am no longer afraid. Nor am I resigned, though I would have every right to be. I tell myself I am simply being modern. One-night stand. A friendly roll in the sack. Nothing heavy, even if the consequences are.

But I want this to be my choice, not something the boys make me do. My choice, now. Not later. Grant, and not some other man.

I kiss him. I am awkward, an ugly duckling when it comes to lovemaking, and Grant is little better. All those smooth moves we had for each other fade away as we fumble at each other's clothes, rocking each other down on the bed as we give up trying to yank off shirts and jackets and jeans, settling instead for a tangle of limbs, cradling each other with hot deep kisses that burn so deep I can feel the slow rise of some cresting pleasure, an ache that makes me twist and writhe. Grant murmurs my name, running his fingers through my hair, while my hands trail down his chest to his belt, his button, his fly. I push my hand inside his jeans and swallow down his gasp with a kiss.

Grant breaks away, chest heaving. "Holy God."

I laugh. "Should you be using the Lord's name in vain?"

"No," he rasps, a slow smile spreading. He rolls us, half-pinning me with his body, and his hands touch my hair again, my face, stroking the outline of my cheeks. His eyes are dark, heavy with hunger, but he does not kiss me. Just stays there, poised, drinking me in.

"You shine so bright," he whispers. "I wish you could see what I see, Maxine. I wish you could see how beautiful your spirit is."

"Not possible," I murmur. "Not me. No light."

"You're wrong." Grant kisses the corner of my mouth. "You're good, Maxine. Down to the core of you, good."

Heat fills my eyes, my face; with it, guilt. I place my hands against his chest and try to push him away. Grant resists, holding me down with his hips and hands. A crease furrows deep between his eyes. "Maxine."

"Let me go," I say to him. "Please."

"Tell me," he replies, unmoving. "What's wrong?"

I close my eyes, silent, anger and disappointment stealing away the warmth inside my body. After a moment I feel Grant shift, his arm stealing around my waist and back, turning me so we both lie on our sides. He snakes his leg around my hip and draws me close and snug. Our noses brush; his lips touch my forehead.

"Tell me," he says again.

I cannot look at him. "There's something you should know. About what might happen if we're together. Now, tomorrow, for any length of time." I hesitate, forming the words inside my head, tasting them, finally afraid. Saying it out loud will make it real. "No matter what we do to protect ourselves, chances are good I will become pregnant."

What a mood-killer. Grant blinks. "Pregnant?"

"As in, with child." I shake my head, trying to pull out of his arms. He refuses to let go. I could force him, but I give up, eyes squeezed shut. "It's part of the magic that makes me what I am. It's to keep the women of my line from . . . cheating the boys out of their future."

"Cheating." His voice carries an edge. "Does that mean the boys are passed on, from mother to child?"

"Mother to daughter. Only daughters."

Grant's chest rises and falls; I listen to his silence, his breathing, his heartbeat, my own heart shrinking and shriveling, my skin crawling. I want to run. I should have run the first time I saw this man. I should never have let this go so far. Damn.

"So we would have a child," he says, finally, softly. "What else aren't you telling me?"

I cannot lie. I could say nothing at all, but I do not want to hurt Grant, to do him the disservice of distrust. I want to believe he is a friend. I want to live the illusion that such a thing is possible for me. To have a friend, even it means he no longer wants me in his bed.

"It's hard," I tell him, my voice breaking on the words. "The moment I have a child my death sentence is signed. I might have a decade, maybe two, but not much longer than that. And I won't die in my sleep. I'll be murdered. Like my mother was, and her mother, and her mother before that. A single line of women running so far behind me I can't see the beginning of them. All victims of a violent end."

Grant flinches, his arms tightening around me. "No."

"Yes. One day the boys will stop protecting me. They will abandon me for my child. And when that happens, the demons I have spent my life hunting will know, and they will kill me. It's the price we pay for the protection we are given. The boys . . . the boys have to survive. And I'm not immortal. I'll get old, maybe sick, and if I die of natural causes before the boys have made the switch . . ."

"They'll die, too?"

"I wasn't always the only Hunter. There were others, a long time ago."

"You could rebel. You could . . . stay celibate."

The catch in his voice almost makes me laugh. "I've done that, but it won't last forever. The boys will make sure I get pregnant. Might hold me down and force a man inside me. Might threaten to take a life if I don't find a man to have sex with. It's happened to some of the other women in my family. Sometimes I wonder if they didn't do that to my mother."

"You said she died."

"Shot in the head. Right in front of me."

Grant shudders. I force myself to look at him, but instead of fear, dismay, all I see is anger, a terrible white-hot fury so chilling I cannot see past the pale of his cheeks, the line of his lips, the cold heat of his eyes.

"You love them," he says in hard voice. "Despite that, you still care about them."

"Family," I whisper. "Family cuts, but it's thicker than blood. They live because of me, and I live because of them. I can't hate them, Grant. Not even for how my mother died. How I'll die. They're too much a part of who I am."

He takes a deep breath, pushing it out, slow. "So if we do this, I'll become a father."

"Probably." I hesitate. "I didn't want to tell you."

"Because you didn't think we would be together long enough for me to find out you're carrying my child? Or because you didn't think I would want to be with you if I knew the truth?" He snorts, some color finally returning to his face. "You don't know me at all, Maxine."

"Sorry," I mutter, my eyes burning, burning like my cheeks, my throat. "I'm so sorry, Grant."

"No." His lips find my forehead again, his hands pushing back my hair, cradling my face. "No, Maxine. This is not your fault. And this is not anything to be scared of. We'll make this work. We'll figure something out. I am not going to let you die before your time."

"You can't stop that."

"There's time," he whispers. "If you want to try."

He almost makes me believe. If faith could be a gift, then this man is capable of giving in spades. But I am afraid, and I do not have his faith, or his belief in my future. I know what I am, and all I have is the present, the past. And it does not matter that the hope in his eyes, his conviction, is addictive. Intoxicating.

I swallow hard. "I am not your responsibility, Grant."

"But you were willing to have a baby with me. Some last-minute choice, huh?" His jaw tightens. "Don't you think I knew what I was getting myself into?"

"No," I say flatly. "I really don't think you did."

"So I didn't know all of it. But I considered at least one possible consequence." His hand slides off my waist and presses gently against my stomach, his voice dropping to a whisper. "Maybe this is rash of me, too. Maybe I could step back, wait another day. Cool off, think this through. Not put you in danger."

"I understand," I murmur, unable to look at him. "Good idea."

"No." He tilts up my chin. "You don't get it, do you? I can't walk away, Maxine. And not . . . not because I want to . . . to just have sex with you. And not because I want to hurt you. Not that. Just the opposite."

"You don't know me, Grant."

"You don't know me, either. Not really. So why are *you* here? Why, when the risks are so great?"

"Because I want you," I whisper. "And I'm not afraid to want you. It feels . . . right."

"No matter what?"

"No matter what," I tell him. "Even if it's just for a night."

"Okay," he breathes. Just like that. *Okay.*

I search his eyes. "You're so calm. Why are you always so calm?"

Grant never answers me. Just wraps his hand around the back of my neck and presses his lips against mine, taking me under with an achingly tender kiss. I almost pull away, almost fight him, but I give up and press against his body, doing everything in my power not to think about what I am doing, to not second-guess myself. No future. Just here. Now. Him.

I stop shaking after our clothes are gone. I stop shaking when I touch him. I stop shaking when he touches me, though another kind of quake rushes through my body as his palms caress my breasts, my stomach, between my thighs. He is a big man, a strong man, though his right leg is the only sore spot; a mangle of muscle and bone, twisted, skinny. I kiss it. I kiss it with my mouth, my fingertips, my hair tumbling over my face to trail a path up his skin. He shivers and groans, writhing beneath me as my tongue finds more to love, hard and hot and long.

And then, somehow, we are inside each other, and there is a bit of pain but nothing more, nothing but a full heavy pleasure as we move against each other, again and again, riding ourselves higher, together, and it feels so good I think I cry out. I think he does the same, neither of us lasting long at all. But we rest, and we touch, and not much later, begin again.

Lost time, Grant calls it.

Not enough time, I say.

In the wee hours of morning, just before dawn, I feel the boys crowd close beneath the covers and hug my naked body. Grant is spooned behind me, snoring softly.

"Sleep," Zee breathes into my ear. "Sleep as we sleep, Maxine. And dream."

I do as he says, and the next time I open my eyes I see sunlight through the window.

My skin is covered in tattoos.

Six

Grant is gone from the bed, but I do not feel particularly abandoned. Not after last night. I roll free of the covers, taking a moment to stare at the chaos behind me. My body is sore, my knees weak. The memories make me smile, though not for long. There are condom wrappers everywhere on the floor, but that is no guarantee when it comes to me. Or at least, that was my mother's warning—the same warning that has ever been written in the old family diaries. I have always been slightly amazed at the lengths my ancestors went to in an attempt to prevent conception. Always failing, though I have to question the resources at their disposal. Maybe this time will be different. Maybe it does not matter. Not anymore.

The door swings open. Grant walks in, dressed in sweats and nothing else. He is leaning on his cane, but in his free hand carries a white mug of something that smells like coffee.

He stops when he sees me, and the appreciation in his eyes makes me smile. I go to him, walking slow, with a sway to my hips that I never thought I would be capable of achieving.

"Love the body art," he murmurs. "Not sure I care much for who makes it."

I glance down. My skin is entirely covered in tattoos:

shades of silver and obsidian, scaled ripples of muscle and limb and tangled claw; here, there, a red eye and a curling fang. The boys cover me from the bottoms of my feet to the pads of my fingertips to the tips of my breasts. I do not have a mirror, but I know the intricate labyrinth of dark lines and bodies ends at the top of my neck, beneath my hair. That my face is clear is a conceit on my part, though in the daytime I am still as protected there, as anywhere else.

Grant hands me the coffee, leaning close to kiss my mouth. His fingers trail down my throat, between my breasts.

"Feels like skin," he says. "Is that really them?"

"In all their glory."

"And you don't know how?"

I shake my head, sipping the coffee. "No one does. There are stories of why, some of which stray into legend more than truth. That humans were first and that the demons came, offering a choice. I don't suppose it matters what kind of choice, just that humans made the wrong one and invited the darkness into their lives. Bad times, after that. And then the Hunters were made, the barriers went up, and all the violence and strife left behind belonged solely to humans. No blame left to cast, except on themselves. And eventually us, the people trying to protect them. Hunters. Demon-runners. Unholy."

Grant frowns. "And there was never any mention of God in those stories? A higher power?"

"I suppose. But not . . . in a direct way."

"Someone made you, though. The barriers, too. The demons didn't go away on their own."

"It took power to do that," I concede. "Immense power."

"But you're not convinced."

"I don't believe in Satan, either," I tell him. "As ironic as that might sound."

"Very. But you do believe there is a ruler over those demons. The Dark Queen."

"She rules only some of them. And there's a difference. One is myth, archetype. The other is real."

"Real as far as you know."

"As far as I've been told. By those she commands."

Grant shrugs, a small smile forming at the corner of his

mouth. "I've never questioned the existence of God. Just the Devil. I've changed my opinion."

"Have you?" I ask him. "And do you think you could convert the epitome of evil, in the same way you think you can change its followers?"

"No," Grant says, after a brief hesitation. "I know my limits."

"Maybe." I smile, trying to take the bite out of my words, and bend down to pick up my jeans. He clears his throat and my smile widens. I like this. Being with someone.

Grant takes the coffee from me, kicks away the jeans with his good leg, and takes me to the bed. We fool around for a while, abandoning the mattress for the shower. There's a plastic seat in the stall to ease the pressure off his leg. I have a good time straddling his lap, though I do not take him inside me. No more condoms. I find other ways to make him call out my name, until Grant twists me so that I face away from him, spreading my legs wide with his hands. He proceeds to return the favor, many times over.

I dress in my jeans and steal an Old Navy sweatshirt from the bottom of Grant's closet. He is in the bathroom, shaving. My hair is wet, tangled, but I tie it into a bun and leave the bedroom, walking barefoot into another world of sunlight and glass and hardwood floors. I notice little things that escaped me the night before; masks and photographs on the brick walls, rocks and sticks and other knickknacks scattered on the tiny tables placed like islands around the couches. Homey touches that remind me of the old farmhouse I shared with my mother, a place I have not returned to in the years since she died. The day after I buried her, I placed all our furniture into storage, locked the diaries and papers in the bank, threw a suitcase into the Mustang, and just took off. Like the old Bon Jovi song. On a steel horse I ride. Wanted dead or alive.

Tall bookcases take up most of the room. Grant's reading material is mainly religious in nature, but not just about Christianity. I see shelves devoted to Judaism, Islam, Buddhism, and Shamanic faiths; myths and legends, archaic texts with odd titles I cannot pronounce, some of which are not even in English.

I hear Grant's cane, but do not turn around until he is directly behind me. I smile. "Some library you have."

"I might have left the priesthood, but not my faith. Even if it has . . . changed over the years."

I say nothing. I am no expert on matters of faith. Being with Grant is the closest I will ever come to such a thing.

We leave his apartment, walking slowly down the stairs and out the metal door. The sun is shining, and the air smells fresh, with only a hint of the sea and the docks. Up and down the street I see row after row of ramshackle brick warehouses, some of which seem to still be in use. Others are under construction. I see billboards announcing the imminent arrival of upscale lofts.

The property I am standing on looks far bigger in the daytime. It also appears to have had its own revival. I glance at Grant. "You own this place? Seems as though it would be pretty pricey for a former priest."

"We both inherited from our parents." Grant points at the squat brick buildings around us. "My mother died from cancer when I was in high school, and my father drank himself to death after she was gone. He had money, though, and the foresight to put a stipulation in his will stating that all his property would be held in trust for me until I left the Church."

"Wasn't he happy you became a priest?"

"Hated the idea. He thought there was too much hypocrisy. And perverts."

"Nice image."

Grant shrugs. "It was a lot of money. Still is. When I was done traveling it didn't seem enough to just live somewhere like a fat cat. I wanted to do more. And this area, five years ago, was a wasteland. I bought this block cheap and converted the space into a shelter and social services office."

"And let me guess . . . you give free concerts, nightly."

He looks at me sideways. "It's helping, Maxine. You wouldn't believe the number of people who have significantly turned their lives around."

"You're walking a fine line, Grant."

"I know," he says. "I know."

Outside, I do not see much in the way of people except for two elderly men in battered overalls who emerge from a back door around the side of the main building off Grant's apartment block. They carry buckets full of gardening tools and greet Grant with big smiles. They look at me with equal, if only slightly less-trusting gazes—focusing briefly on my exposed throat, my hands and forearms, which are dark with those wild tattoos. The men nod once, like it means something, then putter off down the sidewalk with shuffles that are stooped and worn and bespeak old nagging aches in muscle and bone.

From behind the nearby door I hear pots banging, cheerful whistling. I smell grease. Grant, biting back a smile, opens the door for me.

There is a kitchen on the other side—industrial in size and design, with a clean black-and-white tile floor and shining stainless steel appliances. A woman stands at the wide double sink. She is tiny, almost frail, with a nose that resembles a rock slide, full of old breaks and scars. Everything else about her is delicate: her chin, her pale skin, her long hair that is a snowy shade of white. Bangles sing as she moves, and under her arm she holds a small potted plant that bears a suspicious resemblance to cannabis. When the old woman sees us, she lets out a cry.

"Grant!" She dances to him on light feet, her little plant bobbing and weaving as she floats across the floor.

"Mary," he replies, in a voice just as dramatic and grandiose. "Mary, my lamb. It has been only a day, and yet I am nigh swooning for your company."

She giggles, a sound that is surprisingly girlish. "Fred was terribly concerned when you didn't show last night, Grant. I told him not to be, but he gets so caught up."

"Typical." Grant strokes the delicate leaf of the plant she holds out to him. "Fred, what have I told you? I need my own life. So does Mary. You have to let go."

Too late, I think, but the old woman turns her gaze on me, followed by a smile so bright I think it must be carved of sunshine, and she throws her free arm around my shoulders in a hug fierce enough to enter my bones.

"Greetings!" she cries. "So lovely. Who are you?"

"Maxine," I say, wondering when and if it might be polite to disentangle myself from the wiry arm crushing my body.

"Maxine," echoes Mary. "A very strong name. So manly. How nice for you! Please, say hello to Fred."

"Um." I stare at the little plant, and glance at Grant, who is standing behind the old woman. He makes a shooing motion with his hand.

I touch one little leaf and shake it gingerly. "Greetings . . . Fred."

Mary beams. "Would you like something to eat? I'm preparing lunch for all our lost souls. Grant says no one does it better." She leans close, voice dropping to a whisper. "It's because I cook with the love of the Holy Spirit, my dear."

"And, occasionally, some other illegal substances that I hope, sweet Mary, do *not* inadvertently enter today's dessert. Yes?" Grant's smile has an edge. All I can do is stare.

"Oh, of course, Grant." Mary smiles sweetly. "None of Fred's brethren have been sacrificed for today's meal. I take sin seriously."

"That's good," Grant says. "Now, if you'll excuse us, I have more to show Maxine."

"Ah!" Mary releases me. "Good-bye!"

"Bye," I say weakly, and let Grant steer me from the kitchen into another large room filled with tables and empty chairs and oversize windows. I glance over my shoulder at the metal door swinging shut behind us.

"Wow," I breathe. "Was that a cannabis plant she made me pet?"

"Yup," Grant mutters. "She keeps getting the seeds, and I keep making her get rid of the plants. She's stubborn that way."

"And the prospect of arrest doesn't phase her? At all?" Grant just looks at me, and I shrug. "Fine. Is she another one of your experiments?"

He grunts. "How old do you think Mary is?"

"Pushing seventy."

"Not even close. She's only forty-two, Maxine."

"You're kidding."

He shakes his head. "You're seeing her good side. Mary was in terrible shape when she got here. Lost cause, was the general consensus. But I could see she had a good core, so I did my best. Not that it means she'll ever make a full recovery. I think what you just saw is as good as it's going to get."

"She lives here full time?"

Grant smiles. "She livens the place up."

"Apparently so. And last night? Gilda?"

"Former prostitute and drug addict."

"Huh." I smile. "You're a knight in shining armor, Grant Cooperon."

He hugs me against his side. "And you are my lady, Maxine Kiss."

"Yeah," I murmur, all warm. "What a pair."

Grant laughs, leaning down to kiss me, but just as our lips touch, I hear a loud echoing bang, followed by angry shouts.

"That's coming from the men's ward," Grant says, and I do not wait for him; I run, moving swiftly out of the mess hall down a long winding corridor decorated with framed movie posters and bulletin boards organized by want ads and announcements. I glance over my shoulder; Grant is behind me, limping heavily—forehead wrinkled, mouth twisted. He does not tell me to stop.

I hear more shouts, hard language, the crash and shatter of something large, and I slam open a set of metal double doors, rushing into a space full of cots and tables, sofas, yet more windows—and a group of men beating the living shit out of someone. I take a step, prepared to yell, but my voice catches like thorns in my throat.

All the men have auras. All the men are zombies.

I do not know who sees me first, but the fighting suddenly stops—frozen—and every head snaps around to look at me. I see bodies on the ground, bleeding out, needing help, and I do not think—I do not question. I run toward those possessed men. I run fast.

I have never used a weapon against a zombie. No guns, no knives—I have no quarrel with human hosts—but as I near the men I see a flash of steel. Behind me Grant shouts, and I brace myself as a knife arcs down into my gut.

The blade breaks. I stagger. The zombie in front of me takes a step back, all of them staring, confusion and recognition flickering in their eyes. Seven, all shrouded in crowns of darkness that flicker and pulse. Hard gazes. Makes me wonder, again, what it is to be possessed and not realize it. To have a creature inside your head, whispering, compelling urges, and not be able to turn it off. To have it with you and with you until your body becomes nothing but a tool, a living and breathing illusion of free will—a game of manipulation.

Prisoners, puppets, pawns. I suppose I am not much different. Though maybe that can change. Faith is contagious.

I hold up my hands, palms out, staring down the men, all of whom have history etched into their bodies; tattoos, hungry hollows, sinew and leather for skin. They look strong, but it is their minds that are the weapons. The will and intent of the demons inside of them.

"Hunter Fucking Kiss," mutters one of the zombies, a man with a red wool cap pulled down hard over his grizzled head. He makes a move, but I do not give him the benefit of a good feint. I grab his wrist and twist, driving him to his knees as I slam my free palm against his forehead and hold it there, chanting, watching the man's eyes roll white, fluttering like a hard current is sizzling through his lashes. He tries to break free, but the boys are strong in my body, and it is nothing to hold him. I hook the demon and get ready to pull. The other zombies stand watching, none willing to lift a hand to help their brother.

I want to know why they are not running. Not running, like those zombies at Pike Place Market.

Cold fear slams my gut. I am so stupid. I hear Grant hobbling close, and I scream at him to stop. He does not. He stands in the doorway, staring, eyes hard, unforgiving, the slant of his mouth so cold I feel a chill when I look at him. No demon has ever frightened me, but Grant—right at that moment—comes close.

"What is this?" His voice is low, commanding. My skin tingles when I hear him, a prickly rush that reminds me of that first note from his flute. Like something is opening, shifting. *Magic*, I think. *Power.*

"Grant," I say, trying to stay calm. "Grant, turn around and walk out of here. Go to a secure room and lock the door. *Please.* Do it now."

He ignores me, limping forward, and I shove away the zombie in front of me and run, expecting at any moment to hear a gun go off, to see Grant's skull explode in my face like a melon. To go down holding his body, again and again and again.

But no gun is fired, and when I reach Grant he is still alive—alive and impossibly grim. I try to push him out of the room, but he holds his ground.

"No," he tells me in a hard voice. "No, Maxine. This isn't what you think. I know these men. They're regulars here."

"There are demons inside of them, Grant."

"I guess I know that *now*," he replies, but he still does not move, and I tug on his arm. He still pulls back. "No, Maxine. No, I know them. I *know* those men. They won't hurt me."

"Fuck that," I snarl, finally understanding. Makes me furious. I turn back around to face the zombies, who are still watching us, unmoving. Grant grabs my arm. His fingers are loose—I could break free just by shrugging—but I freeze inside his grip, gritting my teeth so hard my jaw screams with pain.

"One chance," he whispers. "Let me find out what is going on. They'll talk to me, Maxine. They don't know I'm aware of what they are."

"They do now," I retort. "The two of us together? You bet your ass they know."

His mouth hardens. "Let me do this my way."

"Your life, your choice," I snap, but there is heat in my eyes, my throat, and I swallow hard, fighting back the pain. Grant moves in front of me, hiding my face from the zombies, making himself a target. I fight him, afraid, but he presses his fingers against my cheek, stilling me.

"I don't want to die," he breathes. "And I don't want you hurt, Maxine. But you have to trust me."

"I trust you," I tell him. "I just think you're too stupid to live."

"Maybe," Grant says. "But God even loves His fools."

He begins to turn away from me. I grab his hand and hold on tight. Step up to his side. He hesitates, then nods once, mouth curving into a smile that is more intimate than any touch; unspoken, secret, a riddle between my heart and his, where the truth is simple and profound: I belong with him. And he belongs with me.

We walk to the zombies. I loosen my hand. No one tries to attack us. They stare at Grant, and they stare at me, and I do not understand why they look at him with deference in their eyes. Respect. When they look at me I see fear, hate—which, at least, is something I understand. I welcome it.

The man with the red cap steps forward. "You shouldn't be here, Mr. Cooperon. Nothing doing that needs your concern."

Big fat lie. I glimpse blood on the tile floor behind their legs. I walk up to the zombies. They do not move. I do not ask. I snap my fingers and point, pouring cold rage into my eyes, making them dead, dead like my mother, like my heart when I think of her. I stare at those demons, unflinching, telling them in silence their futures, and after a moment, they shuffle aside.

I see two young men sprawled on the floor behind them. Bloody, beaten. They are zombies, too. Grant tries to go to them; the man with the red wool cap stretches his arm across the path.

"It's not safe," he rasps. "Bastards came here to hurt you. We caught them outside."

I force the zombie to step back. "You're protecting Grant?"

Red cap says nothing. Just stares at me. Grant says, "Answer her, Rex."

The zombie's lips curl. "You don't know what she is."

"I know she wants to kill you," Grant replies. "You, as in, the demon inside of you. The demon I am speaking to. Yes, I'm aware of that now."

"Weren't you always?" Rex narrows his eyes. "Or just that naive? Not that it matters. We still need you. Still . . . *want* you."

I glance past him at the zombies stretched beaten on the ground. One of them is young, no older than eighteen, with hollow cheeks and brown greasy hair. Red jersey, loose black pants. He hasn't been possessed for long. A new zombie. Fresh meat. I can tell by the strength of his aura. It's not too late for him.

The other is a different story. An older man with coarse black hair cut through with silver. Deep canyons in his face. Conscious, with a burning gaze. The nimbus around his head is dark as coal, so strong it almost throbs. This one belongs to the demon, heart and soul.

I peer into his eyes. His lips peel back over his yellow

teeth; snarling, or just in pain. I do not care, either way. Two other zombies crouch close to hold him down.

"Did you come here to hurt Grant?" I ask the beaten zombie, wondering as I do what is wrong with me. I should not be here. Grant should not be here. I should have dragged him out of here the first moment I saw all the zombies in this room. Demons and their hosts cannot be trusted. Ever.

But I do not move. I have to trust Grant. I have to play this out.

The zombie says nothing. I press my palm to his forehead. He fights, and the ones holding him down share a quick uncertain look.

I stare at the man in the red cap. Rex. "You know what I'm going to do to them." My gaze travels over every watching face. "You know what I could do to all of you. Give me a good reason why I shouldn't."

"There's no reason," says Rex. "Kill them."

Not the answer I was expecting. Grant rests his hand on my shoulder. "Tell me," he says, his voice still holding that soft ring of command. "Tell me what is going on."

"I think you already know." Rex lifts his chin, regarding him with an edge of defiance that is made weak when he is unable to hold Grant's gaze for more than several seconds. "You and your music. You remake us. You turn us into . . . something else."

"Something worth killing over?" Grant asks.

"Yes," says Rex, and there is a heat in his eyes, a passion, that disarms me, makes my skin crawl. I feel like I am looking at someone who has found religion—the fanatical type, of any faith, who says yes without question. Worship—yes. Die—yes. Kill—*yes*.

Grant leans close. "I'm the one you should be trying to kill. You wouldn't be the first. Here I am. Perfect target."

I want to grab him and run. Rex smiles coldly. "If we wanted you dead, Mr. Cooperon, *you would be dead.* But given what you've done to us, we need you alive. Need you to keep playing your music. Keep making the change."

"Change into what?" I ask. "You know what you are. What could Grant *possibly* give you, *ever*, that you would want?"

"Freedom," Rex says, giving me a hard look. "Freedom from our queen."

The boys stir against my skin, tossing in their sleep. I grind my teeth. "Your queen is locked behind the veil. She has no hold over you."

"And you would know?" Rex shakes his head. "You are a Hunter. You kill us, but you know nothing about us."

"I don't have to," I snap. Grant's hand squeezes, but I shrug him off, pointing at the zombies being held down on the ground. "Not everyone feels the way you do. Some are terrified. Some run. Some fight. What makes all of you so different?"

Emotion flickers in the zombie's narrow grizzled gaze. The aura above his head is the weakest shadow I have ever seen a zombie possess, but I do not take it as proof or comfort. The darkness is still there. The demon inside that man knows it.

He is making a choice, whispers a voice inside my head. *He is choosing to be something else. Something different than he was born to be.*

And the thing about choices, I remember, is that not everyone makes the same one.

Grant takes a slow deep breath. "Why do you want freedom from this . . . this queen?"

"Why does anyone want to be free?" Rex gives him a wary look. "She controls us, commands us, sees through our eyes all that we see. Even now she watches, everywhere with us, feeding, taking what we take and using it to make her strong. That is all she cares about, being strong." He touches his head, tapping it twice. "I can feel her. She wants me to kill you."

"Then why resist?" Grant asks. "Why fight for me?"

"Because your music does something to us. You dull the link. Quiet the hunger."

"But it's there," I say, unable to look away from the shadow of that aura. "You still crave the pain your hosts provide."

"I crave yours," Rex says, and Grant steps right up into the zombie's face, knocking him back with a hard shove—surprising everyone, including me. I wait for them to strike back, but not a one—not even Rex—so much as twitches. Even I feel the pressure to stay still, anything to avoid the terrible focus of the man beside me.

"You don't touch her," Grant says, in a voice so cold and strong it cuts. "You never touch her. None of you. And if anyone else tries, you stop them. Protect her like you protected me."

"No," Rex whispers, a light sweaty sheen covering his forehead. "No, we will not do that."

"Then get out," Grant tells him. "Go back to your queen."

Rex shuts his eyes. "She'll kill us. If your influence fades and she regains control—"

"I gave you a choice. Promise not to hurt Maxine. Or leave. It's easy."

"You're asking too much of them," I say. "You don't know the history of my kind and theirs."

"I know they want to be human." Grant tilts his head, eyes narrowed. "Isn't that right, Rex? All of you crave something more. More than just being . . . what was it, Maxine? *Parasites?*"

Don't push them, I beg silently, but Rex does not retaliate. He shuffles backward, the rest of the zombies moving with him, dragging the two on the ground. I run after them, falling to my knees over the young man in the jersey. I drag my hand against his forehead, hook the demon squirming inside his unconscious body, and yank hard. It feels like pulling a raw chicken apart with my bare hands: juicy, cold, dirty. The demon wisp writhes, screaming, begging his brothers for help, but the zombies look on, glancing at each other, shifting from foot to foot. I do not say a word. Just slap the fighting cloud against my forearm, the mouth tattooed there, and apply pressure.

Aaz stirs, dreamily. The demon screams. And then, after a moment, stops. No time wasted—I reach out to the other man, who is still conscious, and exorcise him as well. He fights, but not hard enough, slumping into a deep sleep the moment I make the hook. This time I feed the demon to my other arm. Raw sucks him in.

I look at the zombies, at Rex, who is watching me with cold dispassion. "Leave them."

"No trust?" Rex smiles, reaches beneath the jersey of the young man, and pulls out a handgun. Taps the barrel against his forehead and tucks the weapon into the deep pocket of his jacket. He backs away, and the others follow. No talking, no dissent. Just like the zombies at Pike Place. Working together. Cooperating. Sharing territory.

Except this time all the zombies but Rex look uneasy, afraid—and not just of me.

"Our queen wants you dead, because she fears your power," Rex says, as the men reach the metal double doors. He stands there, framed by the other zombies, his red hat askew over his grizzled head. His eyes are dark, burning. Grant steps close, his hand brushing against mine, our fingers tangling as the zombie watches on, eyes narrowing. He shifts his gaze to me. "But if the two of you are together . . . maybe she's right."

Just not right enough for Rex to do anything about it. He gets out, fast, followed by the others, who hesitate a fraction longer before following. Maybe some second thoughts, after all. That queen of theirs, Blood Mama, must be a big bad bitch to make me—the sole executioner of their kind—look appealing.

Grant lets out a long slow breath, staring at the door. I glance at him sideways. "What happened to Mr. Love and Kindness?"

"I have my limits."

"They wouldn't have been able to hurt me. You could have used them."

He glances down at my stomach. "I wasn't thinking in the short term, Maxine."

I look away, rubbing my neck. "And what if *you* get hurt?"

"I thought you didn't trust them."

"They needed you. That makes its own kind of trust."

"They still need me, Maxine. And if they need me bad enough, they'll come back."

"Which, of course, leads to the problem of what happens after they're done getting what they want."

"One thing at time." Grant sighs, then says, softly, "I knew those men, Maxine. I was making progress. And I still . . . I still believe that they can be helped. I *want* to help them."

"You have helped them," I admit grudgingly. "You've made progress. Enough progress that they decided to save your life. That's something, Grant. I never thought I'd see the day."

Grant squeezes my hand, looking down at the two men sprawled at our feet. "Will they remember anything of what just happened?"

"Not likely. You've heard of selective amnesia and lost time, right?" I raise my eyebrow. "Bingo."

"Seems convenient."

"I suppose, but what they did—what all those men in here just did—is highly unusual. These kinds of demons usually hang back, live like shadows, just . . . whispering. Manifesting urges. What you've seen over the past day or so is much more intense. Takes energy, power, to completely take over a host."

"Where would they get that power?"

"Good question." I chew the inside of my cheek, not fond of the possible answer. "Did Rex or any of those men know you were going to Pike Place last night? Or a month ago, before that other attack?"

Grant nods, his gaze sharpening. "Like I said, those men were my regulars. Rex came first. Ex-con, drug addict. Trouble, right off the bat. Eased up after a while, though. He was . . . responding well. Got a job down at the docks. The other guys came later. Rex said they were . . . friends."

"Sounds like he recruited them."

"Yeah." Grant clears his throat. "My movements wouldn't have been much of a secret."

"Which means, if Rex is to be believed, their queen would have known you were coming. She could have commanded some of her demons to be there waiting."

"But why Pike Place? Why at the market, when there would have been a dozen other places and times that she could have had someone kill me? Doesn't make sense, Maxine. It doesn't even make sense that anyone would wait until now to come here."

He is right. It makes no sense at all. The boys shiver against my skin. Grant wraps his arm over my shoulder and draws me close. "This isn't going to stop, is it? Not until I'm dead."

"Not until we're both dead," I whisper, and press my lips against his shoulder.

Seven

There is no time. The men need medical attention. That, and
the formerly possessed always wake up confused, frightened.
Grant calls 911, and in ten minutes an ambulance arrives, followed closely by the police. We are questioned separately, but
spin stories of surprise and confusion and who-could-do-such-
a-thing. Voices shake. Knees tremble. Adrenaline, riding us
down, just as it should—not entirely an act.

And then the men, still unconscious, are carried out on
stretchers. The police leave. Grant and I go back to his apartment, take off our clothes, and crawl under the covers of his bed,
simply holding each other. I like how his sheets and pillows
smell like the both of us. I like how it feels to have his body tangled heavy and strong around my own, the warm planes and
angles of his face so close I could kiss him by tilting my chin.

So I do, on his jaw. Grant rumbles, almost a purr. "Do that
again, Maxine."

I press my lips against his mouth, and his hands slide up
my back into my hair as he deepens the kiss, crushing me to
his body, winding his legs around my hips. Something hard
and hot presses against my stomach, and I touch him, stroking
lightly, watching Grant's throat tighten, his eyes flutter shut.

His hand trails from my hair to my breast. "You're a bad woman, Maxine."

"My horns hold up my halo."

He laughs, his thumb moving in some very interesting circles that make my back arch and my thighs rub together. "What are we going to do with each other? What are we going to do?"

What started out on a teasing note turns into something softer, darker, and it makes me sigh. "Our options are limited. Run or fight."

"I won't run. I don't want to be prey. I don't think you do, either. Assuming . . . you even want to stay."

His hesitation makes me smile. "I treat men like dirty socks, Grant. Use 'em, then lose 'em."

"Is that so?" His hold around me tightens. "And if I don't want to be lost?"

No more room for jokes. I brush back his hair, stroking the line of his cheek. "Then you won't be. Not ever."

Grant looks at me with such tenderness I forget how to breathe, how to think; all I can do is ride the sudden sharp ache in my heart, a pain that rises thick and pure into my throat, making it hard to breathe.

Life goes on, my mother used to say. *Even if you don't want it to.*

But *I* want it to. My life. My future. Hope. Faith.

And no more running.

I do not know what scares me more.

I wake at sunset, just as the boys are ready to peel off my skin. Grant is not in bed with me. His side of the mattress is cold. My searching hand nudges paper. A note.

I barely notice my tattoos dissolving into smoke as I kick back the covers, scrambling to get up, but before my feet can touch the floor I hear a familiar tap from the other room. Grant, leaning on his cane, pokes his head around the doorway. "Hey, you're awake."

I force myself to breathe, and look down at the paper in my hands. I see the words "going downstairs" and "be right back" and "don't worry, love, G."

I crumple the note and meet his gaze, which is becoming concerned. "I thought you had gone and done something stupid."

"Tempting, but no." Grant's mouth quirks into a wry smile. "I wish I could pound my chest and lock you up, but I'm no superhero, and I value my life."

"Those demons would kill you." I stifle a gasp as the boys peel free, smoke coalescing into flesh before they scatter to the floor, stretching and yawning, claws clicking madly.

"I was thinking more of you killing *me*," he mutters, watching the transformation. Calm. Always so calm. I wonder what it would take to make him lose his nerve for real. He takes a step into the room. In his free hand he holds a wooden flute. I raise my brow.

"I have a plan," Grant tells me. "But it's dangerous. Stupid. And it probably won't work."

"Wooo!" cheer the boys, pumping their little fists into the air.

We eat dinner. Talk. Make love. Hold each other inside the shower, where I wrap my arms around Grant's hard body and hug him so tight I leave bruises. He never complains—just embraces me with his quiet strength, rumbling words I do not understand, but which sound good and warm, like home.

And then, when the hour turns late, we leave. Grant takes his flute. I have the boys.

It is raining, water sheeting down against the windshield with deafening force, blinding my view of the road. Lightning cuts the city skyline, thunder rolling over the empty downtown streets. It is a bad night to be out.

I park the car on First Street, directly in front of Pike Place Market. The steel grates are down, the lights off. Neither of us moves, though the boys melt into the shadows of the backseat. Dek and Mal coil tight around my neck.

Grant fingers the flute. "I suppose we could test my theory in here where it's dry. I've never tried to summon a demon queen from inside a '69 red Mustang. Might make a quick getaway that much easier."

"Having second thoughts?"

"Not really. You said this place is a hot spot, right? Where the veil is thin?"

"And you said you've been playing weekends in this market for months. Just . . . doing your thing." Changing personalities, weaving color into the darkness of human spirits. Work I question, work I would never want him to attempt on me—no matter how good his intentions. "I suppose that explains why you became a threat, if your music somehow made it through the weak spots in the veil. Affecting demons on the other side."

"It may have been enough that I changed demons already here."

I say nothing. Just tap the steering wheel, staring out the window at the rain-battered street. Chew the inside of my cheek, trying to consider the possibilities, the future. My brain goes empty. All I can see is darkness and cold, the shelling water beating the world into a hard drum, a hard pulse, a hard heart.

I touch the door handle. "Ready?"

Grant never answers. Zee explodes from the shadows of the backseat, claws tearing up the leather. Something massive slams into the Mustang's hood, tilting the vehicle up on its front two wheels before dropping us hard to the road. The crash is bone jarring. My seat belt cuts so deep I imagine it touches my spine. Grant shouts my name. Glass shatters, a massive fist punching through the windshield, slamming into his headrest. Zee howls.

I shove open my door and tumble out, dragging Grant over the driver's seat behind me. The rain steals my breath away, as does the hulking figure crouched on the hood, a creature twice my height and triple around. No features, no eyes or nose or ears—just a mass of smoky shadows radiating heat like the rough shell of a hot coal.

Zee melts from the shadows, Aaz and Raw close behind. Dek and Mal loosen their grip around my neck, uncoiling through my hair, whispering words I do not understand. A prickle runs up my spine. I glance over my shoulder.

We are not alone. I see other bodies, darker than night, shambling close like sludge hills with legs. Their skin hisses and steams beneath the rain, and there is a glint of red where their eyes should be.

The demon on top of my car makes a throaty sound and leaps down, concrete cracking beneath its feet. Behind it I see a shimmer that makes me blink hard, wipe rain from my eyes, and stare hard at the hood of my car, which is no longer crumpled and torn—but completely undamaged. The windshield is intact. The only indication there was ever violence is the driver's side door, still hanging open.

"Bogeymen," Zee mutters. "Pain baiters."

Grant lifts the flute to his mouth. The bogey watches the man, measures him. Makes me think of my mother, the zombie who must have sat in darkness outside our home, also watching, also measuring.

I click my fingers, and Zee throws himself at the demon. His claws sink into the frayed darkness of its back, teeth ripping into shadow, tearing out chunks of it like meat. Aaz and Raw cut behind us, yanking spikes from their spines and using them as daggers as they slash through the hulking demons behind us, spraying sparks through the rain, against the cobblestone road.

Grant presses his mouth to the flute, and the trembling notes that pour from the instrument, quicksilver and throaty, make me gasp and the bogies howl. I see no colors, only I *feel*—like riding breathless and wild on the back of a thundercloud—and it is more than music, more than I imagined, more than Grant could explain. Pied Piper, running Hamelin into Hell.

Heat blossoms around the crown of my head. I look up and see a slit in the night sky. An eye, bathed in red; a cut in the veil, a break in the rain. I hear heartbeats, the tumult and chatter of jostling bodies, the world on the other side pressing down and down through the narrow opening. The bogies try to touch that bulge, but the boys hang on like monkeys in banyan trees, swarming and cutting, weighing down those thick arms and legs with their small dense bodies. Looking at me the entire time. Waiting for my call, while I wait for Grant, who falters, the music dying against his lips. An acrid filthy scent fills the air—the miasma, the spit of the Blood Sea.

The bogies disappear. Gone, sparking out—one blink and no more. The boys fall hard to the road, scrabbling and searching. Nothing. I do not bother looking. I reach out and touch

Grant. We lean into each other. I wish he would keep playing his flute—that was the plan—but all I can do is stare.

"Maxine," Grant whispers hoarsely. "There's something I need to tell you. About why I was never afraid."

"Not now," I murmur.

"Now," he says, and the quiet urgency, the fear in his voice, is enough to make me tear my gaze from the sky and watch him tap his temple with a shaking hand. "I had seen you before. Up here. I dreamed your colors, your aura, before I ever met you. And I knew . . ." He stops, his eyes growing hot, bright. "I knew I would love you. I knew then, and I knew it after. I couldn't help myself."

"Grant," I whisper.

"I was afraid of not telling you that," he says. "I'm still afraid."

He presses the flute to his mouth, but only manages to play a high sweet trill before something long and dark snakes from the eye. I move, but not fast enough. The tentacle coils around Grant's throat and raised arms, snapping tight. The flute drops. Grant goes in the opposite direction, kicking wildly, screams muffled as he is hauled like a fish up and up to that red steaming eye. Hooked—just as I hook demons.

I grab his ankles and go with him.

Born again, sliding from the womb into a splash of blood. I open my eyes and see red clouds, red smoke, an expanse of red water running into darkness, boiling and spitting like some hot pustule on the ass of a hissing volcano. The air is foul. Shadows dance around my body.

I hover in the air, my arms tearing from the sockets. My hands are still wrapped around Grant's ankles, and he is being pulled by something I cannot see. Pulled, yet unmoving. Just as I am not moving.

I look down. There is a slit beneath me, and from that slit I see Zee. His little hands clutch my feet. His teeth are bared, the spikes of his hair standing straight up. I can only guess at who is holding his body, anchoring us all.

I hear a whisper, just behind my ear. I cannot turn to look. Too much pain, not enough leverage. I wait, and a moment later a body floats around me, preceded by a wave of darkness: tentacles, shivering, writhing like underwater fronds of seaweed, massive enough to block out the sea and surround, cocoon, weave me into a darkness absolute, where all I know is what my hands know, what my feet know, crushed as they are by another set of small hands that refuse to let me go.

From the darkness, a face emerges, golden and wide and round. Like a doll's head—a simulacrum. Not human, but a rough attempt, and totally devoid of expression. Black eyes, no lids. Slits for nostrils. A small red mouth.

I swallow hard, fighting down fear, focusing on Grant. Grant, who I have not heard make a sound since opening my eyes in this place. His body is so still.

"Hunter Kiss," says the face, a melodious voice, a song of soft vowels and cruel charm. The voice of a queen. Blood Mama. Her lips barely move. "Give him to me, Hunter."

Make me, I tell her silently, and Grant is tugged, sharp. I cry out, but my hands do not slip, not even when a tentacle snakes around my throat, pressing. Dek and Mal, nestled in my hair, attack with hisses and muffled growls. Blood Mama shows no reaction, but a moment later the boys are torn away from me. I scream, watching helplessly as they fall past Zee through the opening in the veil.

Zee howls. Red foam bubbles at the corners of his mouth. Blood Mama's head tilts toward him.

"Little man," she murmurs. "Still paying penance?"

"Get away from him," I snarl, tears running down my face—from the pain, the effort to hold on, my own sense of helplessness. My fingers slip, but only just. I bite back a cry.

"Let go," Blood Mama says again, squeezing my throat. I grit my teeth. She could take him if she wanted, but she has not. She wants me to release him, which is wrong; it must mean something.

"You think too hard," whispers the queen. "Little girl lost. Your mother was never so aimless, nor her mother. Not any woman of your line. Warriors, merciless. Beautiful adversaries. True Hunters. And now you. Soft. Adrift. Letting grief unhinge your life, when the simple truth remains that everyone dies, everyone loses, and your pain is no more special than any other."

I remember my mother wearing a stupid frilly apron, a rare moment of whimsy, singing Happy Birthday. "You killed her."

"I ordered her death, yes. As I have ordered the death of all the women who came before you. As I will order yours, when the time is right."

My throat burns, but not from the tentacle. Blood Mama laughs, quiet. "You want to kill me. You think you *can* kill me."

I think I can try. The darkness around us deepens, folding close against my skin; warm and sticky. Blood Mama's imitation of a face floats so close I can see myself reflected in her black pitiless eyes; shark eyes, doll eyes, glassy and empty.

"Try," she breathes. "Try and we will *all* die. Stupid girl. You wonder why I hunt this man. He is no threat to me. But with his power . . ."

She wants to use him, my mind whispers. *Possess him.*

"Yes," Blood Mama breathes. "Alive, he would never accept me. His mind is too strong. Dead, or close to, he would have no choice."

"Why?" My heart is breaking, right along with my body. "Why would you want his power? There's no one here for you to convert. You can't even leave your prison."

"Can't I?" Blood Mama sways close. "*Can't I*, Hunter?"

I stare, stricken. "Then why haven't you? Why haven't you torn down the veil?"

Her face remains smooth. "There are worse things than my kind, Hunter Kiss. You think you are the only one with a covenant? You think you are the only Hunter?"

My fingers weaken. Grant's leg twitches. I close my eyes, pouring all my strength and will into my hands. Blood Mama's warm breath touches my cheek.

"The veils are weakening," she whispers. "All the veils. And if they break, as they most surely will in time, all will be lost. There are demons who have no love for us. They do not *need* us, in the same way we need you. They eat only death."

The First Ward, I think. *World Reapers.*

"Yes," she breathes. "They will destroy us all."

I have lost the strength to speak out loud. *There must be a way to stop them. They were locked away. Someone did that.*

"And where is that someone?" Blood Mama's eyes glitter. "No, we are alone. All of us. We must fight or die."

I believe her. But that does not mean I want to help her. *Give me Grant.*

"No." Her voice rises—with frustration, perhaps, though I can barely imagine it, not with her power, not with our vulnerability. "The man will serve me here, alive or dead. I will use him against the First Ward. Perhaps he can turn them in the same way he has begun to turn my kind. If not, I will send him back to your world and turn his gift to darkness. Open doorways for my kind into the hearts and minds of humans. Power, Hunter. I need power, if I am to hold the veil."

Grant's foot twitches again. I have trouble breathing. *If you want him that badly, why haven't you taken him from me? Why haven't you tried to hurt me?*

Silence. Zee says something in a language I do not understand, words tumbling from his sharp mouth, running almost into song. Blood Mama looks down at him. She barks back a single word, and Zee begins to laugh. The queen snarls. I hear a cracking sound, like a lash; her tentacles, snapping against the air.

A moment later, Grant begins to descend. It happens so slowly I believe it must be my imagination—until my arms bend and my joints scream with another kind of pain. I hold my breath, trying not to shake as I clutch his ankles, my hands sliding up his legs to his waist as he moves past me. I hug him close, pressed belly to belly, shaking against his chest, savoring its slow rise and fall. I will him to wake. He must speak.

The tentacle around his shoulders and head loosens, as does the shadow constraining my neck. Blood Mama presses close. "Take him. Go."

I stare, stunned. "You'll try again."

"No," she says, the edge of a scream in her voice. "No, I cannot."

Zee tugs on me. I glance down at him, still disbelieving. "Why?"

"Promises," hisses the queen, and a tentacle snakes between Grant and I, pressing hard against my lower belly. "A promise I should never have made."

I do not feel us move, but I feel something wet against my legs and look down again. Zee is gone. Grant and I are knee-deep in the eye of the veil. I glance back at Blood Mama, whose face hovers like a terrible golden moon above my head, her body blocking out sky and sea.

"The First Ward," I say quickly. "When?"

Her masks fractures; an actual crack splitting down the middle of her face. A terrible screaming wind surrounds us, abrading my skin, tearing and cutting. I squint, still trying to watch the queen, listening hard.

If she answers I never hear. Grant and I slip into another world.

I open my eyes to rain. My cheek is pressed against cobblestone. My body aches. Grant is on his back beside me, still breathing, soaked to the bone. I push myself close. It is difficult. My body does not want to move, but I get there, tasting tears.

The boys gather around, Dek and Mal curling warm against my throat, purring. I swallow a sob. "Everyone okay?"

"Same question, same answer," Zee says softly. "Your heart's too big for us cutters."

"Big enough, bad boy." I brush Grant's hair away from his forehead. A hot flush steals over my body, joy mixing with heartache. I try to speak, but my voice breaks. I try again, and this time I choke the words out. "What happened up there, Zee? What did you do?"

"Reminded her."

"Of what? What promise was made?"

"Protection," whispers the demon, sharing a brief look with Aaz and Raw. "Protection she tried to steal from you. Hard earned, hard fought, by those long dead. Protection for those you mark."

"I never marked Grant."

"Yes." Zee places his small hand over my heart. "You did."

Headlights cut the rain. I try to stand, but my body refuses me. So I lie in the road, trusting the boys, too tired to care if they scare the hell out of anyone who sees them.

The car stops just in front of us. A door opens, followed by footsteps. I roll over and look up into a familiar face. Rex.

"This is not a promise," he says, then bends down and grabs Grant's shoulders. Other hands take hold of my body.

The zombies drag us to the car and take us away.

Eight

An hour before dawn, Grant still sleeps. I can stand on my own. Zee, Aaz, and Raw are curled on his sofa, sucking their thumbs, watching *Yogi Bear* on the television. They regress, sometimes. I decide to go for a walk. After a moment, they come with me.

It has stopped raining. I see stars scattered through breaks in the clouds. I crane my neck, staring, but what I remember is red sky, red ocean, and the face of a pitiless doll, a demon, a queen.

A queen who must keep her promises. Whatever those might be. Zee has more explaining to do. Just not now. I am tired. My mind and body hurt. I do not know how my heart feels.

Around the corner of the building, I see a man sitting alone on a bench. I recognize the red hat. In his hands, a bottle of beer.

I walk softly and sit down beside Rex. No warning. The demon inside his body flinches, but the human host never moves a muscle. Zee and the others prowl the shadows; Dek and Mal lean on my ears.

"I suppose you know what happened," I say to him, wondering just how long a human personality can be suppressed by the demonic before being lost forever. I wonder, too, who this grizzled old zombie was before being possessed—and whether I will ever meet him.

Rex grunts. "Our queen is not in the habit of sharing information with her people, especially those who have rejected her."

"You came to get us. I assumed that was a request on her part."

He says nothing, which is all the answer I need. I stand back up. I miss Grant. Absurd, I know—it has been less than five minutes—but the ache is strong, the need, powerful. Like I have to go reattach a limb—or maybe my heart. I walk away.

"I won't be coming back," Rex calls after me. I give him the finger.

Grant is standing in the middle of his apartment when I open the door. He looks terrible, hollow, and when he sees me he stares like his heart is breaking. Takes me off guard, stabs me right down to the core. Grant only manages two steps before he goes down hard, off-balance. No cane. I run, dropping at the last moment and skidding to him on my knees.

"When I woke up . . ." Grant whispers, then stops, shaking his head. "Sorry. I was worried."

I brush back his hair, still breathless from the grief lingering in his eyes. "You thought I was gone. That I left you."

"Or that you were hurt. Dead." He closes his eyes. "I don't remember much of what happened."

So I tell him, and as I talk we lie down on the cold hard floor, curled inside each other's arms. Grant does not ask many questions. What he does ask, I cannot answer. He holds me tight, burying his face in my hair. "This isn't over, is it?"

"No," I murmur, tracing circles against his shoulder. Grant shifts, looking into my eyes. His gaze is solid, strong, warm with compassion. He looks at me like he can see my soul, and I suppose he can.

He untangles himself and slowly stands, tugging on my hand. "Come on. I want to show you something."

Leaning heavily on my arm, we walk to a door built into the back end of his living room. Outside is a fire escape, and we climb the wide metal stairs to a flat expanse of rooftop, the center of which is covered by an immense ragtag array of pots and planters and bird fountains. It is not the most beautiful garden I have ever seen, but it is the most heartfelt. In the center of it are two white plastic chairs facing east. I see a glow against the sky, a sliver of light beneath a line of dark clouds.

We sit down, both of us sighing with relief as we ease our various aches and pains. The boys melt from the shadows and lean against my legs. Grant reaches out and takes my hand. He kisses it, and I scoot my chair closer, close enough to bump, and still that is not enough. I gently dislodge the boys and crawl into his lap. Grant cradles me.

"Another day," he murmurs. "Anything can happen. Something wonderful, Maxine."

"You believe that?"

"We're still here, together. That's miracle enough for me."

"Man of faith," I murmur.

"Man of hope," he replies. "So are you."

I do not know what I am, I tell him silently. I do not understand how I exist, or what my purpose is except to be a prison for creatures that are mine to command, who cannot be killed, who make me a killer. I am a demon hunter. I am a demon.

And I had thought, until tonight, that I held some sliver of the truth of my life, some hard-earned sense of place in this world, however small.

I realize now that even that much was an illusion.

"I've been running for such a long time," I whisper. "I don't have a home. I don't have anything."

"You have me," Grant says.

Claws clutch at my ankles, tugging. My boys wrap their skinny arms around my legs, red eyes glowing. "And us," Zee says, voice reedy and sad. "You have us."

Tears burn. Grant kisses my brow and points at the first blush of dawn. The sun will crest the horizon soon; I can feel it in my bones, a beautiful morning. "Are you ready, Maxine? Are you ready to begin again?"

The boys hold their breath, eyes shuttering closed. I remember my mother, family gone and dead—and now, here, another chance. A miracle. Miracle enough for me.

I think, too, of what Blood Mama said. That there is a war

coming, the same war promised millennia ago when the veil was raised and the demons locked away. A dark future.

But that future is not here yet, and I have love. I love Grant. And I am willing to fight for that love, for him. For us. For the child who will take my place when my time is done.

"Yes," I say, taking his warm hand, pressing it to my lips. "Let's do this."

WILD HEARTS IN ATLANTIS

A Warriors of Poseidon Story

Alyssa Day

One

Bastien surveyed the battlefield, jaw rhythmically clenching and unclenching. "Strategy is everything in war. Watch and learn, youngling."

His opponent narrowed his eyes and studied the field. "Proceed at your own peril, warrior. Know that I will crush you into the ashes of ignominious defeat."

"Oh, for the gods' sake, will you two get on with it, already? I have dibs on the next game, and I have a feeling air hockey and I are going to be very good friends," Denal said, from where he sprawled out on the long, low couch. "You're going *down* to Loser *Town*, ladies, so just hurry it up, already."

Bastien laughed. "Damn, Justice. Looks like your unparalleled rep as a kick-ass warrior may be taking some heat, if little Denal can get away with calling you a lady."

Lord Justice flipped his waist-length braid of blue hair back over his shoulder and sneered. "Seems like he called *you* a lady, too, in case you missed it."

Bastien served a lethal hit straight into Justice's goal. "Hey, I'm golden. When you're nearly seven feet tall, these pitiful insults bounce right off. Atlantis has never seen a warrior the likes of me," he said, grinning. Then he threw his head back and drew in a lungful of pure, sea-filtered air and gazed out over the balcony railing at the glory of Atlantis. White marble buildings gleaming in the liquid gold of magic-created sunlight. Poseidon's Temple the grandest of them all, proudly standing tall in the center with its gold-capped columns. The deep, unfathomable blue of the ocean currents gently gliding past the dome that covered them all.

"It's good to be home," he murmured, almost to himself. He was tired. Hells, they were all tired. The missions to the surface, never less than dangerous, had turned lethal lately. Poseidon's Warriors had protected humanity for more than eleven thousand years, but always in the shadows, under the radar.

Incogfuckingnito, as Ven would say.

Bastien thought back to his training and the words that were burned into his soul—the creed of the Warriors of Poseidon:

All will wait. And watch. And protect.
And serve as first warning on the eve of humanity's destruction.
Then, and only then, Atlantis will rise.
For we are the Warriors of Poseidon, and the mark of the Trident we bear serves as witness to our sacred duty to safeguard mankind.

"Even when they're stupid enough to let vampires into their Congress and shape-shifters into their media," he growled.

Justice raised an eyebrow at him, but before he could make some crack about warriors who talked to themselves, the enormous wooden doors, inlaid with gold, silver, and copper-colored orichalcum, that led from the spacious balcony to the palace's royal audience room, swung slowly open. A warrior strode out to the balcony. Bastien tried not to laugh, as Denal nearly fell off the couch in his haste to stand at attention.

"Lord Vengeance," Denal snapped off, arms rigidly at his side.

Ven never broke stride. "At ease, dude. Seriously, Denal, we've gotta get you over this rookie thing before you drive us all nuts."

Denal's face hardened, and he appeared to age a century's worth of days right before their eyes. "I think being murdered by vampires and then brought back to life as a result of our lady queen's sacrifice is a legitimate entry to the title of seasoned warrior, my prince."

Ven's own face sobered. "And so it is, Denal." Then he grinned again. "But if you call me 'my prince' again, I'm gonna kick your ass."

Bastien figured it was a good time to change the subject. "Speaking of the wedding, when is that blessed event occurring, Ven?"

Ven turned to him, and Bastien realized anew the strain Ven had been under lately. The planes of Ven's face were harsher and more severely drawn than they'd been just weeks before.

Before High Prince Conlan had met Lady Riley and the two of them killed the vampire goddess, Anubisa.

"When does Conlan wed Lady Riley? I'm looking forward to that celebration. Atlantis deserves to ring with joy, after these weeks of plotting out the upcoming war with the vampire–shape-shifter alliance."

Ven glanced around the newly renovated balcony, then shook his head and smiled. "I still can't believe Riley talked Conlan into turning this space into a games room. We've even got foosball. I love that woman."

Justice finally spoke. "Everyone does." He walked over to a support column and leaned against it, the hilt of his ever-present sword rising above one shoulder. "You called it, naming her Lady Sunshine. She spreads light and happiness everywhere she goes," he said, sarcasm drenching his words. "Even a few of the Elders serving on the Council actually smiled at her when she stopped by to mention that they should—oh, *no big deal*—just maybe change the way everything in Atlantis has been done for millennia."

Bastien had heard enough. "Cut it out, Justice. Riley has the heart of a lion, and Poseidon himself named her as Prince Conlan's future wife and queen. Even now she carries Conlan's son. So the sooner we have the wedding, the better for all of us."

Justice narrowed his eyes. "The better for Conlan and Riley, at least. The rest of us? I'm not so sure."

Ven sliced a hand through the air. "I don't want to hear any more of that shit from you, Justice. As one of the Seven, Conlan trusts you to have his back. That includes battling political nightmares, not just bloodsuckers and shape-shifters."

Justice bowed slightly and headed for the door, but Ven called him back. "Stay. It's actually fortuitous I caught you three together, because I need to talk to you all."

"What is it, Ven?" Bastien asked, immediately coming to full alert. He was the most senior of the Seven, and always the most alive when serving his liege. The parts of his soul made for aught else than battle were long-since shriveled and dead inside him. He never minded kicking a little vamp or shape-shifter ass, either.

"We've decided to begin forming our own alliances to try to catch up with the ten-year head start the vamps have on us. Barrabas had his nasty claws in every political intrigue in the country, in his role as Senator Barnes."

Bastien barked out a laugh. "Yeah, and didn't it warm your heart to see how that bloodsucker bought it?"

The four warriors all shuddered simultaneously. Evil three-thousand-year-old vampire or not, there was something about watching a guy get his nuts ripped off that sent a cold chill snaking up your 'nads. When Anubisa had yanked Barrabas's undead heart from his body, it'd almost been a relief.

Ven recovered first. "Yeah. Well, here's the deal. Conlan wants to name an official Atlantean liaison to the shape-shifters."

"Makes sense. The furballs are big on protocol and hierarchy. The alphas of the various prides, streaks, packs, and all the other groups are way less likely to go prickly if they're dealing with somebody they perceive as having status," Bastien said, nodding. "Justice is the perfect choice. Hell, with all that blue hair, he looks half-animal himself."

Ven shot Bastien a look. "It's not Justice, big guy. Conlan wants you to do it."

Bastien's jaw dropped open, then he caught himself and grinned, catching on. "Right. Very funny. Make the all-brawn, no-brains of the organization take on a political role. Sure. Hey, you almost had me, Ven. You're good."

But Ven wasn't smiling. "You're the only one in Atlantis who thinks your value is merely in your physical strength, Bastien. Seems to me Poseidon isn't gonna let you get away with that much longer, but that's between you and the sea god."

Before Bastien could think of a reply, a cold wind swept through the warm, sunny space, then shimmered into shape. Speak of the devil.

Devil—Poseidon's high priest—nigh on the same difference.

Alaric invoked the fear of the sea god in anybody who dared cross his path. Not many did.

Alaric's eerie green eyes glowed with power and then narrowed, as if he were thought-mining Bastien's musings. But nobody these days had the ancient Atlantean power to sift the thoughts of another not soul-melded to him. Or so Bastien hoped.

Alaric finally spoke, fiery gaze boring into Ven. "What the sea god *wills* is beyond your limited knowledge of such affairs. Perhaps you should perform your duty as the King's Vengeance and leave the responsibilities of Poseidon's Temple to me."

Ven inclined his head. "As you say. I'm here to give Bastien his marching orders, since the Council called Conlan back into closed session."

He turned back to Bastien, who was still reeling, trying to process. "You remember that hot ranger you saved from that gang of bikers in Miami a couple of years ago? National Park Service chick? Smelled like a shape-shifter?"

Bastien felt his insides shrivel up a little even as he nodded. "Kat Fiero? Yeah. Vague recollection."

Vague recollection of that day, twenty-one months and three weeks ago.

"Vague recollection, my ass," Ven said, grinning. "It was the one time Mr. Even Keel got his smooth riled."

Too late, Bastien realized he shouldn't have come up with her name so fast, because now everybody else in the room was staring at him. Curious. Considering. Maybe, in Justice's case, mocking.

At least he hadn't said anything *really* stupid.

Like mentioning how the sunlight had kissed her tawny hair into spun gold.

Or how the strength in her tall, perfectly shaped, curvy body had shot him into waking fantasies so explicit he'd had to leave the beachfront bar and walk directly into the ocean, fully clothed, in an attempt to cool down. After he'd battled his way through a half-dozen or so vamps who'd thought to play with a beautiful shape-shifter caught on her own.

Mr. Even Keel. If only they knew. The calm amiability he fought so hard to present to the world was a joke. Decades of battling the evil that stalked humankind had withered the rationality within him. If they only knew how close he'd come to going full-on berserker after discovering what the vampires had done to the babies in that orphanage in Romania, they'd be afraid of him.

Anyone sane *should* be afraid of what he'd turned into, after he'd been forced to clean up the mess.

Babies turned vampire were an abomination, but his soul would never recover from what he'd been forced to do. Three cycles of purification in the Temple had not been enough. Nothing would *ever* be enough to cleanse the stain on his soul. A woman like Kat deserved better than the monster he'd become that day.

"Yeah," he repeated, voice raspy. "I remember her. Mostly how you were hitting on her and she blew you off," he said, trying to turn the heat back on Ven.

Ven grinned. "Yeah, she blew me and my attempts at charm back on our collective asses. Point is, there's a nest of shape-shifters in the Big Cypress National Preserve that's gone rogue, in defiance of the big-shot Florida alpha's edict that they ally with the vamps. We're hoping we can get them on our side. The Big Cypress group is panthers, and the alpha is a truly badass dude named Ethan."

"And Kat?"

"She's our way in, we hope. From what we hear, she's half human. Intel from Quinn."

Bastien slowly nodded. Lady Riley's sister was one of the leaders of the human rebellion against vamp and shape-shifter domination, and she tended to have extremely good information. "That would make sense. Kat seemed . . . different. I could smell the big cat, feel its power under her skin, but it wasn't the same as your run-of-the-mill furball."

Justice whistled. "You felt her cat's power *under her skin*? What else did you *feel*? Just how hot is this chick?"

Gut clenching, Bastien whirled to face Justice and whipped the hockey puck across the room at him. Justice jerked his head to the side, and Bastien watched in horror as the puck buried itself in the wall next to the warrior's face.

"What in the nine hells was that?" Denal whooped, then strode over to pull the puck out of the wall.

It took him three tries.

Bastien felt his face flush hot with shame. A good warrior never lost control. His years of training had drummed *that* into his brain every bit as much as the arts of sword play and battle strategy.

What had come over him?

An image of the curve of Kat's neck flashed into his mind. *Oh, damn.*

He bowed to Justice. "My deepest apologies, Lord Justice. I don't know . . . I—"

Justice cut him off, voice gone a deadly calm. "If you were anyone else, I'd kill you for that. You've saved my ass enough times to earn a free shot. But watch yourself in the future, Bastien."

Alaric glided noiselessly across the room to stand in front of Bastien and stare up into his eyes. The fierce green glow of the priest's gaze seared heat across Bastien's face, and he wondered if Poseidon would use Alaric to strike him down for endangering another of Prince Conlan's elite guard.

Wondered if any punishment the sea god had in his capricious mind could be any more dangerous than facing Kat again. In the nearly four hundred years of his existence, no female had affected him like that one. His duty was to protect humanity, but not once in his long centuries as a warrior had he taken it so very personally.

She wasn't even human.

She was *forbidden*.

The priest finally spoke. "Interesting. This mission will prove very . . . interesting. I may want to visit south Florida soon."

And then Alaric shimmered back into mist and swept right off the balcony, leaving Bastien to face the warriors who were his closest friends—and the mission he wasn't anywhere near qualified to handle.

Oh, yeah. I'm golden.

Two

Kat sat in her Jeep, shirt soaked through with sweat from the heat of south Florida in autumn, and wondered when a simple trip to the grocery store had turned into a test of courage. The thermometer at the bank had read eighty-five degrees, not all that unusual for this time of year, and the wild cat in her wanted to curl up in the sun on a rock somewhere.

Take a nap, maybe.

Take down a sheep or two.

"Yeah, right. Take a break from reality."

The reality in which Kat Fiero, official National Park Service ranger and daughter to the former alpha of the Big Cypress panther coalition, had never once taken down a sheep. Or a goat. Or even a little bitty squirrel.

"Fake shape-shifter, useless excuse for a panther, worthless bitch," she muttered. "Okay, that pretty much covers the range of happiness I'll have to deal with if Fallon or her minions are in there, hanging out in the tuna fish aisle."

She grabbed her wallet from her backpack and shoved it into her shorts pocket, then got out and slammed the door. Eyed the slut-red Jaguar with FALLON1 license plates, felt her lips curl back from her teeth.

The world is going to hell in a coffin, and I have time to worry about what these morons think of me why, exactly?

She thought back to the headlines she'd choked down with bitter coffee and overcooked eggs at Thelma's grill. More bills passing Congress, more extra goodies tacked on to the 2006 Non-Human Species Protection Act, as if the poor humans were any danger to the vamps. Most of 'em cowered in their homes at night, still unable to believe—even after a decade—that the things that went bump in the night were real.

Vampires and shape-shifters both.

Her dad hadn't wanted any of it. "Upsets the natural order of things, Kat," he'd said, again and again. "We're meant to stay in the wild, remain true to our natures. Not play at being reporters and law enforcement and other *civilized* members of society."

But he'd married a human, hadn't he? And then he'd died, still trying to hide how disappointed he was in his only child. The daughter who'd never been able to shift. Not even once.

Now half the rangers she worked with—and a good third of the local paranormal ops unit—were shape-shifters. "Except me," she muttered as she pushed open the door to the store and felt the wonderfully cool currents of air-conditioned air sweep out toward her. "I'm only *half* shape-shifter. I'm just a—"

"Freak!" The voice rang out with unsuppressed glee. "We were just talking about you, ranger freak show."

Kat dropped her hand away from the butt of her service revolver, regretting yet again that bitchiness wasn't grounds for shooting under National Park Service regs. "Fallon. Always a pleasure. Or, wait—never a pleasure, actually."

She watched, eyes narrowed, as the petite—*damn her*—bane of her existence stalked up to her on the kind of five-inch-heeled shoes Kat would never in her life wear. Then she allowed herself a little smugness because Fallon still had to look *up* at her. Being nearly six feet tall wasn't always all bad.

Fallon ran a hand through her masses of black curls, arched her back, and acted like a feline in heat. Which she probably was.

Bitch.

The momentary pride Kat had taken in her height shriveled like her self-esteem, and she went back to feeling like a pudgy Amazon next to the delicate beauty. Somehow, she was sure Fallon knew it, too. Too tall, too strong, just too *everything* for the human males. And too *wrong* for the shifters. Kat would never be the belle of the ball; she was long since resigned to it. But she'd like, just once, to get an invitation to the damn dance. Just once find a man who wasn't intimidated or disgusted by her. She wasn't sure which was worse.

"Are you coming to the gathering tonight? Oh—wait. That's right. You're not really one of us. You're probably not invited," Fallon said, voice dangerously near a purr.

Kat wanted desperately to walk away. Wouldn't give Fallon the satisfaction of seeing her cowardice. "I was invited. Just not interested," she replied, putting all the bored indifference she could manage into her voice.

Fallon arched one eyebrow. "Really? And yet I would have thought your ranger instincts would have gone crazy over the mere idea of us forming an alliance with the Lord High Vampire of the southeast district. I've heard he and his blood pride have *interesting* tastes in entertainment."

Kat had heard the reports. Humans tortured for days, used as playthings for the bastard's sick, perverted pleasure. She clenched her hands into fists, barely realizing that her nails were cutting into her palms. "You're lying," she said flatly. "There's no way Ethan would join forces with the vamps. Especially not Terminus's bunch. The two of them nearly killed each other last year after Terminus played his games with three of Ethan's youngest members."

"Haven't you heard? Terminus is dead. Some new gang in the northeast who've allied with those idiot rebels or something. Anyway, things change." Fallon started to walk off, turned. "Not everything, apparently. Still not a real cat, are you? Tell me, how does it feel to work with wild panthers and realize you'll never, ever be able to become one?"

Kat tightened her lips, knowing anything she said would only prolong the encounter.

Fallon laughed, and the sound of it scraped like shards of glass over an open wound. "Poor little freak Kat, with her pathetic human mother. And really, what were they *thinking* to name you Kat when you'll never be one?"

As Fallon clacked away toward the door on her ridiculous heels, Kat tried to think up a blistering comeback. Unfortunately, the grief burning in her throat blocked the words from coming out, just as the human DNA swirling in her bloodstream blocked the panther from coming out.

Pathetic.

Ethan leaned against the wall nearest to the sealed chamber's door and looked around, fighting every instinct in both of his dual natures in order to appear relaxed and nonchalant. His cat had gone feral beast inside him—wanted to rip through his skin and attack the bloodsuckers in the room. Panthers didn't care much for the smell of dead things that walked around.

But politics was a hunt better played by the human side of his existence. The vamp standing in the center of the room was a master gamesman and expected easy domination over Ethan.

Organos was in for a nasty surprise.

"So, the rumors are true," Organos concluded. "The lost continent of Atlantis is evidently more than a fairy tale for pathetic humans to tell their children. These warriors attacked and destroyed Barrabas and his blood pride, and it is said that Anubisa has gone into hiding."

Ethan smiled, deliberately showing a lot of very sharp teeth. "Hiding? Or did the Atlanteans kill her, too?"

Organos hissed, and his own fangs slid down into place. "You will speak of our goddess with respect, or this alliance will end before it begins. No human could ever defeat Anubisa. She plans strategy far beyond our understanding."

Ethan raised an eyebrow. "Really? She doesn't share strategy with you, either? How exactly is this shape-shifter–vamp alliance going to work if we don't even know what's going on?

"You will know what I know as soon as I know it. Surely you agree that our goal of complete human subjugation is worth a little uncertainty."

Studying the vampire's face was an exercise in futility. Organos gave nothing away with his expressionless features. He could have been made out of cold white marble.

Or else rigor mortis set in about, oh, two or three centuries ago.

His cat shuddered inside him, registering a predator's distaste for carrion. Ethan sent his thoughts inward, soothing and calming the beast. *Soon. We'll be out of here soon, and I'll set you free to roam.*

The cat snarled but subsided within him, a reminder of the constant need for control. The most powerful of the dual-natured stalked the precipice edging total conversion at all times. The danger of going wild was always present. There were too many who had never come back from animal form. Too many of his friends who had fallen prey to the damn humans and their illegal hunting.

When he'd seen the obscenity in Nelson's shop, he'd roared out his anguish and vowed vengeance. Then he'd run outside, gotten as far away as he could before he puked his guts up.

That's when he'd finally agreed to meet with Organos. After he'd seen his cousin—his closest boyhood friend—in his cat form, stuffed and mounted in a taxidermy shop.

No shape-shifter remained in animal form, but for his eyes, after death. That trick required the foulest of black magic. The humans—and at least one black-hearted witch—were going to die.

Growling, he shook his head a little to try to rid himself of the image seared into his brain. He pinned Organos with his gaze. "Total subjugation. Yeah, they've gotta pay."

The vampire glided closer, held out a thin, white-fleshed hand. "Partners?"

Ethan tried not to think about how Hank Fiero would be rolling in his grave at the idea. Tried not to think of Kat Fiero at all. Held out his own hand, repressing his cat's violent revulsion. "Partners."

Three

"What in the nine hells is this?" Bastien rocked back on the heels of his boots and jammed his hands in the pockets of his jeans. "We're meeting a potential liaison to the southeastern shape-shifter contingent at a bar?"

Denal read the words off the rickety-looking neon sign. "It's not just a bar. It's *Thelma's Bar and Grill*."

"Looks like a shithole to me," Justice snarled. "Remind me why, again, I had to come along and babysit you?"

Bastien's lips twitched at the idea of Justice babysitting him. "Right. Your puny six-and-a-half-feet-tall self and what army?"

Justice's pale green eyes gleamed with power, and he raised one hand, palm up, to display a glowing ball of electricity. "None but the priest channel the elements so well as I do, buffoon. Standing nearly seven feet tall merely means you'll make a bigger hole in the ground when I knock you on your ass."

Denal rolled his eyes. "Whatever. If you're done playing, let's get inside and meet this woman. I could go for a beer and five or six cheeseburgers, too."

"You're always hungry, boy," Bastien said, resisting the urge to ruffle Denal's hair. Denal was a man of more than two hundred years, not the boy Bastien had grown accustomed to thinking him. And Denal's death and rebirth had aged the warrior in subtle but very real ways.

Justice brushed by them both and strode toward the door. "Yeah, and anyway, this is shape-shifter country. They probably only serve their meat raw."

As Denal grumbled under his breath and then followed Justice into the bar, Bastien scanned the parking lot again. His senses, honed from intensive training and concentration, picked up the vibrations of both human and shape-shifter alike. Clusters of each, but never together. The residents of Big Cypress were quite markedly segregated.

Question was: By whose design?

Shaking his head again, still baffled that Conlan had chosen him for the delicate job of ambassador, Bastien headed indoors.

Right into the middle of a bar fight.

He ducked a bottle that flew through the air at him and scoped out the room as the bottle smashed on the doorframe behind his head. Justice leaned against the far wall, arms folded negligently in front of him. The blue braid—and the sword hilt rising behind his shoulder—probably accounted for the circle of calm that surrounded him.

Everything about Justice shouted badass. Bastien still couldn't believe he'd thrown a hockey puck at the warrior's head, after Justice had backed him up in countless battles against all manner of shape-shifter and vampire.

A body came flying through the air, and Bastien held out one arm to block the human . . . yes, *human*, he didn't smell like shape-shifter, although it was hard to tell in this craziness. The man's shoulders struck Bastien's arm, and he bounced off and smashed into a table.

"Bastien! Over here!" Bastien turned at the sound of Denal's shout and tried to be surprised to find that the youngest member of the Seven had gotten himself smack in the middle of the battle. Even as he watched, Denal punched one man in the eye, as yet another grabbed the young warrior around the throat.

Denal grinned, lip bleeding. "Finally! A little fun!" he shouted.

Bastien shook his head and moved in a blur of Atlantean

speed to one side of the door, as he caught sight of a man pulling his arm back to throw a dagger in his direction. The door suddenly opened, and the woman who walked through drove all conscious thought out of his brain.

Just the scent of her made him hard.

Her eyes widened as she stared in front of her, and he remembered the dagger. Shot out a hand to catch it. Winced a little as the blade cut his palm, but never took his eyes off her.

As she turned her shocked gaze to him, he bowed deeply. "Lady Katherine Fiero. I am Bastien of Atlantis at your service."

Kat stopped breathing the second she scented him. Her cat purred inside her, seemed almost to stretch and curl its form under Kat's skin, as though the beast wanted to come out and play after all these years of hiding.

It was *him*. The giant of a man she'd met only once, briefly, nearly two years before. The one who'd protected her from a biker gang of vamps intent on making her the object of their bloodsport. He'd cut through them like a panther in its prime through a field of deer, then ignored her fervent thanks and walked away from her. He'd never looked back, striding out of that abandoned building and off into the sunset like some fabled folk hero from childhood stories.

And so he must be, this man she'd never forgotten. He must be the one from Atlantis. When Quinn had described him . . . she hadn't dared to even hope. But it was *him*. *Bastien*.

And he was bowing to her. Bowing and . . . *bleeding*?

She spared a moment to look around the bar. The human–shape-shifter violence that had been roiling in the air for the past several months had come to a head, yet again.

This time, the fools were taking poor Thelma's place apart. It had to stop.

Kat had to stop it.

She looked at the man again—Quinn had said they called themselves Poseidon's Warriors. There could be no doubt to anyone with eyes that the man was a warrior. He had to be seven feet of pure battle-honed muscle. Nobody looked like *that* from working out at a gym once a week. He had thighs the size of tree trunks in that worn denim. And, oh please keep her from drooling, his chest and shoulders were a wall of muscle. God, his biceps were the size of her thighs, and she was no little thing. And his face—oh, his face. Men were not supposed to be so beautiful. It screwed up the natural order of things or something. The cheekbones, and all that luscious black hair that was just a little too long, and . . .

Great, Kat, you're having lustful fantasies while these men are beating each other up and trashing Thelma's bar. Do something, dammit.

Kat's panther snarled inside her, making its desires plain.

The beast wanted to play. It wanted to play wild and dangerous games with this warrior. The panther wasn't chained by the strictures of duty or etiquette. It wanted heat and biting and wild, ravenous sex.

Kat felt the wetness between her thighs, and she flinched a little at the friction caused by her nipples hardening under her shirt. Her face flushed, and she tried, yet again, to focus on the battle raging all around her. She looked up at Bastien, drew in a raspy breath. Opened her mouth and closed it again.

Fierce intelligence burned in his black eyes. Intelligence and something more primal. Was that . . . was that possibly desire?

For her?

Her knees weakened at the thought of it. The seconds that had passed while she stood there, frozen, seemed like hours.

The bottle that crashed against the wall snapped her out of it.

"Damn them. They know this place is Thelma's whole life. Excuse me, sir, but I have to stop this."

He literally snarled. If she hadn't known better, she would have believed he was a shape-shifter, too, from the ferocity of his expression. "There's no fucking way I'm letting you get in the middle of that. In fact, why don't you get out before you get hurt? I'll drive you home, and we can talk about whatever in the nine hells liaisons are supposed to talk about."

He blocked her from the room with his big body, and for one brief second she felt protected. Cherished. Cared for in a way she hadn't been in so long.

Then she pushed that feeling away. She had no time for weakness.

"Thanks for the thought, but this is my job. Now get out of my way," she said, grim purpose in her voice.

His eyes narrowed, and the planes of his gorgeous face hardened even further. He slammed his hands against the wall on either side of her head, pinning her into place with the protection of his body. "You're not—"

"Oh, but I am," she interrupted. Then she held her arms out to her side, palms up, and she let the noise and the fury of the room drop away. She swirled down into the currents of the smooth, clear pond inside her mind. Crystal, liquid peace.

Serenity lapping at the edges of her mind as the waves of the ocean. Even, rhythmic, calming waves.

She inhaled deeply and, as she exhaled, she channeled the peace and calm from within her secret pool and sent it swirling out from her mind and breath and into the air around her.

She opened her eyes and watched the effects. First to succumb, since he was nearest, the warrior staggered back half a step, as though he'd been struck. Then the harsh set to his mouth relaxed, and a measure of calm returned to his eyes. She smiled at him, laid a hand on his arm when he tried to speak, and shook her head. Pointed to the rest of the room.

He turned to face the bar, still protecting her with his body. They watched as Kat's infusion of peace spread through the room. Fists unclenched. Men blinked as though dazed, and put down the bottles, knives, and other weapons they'd been wielding. A collective sigh of unspent rage dampened the roaring emotional ambiance of the room from lethal fury into lethargic lassitude.

A white-haired head popped up from behind the bar, and the tiny woman peered around the room. "Is it over? Kat, that you?" she called, in a slightly shaky voice. "Aw, of course it is. Nobody else has the gift like you do to calm this bunch of jackasses."

Kat ducked under Bastien's arm and started across the room toward Thelma. "Just lucky timing, Thelma. These fine gentlemen were calculating how much money they were going to owe you for the damage, weren't they?"

A pair of the fiercest combatants she'd seen in the brawl hung their heads and nodded. One human, one shape-shifter. So, the crisis was coming to a head faster than she'd thought.

"Thelma, you'll let them know how much to pay? And I think you can all help her clean up this mess, anybody who doesn't need to head over to the ER," she said, pitching her tone to inject an edge of command. Another of her "gifts" she hadn't told anybody about.

"Oh, I've got it covered, Kat," Thelma said. "I'll let you know if anybody doesn't pay up. But why don't you get out of here now? No need to stick around, and you probably ought to get to the meeting."

Kat stifled her bitter reply and managed to smile. "Okay, if you've got this under control."

She knew the residual effects of what she'd done would last for a few hours on all who'd been in range. She wasn't sure exactly how far that range was, but undoubtedly there were some animal predators for a couple hundred yards of the perimeter of the bar who wouldn't feel like doing anything with their prey but snuggling, at least for a short while.

She smiled at the concept and turned toward the Atlantean, shoring up her defenses to keep from reacting like a bimbo at the mere sight of him. He was standing no more than two feet behind her, though she'd never heard him move, even with her shape-shifter senses. The look he was giving her was shrewdly considering, as though he knew she'd done something. He couldn't possibly know *what*, but *something*.

"Shall we go? I'm sure you'd like to get settled in from your journey," she said, wondering what kind of travel arrangements it took to get from a lost continent buried under the ocean somewhere to a nature preserve fifty miles west of Miami. She glanced at his hand, which steadily dripped blood. "We can take care of that, too."

He nodded and glanced to the left and right of her, then almost imperceptibly signaled. Two men she hadn't noticed earlier stepped toward them, picking their way through the dazed and wobbly humans and shape-shifters. Both had the warrior look to them, although one was some sort of goth punk version, with all that blue hair and the sword sticking up behind him. The other looked like somebody's kid brother.

A kid brother who'd seen a lot of battle, she silently amended as she got a look at his eyes.

Then she realized something else, as Bastien slapped the knife down on a table. Not one of the three acted like her little share-the-peace trick had affected them for more than an instant.

Which meant they were even more dangerous than she'd thought.

Four

Bastien was glad Kat's Jeep was open to the night air. If he'd been forced to ride in the car, trapped with the scent of her, for more than five minutes, he might have been driven to desperate measures. Like jumping out and taking his chances with a face plant on the dirt road.

Or asking her to stop the car so he could rip the clothes off her luscious body.

Desperate measures.

But the humid weight of the swamp air and the dense greenery surrounding them served to distract him enough that he could keep his hands—including the one she'd so competently bandaged with the first-aid kit in her backpack—to himself. At least temporarily.

Why did this woman affect him so much? And how was he going to carry out his duties to Atlantis if he didn't get over it? His duty was to protect humans—*all* humans. But he would gladly have channeled the forbidden element of fire itself and incinerated the bar and everyone in it if it had meant protecting Kat. He wanted to carry her back to his home in Atlantis and never, ever let her anywhere near danger again.

A shape-shifter in Atlantis. Ha. Alaric would lose his

freaking mind. And Poseidon . . . oh, his vengeance would be beyond my ability to imagine.

"Where did your friends go?" Her voice broke into his whirling thoughts. Friendly but impersonal. Probably trying to make small talk.

"I sent them to talk to a few contacts we have with the human population of the area," he replied. Then he realized what he'd said and backtracked. She was half-human. Maybe she thought of herself as human? "I'm sorry, I know you're . . . I mean, since you work with the panthers and your father was the alpha, we thought—"

He shoved a hand through his hair and sighed. Again.

She laughed. Like the woman herself, Kat's laugh was sultry and full-bodied. Rich and warm, with an undertone of sex.

Oh, damn. Poseidon, please help your humble warrior here. Because I'm falling down a black pit of lust-induced stupidity.

He clenched his jaw and stared straight ahead, determined not to look at her again until the Jeep stopped.

"What is that noise?"

"What noise?" he countered, senses flaring.

"That weird . . . well, it's almost like a bubbling sound," she said, sounding perplexed. "Like when a pot boils?"

He heard it as soon as she said it, the noise he'd ignored before. The noise he'd *caused*. He'd unconsciously channeled the churning of his frenzied emotions into the nearest source of water. Muttering a few choice words in ancient Atlantean, he drew in a deep breath and sent cooling energy out to the edges of the swamp to stop it from boiling, hoping the change in temperature hadn't lasted long enough to seriously damage any of the nature preserve's flora or fauna.

As the boiling noise stopped, he notice her staring at him, her golden eyes narrowed. "You did that, didn't you? I could feel some kind of energy surge from you."

"You could feel it? What do you mean?" None but an Atlantean, some of the most powerful vampires, or a few of the witches who dabbled in the black arts could feel an Atlantean channel the elements. "Are you a witch? You're surely no vampire. I can feel the heat of your body from here."

Her pinks burned a hot pink for a moment, and she ducked

her head. "You, ah, well. No, I'm certainly not a witch. Why? And quit distracting me, anyway. What did you do to the water?"

"It's an Atlantean thing. We channel the elements, especially water. Occasionally, strong negative emotion will siphon off into the nearest water source. I fixed it." He realized his voice was gruff, but damned if he'd wanted to show weakness on his first day as an ambassador. What had Conlan been thinking? Perhaps love *had* addled the prince's brain, as Justice had implied.

Bastien waited, but she remained silent for a while, headlights picking out the bumpy road in front of them. He sank into his own musings, dire expectations of the dozens of ways he could fail his prince in this mission. He was made for battle. For crushing the enemies of Atlantis and of humanity. Not for delicate political negotiations.

"Is something wrong?" Her voice was hesitant, but the amusement was still there. "You seem to be heaving a lot of deep sighs over there. I didn't hurt your manly pride, did I?"

"My *what*?"

"Hey, I live and work with a whole heck of a lot of the most alpha of *all* alpha males on the planet. I know frustrated pride when I see it."

He glanced at her and glimpsed her perfectly calm expression. He also noticed her white-knuckled grasp of the steering wheel.

She was *afraid* of him. The knowledge twisted painfully in his chest.

"I'm sorry, Katherine. Miss Fiero. Ranger Fiero," he stumbled over the words, in his haste to get them out. "What *do* you want me to call you?"

She smiled and relaxed her grip on the steering wheel. "Kat is fine. And you are Bastien. Am I pronouncing that right?"

Something inside him made a weird flipping movement when she said his name. He ignored it. Indigestion, probably.

"Yeah, that's it. Mom loved France in the 1500s. She gave us all names from that time period and area. Phillippe, Marie, Antoine, and me. I'm the baby."

She whistled. "Some baby. What are you, a family of

giants?" Then she winced. "Hey, I'm sorry. If anybody shouldn't make cracks about size, it's me. I'm practically a freak of nature."

He could almost feel the pain that washed over her bitter words. Wanted to kill whoever'd caused it. Unclenched his fists and wondered if he were losing his mind.

Turning in his seat to face her as she pulled into the driveway of a small house, he slowly looked her up and down. "If an enemy approaches with such obviously deceitful ploys, you gain the advantage in any battle strategy."

She turned off the ignition and set the parking brake, then tilted her head to stare at him with those spectacular amber eyes. "What are you talking about?"

"In the vernacular, anybody who sold you such a line of crap is a fool, and you will easily kick his ass." He lifted a hand to touch a strand of the tawny golden hair that had escaped her braid. "You are gloriously lovely and would grace the arm of even royalty, were any mere man to deserve you."

The thought of Ven, brother to the high prince, approaching Kat crossed his mind, and he had to clench his teeth against the searing jealousy.

Yep. Losing it.

Kat's eyes widened, and her pupils dilated until she looked almost more like her namesake panther than she did human. "What? You—nobody talks like that. I mean, are you some kind of poet? They sent me the poetry ambassador? But you look like a warrior—"

She stopped. Smacked herself in the forehead. "Right. You were mocking me. I get it. Well, I'm used to it, so don't be too impressed with yourself. Been there, done that, got the tracking collar to prove it."

Before Bastien could stop her, she was out of the Jeep. He slammed out of his side of the car and focused his energy to flash to the front of the Jeep. He caught her arm as she tried to pass, pulled her toward him with barely leashed fury. "Never accuse me of mocking you again, I implore you."

He stared down into the depths of her golden eyes and sank into her. Sank into her soul.

Was suddenly, desperately ashamed. He released her arm and took a step back. Bowed. "I offer my sincerest apologies,

Lady Katherine. I cannot begin to explain what has come over me that I would offer insult or harm to a female. The thought that you believed I would seek to harm you with my words was suddenly more than I could stand."

She stared at him, rubbing the spot on her arm where he'd grabbed her. "What—I don't know what to do about you. I planned to offer you the spare room in my home for the night, but I'm not sure that would be a good idea."

His body tightened at the thought of resting so near to her. Seeing her out of that uniform, her wealth of hair spread across his pillow. He slowly exhaled, fought again for control. Resolved to seek counsel from Alaric as soon as possible. "I will sleep under the stars so as not to inconvenience you again. Please do not let my impertinent actions threaten your view of my mission or my people."

She stared at him for a long minute, and then a reluctant smile tugged at the corners of her mouth. "Fair enough. If the entire ranger service were judged by my bad tempers, we'd be out of business."

She turned toward the house, headed for the door. He stood, unmoving, watching the sinuous grace of her walk. Her rounded hips that would fill his hands.

She suddenly glanced back at him. "Well, come on. You can have the guest room if you promise to behave. You did try to protect me from those thugs, after all. There is . . . there is the small matter of an old debt, as well." She dropped her gaze, not meeting his eyes.

As invitations go, it had been neither the warmest nor the most encouraging he'd heard in his nearly four hundred years. But surely none had ever been more welcome. He swung his duffel out of the back of the Jeep, then followed her to the door, shaking his head.

The poetry ambassador. Wait till Justice hears that one. On second thought, maybe I'll just keep it to myself.

Five

Kat tossed her keys on the table and tried to force her neck muscles to relax. Every instinct she had—both human and feline—was on the alert, revved up into a heightened state of anticipation. And, though admitting it was painful, arousal.

All because of the man—no, the *Atlantean*—following her into her house.

And she couldn't figure it out. It wasn't like she'd never seen a sexy man before. Ethan, for example, was flat-out gorgeous. If you liked your men long, lean, hard-bodied and arrogantly alpha, that is.

She had a feeling her tastes ran more to the poetic warrior/ambassador type.

She groaned. "I've gotta get past this."

"Excuse me?" Even his voice was killer. Low and sexy, with a lilting cadence that sounded a bit like a distant cousin to the Gaelic she'd often heard spoken by park visitors from Ireland.

Squaring her shoulders, she turned to face him. "I have to check on the cubs. I'll be back in a moment."

It's not running away when I really do need to check on the babies. It's not.

She kept repeating that to herself all the way down the hall, hoping that soon she'd believe it.

Bastien dropped his bag on the floor near the overstuffed couch, wondering what he should do next. She probably wanted some space from the crazy fool he'd acted like in the car. He couldn't blame her.

He looked around at the small but cozy room, noting the pictures of what must be her family on a bookshelf. He crossed to it and picked up a frame, recognizing Kat's strong features and height in the man who stood with his arm around a fragile-looking woman who held a baby. Baby Kat, maybe? The woman had Kat's golden coloring, but was a tiny thing. Quinn had said Kat's mother was human. Wonder how hard that had been, growing up as the half-breed kid of the alpha?

A muffled shriek from the back of the house jolted him to attention, and he shoved the frame back on the shelf and took off at a dead run down the hall, automatically reaching for the daggers he wasn't wearing. He'd stashed them in the duffel bag in deference to his hostess; that little courtesy might get him killed. No time to get them now. She might be—

"Kat?" He hit the end of the corridor and burst into the doorway with light spilling out, only to see a totally unexpected sight: Kat sat on the floor, laughing, while four clumsy panther cubs crawled and rolled all over her. Bastien stared at her and felt the breath leave his lungs.

Serious Kat was beautiful.

Laughing Kat was a goddess.

She looked up at him, still smiling. "I'm sorry. Did you hear me yell?" She held up the largest of the four, a male. The cubs had cinnamon-colored reddish coats and white undersides and a funny kink in the end of their tails. "He's trying to prove he's fiercer than his three sisters, and nipped my finger pretty hard, didn't you baby?"

When she bent her forehead to rub it against the cub's, Bastien suddenly understood exactly why the creature started purring. He'd purr himself if he could get her to rub his belly.

"They're beautiful," he said, and meant it. "I've never seen panther cubs before. Are they—I mean—"

She laughed again, but this time her laughter held a note of bitterness. "No, they're not shape-shifters. These are full panthers. And for a while, it was touch and go whether *anybody* would ever see a Florida panther cub again, the way the humans were murdering them."

"Poachers?" He sat on the floor, cautiously held out a hand to the two cubs nearest him. One of them ignored him completely and began to wash her face with one tiny paw, while the other slunk into stalking mode, jumped on his hand, and ferociously attacked his shirt sleeve.

"No, not poachers, although we have to fight them now, too. Believe it or not, it was perfectly legal to hunt these incredible animals as recently as 1967, when the U.S. Department of the Interior listed them as endangered. Damn near too late, too. They were hunted to near extinction by around 1955." She leaned back against the wall and stretched.

Bastien tried not to be distracted by how long her legs were. "But they're doing better now?"

She nodded, face still grim. "Better. Still not good enough. An agreement with the Texas cougar coalition back in ninety-five helped. We introduced eight female Texas cougars into our panther population to help with the potential inbreeding issue."

The male cub curled up on her lap and fell asleep, and Kat absently scratched his ears. "Better and better, still not optimal. Plus, we're stuck with more of the Texas females than we ever wanted," she said bitterly.

The change in her tone puzzled him. "I thought they were important to your own cats?"

Kat blinked, then seemed to realize what she'd said. "Oh, never mind. I was thinking of entirely another type of Texas cat that's shown up here. One named Fallon, to be precise."

He raised an eyebrow, and she responded to his unspoken question. "We . . . *imported* several Texas females ourselves, for similar reasons," she said, not meeting his eyes. "One in particular, Fallon, doesn't have much respect for anybody who's not a purebred, and she's not shy about showing it. Unfortunately, Ethan took her to mate, so . . ."

As her voice trailed off, he read the truth between the lines. Fallon was an evil bitch who rubbed Kat's nose in her shortcomings at every opportunity. Figuratively speaking. Suddenly, his hands itched to stroke Kat's hair, to offer comfort of some kind.

Again, not a damn bit like him.

The delight Kat had shown while playing with the cubs evaporated, and she stood up abruptly. "I'll show you to your room, and we can get started in the morning. We'll certainly have a lot to talk about with Ethan, from what I hear about the big meeting tonight."

He gently disengaged the cub's teeth from his sleeve and set it on the floor, then stood as well. Kat stopped, inches in front of him, and stood as if trapped. The room shrank around them, and he felt his throat drying up as he looked down into her eyes yet again. "Kat? I—"

"Door," she blurted out. "You're blocking the door."

"Oh. Sorry. Door." He moved aside and, for the second time that evening, she fled from him.

He smiled slowly as he watched her. If he'd been a predator, the sight of her flight would have incited him to the hunt. He took his time before following her down the hall, waiting for the urgent hardening of his body to subside. "We may be in trouble, Lady Kat," he murmured to himself. The cubs on the floor gazed sleepily up at him. "Because I'm suddenly feeling very predatory."

Alaric shimmered into mist and soared away from the ranger's cottage, disturbed by what he'd sensed from the shape-shifter with Bastien. In a burst of speed, he shot up and out and didn't descend until he was floating above the midnight blue waves of the Atlantic Ocean. As he spiraled down into the water, regaining his form on the way, he channeled the magic of the portal into Atlantis.

Grimly hoped that the portal would cooperate. It had a decidedly capricious nature, much akin to that of the sea god himself.

Fortunately for the urgency of his mission, the portal opened immediately and he stepped through onto Atlantean soil. Immediately felt the peace of his homeland rush through him, sweeping through the corroded corners of his soul.

Though not even the peace of Atlantis could fill the emptiness of some losses. Some wounds would never heal. Her enormous eyes flashed into his mind, and he nearly flinched.

Quinn.

His eyes gleamed with power, startling the two portal guards who'd fallen back at his entrance. They bowed deeply. "Alaric. Prince Conlan sent for you," one ventured, not meeting his eyes.

He nodded and headed for the palace. The news that Bastien's shape-shifter liaison almost certainly had Atlantean blood in her superseded his own pathetic longings for a human he could never have.

Quinn had made that clear, as if his own duties did not dictate the same.

Tangled up in his own black mood, he failed to sense Conlan until the prince flashed into form before him on the path. "What news, Alaric?"

Alaric lifted his head, masking the bleakness of his thoughts to calm control and arranging his expression to reflect the same. "There is a problem. Our shape-shifter has Atlantean blood in her."

"What? Are you sure?" Conlan ran a hand through his hair. "How is this even possible, in a shape-shifter?"

Alaric raised one eyebrow. "Considering the nature of your beloved and her sister, I am unsure as to why you are so surprised by this development," he said sardonically.

"But a shape-shifter? Is it even possible for an Atlantean to breed with a shape-shifter?"

"Clearly it is, at least if the mating involves a human with slight traces of Atlantean DNA from an ancestor who was born more than eleven thousand years ago."

Conlan looked at Alaric and nodded. "You were right."

"I am always right. Can you be more specific?"

Conlan's lips twitched in a ghost of a smile. "When we met Riley and Quinn, you said everything was changing. After millennia of fighting the shape-shifters on behalf of humanity, now you tell me that they—at least some of them— might be our descendants."

"It's difficult to know who to battle, when the identities of the combatants switch in the middle of the game," Conlan continued.

"Yet it is even worse than you know, my prince." Alaric closed his eyes and sent his energy winging out from his body to refresh itself in the air and waters of Atlantis. As the pure power of the sustaining elements of his home rushed through his body, he felt the energy grow within him until a shining nimbus of energy glowed around his entire body.

Conlan folded his arms. "That bad?"

"Worse. Bastien's little shape-shifter may well be just that—*Bastien's* shape-shifter."

"You don't mean—"

"I do. Their energies parallel. They have the potential to reach the soul meld."

Conlan's face hardened. "To the palace, then. We have much to discuss. I don't know if I can allow that."

Alaric laughed, but fell into step with his prince. "Think on how you feel about Riley. Not even Poseidon himself could have barred you from your desire to unite with her. With Bastien and his shape-shifter, you may not have any choice."

Six

"You're going to have to tell me about it sometime," Bastien said, following Kat down a muddy, overgrown path. She'd explained that they were at the very beginning of the dry season, and the path had been covered by as much as three feet of water during the height of the May through October rainy season. They'd passed through stands of dwarf cypress and pinelands, mostly in silence, while she quite determinedly ignored him and he tried desperately to think of something liaison-like to say.

Since he still wasn't sure what a liaison did, he was good for trying Denal's advice to try to "build a bridge of understanding" between their two cultures. What better way to do that than by hiking a dozen-mile roundtrip path through humid swamp country? Yeah, so irony wasn't his strong suit, no more than diplomacy.

Yet as he gazed at the curved backs of Kat's endless legs, he realized he could think of quite a few better ways to build bridges.

"Tell you what?" she called back, not looking at him. She wore her uniform and her official status like a shield against him today, and he'd seen no trace at all of the breathless woman who'd run from him the night before. Instead, he'd heard commanding intelligence in her telephone conversations with various members of her ranger force and the local paranormal ops unit.

From the way her phone had rung incessantly, and the side of the conversations he'd overheard, both groups respected her insights and her authority. He'd seen the deference in the actions of the zoological staff who had come to transport the cubs to a secure facility for care and raising. She'd said goodbye to them with sadness, and in her kindness and play with the cubs he'd seen a flash of the mother she would one day become.

The knowledge of her bearing another man's child sent a stabbing pain through him that he refused to contemplate.

This hike was an attempt to investigate a vague report of trouble in the area that had been filed the night before, before their scheduled meeting with Ethan, the panther pride's alpha.

But he was still curious. "Tell me about your gift."

She stopped, finally turning to face him. "What are you talking about?" Honest confusion clouded her eyes, and she put her hands on her hips. Six miles of walking, and she wasn't even winded. She had warrior spirit in her, his woman.

The woman. Not *his* woman. *The* woman. *Dammit.*

"Your gift. The ability to calm aggression. Is this a shape-shifter ability that has been kept secret before?"

She blinked, then laughed bitterly. "Gift? Right. You mean curse. The lovely ability I have to calm hostility and aggression in everyone, including myself. The *gift* that keeps me from ever becoming a true shape-shifter."

Somehow, he felt the fury radiating from her. He *saw* the evidence—the clenched jaw, the narrowed eyes, the hands fisted on her hips. But he *felt* the rage and pain, somehow inside himself. Impossible. But true. He tried to form a coherent question. "How does it—"

She cut him off. "How do you think we get in touch with our animal sides? We tap our animal instincts. A panther is a true predator. I can't reach the predatory side of myself, dual-natured or not, when my *gift* automatically switches on to calm any aggression anywhere around me."

Kat pulled her hat off, wiped her forehead with the back of

her hand. "That includes, in case you were wondering, any of my own aggression."

He flinched at the anguish searing through him. Wondered how he could possibly feel her pain burning in his blood. "Kat, I—" But even as he formed the words, a blanket of calm muffled her emotions.

She sliced her hand through the air, dismissive. "No. I didn't tell you because I want your pity. Just thought I should let our Atlantean liaison know that I'm a poor choice to be your counterpart. I'm a half-breed who will never truly be a panther. You'd be better off with somebody else."

He reached out, couldn't help himself. Touched the curve of her cheek with his fingertips. "Quinn said *you*. You were the one. Prince Conlan agreed. And this is my first assignment as liaison, so perhaps we can figure this out together."

She seemed to hold her breath, staring up at him. He could lose himself in her gaze. Sink into the warmth of her amazing mouth and spend the next hour or seven kissing her. Touching her. Plunging into her.

Her face suddenly pinkened as though she could read his entirely *unliaisonlike* thoughts, and she took a jerky step back from him. "Well, um, okay. We—we've checked this path, and there's no sign of the trouble that—"

Her head snapped up, and she lifted her face into the sluggish breeze, as if she were scenting the wind. "Do you smell that?" she whispered, the lines of her face gone hard, her eyes feral.

He shook his head. "All I smell is swampland. What do you—" he broke off, Atlantean senses sharpening. His sense of smell may not be as keen as a panther's, but his hearing was preternaturally sharp. "Moaning. That way." He pointed through a grove of trees and took off at a dead run. The moaning had sounded human.

Even in human form, Kat moved like the panther she was and seemed almost to flow through the underbrush to meet him as they found the source of the moaning. It was a shapeshifter—another panther. The man stared wildly up at them, throat drenched in scarlet blood from the wounds that ripped through the side of his neck. "Kat? It was Terminus," he said, voice rasping with the effort. "Tell Ethan. Terminus did this."

Kat dropped to her knees next to the man, tears streaming down her face, already barking orders into her radio. She gave their location, then dropped the radio on the ground and reached for the man's wrist, trying to check his pulse. "Nicky? No, Nicky, no. You have to hang on. We'll get help, I promise."

Tears streamed down her face, and Bastien stood there, helpless with rage. Wanting fiercely to grab her, throw her over his shoulder, and spirit her away from any possible danger. Knowing he couldn't. He fisted his hands on the hilts of his daggers and scanned the area, though his senses told him the attackers were long gone. Those were vampire bite marks, and the morning sun burning down was sufficient evidence that the vampires had gone to ground.

Nicky held up a hand to Kat, and she clasped it in both of her own. "I'm sorry, Kat," he managed, hoarse voice fading even as the light in his eyes did the same. Bastien watched as the man's eyes changed. Turned to panther eyes. His death was fast approaching.

Kat shook her head wildly back and forth. "No. You tell me you're sorry later, when you're better," she commanded.

"You deserve to know, Kat. Ethan . . . Ethan wants you. His plan . . . his . . ." Nicky's chest heaved in a shuddering gasp, and then his head fell to the side and his hand slid limply out of Kat's grasp.

Kat lifted her head to stare at Bastien, agony in every line of her tear-stained face. "But it's Nicky. He can't be dead. He's my friend."

Bastien couldn't stop himself. He knelt to sweep her into his arms and lifted her, cradling her to his chest. It was imperative that he soothe her; his soul demanded it. "Shhh. I am so sorry for the loss of your friend. May Poseidon and the gods of your ancestors watch over him on his journey into the light."

He bent his forehead to touch hers, trying to transmit his sympathy and sorrow for her loss. Wishing he could take the pain into himself and protect her from it.

She clutched his shirt and gave in to a firestorm of sobbing, but it lasted less than a single minute. Then, abruptly, her tears stopped. Her breathing slowed down from its frantic pace until it was rhythmic again. Measured. Calm.

She looked up at him, and the force of the anguish in her eyes dimmed, as he stared into them. "Please put me down now," she said, clearly trying to pull her dignity around her.

His arms tightened involuntarily, but he forced himself to release her. He gently set her down, so that she stood on the path before him.

"You see," she said, utterly calm. Features utterly still. "I am not merely half shape-shifter. I am half human. My *gift*, as you call it, blocks me even from the wholly human emotion of mourning for a childhood friend. I'm neither human nor shape-shifter, but a bastard hybrid—half of each."

Her lips twisted with evident self-disgust. "And half of nothing is still nothing."

Before he could speak, he heard the hum of the all-terrain vehicles thundering up the path behind them. Voices calling out for Kat. She shouted out to them, and the opportunity was lost.

But Kat's gift apparently only worked on aggression. Because the torment racking through Bastien at the sight of her pain and self-loathing didn't abate in the slightest.

Seven

Bastien entered the enormous house designated as the home and headquarters of the Florida panther alpha, walking slightly in front of Kat. He didn't like what he'd heard of this Ethan character, and every protective instinct he'd ever possessed was on overload.

The sensations of predator and violence permeating the house didn't help, either. He tuned his senses to high alert and stopped, waiting.

Kat, walking with her head down, bumped into him and stopped. He glanced down at her, and his breath caught in his throat at the sight of her slumped shoulders and the tortured sorrow in her gaze. "What is it? Why are we stopping? Ethan said to meet him in the pool room," she said, voice low and hoarse.

"Really? One of his own is murdered, and he has time to play a game or two of pool? Not much of a leader, is he?" Bastien heard the sharp sarcasm in his own voice and realized it might not be the proper tone for a liaison to take. Then the atmosphere in the airy entrance hall changed a split second before he sensed the danger and whirled to face it, daggers drawn, body poised in front of Kat.

The man standing in the entranceway was completely familiar to Bastien, though he'd never seen him before. Three centuries of protecting humankind from shape-shifters had taught him a few lessons. This man was the alpha. It was clear in his stance—shoulders thrown back, legs apart. Head thrust aggressively forward.

This had to be Ethan, and he expected instant subservience. Too fucking bad.

Kat moved to walk around him, and Bastien put out a hand to block her. "Perhaps you could introduce us," he said, eyes never leaving Ethan.

Ethan's lips drew back from his teeth a little, but he said nothing in response to Bastien's comment. Simply folded his arms across his chest and waited.

Kat pushed Bastien's arm down and looked up at him. "Ethan is the alpha of my pride," she said, impatience in her voice. "You don't need to protect me from him."

"Oh, is that what he's doing?" the shape-shifter's voice was silky. "Maybe you could tell your friend that you're mine, and he interferes with pride business at his own risk."

The fine hairs on the back of Bastien's neck went up at the words. "I know about pride hierarchy, shifter. Be advised that Kat belongs to no man, least of all one who allows his female to attack Kat with her nastiness."

He heard Kat's sharp gasp at his words and figured he'd pay for them later. But something deep in his soul had rebelled at hearing the man refer to Kat as *his*.

She's mine.

Ethan snarled and shot ten feet toward them in one giant leap. Bastien raised his daggers and prepared for battle. But Kat stepped between them, holding her hands up. "Don't make me use my secret weapon," she said, weariness infusing her voice. "Don't we have better things to do when Nicky . . . when he—"

Bastien waited for the alpha to stand down. The man's muscles tightened and then relaxed, and he inclined his head to Kat and Bastien. Bastien thrust his daggers back in their sheaths, then put his arm around Kat's shoulders. "You are correct, yet again."

He squared his shoulders and held out a hand to Ethan.

"My apologies. I mean to offer insult neither to your family nor to your honor, and I offer sincere condolences on the loss of your pride-brother. I am Bastien from Atlantis, and we need to talk."

Ethan waited a long moment, then grasped Bastien's hand and shook it. "No apologies are necessary. I can understand why a man—or an Atlantean—would want to defend Kat's honor. She is one of our pride's greatest treasures. Her . . . *gift* is of incalculable value to our defenses."

Ethan's eyes narrowed as he stared pointedly at Bastien's arm resting on Kat's shoulder. The smoldering possession in the way Ethan looked at Kat made Bastien want to smash something. Or someone.

Kat spoke up again. "We need to talk about Nicky, if you two are done marking your territory. Which, I might remind you, does *not* include me."

Ethan evidently agreed, at least to the part about the need for a conversation, since he held up a hand to direct them to the room from which he'd just entered the hallway. Bastien smiled his best liaison smile. "After you."

Ethan's lips twitched in a half-smile, and he strode in front of them toward the doorway.

Bastien reluctantly released Kat's shoulders, but stopped her gently when she began to follow the shape-shifter. "Are you well?"

"No. No, I'm not *well* in any way," she said. "But we need to do this."

Bastien followed her through the doorway into an enormous room dominated by an Olympic-sized swimming pool. Ah. The *pool* room. Someone was doing laps down the middle. He raised one eyebrow at the sight. "I didn't know panthers even liked water."

Ethan shrugged. "We like it well enough as cats, but I've found that most of us love it in our human form. And the benefits of being the man who owns the pool are obvious." He jerked his chin toward the edge of the pool nearest them, where a nude woman stood up in the water, lifted her head, and shook droplets from her hair. Her eyes sharpened when she saw them.

"Ah, it's Kat," she said. Her voice dripped menace even as

her hair dripped chlorinated water. "I heard about Nicky. He was a friend of yours, wasn't he?"

Beside him, Kat had noticeably flinched at the sight of the woman, but answered in a quiet tone. "Yes, Fallon. He was."

So this was Fallon. Bastien found himself wanting to unsheathe his daggers again. Anubisa, the evil goddess of the vampires, had taught him that females could be far more deadly than males—of any species.

Kat abruptly turned to Ethan and positioned her back to the pool. Bastien wondered if it were deliberate. He kept an eye on the female in the water and noticed that Fallon's lips curled back from a mouthful of sharp-looking teeth as she silently hissed at Kat.

Deadly, indeed.

"Ethan, Nicky told us that Terminus did this to him. Before he died—" Kat's voice broke.

Bastien touched her arm, then gently pulled her back against him. "He did say that, but he was wrong. We destroyed Terminus several weeks ago. He is permanently dead this time."

Ethan's attention snapped to Bastien. "You destroyed one of the most powerful vampires in the United States? You said 'we.' Who is 'we'?"

"Prince Conlan of Atlantis and those of us who form his elite guard. Terminus and several of his minions attacked us. Trust me, Terminus is no more. And not *one* of the most powerful, but two, are now permanently dead. We also watched Anubisa slay Barrabas, her servant, and then our prince and his betrothed destroyed Anubisa."

A splashing noise from the pool alerted Bastien. He jerked his head around to gauge the threat from Fallon and was surprised by the sight of her very naked, very female form climbing out of the pool. Part of him enjoyed the show. Another, much larger, part of him wondered why he didn't enjoy it more than he did.

The feel of the woman almost imperceptibly trembling in his arms answered his question. Something about Kat made him think of dangerous words. Words like *protect. Comfort. Cherish.*

Fallon stalked across the floor, arrogantly flaunting her

nudity. Clearly putting on a show for Kat. When she reached Ethan, she draped herself around him.

"He claims to have destroyed Terminus, but what do we know of him? Terminus was more powerful even than Organos," she sneered. "We would be foolish to believe this so-called Atlantis man."

Ethan pushed her away, and Fallon snarled at him. Bastien watched the interchange and wondered how much of it was a display presented solely for his benefit. Or, he amended silently, for *Kat's* benefit. The sorrow that had radiated from Kat darkened and soured into an almost-helpless rage, but even as he felt her emotions slicing through him, they changed. Dampened back to calm. Her gift was at work again.

"I am a Warrior of Poseidon. I am here to offer alliance to the East Coast shape-shifters, beginning with your panthers, on the advice of one who knows you," Bastien said. "I offer my help in the investigation of your dead colleague. We have much experience in these matters."

"Experience in what matters? Killing shape-shifters?" Fallon spat the words at him. "We've heard of you. Learned that the Atlanteans of legend have been walking the earth for millennia, killing our kind on behalf of the pathetic single-natured humans. We don't need or want help from the likes of you."

Before Bastien could respond, Ethan roared. It was the full, throaty roar of a male panther in his prime, and the force of it sent Fallon cringing to her knees before him. Kat bowed her head, as well, and Bastien hated the submissive gesture.

Hated the idea that Kat would submit to Ethan for even a single second—in any possible way. He stepped around her to face Ethan. To the nine *hells* with politics. He was up for a little one-on-one ass kicking.

"One known as Jack claims to have fought beside your prince against Barrabas. Do you know of this?" Ethan directed the question to Bastien.

"Yes. I was there."

"Did Jack shift to his panther form when you battled the bloodsuckers?" Ethan glanced to his right, and Bastien was left with the sure knowledge that an army of shape-shifters stood in the shadows ready to kill him if he answered incorrectly.

Kat started to speak, but Bastien cut her off, recognizing the trick question. "No, he did not. But he shifted into a tiger, damn near ten feet long."

Ethan's shoulders relaxed, and the tension in the room noticeably decreased. "Yes. The tiger spoke well of you. Said 'the tall one is a fucking fighting machine,'" Ethan admitted. "Told me you were a good one to have around if the world needed saving."

Bastien grinned. "I feel the same way about him. I'm a lot better at battles than I am at politics, but my prince assigned me this mission. Therefore, I *will* successfully complete it."

Ethan stared at him, considering, for a long beat. Then he threw back his head and laughed, though the laughter was acid-like in its bitterness. "I think I'm going to like you, Atlantean. Now let's head to my conference room to talk."

As the shape-shifter headed down the hall, Bastien noticed that he never looked back at the naked woman still huddling on the floor. Kat very carefully gave Fallon a wide berth as she walked around her and followed Ethan. However, Bastien's ingrained standards of courtesy did not include leaving a naked woman to shiver on the floor. He held out a hand to help her up, his face impassive in an attempt to preserve what shreds of her dignity she had left.

She hissed at him and flung herself back and away from his hand. "Get away from me, you murderous bastard. We know what you are. You can't undo thousands of years of murdering my kind by making—or pretending to make—one or two deceitful alliances."

She stood up and glared at him, hatred and fury radiating from every line of her body. "Tell that freak bitch to stay away from Ethan, too. He's mine. No matter how much he thinks he wants her, he must mate with me for the purity of the species. What good is a half-breed to the alpha of our pride?" She spat on the floor and then turned on her heel and sprinted away from him and through the door that led back to the hallway.

Bastien's entire body clenched at the implications of her words. Ethan, the pride's alpha, wanted Kat. The dying shifter had said the same. Did Bastien, as the Atlantean liaison, have any right to interfere with that?

Every cell in his body rebelled at the thought. Not Kat. Kat belonged to *herself*. She wasn't a pawn in some ancient hierarchy of shape-shifter politics.

Something primal stirred deep in the blackness of his soul. *Fuck politics. There is no way he will ever put his hands on her. I'll kill him first.*

"Bastien?" Kat stood in the doorway. "Are you—oh, my God. What are you doing?"

He looked at where she was pointing. At the water steaming and hissing as it lapped at the edges of the swimming pool. Just the mere thought of another man's hands on Kat's body had done that. He'd channeled sheer, potent rage through his command over the element of water.

Ethan's voice, calling from somewhere out of sight down the hall, cut through Bastien's dazed thoughts. "Kat? I need you."

And, even as Bastien forced his hands to unclench, the water in the pool began to boil.

The conference room was as spare as the entry and pool room had been ornate. A man worked here, it was evident. A leader. The wooden tabletops were covered with documents and maps.

"Plotting strategy?" Bastien stepped closer to the table holding the largest maps, and Ethan smoothly placed himself between Bastien and his goal.

"Not strategy so much as options," Ethan said smoothly, the amusement in his eyes defying anyone to challenge him.

For the present, there would not be a challenge. Atlantis needed Ethan and his shifters. One step at a time, then.

"What options if you join with vampires, your oldest enemies, against humanity?" Bastien demanded. "Even as some of you are part human."

Kat made a sound; of protest, maybe. Denial. But no shape-shifter was part *vampire*, that much was irrefutable.

Ethan leaned back against the table, projecting a studied image of nonchalance. But the rage in his eyes belied his calm pose. "I don't want to hear your opinions on my options, Atlantean. You didn't face the blasphemy of your brother-cousin, trapped in his animal form in death, *stuffed and mounted* in a shop!"

Kat gasped. "No! Nelson's shop?"

Ethan inclined his head, jaw clenching.

She shook her head, as if willing the vicious image from her mind. "No, that's not—then we have a black coven here?" She snapped her head up, pinned Ethan with her gaze. "The fire? That was you?"

"I burned it. If Nelson had been there, I would have burned him with it." He stood proud, uncompromising.

Bastien almost unwillingly admired him for it. "Had the same happened to one of my brother warriors, I would have felt much the same. Your revenge is understandable. Forming an alliance with the bloodsuckers out of vengeance or spite is not."

Ethan rose in a swift, fluid motion, the muscles in his body acting in concert to display his predatory nature. "But we should ally with you instead? The death squad of vigilantes in black who have murdered our kind for centuries? For millennia?"

Bastien never even flinched. "Are we really, panther? Have we ever acted against you or yours? Against Kat's father or his father before him? The Warriors of Poseidon only intervene when mankind is threatened. It is our mission, our duty, and our sacred oath. Those shape-shifter prides like your own who have never threatened humans have never known our vengeance."

Kat spoke up. "He's right, Ethan. Our only knowledge of Atlantis is shrouded in the myths and stories of our people. We've heard of the warrior vigilantes, but they've never come against us."

Ethan bared his teeth in a silent snarl, a low, grumbling noise issuing from his throat, and Kat backed up until she stood beside Bastien again. He pulled her against him and felt the slight trembling run through her body. Vowed to make someone pay for making her feel anything but happiness. Maybe even the *someone* standing in front of him.

"No, we have never threatened humans, but they have

nearly hunted *us* to extinction," Ethan growled. "Not only our pure animal brethren, but our own pride. Now they work with the black covens to trap us in death for sport. Why would I not form an alliance with Organos?"

Bastien played his trump card, judging the time right to share the information Alaric had told only to him before he, Justice, and Denal had left Atlantis. "Because Organos plays you for a fool. He is the one working with the black sorcerers."

Kat gasped again, this time moving away from Bastien. Ethan merely narrowed his eyes. "What proof do you have of this? Why would I believe you?"

"I have the word straight from Poseidon's high priest. He does not lie."

"So you say," Ethan said, shrugging. "But I have no knowledge of your priest. Where is your evidence?"

Bastien's hands grasped the handles of his daggers at the implied slight to his honor, then he slowly removed them. "Liaison," he reminded himself, shaking his head. "I'm tempted to challenge you to battle for that remark, shifter, but I must remember my sworn duty. So I will provide you this evidence you require. Will you grant me the courtesy of waiting before you proceed with an alliance with Organos and his blood pride?"

Ethan slowly nodded. "Forty-eight hours. I will give you that much time to prove you're right about this. And if you are—" He smiled so fiercely that Bastien could well understand how the man was alpha of such a fierce coalition of shape-shifters. "If you're right, and the vampires are killing my people, then we'll *end* them."

Bastien's smile matched the ferocity of Ethan's. "As your liaison, I can officially assure you that I will be right there beside you when that time comes. Even us political types need to battle a few vampires now and then."

Ethan's ringing laughter followed them down the hall as they made their way out of his house. Kat looked up at Bastien, wonder and consideration in her eyes. "I'd almost say he likes you. And he doesn't like any outsiders. Ever."

"He is a fierce warrior who seeks to protect his people. I respect him, as well," he replied, never breaking his stride.

But, as they walked out into the fading sunshine that mocked the darkness of his mission, he realized the truth behind his words. Although he respected Ethan, he would not hesitate to bring him down unless Ethan called off the alliance with the vampires.

Or if he attempts any claim on Kat, a voice in his mind demanded.

That remains to be seen. Okay, my Lord Poseidon, now would be a really great time to take pity on your warrior and share your plans with me.

Unfortunately, as was so often the case with gods, the only response was a faint, mocking laughter that echoed in his mind.

Eight

Kat put the grocery bag on her kitchen table and stared almost blindly at it, as if somewhere in the grain of the brown paper lay the secret to resolving the crises that had smashed into her carefully structured life.

One of the few friends I had left in the world dead—murdered? Check.

Ethan admitting he formed an alliance with the vampires? Check.

Fallon hating my guts and probably going to try to kill me after I saw him humiliate her? Check.

Alone in my house with bags full of food I don't know how to cook and a huge Atlantean male who seems to want something from me? Something I'm not prepared to give?

Check. And check. And check.

"Damn."

"You don't like steak?" His voice was mild, but the sound of it still startled her. Something in the tone of it—rough, but gentle—sent chills down her spine. Not chills of fear, but just the opposite. Attraction. Desire.

Wanting.

She felt that peculiar sensation again, as if the animal side of her nature were finally waking up from a hibernation that had lasted all of Kat's life. If it hadn't been so impossible, she might even have believed that she was on the verge of shifting.

"Kat?" Bastien's voice cut into her thoughts again, and this time he sounded concerned. She needed to pay attention. To make an attempt to form coherent sentences.

"I'm sorry. It's been a long day. Nicky . . . I think I need to take a shower and just rest." The thought of a shower was so tempting she nearly cried. But she had a guest. He must want to clean up, too. "You should go take the first shower. I'm sure you want to rinse the day off, too."

She turned and tried to smile, but the idea of Bastien naked and wet in the shower spiked her imagination to a dangerous heat. She had to fight herself to keep from jumping on him.

He flashed that incredible smile at her, and for an instant it was there again. That gleam of fire in his eyes. But then it was gone, and his expression was back to his Mr. Liaison cool calm again. "No, but thank you for the kindness," he said, bowing slightly. All courtesy and gallantry, when what she wanted from him was heat and fire. Passion that could make her forget the sight of Nicky's eyes glazing over to lifelessness.

She shook her head to rid it of the image. "I'll just go first, then. We can figure out dinner in a while."

But, having said that, she couldn't force herself to move. A strand of his hair had fallen across his cheek as he bent his head and unpacked the groceries, and she stared at the glossy blackness of it, wanting nothing more than to raise her hand and smooth it back from his face. To step into his arms and, for once in her *be strong, be brave, be self-reliant, be independent* life—just for one damn time—let someone else be strong.

To let *him* be strong. Just for a moment.

He looked up and caught her staring at him. Must have read something in her eyes. Took a step toward her. "Kat, there's something I need to—"

"No! I mean, no, there's nothing," she heard herself babbling but was powerless to stop. "Well, you should just, I'll go. Now. I'll—"

He blinked, probably wondering who the crazy woman

was and what she'd done with Kat, and the sheer humiliation of it all snapped her weird paralysis, and she ran. Ran again, by way of stumbling down the hall to the bathroom. Ran away from the first man who'd ever made her feel safe.

Bastien pushed open the door and headed outside. He knew he wasn't imagining it. There had been a moment. A capital M Moment, right there in the kitchen. Whatever it was that had taken over his mind and senses, Kat had felt it, too. At least for a single moment. And then she'd run away from him. Again.

"It's so terrific, this effect I have on women," he muttered. Then he forced himself to reach for the calm center of his serenity—the center that seemed to explode into fractured shards whenever he was around Kat. Drew in a lungful of the humid evening air and stripped off his shirt and pants. He had need of a shower. Maybe an hour or two under icy water would help the current state of his painfully aroused body.

He was Atlantean. He had no need for pipes and plumbing to find the water to cleanse his body. Legs spread apart, he lifted his face to the evening sky. Raised his arms, palms up, and called to the sea. Called to the water all around him. Called to the elements to purify the water and bring it to him.

He laughed, delighted still, after hundreds of years, as the water rushed to do his bidding. He'd learned a few tricks over the centuries, and he manipulated the currents of water as they danced and swirled in the air around him. Ribbons of water sparkled and shimmered as they curved around and over him to wash the sweat and dirt of the day from his body.

The coolness of the water soothed his overheated skin, calmed the nerve endings jumping and jangling under his skin, and caressed the fiercely hardened erection that jutted up against his body. Everything about Kat—her luscious curves, her scent of sunshine and forest, and her silky cinnamon and sunshine hair—had him walking around in a state of permanent arousal. But the look in her eyes in the kitchen had made him want to lift her onto the table right there and then. Rip the clothes from her body and drive into her. Claim her heat and her wetness for his rightful place, and then spend the next ten or fifty years holding her.

But wanting to *claim* her was wrong. It made him no better than Ethan. Not to mention the slight problem that she was half shape-shifter. Poseidon didn't exactly allow his warriors to interact with the dual-natured. He spared a thought for Alaric's reaction to the news that Bastien had mated with a shape-shifter, and grimaced.

Not that it mattered. Kat had made it clear that she wanted nothing to do with him, after all, when she went running down the hall. Bastien sent his senses into the elements and adjusted the temperature of the water sluicing down his body. He needed it to be icy.

Kat finished toweling the water from her hair and wrapped the robe more firmly around herself. She'd been too distracted by Bastien to think of clean clothes when she'd escaped into the bathroom. Only ten steps, though. She only needed to make it ten steps down the hall to her bedroom without him seeing her.

"Oh, get a grip," she lectured her reflection in the steamy mirror. "It's not like he's going to grab you and ravish you. He's a perfect gentleman."

Her reflection seemed to have its own thoughts on the matter, though, because it made a face back at Kat. "Yeah, I know," she told herself. "Damn the luck, right? And, really, the only worry is that I'll jump on *him*."

She pushed open the bathroom door, realizing that talking to herself in the mirror—and, worse, expecting her reflection to talk back—was a slim stick of beef jerky away from the crazy machine. She peeked down the hall for a glimpse of her guest, but the coast was clear.

As she slipped into the hall, she heard the sound of rain outside. "That's odd. We had sunshine in the forecast for the next three days," she murmured, then pushed aside the cotton curtain that covered the small hallway window and looked outside.

Her knees turned to water. She had to grab the windowsill to hold herself up, because the object of her more heated shower fantasies was standing in the middle of her yard. Stark naked. And, from what she could tell, he was somehow magically causing water to dance around and caress every inch of his incredibly firm, muscled body.

She stood there, frozen, and watched the playful loops and curls of water twirl over his thickly curved biceps and down the muscled planes of his back to his, oh, dear heavens, firm, tight, and gorgeous butt. She watched the water continue down the corded muscles of his huge thighs and the length of his long, long legs and heard a low, growling noise. It took her a moment to realize that the sound came from *her*. She wanted to *lick* him. The cat inside her sat up and begged at the idea.

Kat's mouth dried out as she continued to watch him, unable to tear herself away. He turned, and she caught sight of his huge chest and the silky hair that arrowed down his abdomen to the erection that was as fierce and strong and huge as the rest of him. The heated emotions of her inner cat got tangled up with her own, more human, thoughts, and all she could think was *yes, yes, oh, that, I want that, I want to lick him and bite him and I want to play, and I want to feel him pounding inside me with that, oh, please, oh, please, I'm so cold, I've always been so cold, I want that heat.* A warm torrent of silky wet heat dripped between her thighs at the thought, at the sheer aching desire of it, and she moaned, digging her nails into the wood of the windowsill.

And he turned, sparkling with the luminescence of the water surrounding him, and looked straight into her eyes.

Bastien felt her watching him. Knew she was behind the window. The feral warrior who lurked behind the amiable mask he showed the world roared inside him, wanting to get to her. Wanting to possess her. Needing to at least show her exactly what she did to him.

It wasn't gallant or courteous or gentle. It was sheer raw need pouring through him at the thought of her watching him. He turned to face her house and the window where he knew she stood. Planted his feet and let her see him. All of him. Let her see his fierce arousal—his desire for her. Only for her.

Felt his legs tremble with the force of his longing. When he met her gaze through the glass, the shock of awareness sparked and burned through his veins. She wanted him, too.

Grimly determined, he released the water he'd been channeling and headed for the steps to her house. Prayed she wouldn't deny him. But realized, with the sliver of rational thought left to him, that they might both be better off if she did.

Nine

Kat knew the second Bastien made the decision. She saw his eyes change; saw them darken with a heat that mirrored her own. Watched in awe as the tendrils of water sparkling around him suddenly pulsed with a shimmering blue green light. Nearly fell to her knees when he started for her door.

What had she unleashed, and why was it exhilaration rather than fear that swept through her? She shivered at the prospect of tasting passion in the arms of a warrior who'd stepped straight out of a legend. She heard the door bang open, and the sound sent shockwaves trembling through her.

Clutching the folds of her robe at her throat, she didn't even pretend to back away. She wanted him—oh, dear God in heaven, how she wanted him—and he was coming. Stalking down the hall toward her with the arrogant pride of a warrior and the lethal menace of a predator. She didn't know which aroused her more. The cat inside her snarled its mingled defiance and desire, while the woman made a low, moaning sound in her throat.

He stopped, mere inches away, and looked down at her. His jaw clenched with the effort it cost him to remain still; to keep from touching her. The passion in his eyes seared into her, and she felt the melting in her core as it dripped warm, creamy wetness onto her thighs. He still said nothing, but the faint trembling shudder that shook through his body reassured her. This was no ravager to take without permission. He wanted her, but he waited.

The knowledge of her power over this warrior from ancient prophecy thrilled her beyond any desire she'd ever felt, and she had to put her hands out to his chest to hold herself upright. "Yes," she whispered. "Yes."

Bastien heard her surrender and threw his head back and roared out his claim. He had channeled the fury of lightning itself before, but had never known this searing fire that burned through his blood. The hunger echoed in his pulse and in hers, which he heard quickening as he reached out to her. Finally, *finally* put his hands in that wealth of glorious hair and gently wrapped one palm around the back of her head to pull her to him.

"Kat," he murmured. "Lady Kat, do you say yes to me? If yes, you will be mine for this night."

She stared up at him, and the shape of her eyes was somehow lengthened, her pupils changed. The mysteries of womanhood and of her dual nature were reflected in her eyes. "Yes, Bastien. I say *yes*. I need to feel alive."

He paused, though nearly driven mad by her words. "I would not take advantage of your sorrow, my lady," he said roughly. "As a scion of Atlantis, I may call down an hour or two more of cold shower to ease this fire you create inside me."

She smiled at the image created in her mind and shook her head, then put a finger against his lips. "No, Atlantean. I do not say yes merely out of my sorrow, but from the need I have for you." She ducked her head and then raised it to meet his gaze. "The need I have felt since I first met you, two years ago."

The courage and desire shining in her eyes released him from the bounds of restraint, and he lifted her into his arms. Bent his head to kiss her, knowing even as he did that he was lost. When his lips touched her, a touchstone deep inside his soul unleashed a torrent like unto the one that had driven Atlantis to its undersea destiny.

More, more.

An ember of sanity struggled to surface, bearing thoughts of Poseidon, Conlan, and Atlantis. Duty and honor and mission.

But desire swamped sanity. Longing triumphed over logic. He needed, by the gods, he *needed*, and he had never needed anything in his four centuries as he needed the taste of this woman.

He swept his tongue into her mouth and kissed her with all the desperate wanting she provoked in him, and wonder of wonders, *she kissed him back*.

Kat's mind raged at the feel of him, the heat of him, and the steel of muscle under skin that trembled at her touch. She caught her breath at the first touch of his lips and was lost. Her breath, his breath, they mingled together in a kiss that lasted longer than an eternity, shorter than a thought. Caught up in the strength of his powerful arms, she melted against him, sank into his strength, surrendered her willing spirit to him.

This moment was hers, no matter what may follow it. *He* was hers, if only for a night. She smiled against his lips, and her cat purred inside her. For one moment trapped in starlight, wrapped in desire, the two sides of her dual-natured existence came together as one.

"You are mine, then, for this night? You freely give yourself into my care?" he asked, no, *demanded* of her.

The fierce longing in his tone carried any lingering hesitation away on its currents. She was desired, and she desired. Nothing had ever felt so right to her as this one moment, her body wrapped in the arms of a warrior.

"I am yours," she said, relinquishing her control and trusting him with everything she had. "I am yours."

Bastien did not ask again. He'd been granted permission, now it was in him to take. To *take* and to *give* and to bring an end to this pain of wanting that had swamped him since he'd first caught sight of her face, terrified but filled with grim resolve, two years past.

He lifted her off the floor and, hands firmly grasping her rounded hips, swung around to find her bedroom. She gasped and he took her mouth again, plundering. Possessing.

Mine. The voice in his head demanded he claim her, mark her, brand her as his own.

Cherish her, protect her, keep her for the long centuries of my existence.

His body demanded something more urgent and immediate. He hardened even further against her, his cock straining against the robe she wore, as he reached her bed. He slowly released her to slide down his body and reached between them to untie the cord that kept him from feeling her shower-damp skin against his heated flesh.

As he pushed the edges of her garment from her shoulders, the creamy skin thus revealed damn near brought him to his knees before her. He pulled in a sharp breath and then reconsidered.

"On my knees seems a fitting tribute to your beauty, my lady Kat," he murmured against her hair, against her throat, against the swell of her breasts as he sank to the floor in front of her.

She bent and cupped his face between her hands, golden eyes huge in her pale face. "But—"

"Shh," he whispered. "Let me learn the secrets of your body. Let me touch you and taste you and know you." He captured the tip of one breast in his mouth and licked and suckled on it, gently at first, then strongly, until she moaned and made a helpless thrusting motion with her hips.

Then he transferred his mouth to her other breast and replaced his lips with his fingers on the first, gently squeezing and lightly pinching the nipple as he sucked on its twin, until he heard her moaning again, this time his name. She twined her fingers in his hair and pulled.

"Please, please."

He looked up at her, and the soft flush of her skin combined with the heat in her eyes to undo him. He had no more thought for gentle seduction, but only for taking. For driving into her until she could never get him out.

For claiming.

He tested her readiness with a finger, nearly crying out at the hot wetness that welcomed him into her body. He bent his head to her nipple again and drove two fingers inside her. This time it was she who cried out, bucking against his hand.

In one motion, he stood and lifted her, then twisted to fall back upon her bed with her on top of him. He held her head to his and plundered her mouth once more, with his fingers still steadily thrusting inside her. Then he rolled over so that he straddled her body. "I need you now, my lady. I must offer my apologies for reverting to the haste of my youth, but I find that I need to be inside the heat of your body more than I need to find my next breath."

She stared up at him for a long moment, body shuddering in reaction to her desire and the motion of his fingers across the pearl at the junction of her heat. He had a moment to wonder at the secrets hidden deep in the amber of her eyes, before she slowly smiled and lifted her legs to clasp around his back. "I need you, too, my poet warrior. And remember that I'm not the only one surrendering, here."

He moved his hand to guide the head of his cock against the slick wetness of her opening, and then he put his hands on the bed on either side of her as he bent to kiss her yet again. "Gladly do I surrender, Kat Fiero," he whispered, and then he threw back his head and roared his possession as he drove into her with one stroke, not stopping until the base of his cock thrust against her pelvis.

She arched up and into his body and screamed, an eerie sound that had as much of panther in it as woman, and then she dug her nails into his back and clung to him, thrusting into him in time with his movements. "Oh, yes, please, now," she said, more demand than plea.

"Yes, *mi amara*, I am pleased to comply," he said, voice rough with the effort of forming coherent speech. He drove into her, harder and faster, gone partly mad with hunger and a desperate, terrible passion.

Knowing he would defy Poseidon himself for this woman.

He felt the moment she approached the precipice; her entire body tightened around his own. He thrust, impossibly hardening beyond any limits his body had ever known.

As he drove her up and over the edge into the abyss, she looked into his eyes, into his soul, and uttered a single word. His name.

"Bastien," she murmured, and he was lost.

The stars that surely had shone upon Atlantis in its glory days exploded behind his eyes and in his blood and—for a moment, a long moment, an incalculable moment—he felt her inside him as jewels burst in his brain to color his world.

A rift opened in the fabric of his universe, a fissure in his bleak solitude, and she slid in, warm and silken as a summer rain on the ocean waves. Her essence opened itself to him as the unfurling of a bed of sea stars, and it tempered the bleakness of his hardened soul. Hopefulness met grim resolve, compassion met implacable duty. Her kindness entwined itself in the dark, crabbed spaces of his black soul and somehow lighted the path to absolution.

He was lost, and yet she had found him, and he would never, ever be the same.

Ten

"What just happened?" Kat lay—okay, she was collapsed, in fact—halfway on top of Bastien with her legs hanging over the edge of the bed. She was trying not to admit to herself that she was entirely freaked out. Basically, this was the first time she'd made love, since a few ineffectual fumblings in college. Oh, yeah, and the sky had exploded in her brain.

Nothing out of the ordinary. Just an unbelievably passionate interlude with a four-hundred-year-old warrior from the lost continent of Atlantis.

Bastien's voice rumbled in his chest, under her head. "That, my lady, was a passion unmatched in my history."

He sounded as exhausted as she felt. Kat smiled, fiercely glad of it. "Truly?" She turned to look at him. "There had to be a lot of women in so much history."

He raised an eyebrow and reached to pull her up so that her head rested on his shoulder and she fit snug against his side, her leg resting on his thigh. "Not nearly as many as you might think. When one is bound by inexorable duty and mission, one loses the taste for dalliance."

She tried to pull away from him, but his arm tightened around her. "Is that all I am? A dalliance?" She hated the note of uncertainty in her voice even as she heard the words tumble out, so she tried to laugh it off. "Well, that was a pretty terrific dalliance. That should hold us both for a while, until we find somebody else to dally with, right?"

He sat up abruptly, drawing her to sit beside him. "If that is what you think, you are utterly mistaken," he said flatly. "There will be no other dalliance, *mi amara*, for either of us. Please do not speak of it again."

She blinked. "Okay, *that* was unexpected. After your brave words in front of Ethan, are you now suggesting that I surrender my independence to you? And what is *mi amara*?"

"Your surrender, as mine, was not of your independence but of your solitude, I think," he said, pulling the blanket around her when she shivered at the cool currents of air-conditioned air blowing on her bare skin. He laced his fingers in hers, and she looked down at their joined hands, marveling that she could feel so completely safe and cherished—so *right*—in the arms of a man she barely knew.

And yet . . . somehow there had been that moment of knowing. That moment when her soul had seemed to wing its way out of her body and twine its way through Bastien's heart, the same way their fingers were joined together now. She'd known him on a level far deeper than she'd ever known another living soul; known the pain he'd faced, the battles he'd fought, and the black acts he'd been forced to commit on behalf of humanity.

He believed he was damned for it. Damned to the nine hells, whatever that meant. Having caught a glimpse of his despair, she could guess, though.

The mere thought of it terrified her. But before she could find words to tell him why the idea was bad, awful, and just wrong in so many ways, he spoke first.

"I am wrong for you." His black eyes were filled with pain as his words echoed her thoughts. "I have done so many things, caused so much death and destruction in the name of my mission—in the name of my god—that I can never undo."

She leaned against him, driven by the despair in his tone to offer comfort instead of rejection. Her heart rebelled at the thought of turning away from him. "What you have done, you have done as part of your duty to protect, haven't you?"

He nodded, caught her hand in his and kissed her finger-tips. "Yes, but all Atlanteans have free will, *mi amara*. It was my choice to serve as a warrior of Poseidon. The sea god marks each of us at our dedication ceremony," he replied, touching a hand to the strange symbol marked high on the right side of his chest.

She traced its outline with her fingers. "What does it mean?"

"It offers testimony to my vow to protect mankind. The circle represents all the peoples of the world. Intersecting it is the pyramid of knowledge deeded to them by the ancients. The silhouette of Poseidon's Trident bisects them both."

He smiled crookedly. "Even one good only for his strength has the opportunity to serve well in Poseidon's service."

"Why do you do that? Why do you discount your intelligence?" she asked, brows drawing together. "Your strength is not all that you are. Somehow, I have seen inside you to the fierce intelligence you don't admit even to yourself. You plan and question and plot strategy with the best of them, don't you?"

"But—"

She cut him off, nodding sagely. "Oh. Your prince isn't very smart, though, is he?"

"What? Prince Conlan is a brilliant leader. His—"

"Really?" she said, tilting her head. "So Prince Brilliant chose you as liaison, huh? Guess he must have known what he was doing."

He gently tucked a strand of her hair behind her ear. "You are also very wise, are you not? Fierce in your defense of one as unworthy as me. Had my heart not been captured to your will before, you would have just won it."

She trembled, unable to breathe. "Your heart?"

"From the day of my vow until this night, I have never found reason to question my loyalty to my duty. But looking at you, holding you in my arms . . ."

"And *mi amara*?"

"Means my beloved."

Heat rushed through her at the words and at the expression on his face—that of stark possession mingled with fierce longing. "Shh," she said, laughing a little, trying to pretend her universe hadn't just turned upside down. "There is no need to question anything right now. We never question loyalty on an empty stomach, right?"

He blinked, then shouted with laughter. Something chained in her heart broke free at the sound of his unfettered joy. "Ah, yes, my little cat. I am indeed hungry. But it is not for the food we purchased."

In an instant, he had her on her back and underneath him as he grinned joyously down at her. "I'm of a mind to sample my dessert first this night."

It was a long, long time before she was able to form another lucid thought.

Bastien watched Kat as she lay sleeping and wondered why Poseidon had seen fit to bless him with this woman. He could never deserve her.

No, but the gods do not give only what we deserve. It is the nature of their caprice. And perhaps she is not for me.

Everything in him rebelled at the thought. Perhaps she was not meant for him, but that did not mean he would ever give her up. If Prince Conlan could break with eleven thousand years of tradition and marry a human, surely he—not royal by a single cell of his makeup—could make his own choice, as well?

If she will have me, I will be hers.

As he stared down at her, the emotion welling inside him forced the words up from his heart. From his soul. Words that he spoke in his native tongue, ancient Atlantean, as if to underscore his vow:

I offer my sword, my heart, and my life to protect your own
From now until the last drop of ocean has vanished from
the earth
You are my soul.

She stirred in her sleep, but didn't waken. Simply uttering the words had freed something in his heart and stirred his body to urgency again. He leaned over her, tempted to wake her and join with her once more, but decided to let her rest. To put her needs ahead of his own.

Oh, boy. Next I'll be taking out the garbage and shopping for curtains.

Grinning, not nearly as bothered by the thought as he should have been, his thoughts turned to something nearly as important as love—food.

He rose silently from the bed, intent on stealing into the kitchen and preparing a feast for her while she slept. She had mentioned a hunger other than the one they had sated so well together. Let her learn that he had other skills than death and justice.

He was a fantastic cook. And what was the old saying? The way to a shape-shifter's heart was through her belly?

Laughing softly, he drew on a pair of jeans and a T-shirt from his bag and headed for the kitchen. Humming to himself, enjoying the peaceful and contented aftermath of his body's fierce spending in hers, he reached in a cupboard for a pan and nearly missed the quiet call of Justice's voice in his mind. *Bastien? You brick-headed ox, are you in there?*

He accessed the mental pathway that only Atlanteans knew, save for Riley and her sister, and reached out to his fellow warrior. *I am. Do you have something to report?*

We're on your front step. You're going to want to hear this.

He strode to the front door and opened it to find Justice and Denal waiting for him. The dangerous cast to Justice's expression sent ice racing up Bastien's spine. "What is it?"

Denal looked him up and down and whistled quietly. "Ho, boy. What have you been up to? Or should I say *who* have you been up to?"

Bastien never changed expression, but lifted the youngling

into the air by means of a hand around his throat. "Perhaps you will refrain from any further disparaging remark about Lady Kat," he said, mild voice at odds with his actions.

Denal nodded slightly as his face turned red, and Bastien lowered him to the ground. Justice's eyes narrowed. "Why does this smell like trouble, my friend? She is a shape-shifter and well you know it."

Bastien inclined his head. "There are few things I seem to know anymore, but one of them is that Kat is my destined mate. How I resolve the conflict that brings is between me and Poseidon."

Justice laughed, not unkindly. "Oh, Bastien. You have depths none of us dreamed of. And I'm guessing Alaric and Conlan will have a few things to say about it."

Bastien shook his head. "We will discuss this later, if at all. What news do you bring?"

"It's Organos," Denal said, rubbing his throat and looking warily at Bastien. "His so-called alliance with Ethan is a lie, just as Alaric said. He plans to use vamp mind control to bring all the shape-shifters on the East Coast under his thrall."

Bastien leaned against the porch railing. "Mind control? This has never worked on large populations of shape-shifters, or we would have had armies of them to fight throughout the centuries."

"Evidently Terminus and Organos learned some new tricks from some scrolls Anubisa gave to them and Barrabas before Conlan and Riley dusted him," Justice drawled. "They're trying it out in a small way now. Today Florida, tomorrow the world, sort of thing."

"We need proof," Bastien said, remembering his pledge to Ethan. "The alpha gave me forty-eight hours to bring him proof, or else he allies with Organos."

Justice swore under his breath. "Yeah, about that. We had a nice little bloodsucker who sang like an undead canary, but he was so terrified of what the big bad O might do to him that he staked himself."

Denal grimaced. "Yeah, right in the car. It was disgusting. I hope I don't get charged for a cleaning by the rental company."

Bastien and Justice both turned to stare at the young warrior, who squirmed a little under their incredulous stares. "Okay,

okay, I get it, end of the world more important than my rental car agreement."

Justice rolled his eyes, then turned back to Bastien. "In any event, we will need to go back to the source, so to speak, a dive bar in Miami, and get another songbird if you need proof."

"And keep any sharp wooden objects away from this one?" Bastien prodded. "In the meantime, I'll arrange a meeting with Ethan to let him know what you found out and what's going on now. Once you bring me the evidence, you can report back to Atlantis and relay the news to Conlan, Ven, and Alaric."

Justice grinned at him, not moving an inch.

"What?" he asked, impatient to be moving. Doing something to protect Kat and her pride of panthers.

"For one so reluctant to take up the mantle of authority, you wear it well," Justice said, still grinning.

Bastien paused, realization dawning. In the past, he might have looked to Justice to form their strategy. He glanced at the house. The knowledge that Kat slept inside, still wrapped in the scent of his body, had forged steel in his mind to match that in his spine.

He was a leader now, and a leader could not give in to petty annoyances. He bowed slightly to Denal. "My apologies, my friend. I should have informed you of my feelings before expecting you to respect them."

Denal rubbed his throat again, more dramatically, then flashed his boyish smile. "No problem, man. It's worth it to see the mighty warrior laid low by a kitty cat." He ducked back, still grinning, before Bastien could smack the back of his head.

Justice leaped off the porch first. "To work, then. We shall return with all haste with your proof, Bastien. Happy hunting."

Denal was close behind him. "Say hello to the lovely ranger from me, Bastien," he called out. Then both shimmered into mist and soared over the trees toward the ocean.

Bastien watched them for a moment, then went into the house to wake Kat. Middle of the night or no, he needed to visit the pride's alpha. *Now.*

Eleven

Kat rose slowly through several layers of warm, contented languor to the sound of her name and the feel of hands gently rubbing her shoulders. "Kat, you have to wake up," the husky voice insisted. Sexy voice.

Bastien's voice. Her eyes flew open, and she looked up at his face. Not a dream, then. It had been real. *He* was real. "What is it? *When* is it? I'm starved," she murmured, reaching to touch his cheek with her hand. Then she blushed, remembering where the last conversation about hunger had ended up. "I mean, for dinner, not—"

He smiled, caught her hand, and pressed a kiss into the palm of her hand. "I would love to hear more of your hungers. I had intended to cook for you, also. But we must call on Ethan for a meeting."

She sat up, instantly awake. "What happened?"

He sat back, face drawn in harsh lines. "Organos. Perhaps Ethan will heed my warnings this time, now that I have learned the true nature of Organos's plan."

"Which is?"

"To mind-thrall your pride. First you, and then scores of

others. Once you are imprisoned by the vampires, humanity will be unable to win free of utter subjugation."

She shot out of bed, mind whirling, and pulled on the nearest clothes to hand, a pair of khaki pants and an old T-shirt. "Slavery," she said flatly. "Just what my father never wanted. If we enslave the humans, and the vampires enslave us, the world truly will end, won't it?"

In some corner of her mind, she distantly noted that by "us" she had aligned herself with her shape-shifter pride. Irrevocably.

Startlingly, he smiled as he stood. "You forget Atlantis, which is perhaps normal, considering you have so little experience with us. But we will fight the bloodsucker plan with everything in us, and the warriors of Poseidon are not an easy foe to defeat. Even now, Justice and Denal are on their way to gain proof of this plan that will satisfy Ethan."

She ran to him and hugged him, suddenly afraid that their moment would never return. Tears burned her eyes at the thought, but she furiously fought them back. A warrior deserved a woman worthy of him.

He kissed her, hard, and then grasped her shoulders and held her from him. "You need to get out of here. Now. I will not allow you to be in any danger. If you were to be harmed, my heart would shrivel within me, more barren than ever before."

The tears spilled over, but she was shaking her head *no* before he finished speaking. "Ask me anything else, Bastien. But I will not and cannot leave you, nor my family. If my gift for calm was ever good for anything, it must be now."

"Does it work on vampires?"

She blinked for a moment, and then her heart plunged down to her feet. "I don't—I've never tried it on a vampire. I don't know if it works or not."

His mouth flattened into a grim line. "I would doubt very much that it will, Kat. Vamps are immune to much that affects humans, shifters, and the children of Poseidon. They are already dead and thus impervious to many weapons dangerous to the living."

She cast around for a response more reassuring than *we'll have to find out*, or something equally inane, when they heard it. A high-pitched, female—or feline—scream.

The meaty thud that followed it.

The booming echo of a voice so purely evil that it burned the edges of her mind. "Come out, man from Atlantis. Come out, half-breed. It's time to play."

Terror turned her blood to ice. "Bastien, I know that voice. I've heard it before. That's Organos."

He shot over to the window to look outside, then turned to face her. "Stay here. Do not, under any circumstances, look outside. I would spare you that, at least."

Then, before she could protest, he pressed one last kiss to her lips, shimmered into sparkling mist, and vanished.

Twelve

Bastien shimmered through the house, stopping only to retrieve his weapons, then returned to mist to fly through the open doorway and into the sky in front of Kat's house. He prayed to all the gods of his ancestors that she would listen to him and stay hidden. He did not want her to see the broken body on the ground. She'd held no love for Fallon, but Kat was far too compassionate to wish to see her like this, sightless eyes staring into the night.

He cast his senses out, while still in mist form, in an attempt to find the master vampire. Finally, he was forced to admit defeat and return to his corporeal form as he spiraled down to stand, daggers ready, in front of the house. "Do you fear me, then, evil one?" he called, shouting out his challenge.

The chilling laughter materialized before its source. "Fear you, Atlantean? I think not. You are a minor annoyance, a boil on my ass, nothing more. I didn't even bother to bring any of my blood pride along to deal with such a minor irritant."

Bastien impassively measured the vampire who floated down to the earth not a dozen feet from him. From the ghostly white pallor of his skin to the red fire flaring in his eyes, this one's every feature proclaimed his dangerous nature.

"A cape? Really? Isn't that a little out of fashion?" He kept his voice level and amused, knowing that nothing knocked a master vampire off balance faster than facing one who was unafraid.

True to form, the vamp hissed with rage. "You *dare*? Do you see what I did to the pathetic alpha's mate? She wanted to strike a bargain with me, can you countenance it? A puny female cat daring to match wits with one of more than a thousand years of power?"

"She was a fool." Bastien slowly dropped one dagger to the ground, retaining the dagger in his left hand, and drew his sword with his right. "I am not."

"Yet you do not ask the nature of the bargain," the vampire mused, slitted eyes watching every move Bastien made. "Are you that confident or merely that stupid?"

"Perhaps you should decide, undead one," Bastien returned calmly, uninterested in being drawn into wordplay with the creature.

The vampire laughed, and the sound of it skittered down Bastien's spine like the chittering of a horde of death beetles in ancient Egypt. Death whispered in its wake. "Oh, but I want you to hear this. I smell the half-breed whore's pussy on you, so you might find it of interest."

Snapping his head up, Bastien fought to contain his rage. Barely restrained himself from charging at Organos's filthy head, sword raised to slice the undead head from its neck. He clenched his jaw and said nothing, but called water to form ice shards and flung them at Organos, aiming to slice the vamp's head from its neck.

The vamp laughed and lifted one hand to deflect the ice. It melted in midair. "This one begged me to suck the life out of your half-breed. Although I killed Fallon for her boldness, it might amuse me to turn the ranger to my use. I can think of many uses for a beautiful woman in thrall, especially one who has the strength of both of her natures to help her survive my darker urges."

A haze of violent rage, so dark a red it was nearly purple, spilled over Bastien's vision, as fury blazed through him. "You will not have her," he roared. He leaped straight into the darkened night sky, calling upon the element of air to drive him toward his enemy.

Organos sneered and waved a hand in front of himself before disappearing and reappearing directly behind Bastien. The agony of a dagger between the ribs brought Bastien crashing down to his knees on the hard ground, his sword falling from suddenly nerveless fingers.

"Simple enough to defeat an Atlantean, then. I wonder at Terminus's weakness, if the rumors are in fact true?" Organos said, voice filled with scorn and contempt as he floated down to stand before Bastien, then reached down to snatch his sword from the ground. "Perhaps I will preserve your head to grace my wall."

As the vampire raised Bastien's own sword to kill him, the warrior gathered himself for one last, desperate attack.

The sound of her voice stopped them both. "Oh, Organos, you can do better than that. You can have me, willing, if you let the Atlantean go."

Bastien looked up at Kat, standing defenseless before the ancient vampire, and his heart shriveled in his chest.

Kat feigned bravery, when really all she wanted to do was curl up and hide. Fallon, though no friend, especially after what she'd just overheard, had not deserved to die like this. The first man she'd ever loved knelt, bleeding, on the ground in the shadow of a master vamp's upraised sword.

She admitted it to herself, though it made no sense. Somehow she'd already fallen in love with this fierce warrior. "There's no way I'm going to let him die," she muttered.

Then, louder, she repeated her offer. "What fun is an enthralled mistress, shifter or no? Wouldn't I pretty much just lie there?"

She ignored Bastien's roar of protest, didn't allow herself to even glance at him. "Let him go, and I promise to play all the dirty games you like, vampire."

Staring straight at him, eyes open and alert, she thrust waves of peace and calm at Organos with everything she had. Futile, perhaps, but she had to try. Something in her head snapped at the force of it, and she felt blood trickle from one nostril.

Organos never even blinked. He stepped back a pace from Bastien, clearly wary only of the fallen warrior and not of anything she had done, then flicked a considering look her way. "You will play my games regardless of your volition, whore. What makes you think I do not prefer it to be while you are in thrall to my whim? I know of your so-called gift," he sneered. "Even should you wish it, you would be unable to defy me. And such trifles do not work against my kind."

Hopelessness and terror threatened to overwhelm her. A life of mindless zombie-like servitude to a vampire loomed worse than death and, for a moment, her courage deserted her. As she tried to force words past the lump of pure horror lodged in her throat, she felt the first whispers of calm smooth out the edges of her fear, as her *gift* made its appearance.

No! Not now! I cannot afford calm! What I need is rage!

She clenched her hands into fists, driving her fingernails into her palms until they bled, fighting with every ounce of her will against her gift. Against her *curse*.

Prayed to the goddess of all shape-shifters for a boon.

For a *miracle*.

Bastien made some slight movement, nearly imperceptible, but Organos hissed and turned his focus to him, losing interest in her. She was beneath his notice, and she knew it.

Not quite a shape-shifter. Not quite human. Not quite good enough for anything. Where was her miracle?

THEY ALWAYS CALL UPON ME WHEN IN NEED OF A MIRACLE, THE DESCENDANTS OF MY SEED, DO THEY NOT?

The voice in her head was bored and mocking, but some glimmer of warmth and amusement swirled through her mind with it.

Who are you, and what are you doing in my head? She glanced down at Bastien, but his gaze was locked on Organos. And it wasn't Bastien's voice. No, it was someone more . . . more . . .

YES. MORE. AND MORE AND MORE AND MORE. I AM

POSEIDON, GREAT-GRANDDAUGHTER CROSSED WITH BEAST.

Kat tried to think, but it was too much. Organos was going to kill Bastien any moment, and somebody was hijacking her brain. Some . . . some . . .

Oh. My. God. Are you—

YES. I AM YOUR GOD AND THE GOD OF ALL ATLANTEANS. I AM POSEIDON, RULER OF THE SEA. AND YOU ARE OF MINE AND YOUR COURAGE INTERESTS ME. LET US SEE HOW YOU DO WITHOUT THE IMPEDIMENT OF YOUR GIFT.

The voice—the *presence*—withdrew, but something in Kat snapped. Organos wouldn't lay a single claw on Bastien. No more would she put up with this worthless half-life.

No more! Rage, clean and icy pure, shot through her in a torrent of fire and roaring fury. The cat within her, so long imprisoned by her human side's unnatural calm, bellowed its defiance.

Kat clenched her teeth against making any audible sound as she watched Organos slowly raise the sword again, taking his sweet time about it, toying with Bastien before he murdered him.

But the panther inside Kat had no patience left in it. It crashed its way through her, cracking bones and contorting flesh as it leaped for its prey. In mid-leap, a feat so difficult that only the most powerful shifters could accomplish it, Kat changed fully from human to cat, lunging for the vampire's bared neck.

Even as she flew through the air, claws extended, she saw Bastien launch himself at Organos. She raised one mighty paw in the air, glorying at the freedom and power of this new body, and smashed her paw down on the vampire's neck, ripping his head nearly off of his body.

Even as she fell, rolling, to the ground, she saw Bastien plunge his dagger into Organos's heart. She screamed a feral cry of rage and triumph, shooting up to a crouch in front of the vampire, ready to rend and tear.

Bastien threw himself on her and pushed her back, as Organos dissolved into a flood of acidic slime. She snarled at him, but retracted her claws, retaining her sense of who she was.

Not panther, but woman. Dual-natured, but human still.

He stared into her eyes, and she wondered what he saw. Wondered if his budding feelings for her would turn to disgust, now that she was truly one of the race his kind had fought for millennia.

He reached up to cup her face in his hands, bent his forehead to briefly touch hers. "I am forever in debt for your attempted sacrifice and your courage, my lady."

He stood, a coiled spring of power. "Yet if you ever put yourself in danger again, I will lock you up and never let you out," he said roughly. "My heart died in my chest at the thought of any harm coming to you."

She snarled again, then stalked her way around him, reveling in the feel of her new body. Her new power. But a glance at him stopped her in her tracks. The passion that shone in his eyes—the *love*—speared her with its intensity. The cat relinquished its hold, and the woman returned.

Muscles and bone reshaped themselves, but Kat knew the feel of it now. Knew she could shift again, and was glad.

She rose, proudly nude, her clothes shredded by the shift, to stand in front of him. He smiled that slow, dangerous smile of his and swept her up to cradle her in his arms. "You are mine, little shifter. And no enemy will ever take you from me."

She put her arms around his neck and smiled. "Goes both ways, Atlantean. You're mine, too." Then her smile faded. "But we've got a lot of problems to face. We must tell Ethan about Fallon and arrange for her funeral." Her voice broke. "And Nicky's."

Bastien's head suddenly snapped up, and he released her and unsheathed his daggers. "Show yourself," he shouted to the darker shadows at the edge of the lawn.

An enormous panther hurled itself toward them, shifting as it ran, and then Ethan stood before them, fully dressed.

I have to learn that, she thought absently, suddenly aware of her nudity. Bastien ripped his shirt from his body and handed it to her. As she drew it over her head, the hem falling nearly to her knees, she heard the unspeakably weary voice of her pride alpha.

"You don't need to tell me anything. I'm here," Ethan said, looking down at the body of his dead mate. "I wish I could feel nothing for this death, considering how cheaply she purchased it for herself and her traitorous acts."

"Death is never to be taken lightly, and you cared for this woman," Bastien replied, pulling Kat close. "I am sorry for your loss. She was, perhaps, misled."

"My people intercepted yours in their search for 'the evidence, part two,' as your warrior called it," Ethan continued. "Together, they found several newly formed vampires willing to sell Organos out in hopes our people would let them live. Your intelligence was correct. We have the names of the practitioners in the black coven who helped him, as well."

"Did they?" Kat asked.

"Did they what?"

"Let the vampires live."

Death itself gleamed in Ethan's feral eyes. "No, they did not. Neither will we suffer the witches to live."

Bastien raised an eyebrow. "Quoting the Bible?"

"Our form of religion does not differ so much from Christianity, Atlantean," Ethan said. "I would welcome the opportunity to discuss your ideology with your priest some day."

"As I am sure he would, with you. In more peaceful times."

Kat shivered. "That's what we need to pray for, all of us. More peaceful times."

Bastien wrapped his arms around her. "Pray and fight. Whatever Poseidon and your own gods require."

The sound of an approaching vehicle grew closer. "That will be my people. I will call a council to discuss these matters. But you may be sure that we will be on your side in the coming war, Bastien."

"A war that we will win, Ethan. Strong allies and the side of justice must prevail."

The men clasped arms, and then Ethan looked down at Kat. "I see that you have made your choice, my Kat who is my Kat no more."

"I was never your Kat, Ethan. You made your choice, as I've made mine," she said. "I, too, am sorry for your loss. No matter what she was or did, she didn't deserve this. I'm glad we killed Organos to avenge her."

Bastien made a grumbling sound. "You were indeed formidable as a panther."

Ethan's eyes flared with interest. "This, too, is something I want to see and hear about. But another time." He bent to lift Fallon's broken body into his arms, as the headlights flashed in the driveway.

"Another time," Kat echoed sadly. She and Bastien stood watching as Ethan drove off with his dead mate's body. Then she turned to face her own mate, as she now knew him to be.

"I heard your sea god in my head," she told him, smiling a little. "He seems to think I'm his long-lost great-granddaughter or something."

Bastien's eyes widened in wonder. "Poseidon spoke to you?"

"Yes, and I think he did more than that. I think he helped me break through my gift to bring my panther out."

"He does always admire courage, Poseidon," Bastien admitted. "But now, we have much to do."

"First off, I need to get dressed," she pointed out.

He laughed and swept her into his arms. "That would not be my first choice, lovely one."

"Bastien, we need to sit in on that council," she said, although she wished she could spend the next week hiding out in her bedroom with him.

"And Prince Conlan must learn of these matters," Bastien added, walking toward the house with her in his arms.

"We have to break this mind-thrall thing, and keep my people safe from it. Oh, and you need to get over your 'I'm the warrior, you hide in the bedroom' issues."

He growled, then pressed a kiss to her lips as he went through the door, kicking it shut behind them. "I'll ignore that for now. We need to hammer out an alliance between your people and Atlantis, so your rogue shifters stop preying on humans."

She sighed, rested her head on his shoulder. "This is no 'I hate my potential mother-in-law' petty problem between us, Bastien. Our problems might be—"

He kissed her again, thoroughly this time. By the time he

raised his head, they were both trembling. "Our problems are the world's problems, *mi amara*. Even as we solve them, so do we secure the future of all of our races."

She smiled, daring to hope. "Together?"

Her warrior tightened his arms around her. "Together."

Turn the page for a preview of the next lupi novel
from *USA Today* bestselling author
Eileen Wilks

MORTAL SINS

Available in February 2009 from Berkley Sensation!

Southern air holds on to scent. Scent is vapor, after all, a chemical mist freed by heat to hang, trapped, in moist air. In his other form, Rule knew this.

In this form he knew only the richness. His world was more scent than sight as he raced through silver-shadowed woods, through air heavy with moisture and fragrance. Layers and layers of green overlaid the complex stew of water from a nearby stream with its notes of kudzu, rock, and fish. Rhododendron's subtle vanilla scent jumbled with moss, with dogwood and buckeye and the sugary scent of maple, punctuated by the cool tang of pine.

But it was the musk, blood, and fur scent of raccoon he chased.

A three-quarter moon hung high overhead as he leaped the stream, muscles reaching in exhilarated approximation of flight. He landed almost on top of his prey—but his hind feet skidded in slick red clay. A second later, the raccoon shot up a tree.

He shook his head. Damned raccoons always climbed if they got a chance. He didn't begrudge the animal its escape but wished he'd had more of a chase first.

Deer do not climb trees. He decided to course for that scent.

Coursing was as much excuse as action. He'd eaten well before Changing, so hunger was distant; the real delight was simply being in motion, reading the world through nose, ears, the pads of his feet.

The human part of him remained, a familiar slice of "I" that was not-wolf. He remembered his two-legged thoughts and experiences; they simply ceased to matter as much. Not when air slid through him like hot silk, pregnant with a thousand flavors. It was probably the human part that felt a pang for the wonders of these southern woods, remembering the hotter, drier land claimed by his clan in southern California. His grandfather had made the decision to buy land there for Nokolai's clanhome. In that place and time, the land had been cheap.

It had been a sound decision. The clan had prospered in California. But at Nokolai Clanhome, wolves ran on rocks scattered over hard-baked ground, not on a thick bed of needles and moss through tree shadows surprised here and there by the tumble of a stream.

Rule had run as wolf in many places, yet there was something special about this night, these woods. Something new. He'd never run here as a wolf before. Not with Leidolf's clanhome so near.

The spike of worry was real, but fleeting. Wolves understand fear. Worry is too mental, too predicated on the future, to hold their attention. The slice of him that remained man wanted to hold on to that worry, gnawing it like a bone that refused to crack. The wolf was more interested in the day-old spoor of an opossum.

This was why he ran tonight: too much worrying, too much gnawing at problems that refused to crack open and release their marrow. He'd learned the hard way that the man needed the wolf at least as much as the wolf needed the man. These woods were sweet. He'd find no answers in them, but tonight he wasn't seeking answers.

Lily said they hadn't come up with the right questions yet.

Rule paused, head lifted. Thought of her was sweet to both man and wolf. If only she could . . .

He twitched his ear as if a fly had bitten it. Foolishness. Both his natures agreed on that. Things were as they were, not as he might wish them to be. Females did not Change.

An hour later he'd found no deer, though he'd crossed their trails often enough, along with many others—a pack of feral dogs, a copperhead, another raccoon. Perhaps he'd been more interested in the distractions than the hunt, when there were no clanmates to join the chase. He wished Benedict was here, or Sammy, or Cullen . . . wished, though he tried not to, for Lily. She could never share this with him.

His son would. Not yet, but in a few years. His son, who slept in a nearby town tonight—a town that would not be Toby's home much longer. In four days they would meet with the judge for the custody hearing, and as long as Toby's grandmother didn't change her mind . . .

She wouldn't. She *couldn't*.

Feelings thundered through him, a primal cacophony of bliss, fear, jubilation. Rule lifted his nose to the moon and joined in Her song. Then he flicked his tail and took off at a lope, tongue lolling in the heat.

At the base of a low hill he found another scent. The chemical message was old but unmistakable. At some point in the last few months, a Leidolf wolf had marked the spot with urine. Something more visceral than recognition stirred as the portion of new mantle he carried rose, *knowing* the scent. Welcoming it.

Briefly, he was confused. Always before that scent had meant enemy. But the message of the power curled within him was clear: this wolf was *his*.

The man understood this change, had expected it, and memory supplied the reasons, so the wolf acknowledged the change and moved on. He wound up the little hill, bathed in the aural ocean of cricket song, anticipating grass. His nose informed him of a grassy place nearby, a spot where some alteration in soil had discouraged trees.

He liked grass. Perhaps it would be tall and home to mice. Mice were small and tricky, but they crunched nicely.

A thought sifted through him, arising from both ways of being: a few months ago he wouldn't have noticed a scent trace as old as that left by the Leidolf wolf. Had the new mantle coiled in his belly made it possible to sort that scent? Or was it because there were two mantles now? Perhaps this night, these woods, were unusually magical because he carried more magic within him.

He would consider that in his other form, which was better suited to thinking. For now . . . at the crest of the hill he checked with the moon, aware of time passing and a woman who waited in the small town nearby . . . Asleep? Probably. He'd told her he would be gone most of the night.

Part of him thought this was a poor way to spend the night when he could have been in her bed, but there was grass ahead, the chance of a mouse or three. He was here, not there, and it was impossible to regret the night.

It was growing late, though. The fireflies had turned off their glowsticks and the moon was descending. He would investigate the tall grass, he decided. Then he'd return to the place he'd left his clothing and to the shape that fit those clothes.

The grass was indeed tall and the pungent smell of mice greeted him as he approached the tiny meadow. Rabbits, too, but rabbits were for daytime, since they seldom ventured out of their burrows in the dark.

A breeze rose, whispering in the grass and carrying a host of smells. He paused, curious, and tested the air.

Was that . . . ? Corruption, yes, the stench of rot was unmistakable, though faint and distant. It meant little. Animals died in the woods. Besides, the smell came from the general direction of the highway. Animals were hit by cars even more often than they died naturally. But was it an animal?

The mantles might help him find out

They slept now. He wouldn't call them up, not even just the one he considered truly his—that portion of the Nokolai mantle his father had given him years ago. To call one meant both answered, and he'd been warned. Drawing strongly on the portion he held of the other clan's mantle could kill the mantle's true holder, who clung so narrowly to life.

Not that Rule objected to Victor Frey's death. In other circumstances he'd celebrate it, but he didn't want the clan that would come to him with Victor's dying. And neither he nor Nokolai needed the ruckus that would follow.

Could he use the mantles without actually calling them up?

The wolf thought so. The man, troubled by instinct or too much thinking, wanted to try.

With a wisp of attention, Rule woke the twin powers in his gut. He focused again on the trace of scent carried by the breeze, not so much using the mantles as including them in his intention.

That scent sharpened in his nostrils immediately. Not a dog hit by a car, no. Nor a deer brought down by disease. Though the rot stench overpowered the rest, he was almost sure the body he smelled had never walked four-footed.

Go. The breeze might die, or this new acuity fade. *Go. Find out.*

He launched himself into a run.

Wolves are largely indifferent to death as long as it doesn't threaten them or theirs. The body he chased was certainly dead, so the wolf felt no urgency. But the man did. Rule ran for over a mile—not full-out, not over unfamiliar terrain with no immediate danger or prey. But he was fast in this form, faster than a born wolf.

By the time he slowed, he knew he'd been right about the highway. He heard cars cruising perhaps half a mile ahead . . . not many. It wasn't a major highway.

But what he sought lay within the woods. The rankness made his lip curl back from his teeth as he approached. Some other scent hid beneath the stench, but even with the mantles' help he couldn't sort it clearly, smothered as it was by putre-faction. Whatever it was, it brought up his hackles and started a growl in his throat.

Unlike some predators, wolves don't sideline as scav-engers; only one on the brink of starvation would consider eating meat this rotten. And Rule was too much of a man even now to feel anything but a sad sort of horror at what lay in a shallow ditch between a pair of oaks.

Not all beasts are so picky, however. And he hadn't been the first to find them.